JAMESON HOTEL

THE DARK SUITE SERIES
PARTS ONE, TWO & THREE

AVEN JAYCE

Mirror Call Press

Jameson Hotel

SECOND EDITION, MAY 2016

A&M Michigan Editing
Cover Image by Alenaviad
Cover and Book Design by Triple J Marketing
Published by Mirror Call Press

Published and printed in the United States
ISBN 978-0990498551

www.facebook.com/AvenJayceAuthor

For Michelle McGinty

Welcome to the JAMESON. This HOTEL contains explicit sexual content, strong language, drugs, violence, and murder...

... plus a touch of humor.

PART ONE

PROLOGUE

E ager for a change after losing custody of my son and half of my possessions in an epic and savage divorce battle, I sold my porn company, my house, and the remainder of my belongings to escape the shithole, dehydrated city of Las Vegas.

I spent the next two years arguing with architects, and countless months trying to get the proper building permits until I was finally approved to have a hotel built on a piece of land between Carson City and Sacramento. It's a three-story structure with a rustic log cabin exterior that melds with the landscape, and an interior that's elegantly decked out, comprised of dark-toned walls and rich earthy hues in the carpets and wood floors. With high-end furnishings from the ground up, gold and red accents in the corridors, and fresh Mariposa lilies strategically arranged in every room, I've heard it referred to as luxurious and stately, similar to a manor house.

Located just off Route 50, my hotel is burrowed in the high pines of the Sierra Nevada Mountains. Replete with a remarkable view of Lake Tahoe, it's a place for anyone in need of an escape from their polluted urban life of fast food, gadgets, car exhaust, and nine-hour days in front of a digital blue screen.

I thought my time away from the porn industry and casinos might sway my ex-wife to lighten up about my visitation rights with my kid, Jack, who I never get to see. However, I'm beginning to realize that as the son of the former king of porn, Paul Jameson, a psychopath who ended up face down with a bullet through his head, *his* past will always be a part of *my* present. My ex-wife is fully aware of the disturbing life my father led, and now that we're no longer together, she's using it against me, keeping my son at a distance. She also believes I'm turning into a shielded, voyeuristic, mentally ill man just like he was, and she could very well be right. What she doesn't understand is that I not only inherited part of my father's estate, but his enemies as well, and I need to protect myself.

Hiding behind every slot machine back in Vegas and now in these tall mountain pines is someone who's out to kill me. I don't trust a soul. Even at six thousand feet, with only one long road in and out of my hotel, I know that someday, someone's going to arrive and seek vengeance for my father's fucked up behavior. I *am* a bit guarded.

I have cameras around my entire property, in the lobby, restaurant, pool area, gym, laundry room, in all of the corridors, the executive suites, and even some of the standard-stay rooms. While I know I can't legally observe and record my guests in their rooms, what they don't know can't hurt them. As far as I'm concerned, it's a security issue and one I don't take lightly, not after witnessing some of the shit that went down within my father's porn company. And, I hate to admit this, but sometimes watching people screw in my hotel hardens my dick.

People traveling through these parts are mostly vacationers hitting the ski slopes during the winter or hiking and boating during the summer. They're looking for a serene setting—to inhale the mountain air and put their four hundred dollar a night bed to good use—fucking like wild beasts every chance they get. With all the cameras in and around this place, I can catch them sucking cock and eating pussy any time of the night or day. And the best part is it's goddamn real, not a bunch of worn-out porn stars paid to mechanically perform. It's fucking hot. Shit, even the baggy old asshats that wander into my hotel get it on with their K-Y Jelly for at least one night during their stay.

I've also caught my staff screwing around on their breaks. Housekeeping, restaurant workers, the doormen and baggage handlers, my maintenance and grounds crew, every damn one of them have banged someone at least once in this hotel, mainly one another, but sometimes the guests. The chief badass offenders are my pool boys; three guys who are fresh out of high school. And at eighteen, their dicks are hard 24/7.

I may need to change the name of my place from Jameson Hotel to Brothel in the Pines and, in all honesty, I'm just as guilty as the rest of the whorish men and women who hang around here. For Pete's sake, I'm not going to live my life without pussy.

And just to be clear, I don't take shit from anyone. People who fuck with me never check out. Lake Tahoe is the third deepest lake in the United States with an average depth of a thousand feet. If some swine finds himself sinking to the bottom with a concrete block tied around his chest it's because he was a threat to someone I care about, in which case he's never going to be found. Trust me on that one.

I'm Mark Jameson.

Oh, and welcome to my hotel.

AFTERNOON

The face that stares back at me in the bathroom mirror is more foe than friend. Six-feet tall with blond hair, blue eyes, high cheekbones, and a chiseled jawline, I've been told time and time again that I look like a model. I'm the living, breathing, shitting version of Malibu Ken, only I dress a hell of a lot better and I don't have a vinyl bulge for a dick. I also don't believe there was ever a Ken doll sold that was deranged. There's no *Killer Ken* in the toy stores, and certainly no *Fuck Her in the Ass Ken,* so I've got a leg up on Barbie's little squirrel monkey.

But this face I keep gazing at each day... the quixotic man who enjoys fine suits over Bermuda shorts even in eighty-degree weather, the one who is past his prime in the midst of a mid-life crisis, if *that* man had his way he'd look like his father—dark features, beady rodent eyes, large build, with fists of steel and the laugh of a villain. Evil surged from every pore of my dad and anyone within a hundred-mile radius sensed his wickedness. His presence was unsettling to all.

Still, when I walk into a room, women pant while men stand and want to shake my hand like I'm some fucking prince. My features are the antithesis of the malicious man I've become. I didn't inherit my father's mob boss appearance, but I did end up with his cruel, heartless, and merciless genes.

And my looks are the reason it's so easy to get away with all the shit that happens in my hotel. I look like an innocent, good-natured Boy Scout, and most of the time I'm calm in public. The ruthlessness of my inner core only materializes behind closed doors.

"Mark, you said you'd be right back. Fuck's sake, I'm drying out over here. Come back to bed."

"Use your fucking fingers 'til I'm finished, alright?"

New guests arrive each day and I have my choice of some strikingly beautiful rich women—lips plumped full of Botox, high-heels clicking on my lobby floor, their asses snug and swaying in skin-tight dresses, ready for a day of shopping, gambling, and sightseeing in town. Shit, they all remind me of my wenchy ex-wife and I couldn't care less about any of them. Right now, I want the one who's in my bed.

Julia.

I've had some mind-blowing oral suck fests with her; a foul-mouthed blonde with long hair, nice tits, and a pretty smile who works nights at the front desk. I asked her to arrive an hour early today so I could take her to my private suite for an afternoon fuck before her shift begins, hoping to finally get my dick wet, but she still refuses to open her legs for anything other than my tongue.

She's twenty-two and far from being worn out, getting the dick-stick from a measly two inadequate guys in her life. She makes me feel like I'm a teenager in the back seat of a car, begging my prom date to spread 'em wide. I hover over her, but as soon as my cock touches her skin she clutches it and takes it in her mouth, never letting my tip get close to her pussy. And when cum dribbles down her chin, she takes my hand and forces it into action for her own pleasure. She's been driving me mad.

"I'm about to cum. Finish me off, please!"

I knew the moment she walked into my office for an interview that I'd have her modelesque body in my bed before anyone else in this hotel laid a hand on her, but if I could've predicted that a noose would start tightening around my neck because I have feelings for...

"What the fuck was that?" She rushes over to the bathroom door. "Mark?"

I admire the broken glass with a grin. "It was nothing."

She looks in and gasps at the shards in the sink and surrounding my bare feet while the blood that flows from my cut hand drips onto the tile floor.

"What the hell happened?"

"I guess I shut the medicine cabinet too hastily. Sorry about that." I wrap a towel around the cut and step away from the glass. "Come on, let's finish this."

"Are you crazy? You wanna fool around while your make-shift bandage becomes soaked with blood... no way, no thanks." She turns away and I grip her soft suntanned shoulder, bringing her body back to mine.

"Look," I whisper and block her path to her clothing. "We're not finished. I respect the fact that you want to wait to feel my cock deep inside you, but you don't have all the control when you're in my room. Let me hear you cum. Now get back in my bed so I can make that happen," I say softly, steadily, and flash my warmest smile, hiding my desire to throw another punch toward my sneering reflection.

"What were you doing in there, anyway?" she asks, sitting on the edge of the bed and spreading her legs like an open nut cracker, waiting to crush my head between her inner thighs.

I smile when I kneel before her, grabbing her hips and sliding her smooth twat closer to my mouth.

"Lean back."

"No, I want to watch," she whispers, caressing my chin with her finger. "Pretend your hands are tied behind your back so I don't have to see the blood. And keep your eyes open for me."

I'm giving her far too much control today and I think her clit needs to be teased as payback for leaving my dick in a continuous state of craving.

My tongue is soft and warm, not bristly and cold like most men, and as it glides effortlessly from her ass upward, between her folds and over her clit, she lets out a heavy moan.

"Were you about to cum a few minutes ago?" I ask, as my heated breath travels over the saliva I deposited on her flesh, causing her to shudder in sexual frustration.

"One lick's not enough," she states, staring into my eyes.

I lean forward with my hands behind my back, gazing at her diamond shaped young face and begin a powerful massage of her pussy.

"That's perfect," she says.

With a twist of my hair between her fingers, my head is quickly restrained in a tight grip. Her eyes become distant indicating an orgasm's on the rise. Distorted whimpering sounds leave her mouth, echoing off every wall of my two-story suite.

"More," she begs.

"Plead," I whisper. "Tell me you want all of me, including my dick."

I pause and wait, but she doesn't say it.

"How can you hold out like this?" I ask, reaching under my bed for my strap-on facemask. Still, she doesn't answer. Fuck, I'll get inside her one way or another.

The toy fits securely over my head and once it's in place the giant cock bobs in front of her hole.

"What the shit, Mark? A man with a dick hanging off his face doesn't turn me on. If anything, it's frightening."

"Release my hair and lean the fuck back or you can

get dressed and go to work with a twitching pussy. I gave you a few minutes of power, now let me have some fun."

She smiles and falls backward, "yes sir."

I lower the strap-on to my chin, leaving my mouth exposed and my tongue free for pleasure. Hell, if she lets me do this, my actual cock will be in her within a day.

"Whoa," she whispers as the black latex dick starts to slide inside. "Holy shit. Stop!" She grips the shaft and pushes it away. "Not yet. I'm not ready."

I'd love to ram it inside and get it over with, but I do respect the words "stop" and "no" from a woman, so instead I lower the stiff toy against her ass and out of the way while my tongue swiftly does its duty. Licking, swirling, and flicking until...

"Uh, uh, uh, Mark."

That's right, at this moment she's completely vulnerable. I believe if you're going to kill someone, you need to do it when they're in this state. When the person you're with can't move, speak, breathe, or open an eye, and when they don't remember their name or what day it is.

"You good?" I ask, pulling off the latex shaft, disappointed I'm still locked out. "I hope you let me loosen you up later tonight."

"Christ, that was strong. Nice moves, by the way." She breathes heavily and looks at me. "You think I'll be in your suite again this evening?"

"If I ask, you'll *come*."

"You haven't even kissed me today."

"You know I hate that shit," I mutter. "It makes me feel weak." I unwrap the towel and see that the cut's not as deep as I originally thought and shouldn't require stitches. "You're attractive and sexy, Julia, but my mouth only enjoys certain kinds of lips."

"You're such a nutsack. I'm not letting you fuck me if you can't even dish out a simple kiss. And you know I prefer Jules to Julia."

"Nutsack?" She's so young. "That sounds like something my son would say. Get dressed and get to work. It's almost three."

"Did you hear me? Call me Jules, okay? It's been my nickname since I was a baby."

"I'll try, but Julia sounds more sophisticated."

"You mean older, right?"

"No, that's *not* what I mean... and I'll call you whatever feels right at the moment."

She gives me the finger. "Great, so I can call you dickhead because that's what suits you at *every* moment."

I toss her clothing on the bed, slip into my boxers, and head to the bathroom for a bandage. I'm sure my hair looks like shit from her finger play and the skin around my mouth has indentations from the strap-on. I'll have to wait a while before I make an appearance in the lobby.

"You're fully booked tonight," she says, helping me put on my white dress shirt. She buttons it slowly, feeling my abs as I place the bandage on my hand. "I noticed on the schedule that you're interviewing for a

11

new security guy this evening. Did you fire one of—"

"Don't ask so many questions."

She drops her arms hastily and sighs. "Fine. No kissing and no talking. You're not getting very far with me, Mark."

She snatches her purse off a table and starts to head out. "If you want some inside information that might help you with your decision, I met one of the guys who applied. He's huge, bigger than your last man and seems pleasant."

"Name?" I snap my fingers. "What's his name?"

"Dayne something."

My hand is glued to her forearm before she can take another step. "What the fuck did you say?" I push her up against the wall. "How do you know Dayne?"

She stutters while trying to respond. "I... I don't." Her eyes glance at my firm grip. She's pissed. Damn it, I fucked up.

I release her and rest my hand on her shoulder.

"I don't know him!" she shouts. "And don't you ever be physically cruel with me!"

"I barely touched you!"

"I'm out of here, you crazy shit." She races down to my living area and slams the door on her way out.

"I barely touched her." I exhale and stare at the empty room, the blood, my hand, and the shattered glass on the floor. I lean against the wall and lower my head. I've never been this irate and manic in the past. Mentally, I'm losing it.

"I'm a troll, fol-de-rol."

When you sing about trolls you have to remember to pronounce each word slowly, using only your deepest voice.

"I'm a troll, fol-de-rol... and I'll eat... you... for supper."

Hell, that afternoon didn't go as planned.

EVENING ARRIVALS

I can't believe Julia's still here after I forced her up against the wall. It can't be because she loves this job. I'd say she either can't afford to quit or she might, even after a shitty afternoon, have feelings for me.

She looks radiant in her Jameson Hotel blazer under the shimmering lights. When the guests move away from the desk, she checks her cleavage then adjusts her tits while I grin and mimic her actions with my dick.

I haven't apologized yet. I've been in my windowless office; a room off my private suite, viewing security cams, thinking, waiting, and watching for the big man to arrive. Dayne Rosen.

I know him well. He and his twin, Doron, were my dad's bodyguards for years. After my father was killed, the two of them found themselves serving a decade in prison, for a good many reasons.

That fucker. He's here.

He approaches Julia and shakes her hand. Her warm smile and his eyes falling to her tits slice my gut open. She waves in the direction of the lobby seating area that's in front of the stone fireplace and he settles in.

The piece of shit looks like an ox wearing a cheap suit.

He studies the room, the staff, the front desk, my doormen, then detects the cameras. One... two... three... and number four... he looks directly at me and winks.

What a bastard. This is exactly what he's trained to do, and I hate it that he's so fucking good.

I place my gun in the back of my pants and take a deep breath before walking downstairs. I'm not a fool. Dayne's here because he wants me dead or because he's looking to take down my sister and her husband. This is about revenge, not a job, and as far as I'm concerned, I'm tired of the Jamesons and Rosens acting like the Hatfields and the McCoys. My father's dead, his father's dead, and even though they both deserved what they got, it's time for the rest of us to move on.

Yeah, right. All I can think about on the way down is killing the dumb fuck.

The business office behind the front desk has a back door that I use so I don't have to walk through the lobby. I'm not going to be caught off guard by this guy.

I call the front desk so I can get this over with as quickly as possible. "Julia, tell Mr. Rosen I'm ready for him. Use those exact words."

"Not a problem."

She hangs up and a minute later his figure fills the office doorway.

"Mark." He nods, not in the least bit surprised

when I remove the gun from behind my back and point it at his head. I motion with it for him to take a seat, which he does after closing the door.

"Tell me why the fuck you're in my hotel. Make it quick."

His laughter pisses me off so I send the slide of the gun forward to put an end to that shit.

"Alright." He raises his hands. "Chill the fuck out, man. You need a new security guy, right?"

"Not a Rosen."

"We're the finest around... *I'm* the finest around and you know it."

"I'm not looking for a *Rosen*," I repeat. "And I don't need a bodyguard, which is what you really are. The job's to watch over the grounds, inside and out, and to give my guests a feeling of security, nothing more. You'd be better off in Vegas."

He lowers his hands and leans back in the chair with a straight face. I notice how dirty he looks, which is unusual for him. His short graying hair is greasy and the stubble on his face is nicked off in places like he used a dull razor. And the scent he brought into this office, Jesus, it's a combination of sweat and steamed broccoli. In other words, the man's a walking sewer.

"I got out of prison last month," he says in a deep voice. "Things haven't been easy. People in Vegas, the ones that matter, those guys won't hire me. They know I worked for Paul."

"Yeah, well Paul's dead. You did a terrible job

protecting him, now didn't you? Why would I hire a guy who couldn't keep my father safe?"

"Listen, douchebag—"

I stand with the gun still pointed at his head. "No, you listen. I know my father deserved a bullet in his head, but it's high time someone put one in yours. When the detectives came in to investigate his death and found the footage that showed what you did to people, including my sister, I didn't feel one bit sorry that you got arrested and I sure as fuck don't feel sorry for your whiny ass now! You drugged my sister and tattooed her flesh with my father's porn company name. What a piece of shit you are. I bet you would've killed my dad too, but someone beat you to it."

"Fuck that, everyone wanted him dead, Mark. He was a brute with no regrets for mistreating his porn stars, including the young teenagers he fucked. He only cared about himself. I was loyal to the sick bastard until the day he died." His face remains expressionless while his mouth spews hatred. "You're right, I wanted him dead and I could've killed him, but I didn't."

I laugh at his pokerfaced confession. "Those words aren't going to get you this job."

"Mark, you know everything about me. I need this." He takes a deep breath. "My brother got out of prison before I did and he went back to his wife, and my sister won't give me the time of day. Neither will speak to me. I've been run out of Vegas... fuck, just give me a chance. Your dad would've taken me back."

"Don't play those games." I shake my head and sit. "He wasn't stable in the end and he would've hired a fucking flamingo if it walked through the door."

Dayne scratches his head and looks around the room; eyeing the camera I have above the desk then checking the time on a non-existent watch. Must be a habit for him to look at his bare wrist.

"No one will hire an aging a-hole who just got out of prison," he says with a direct stare into my eyes. "I'm sorry about your sister. Is she doing okay these days?"

"Haven't a clue. I think we're finished here, Dayne."

"She still living in St. Louis with her douchebag husband?"

I stand and point to the door, but he doesn't move. His nostrils flare and I sense the real Dayne Rosen emerging, the animal I remember from when I was just a twenty-something-year-old kid. The guy who would use me as a punching bag and call me a pussy if I ever complained to my father.

He lounges forward and grips my hand as the tip of my gun presses into his chest.

"You can be dead in two seconds," I whisper.

"You too, dickface. I can turn this gun around in no time."

"Why are you really here, Dayne?"

"I want to know what happened to *my* father, you little prick."

I knew this was coming.

"A suicide, right? That's what I was told when I was

in the big house. Bull-fucking-shit!" He raises his voice and spit flies from his mouth.

"Mr. Jameson?" Julia knocks on the door. "I'm sorry to interrupt, but I have an emergency."

"Nice." Dayne smirks. "You've got that little pussy trained well. Does she also wipe your ass for you after you take a shit?"

"Get out," I fume. "Get the *fuck* out of here."

He steps back and releases my hand, but leaves me with the eeriest grin.

"Call your baby sister and tell her I'm coming for her and her family. That tattoo I inked on her shoulder cost ten years of my life, and I'm gonna cut it off and keep her flesh in my pocket until the day I die. And if her husband had anything to do with my father's death, his balls are coming off and getting shoved in his mouth."

"Mr. Jameson?" This time Julia opens the door and pokes her head inside. "I need help, please." She enters the room as Dayne steps out.

"Motherfucker," I say under my breath, still holding my gun. She knows I carry it whenever I leave my suite, but she's never seen it out and ready for use.

"You okay? The new arrivals kept looking back this way when they heard the arguing and cursing. It's not like you to act like this in public."

"Shit." I exhale, rubbing my chin with my gun.

"Mark, don't point that thing at your face. Is it loaded?"

"Don't boss me around, alright? Now what's your emergency?"

She looks at me like I'm crazy and goes back to work without saying a word.

"Julia," I call out, with no response. No woman's ever put me in my place like she has. "Jules, come back, I need to talk to you."

She leans against the doorframe with a hand on her hip and says, "Thanks for calling me Jules. It's about time."

"I told you it's whatever feels right at the moment. Did he leave?"

"Yeah, he walked right out."

"You said you met him. Where? Was he here?"

"No, at Kick's Bar, downtown."

"What the fuck were you..." I stop before I come across as being jealous, but by her satisfied expression I can tell she got the picture. "Stay away from him. He's dangerous."

"Is that an order, Mr. Jameson?" Her hand stays on her hip like she rules the room.

"Close the door," I whisper.

She steps inside and closes the solid oak door then places two hands on my desk and leans forward. Her tits fall out of her blazer in a hanging tease.

"I apologize for being a dick earlier," I say softly, forcing myself to look away from her chest and into her eyes. "I just don't want anything to happen to the people I care about. You understand?"

She gives me a quick nod.

"I'm frustrated that he's in town," I continue, "but that's not an excuse to take it out on you."

"You're passive aggressive," she whispers back. "Or maybe even bipolar or worse."

I shake my head. "No, don't say that shit about me."

"Someone should. You can be sugary sweet one second and bite my head off the next. It's kind of scary, you know?"

"Then why the fuck are you here? Why did you come in early today to see me if you feel this way?"

"Shh." She places a finger over my mouth and I look back to her bouncy tits. "You know, Mark, someone needs to help you."

"And you think you're the one?" I grin and guide her to my chair. She straddles my waist as I reach under her blazer, unable to get enough of her young tits.

Fuck, I'm hard again.

"Chloe's working the front with you tonight, right?"

"Yeah, but I'm not going to fool around back here when she's ten feet away."

I caress her cheek and bring her lips to mine. Our tongues play and she sighs when I bite her bottom lip on the way out. "You're having dinner with me when your shift's over. Let me apologize again, the right way. Nine o'clock."

Her honey colored eyes gleam from my unexpected kiss, which are few and far between.

"And promise me you'll never speak to Dayne Rosen again. Okay?"

She nods. "You think your other two interviews will be the same as the last?"

"Doubt it. I plan on hiring them both."

"Will you tell me more about Dayne tonight?"

"He's not the best subject to bring up during dinner, besides, I'd just as soon discuss getting you back in my bed." I slap her ass as she stands.

"I'll send the next guy in when he arrives."

"Give me about five minutes. I need to do something first," I say, pulling my dress shirt out of my pants to cover my erection.

She looks down and smiles, thinking I'm gonna jerk off, which isn't what I'm about to do.

"Save it for later," she whispers on her way out.

I leave the office quickly and take the elevator to the second floor. My hotel has two sets of living quarters on opposite ends. Both are two thousand square feet, two bedroom, two bath, and two-story units. I have a thing for two's, being born on February second, owning two black Toyota Tacomas, two boats, and two guns, having nephews who are twins, and a collection of twenty-two switchblades. It's all been good luck. All except my encounters with the Rosen twins, the only *two's* in this world that appear to be vile, at least in my opinion.

The private suites are similar to living in a penthouse in that they're safe from assholes like Dayne. They each have a steel door that's equipped with an electronic keypad. One has no other way in or out except through a sliding glass door off the master bedroom, which leads to a large deck with a view of the mountains, but also includes a forty-foot drop to the ground below. The door opens to a view of paradise and nothing else. I made sure these two suites were private enough to let a person live in seclusion, even during the height of tourist season.

A slight difference is that my suite has a set of stairs leading to a private underground four-car parking garage, two spaces for my trucks and two that are currently empty—used for winter boat storage. The private garage allows me to come and go without being seen. To hell if I'm going to park my vehicles in the guest or staff parking lots...

I see the door.

It's been a week since I've approached this suite. My staff thinks I use it for storage, which was true up until about three weeks ago. Now it's occupied with something I find most precious.

I could call, but I need to see someone's face instead of having a discussion through our cell phone watches.

I knock once, a hard pound, and wait.

There's one knock in return, then silence.

Placing my head against the door, I whisper my first warning...

"He's here."

• • •

Nights are my mornings...

I don't sleep more than a few hours each night because of troubling thoughts and an overactive cock. I have two unstable heads dominating my life and both get a thrill from suffocating my softer side. I want to tame them for Julia, but at the same time I'd rather come across as her alpha, than as a pussy with a heart.

Damn, look at her applying a fresh coat of dark lipstick for my dick and me. I can't wait for that precious mouth to open wide later. And there's something about seeing my name embroidered over the chest of my staff, especially hers, the name Jameson bouncing with each movement makes me feel all-powerful.

She sees me and I let out a faint laugh. It's not for her, but because I just realized those embroidered names remind me of the tattoos my father forced his porn stars to get on their shoulders, labeling them as Jameson Industries whores. I even have one of the company tats on my shoulder. And according to Jules, I'm an egotistical bastard to have my last name inked on my body.

I'm fine with that assumption. She doesn't need to know the truth as to why it's there.

"Hey, where're we going?"

I raise my hand in the direction of the back hall and she lowers her purse in disappointment.

"Really, Mark? Taking me to your own restaurant isn't taking me *out* for dinner."

"Of course it is." I grin. "You joining me or not?"

Her eyes roll as we walk side-by-side on the red and gold carpet to the dark wooden doors, reminiscent of a castle entrance. She's always in heels, even when she's in my bed. Without them, I'd guess she's about three inches shorter than me.

"After you," I say, letting her enter first.

"Why so nice all of a sudden?" she asks with a look of suspicion and disbelief.

My main hostess leads the way to my usual table and pours two glasses of wine. It's a quiet spot, just off the main room, with floor to ceiling windows that are perfect for viewing the lake.

"Stunning," she whispers with her first sip of wine. "My parents own a boat, but I haven't been out on the water in over a year. Do you have one?"

"Two."

"Two boats, why?"

"Just in case one breaks down." I snap my fingers for a basket of bread and pour a second glass of wine after chugging the first in under a minute.

"Are you getting wasted tonight or are you hoping I will, so I'll be less protective of my foxhole?" she jokes.

I pull her chair closer and devote my hand to her athletic thigh. Julia's different from most of the women I've been with. Besides the fact that her skin is never cold or dry and she seems at ease with her clothing and makeup, in such a way that those things come naturally to her, she also says what's on her mind. And when she can't answer, she keeps silent, which is a hell of a lot better than telling lies.

"Your other two interviews seemed to go well, at least I think they did since there wasn't anymore yelling after that guy Dayne left. Did you find someone?"

"Yeah, two. Both experienced with open schedules. They'll start immediately."

She nods. "Are you worried about your staff talking about us?"

"Obviously not if I brought you here. Does it bother you?"

"No, if anything it makes me feel special, like I'm here for something other than to give you head."

She chews a piece of bread and smiles at the decor, admiring the lush carpet, fine linens, and the Mariposa lily next to our wine glasses, then her heel inches under my pants. "It's working, Mark Jameson," she whispers.

"What is?" I ask innocently, knowing full well I brought her someplace romantic to get laid.

I'm given a second sign when she slides my hand under her skirt. Fuck, women my age never get this wet. I can feel how slick she is through her underwear. It *is* working.

"So you've been holding out for this? Dinner with a lakeside view?" I ask.

"No, but it helps."

I nod. "Why don't tell me what's on your mind then? I'm curious as to what I'm doing wrong. You said it helps, but something's still missing."

"Don't laugh." Her tone is serious. "It's not you, Mark. The last two guys left after they got it. I'm jinxed that way. And since they're the only two I've been with, it makes sense to believe you won't come back for seconds either."

"That's fucking bullshit, Jules. Trust me, I'll be back for seconds and thirds. I like pussy, a lot. If I could handle the pain, I'd have a pussy tattooed on my dick so I could fuck it everyday. You'll be begging for a break... not wondering why I left."

"But..." She looks around with hesitation.

"What?" I demand an answer.

Her delicate hand covers mine before she hides it away. "Chloe and a few of the other women have mentioned they've fucked you. You've been with *a lot* of your staff."

I start to speak but she raises her hand for a chance to continue.

"I understand you've got a dick and you want to use it and it doesn't really bother me that you've been with a lot of people, I mean..." She sighs. "How old are you?"

"Late thirties."

"Yeah, so you have a lot of experience, that's okay, but what I *am* bothered by is the fact that you didn't stay with anyone. Why? What happened?"

"I didn't give a shit about them. That's what happened."

She flashes her *I knew it* expression. "I'd prefer to get my mouth used and tossed away instead of my pussy, and with the answer you just gave me, I can tell that's what would happen."

"Look." I exhale and take a gulp of wine, wanting to tell her I could have some random woman bent over a chair in my suite within the hour, but because of her I'm giving up on that shit for now. One-nighters lately are beyond boring and I'm up for a new challenge. I've been working my ass off for Julia's warm pussy and I can tell I'm not wasting my time.

"Look what? You didn't finish your sentence," she says, setting her wine down. I watch her unfold her napkin and place it on her lap then turn toward the lake.

"It's not just about my dick getting inside some of the staff. What else is stopping you?"

She looks surprised that I know her so well.

"You're stunning, Jules. The type of woman who walks into a room and heads turn, which means I'm not the only guy around who's noticed you, especially if you've been to Kick's Bar. I'm sure a few men were admiring your ass at that place. Right?"

Her face turns red and she shrugs. "So?"

"I bet those men don't have workers they've fucked, but I haven't heard about you sleeping with them, so it's not just about me. You're not giving it to anyone else either. Why?"

"Maybe I'm not a slut."

Smirking, I lean back while our dinner arrives and wait for her to take the first bite before I begin. I'm always served the daily special for my evening meal and having that planned in advance with the kitchen staff is better than wasting time with my head in a menu. It's also nice that Julia didn't complain about not having a choice.

"You find that amusing?" she asks while nursing her wine.

"Well, you're not a prude."

She halts my hand from cutting into the meat on my plate then moves the conversation away from herself. "Tell me why that guy Dayne was arguing with you earlier."

My face feels warm as I push her hand away and continue cutting my food, slowly at first, but then with more power and aggravation. "It's a family issue and none of your concern."

"Gah. Saying one wrong thing puts you in a sour mood. So he's family? Like, your dad or uncle or something?"

I slam my silverware on the table and throw back my second glass of wine.

"Sorry I asked," she says softly.

"You're too young and innocent to understand, so give it a fucking rest. I already told you I didn't want to talk about him tonight anyway."

"I forgot, we can only talk about sex," she fires back. "You think I'm young and innocent, well let me tell you something, I've been through hell too and my trust in men disappeared when my last 'boyfriend' held me down and stuck a freaking hairbrush handle inside me as punishment for not putting out on our second date."

"Excuse me," I whisper.

"That's right, he flew into a rage, took the brush off my dresser and stuck it in. I let him fuck me that night so he'd stop abusing me with the brush, and when it was over he said he didn't want to deal with my drama. I never saw him again."

I loosen my tie then unbutton my suit jacket, unable to breathe. She won't look at me and when I raise her chin with my finger a tear rolls down her cheek. Shit.

"Were you hurt?" I question. "Besides emotionally."

Her head's down while my eyes look to the ceiling, away from her tight lips and shaking head.

"No," she whispers. "He wanted to humiliate me and nothing more."

I have white knuckles and a clenched jaw. "No, trust me, the fucker wanted to do more than humiliate you. Did you press charges?"

She shakes her head again. "I wanted that night to disappear from my memory, not relive it with a detective, besides, I told him we could do it. I agreed to it."

My fist slams the top of the table transmitting my fury to her and the rattling dinnerware.

"I'll be right back, don't go anywhere," I say, rushing away from the table, through the kitchen, past my staff, and out the back door in need of fresh air.

"Fucking son of a bitch."

I pace with my head down, hands in my pockets,

and listen to the fall leaves crunch under my shoes. What the fuck am I getting myself into? This isn't the right time for this, not with Dayne here. I need to stay focused on him, and now I have this situation to deal with.

"Fuck, fuck, fuck, those words were selfish." I bite my lip in anger and frustration. "That scumwad," I whisper. There's nothing I hate more than a rapist. I'm a prick and I know I can be an abusive ass, but I'd never sink so low... I'd never rape a woman... unlike my father. That's one trait he didn't pass down to me; the other is having a man do his dirty work for him. I'm not hiring some chump to teach people a lesson. I'll take care of business when necessary with my own two hands.

Some people are pussies.

I take a slow walk around the outer edge of the pool, inhaling the heady scent of the mountain pines. Slow and calm. Breathe steadily, Mark. Take a moment to think and chill out.

The sky is clear, full of stars, and the moon's reflection dances on top of the water; it's beautiful, unlike life.

My outdoor pool is heated year round and has blue lights shining upward from the bottom. Guests can enjoy a relaxing swim even in the dead of winter. The lone swimmer this evening disappears in the rising steam from the water's surface then reappears in the shallow end by the stairs. At this time of the night people swim at their own risk, but during the day when the pool is full of bobbing heads, my pool boys keep a watchful eye out for safety.

I need to figure this shit out. Either I step up to the plate and start a real relationship with this woman or I walk away, and I know I can't do that. I'd be like the last piece of shit in her life that said he didn't need the drama. Well, fuck that. Life without drama isn't living. It's like spending your days in a fucking coma. And it's amusing that earlier she said someone needed to help *me* when she's been wrestling with her past as well.

"Mark?" Her soft voice glides to my ears. "I'm not all that hungry, I think I'm just gonna go, but thanks, it was nice."

I can tell she hasn't calmed down. I haven't known her for long, but from some of the shit I've put her through, I do know she's not a crybaby or a weak woman. She'll bitch me out before she cries, so the tears a few minutes ago were an eye opener.

"I'm worried about you, Jules, stay and talk to me. I want to know more about this situation. Tell me about the guy. What's his name?"

She watches the guest step out of the pool, wrap a towel around her waist then walk away, giving us some privacy.

"It was over a year ago and I shouldn't have brought it up, forget it. I feel like I threw it in your face to punish you..." She starts to leave and my heart sinks to the bottom of the pool. My mouth won't open to call her back, and at this moment it's clear that this woman weakens my soul. I'm obsessed with her every word, movement, and breath. She can't disappear.

"Wait." I walk up to her and place my hand on the curve of her hip, looking into her eyes with an apologetic expression on my face. Something inside me wants to hold her, and another part can't wait for her to leave so I can find this guy and rip his head off. I hide that conflicting split and try to get the information I need. "I blew up in there, as usual, you know that about me, but I'm dead serious when I say I want you to stay. I'll keep my cool."

"Another time," she says.

I exhale and ask a final question. "Tell me where you met this guy."

She pulls a set of car keys from her purse and stands before me with a straight face. "He was my boss at Mountain Bread in town. I worked the morning shift with him until that crap happened. Then I quit. And if I were smart, I would've learned from that mistake... I shouldn't fall in love with the man I work for." She turns away and walks along the pool's edge to the side gate and disappears around the building, on her way to the employee parking lot.

I take one last leisurely walk around the pool and look up at the dark windows of my suite, then at the fully lit private suite on the opposite end of the hotel. There aren't supposed to be any lights on and I'm annoyed that my instructions are being ignored. A silhouette appears for a brief moment, then the lights go out and the figure dissolves into the darkness. It better stay that way.

I'm a protector. Most people think I'm an uncaring, self-centered man, but the reality is I live my life as a guardian over my family and friends. I took on that role at a young age because neither one of my parents ever did.

I was engaged when my father approached me with an extravagant offer to work for him in his porn company. I already had a decent job in my hometown of Philly and didn't want to relocate my fiancé away from her family, but I also wanted to make the big bucks to support her, especially since I had just knocked her up. I visited my dad on and off in Vegas, learning the in's and out's of his business before he gave me an opportunity to run one of his remote locations from home. For a while it was simple and honest work, developing and managing online porn sites, but then I started attending some of his private parties and got sucked into his world. They were intense and like nothing I'd ever experienced, with an overabundance of drugs, booze, and naked women hanging on my arm. No one knew I was Paul's son except for his bodyguards. My porn name was Marcus Wild, and after a while I fell so deeply into his company I ended up becoming one of his biggest online stars whenever I visited—sleeping with both men and women, and cheating on my wife. My childhood and teens were spent with a mother who was mentally ill and abusive, and my twenties were spent hanging around a father who taught me how to kill and expected me to stick my dick into anything and everything that moved.

Heck, I hope the next generation of Jamesons isn't this fucked up.

I check on my staff in the kitchen, front desk, and my head security guard, letting all of them know about the two new guys I hired before taking off to my suite.

Dayne's not coming back tonight. He knows I'm on guard and he'll want to ask more questions about his father's suicide and my sister's whereabouts before he takes action. He's also the type of man who'll punish my family without veering off path, meaning he's not going to take anything out on my staff or Julia. He won't complicate what he came here to do by involving random victims. It's just not his style. He wants answers and to settle some ongoing conflict with my family. And hell, for all I know he could be on his way to my sister's home in St. Louis. Her husband owns a wine bar, the only one in the city, which makes them easy to find. But I know for a fact she's been counting the years, months, and days of Dayne's release. She's prepared.

I type my code into my keypad and enter my suite, tossing my jacket over my dining room chair and mixing myself a scotch and soda before heading into my office.

Someone in this town is about to meet his maker.

DEPARTURE

It's rare for me to leave my hotel. I have everything I want and need in there, a warm bed, liquor and food, and a woman who I believe professed her love for me last night. It's paradise compared to jogging in the cold along one of the southern Lake Tahoe trails, watching my breath float into the early light while my cock's a shrunken head hiding beneath my sweats.

I pull back one of my black leather gloves to check the time. Six o'clock. No one's out this early except for one lone soul about fifteen feet ahead. We're just two men out for a little exercise on a frigid morning.

"I'm a troll," I sing softly.

He turns his head while keeping his pace, then, sensing a threat, speeds up.

"I'm a troll, fol-de-rol," I say with quickening steps. *"Now... I'm coming... to gobble... you up..."* My sentences break apart as I run faster to catch my prey.

He sprints ahead but the trail ends, leaving him with a split second decision to turn around and face me, or head into the pines.

"I'm... a troll." I'm quicker, bigger, stronger, than this little shit.

My switchblade juts from my hand, my heart pumps and blood rushes through my veins, extending my dick. The hunt always causes an erection... I love this feeling... the kill... fuck, I'm in. My blade slips inside his warm gut and blood coats his sweatshirt. It's like penetrating a virgin.

"Uh!" he yelps with wide eyes and an open mouth.

I bring him closer and sing despondently while he takes his final breaths.

"And I'll eat..." My knife jerks upward and twists.

"You..." Pulling out, he falls to the ground.

"For supper."

Rot in Hell, you dumb fuck.

MORNING

T hat was a masterful morning.

It's been years since I've had good reason to take a man down, and from start to finish, it played out without a hitch. I truly believe ridding the world of scum is a good deed. It's not wrong to kill a man who's hurt others or who has the potential to harm again. I'm a vigilante for those I hold dear and it was the right thing to do. My greatest strength is to defend and protect, and Julia's one lucky woman to have me around.

The guy's name was Roland Lorne, manager of Mountain Bread, avid fisherman, skier (both water and snow), only child to William and Stacy of Carson City; a Republican in his early thirties, with a love for 'Star Trek, Big Titties, and Beer.' That's what I found on Facebook after scoring his name from the Mountain Bread website. The moron also posted his daily run, including a map, distance, and the time of the day he jogged, open for the entire world to view. I've tracked a few people this way and it's usually the ones with low IQ's or inflated egos who leave their profile settings public. I knew I had the right guy, plus, he never deleted the selfie of Julia and him from their first date over a year ago, along with the twenty other women since then.

After he was dead I found a slim wallet zipped in his back pocket, put blood on it, and jogged the two miles back to town where my Tacoma was parked. The jog was the most difficult part. The sneakers I wore were a pair left behind by one of our guests and they were a size too small. I set them, the wallet, and the bloody blade on a bench in the small downtown park, close to a homeless guy who was sleeping under a blanket by a tree. I waited in my truck until he got up, watching with a grin as he found the items.

It was like he read my mind. He opened the wallet first and got blood on his hand, wiped it clean on his shirt then placed it in his back pocket. Then he opened the blade, wiped the blood from that onto his sleeve and pocketed it as well. The sneakers were too small but he wore them anyway then packed up his blanket, put his old shoes in his backpack, and walked off.

Fucking brilliant.

The homeless are usually the first to be questioned in this town and if he gets charged and sent to prison, he'll have free meals and a warm bed for twenty-five years. That has to be better than eating rotting table scraps from dumpsters or ending up frozen to the sidewalk on a minus twenty-degree winter night. Others may disagree, but this slaughter seems like a win-win for all. A dickhead's never going to hurt another woman, a homeless guy is finally going to get taxpayers to take care of him, and I get the girl.

Goddamn, I feel amazing.

Even without the bum, South Lake Tahoe's traffic count is fifteen thousand cars a day with people on their way to California or headed in the opposite direction to the casinos, not to mention the daily influx of tourists who stay the night then disappear come morning. I bet at least two killers drive through these parts on any given day.

I mean, other than Dayne Rosen and me.

When I got back to my suite, I burned my black leather gloves, then turned on the driveway security cameras before relaxing on the sofa for a moment with a glass of juice and a piece of dry toast.

And now, I've been unable to wipe the grin from my face for hours and I'm too fucking wired to sleep. All I can do to waste some time is take a hot shower to loosen my tight muscles then try to get my ass moving for the day.

I stand with my hands pressed against the marble tiled wall with my eyes closed and the water streaming down my face. "I'm a badass, Dad," I whisper. "A fucking badass, just like you always wanted."

• • •

"You have the face of a pansy," my father says while gripping the back of my neck, forcing me to stare into the

bathroom mirror. "Look at yourself, a fucking fair-haired, blue-eyed, replica of your mother. I don't even think you're mine."

A tear rolls down my cheek that I quickly wipe away. "You never say these things to Sophie," I whimper, starting to feel sickened by my appearance.

"Your sister's beautiful. She came out with dark hair and chestnut eyes like me. A badass. The Jameson genes are evident in her. What happened to you, Mark? You look like a fucking sunflower." He clutches my chin and lifts my head so I can't turn away. "How the fuck are you going to survive being such a pretty boy? Men will call you a faggot."

"Dad, stop. You're hurting me."

He smacks the top of my head and backs away. "Look in the mirror and say you're a badass."

"I don't want to," I whisper.

"You need to toughen up on the inside, or maybe I should break your nose so don't look so feminine. That might help."

I put my hand over my face in defense and he laughs.

"Oh, my little Marky." He shakes his head. "Your eyelashes are longer and darker than a woman wearing thick mascara and your lips look like they have a coat of pink lipstick on them."

I turn to the mirror with a furrowed brow and scrunch my nose at my reflection.

"Better. Now make a fist and say you're a badass."

"I'm a badass," I whisper.

He laughs and calls me a loser under his breath.

"Sophia, come here," he calls out. "Sophia!"

A moment later my little sister pokes her head through the bathroom door and giggles.

"Hey, kiddo. Are you tough?" my father asks.

She raises her arms, pretending to make two muscles, tightens her lips and yells, "Me badass! Rarrr!" Then runs off in laughter.

"That's my kid," he says with a second slap to my head before he leaves me alone to face my reflection.

• • •

My Calvin Klein face ended up making my father a shitload of money when I was one of his porn stars, and his constant verbal abuse turned me into the mean-tempered asshole he wanted, but I never pleased him enough to be called his son.

And he wouldn't be proud of me now, either. Not if he found out I killed a guy because of a woman.

He'd say, *It was over pussy? What the fuck's wrong with you?*

I wrap a towel around my waist and put a fresh bandage on my knuckle, but avoid the new mirror my maintenance team installed yesterday.

A text came in from Jules while I was in the shower—an unnecessary apology.

Sorry 'bout last night. Didn't mean to make this all about me. Do over?

I text her back. *Need you here. Come talk to me.*

Twenty minutes. She responds.

My growing erection twitches under the towel. I can't wait to touch her, smell her, slip my fingers inside her and lick her pussy.

Two pieces of pine are placed on the fire and my window shades are closed. The room is comfortable, quiet, and warm. I *do* plan on having a conversation with her, but I know we won't make it past my living room if I decide to kiss her, and I think she may be deserving of a kiss today.

I keep a watchful eye for her from my office cams, checking on the rest of the hotel as I wait. One of my pool boys is netting the Aspen leaves from the water, a few people are eating lunch, and a woman sits alone at the restaurant bar, which won't be open for a few more hours. She's either an alcoholic or looking for solitude. The lobby's quiet, checkout's over, and check-in's not for a while. All is well... wait... for Christ's sake.

I zoom in on the staff parking lot and see Julia's car. She's in the back seat with her feet in the air, slipping out of a pair of jeans and into her work clothes. For a moment, I think she's screwing around with some asshole, but after fixing her shiny blonde hair in the rear view mirror, she steps out with a towel and a small bag... alone. I follow her with the cam to the pool changing area, where she walks into the women's room.

"Why are you getting dressed in your car?" I whisper. "Where are you coming from?"

I wait patiently until she reappears and walks

outside, tossing the bag and towel into the backseat.

"Fuck," I mumble, pushing my chair away from the desk. I put on a dress shirt and hear a knock on the door, answering it while still buttoning the front.

"Nice." She smiles with bright red lips. "Leave it open. Actually, take it off, the towel too. I owe you *something* after taking off last night, don't you think?"

She walks in and I lock the door, continuing to button my shirt without answering.

"Mark," she says and stops my hand. "Don't give me the silent treatment, I'm sorry, okay?"

The expression on her face is always genuine. Whether she's in a loving mood, enraged, or apologetic, it's never forced. I love that about her.

I take two soda waters from my fridge and she gladly accepts one of them.

"We should talk," I say softly. "I have some questions before we fool around... if we fool around." I motion to my sofa and she takes a seat. I'm no longer aroused after seeing her use my hotel like it's a... hotel.

"His name's Roland," she says. "I was hoping by now you would've let that conversation from last night go."

I play along, acting like I don't know anything about the guy.

"Who? The guy who hurt you?"

"Yes."

"Roland sounds like the name of a pet pig... and I *will* let it go temporarily, but that doesn't mean I'm not pissed about it." As I'm sure she expects me to be.

She nods and whispers, "Thank you."

"But we have other things to discuss." I exhale, placing my drink on one of my end tables.

"It's alright, Mark, I understand."

"Understand what?" I face her with my arm resting on the back of the sofa.

"That you can't be with me anymore because I have weird baggage. I don't blame you."

"That's not what I was going to say."

"Really?" She's hopeful. "Then what?"

I slide her closer and trail my finger along her forehead, temple, cheek, to her small chin, then around to the back of her neck, bringing her mouth to mine. Her skin smells like a fresh spritz of flowery perfume and her lips taste like peppermint. Two kisses in less than a day... Jesus, I'm losing it.

Her hand works its way under my towel but she sighs when she finds my cock flaccid.

"Tell me something, Jules." I look deeply into her eyes and my caressing hand on the back of her neck changes to a firm grip. "Where'd you sleep last night?"

She tries to pull back but I refuse to loosen my hold.

"What does it matter?" She pushes my arm away and rubs her neck. "As far as I can tell, we're not in a relationship, so I shouldn't have to answer that question, especially since you never open up about anything in *your* life."

"Bullshit." I stand and put another log on the fire.

"That's complete bullshit," I repeat, needing to keep my hands occupied or something's gonna break. "It matters to me and just because I didn't want to discuss Dayne doesn't mean that the rest of my life is off limits."

"Let me repeat," she says assertively. "I think we have a good time fooling around with one another, but there hasn't been much else to make this—"

"I asked you to dinner last night."

"Yeah, and you got moody and left me alone." She crosses her slim legs and leans forward.

"So... you're saying you want to date, like we're in high school or something. Hell, the last person I dated was my ex-wife and that was over fifteen years ago. I'm a grown man, Jules. I'm not going to—"

"So you just fuck people? See, that's exactly what I'm talking about. Don't get me wrong, I love sucking your cock, Mark, and if that's all you ever want from me, fine, but every once in a while I see something in your eyes that tells me there might be more to all of this. Perhaps that's all just wishful thinking on my part," she says with uncertainty.

Put up or shut up time. I should've done this last night.

"Everyone in this hotel always talks about your good looks, but I notice other things about you, like the fact that you're a smart businessman, and when I hear you talk to vendors and some of the guests you come across as intelligent and knowledgeable about what's going on in the world. A lot of people don't give a shit about things outside their hometown. You're not one of them."

"Stop," I whisper, losing my train of thought.

"You're a warrior in the bedroom." She smiles. "A domineering fucker, but you've revealed a softer side that's been hidden away. The fact that you care about my past and that someone hurt me was a telling sign last night."

"Enough."

"I also find you mysterious, a little dangerous, and haunting my every thought." She stands and moves closer. "And your fingers mimic your words, sometimes gentle and calm reaching deep inside me." She takes my hand and slides it under her skirt. "And other times they can be disciplinary and cruel."

I breathe heavily and slip one inside her warm body. She moans and closes her eyes.

"Discipline me, Mark." Her head rests against my chest as my finger glides around her pussy. "Punish me for falling for you."

"Fuckin' A," I respond to her leering tone with a hard swallow. Hell, this woman got me stiff in thirty seconds. "Look at me," I command.

She obeys with a roused expression and unbuttons my shirt. My nipples are sucked and kissed with great desire.

"Jules, tell me where you slept last night. I need to know."

She unzips then drops her skirt, taking off her sweater and bra, standing with only a thong on her body.

I drop my towel as she positions her chest over the arm of the sofa, her head down and ass high in the air.

"Give me the works," she whispers. "I don't want to feel like I'm a part of your life when I'm not. Hurt me so that I hate you." She looks at me with pleading eyes, waiting to feel pain.

"Never."

She rises slowly from my response, wanting to hear more.

"You know I'm a sucker for this type of play, but only because it's always been pleasurable for both of us. I can't give you what you're asking for right now." I wrap my towel back around my waist. "It's not what *I* want."

HOOKED

Julia's reeled me in and now she has me in a small white bucket, unable to swim away and with little room to turn around. Jumping out at this point would only leave me flopping on the ground and gasping for air. All I can do is stay and wait for her to prepare my body to be pan fried, eaten, and shit out.

I'm rather fond of her.

She pulled that act so my true colors would show, thinking she'd be a sneaky little bitch when all along I knew what she was doing. By her blissful expression, I could tell she was pleased with my response and is now fully aware my dick isn't going to disappear after one dip. She trusts me. And thankfully I didn't have to say much for her to finally get the drift. The term 'dating' is something she needs to erase from her vocabulary, but seeing one another is fine. Those were my words.

I want to see you.

I have to laugh at the irony of being bound to a woman who I haven't even fucked yet.

And I was clear when I put my towel back on that

her response about her whereabouts angered the fuck out of me—enough that our playtime before work was over before it even began.

I'm running on a meager three hours of sleep. The adrenaline from the kill has worn off and I've spent six hours in my office, going over the budget and financial records with my hotel manager, and trying to figure out where the fuck Dayne's staying or if he's even in town.

I didn't expect to see him yesterday, but am surprised he didn't show his face again today. He wants me to get all fidgety and paranoid, which isn't going to happen. And I may have shed one of my blades after the last kill, but I have plenty more. One of them surely has his name on it.

Nine o'clock.

I watched Julia throughout the evening, but kept my distance so I could get some work accomplished. She knew I was busy and it's not unusual for us to have days apart or even not cross paths, which means she's also unsuspecting of my truck trailing three cars behind hers, along Route 50, after her shift ends.

It's dark and with the headlights shining in her rear view mirror, it would be impossible for her to spot the pursuit. She's left me no choice but to find the answers myself.

After a five-minute drive we arrive in town. She circles the downtown shopping area before parking behind an old church. I pull into a lot across the street and watch from my truck as she tugs on the side door of the stone building, then the front, with no luck. Both are locked. She returns to her car, defeated.

"I knew it," I whisper.

I send her a text.

Plans tonight?

She smiles when she reads the message, but after staring at her cell for a few minutes, she puts it away and never responds.

"Now where to?"

I pursue at a distance from the church to one of the handful of secluded lakefront parks. It's closed, but she drives her beat up Toyota Corolla around the barricade and vanishes down the dark road.

"Fuck, Jules." I squeeze my Tacoma through the same space; barely making it without a scratch, then turn off my lights and park next to the first picnic area I see. She won't be far from here, the park's not very big, and she'll have to come back this way if she decides to leave.

I pull out my gun, concerned more about the bears than the drifters in this area, and maintain a steady pace off the pavement to quiet my footfalls.

The lights of her car ignite the lake ahead where she's parked next to a small restroom. She takes a sleeping bag from her trunk, turns off the engine, and settles into the backseat. She needs her neck ringed for being such a fucking dumbass. This area sucks for a young woman to be all alone, not to mention the low temperature. She's going to freeze.

To hell if I'll let this happen. I text a warning so

she's prepared.

Don't be scared. I'm here.

Her cell illuminates the inside of her car and a second later her head appears over the back seat, searching for a man approaching in the dark.

She opens her door with a doleful expression from being caught.

I slide in next to her and she locks us inside. There's a steak knife next to my foot, something she probably uses for protection. Other random items, mostly clothing, jewelry, and packaged food are also on the floor and passenger seat.

I'm silent, waiting for my heart to slow, my gut to relax, and my head to unwind. She's not staying here.

"What the fuck are you doing?" My mouth is taut with fury and even though I'm whispering, she knows I'm upset.

"I can't believe you followed me."

"You should've answered me earlier."

"Maybe where I sleep is none of your business."

"Don't fuck with me. You can't sleep here, Jules. I won't allow it."

"Well, the police have a shit fit when I sleep in the shopping center parking lots."

I throw my head back and exhale. "Fuck. How long have you been living in your car?"

"A while."

"A month? Two months? Fucking talk to me."

"Alright. Since last spring." She raises her voice.

"Why?"

"Why?" She looks speechless that I would ask such a question. "What? Do you think I'm a druggie or something? Think about it, Mark. I work thirty hours a week and make twelve dollars an hour. After taxes I'm living on twelve hundred a month. I have to buy food and gas; pay for my car insurance, health care, my P.O. box and a storage unit. I have a student loan too. It's not enough. I can't afford an apartment right now and I haven't been able to find a second job."

"Don't you have any friends... family... and what the hell did you think you were going to do in the winter? You'll freeze to death!" I yell. "And why didn't you tell me? This is total bullshit."

"Christ, don't you get it? I stay with friends sometimes, but I can't do it every night. They can't support me. And my parents said I needed to figure things out on my own. They can't support me either. I can tell you come from money. You wouldn't understand." She sighs.

I place my gun and coat on the floor and put my hands on the back of my neck. I breathe deeply, feeling restricted at the moment, and needing to regain my composure. She hasn't a clue about my past. No one does except my sister. We were dirt poor after my father left and had to scrape by just to eat. If my mother could've figured out a way to sell the two of us for a little extra cash, she would have. It wasn't until I was out of high school that my father reappeared with the big bucks from his casinos and porn company.

She places a hand on my leg. "Mark, I'll be fine. No need to pity me. Now take your pursed lips and go home."

A snicker suddenly transforms my stern face. "Don't be ridiculous, I'm not leaving you here. You can stay with me tonight. Tomorrow I'll set you up with your own room so you can have a little privacy and not have to worry about me attacking your tits all day."

"Mark, I..."

"I'm not ready for us to live together, but that doesn't mean I can handle you living in this car." I take her hand. "For fuck's sake, Jules, I own my own hotel. Start your engine and get your ass back there. This isn't a debate, it's a demand."

Her head shakes as she tries to restrain a grin. "Are you seriously going to do this... for me?" My waist is straddled and her hands grip my shoulders with sheer excitement. "I get to spend the night? Like sleep over? You're not talking about a night of fooling around then I get dressed and leave... but a night where I can *stay?*"

"I thought we already had this conversation today."

"You haven't said the actual words," she whispers, leaning in and nibbling at my ear. Her hand caresses my dick and I lower my body in the seat to give her more headroom.

"I think I've said plenty." I touch the side of her face and her massaging hand over my pants has me fully erect. "You need to be careful what you wish for anyway.

Once you're in my life, I'll be keeping an eye on you at all times." I smirk. "I can be a controlling bastard."

"I like that about you." She unbuttons my shirt then pulls off her sweater and unsnaps her bra. "I'm ready to be under your control."

Her tits are quickly in my hands and I wonder who truly holds all of the power, her or me.

My cock's engorged as she rises on the seat, allowing me to slide my pants down. I never imagined at my age being in the back seat of a Corolla with a twenty-two-year-old on my lap, her tits in my face, and my pants wrapped around my ankles. I hope the fucking cops don't show up.

"Mark," she whispers in my ear. "I said I'm ready to be under your control."

Oh shit.

Her back is on the seat, legs up, feet against the window, and a condom's out of my wallet in less than five seconds.

"You don't have to put out because I'm giving you a place to stay. You're not my whore."

She pulls me down and grips my hips. "I was waiting for you to show that you cared."

Holding the back of her head with two hands, I fixate on her eyes to make sure this is *really* what she wants.

"Do it," she whispers.

Fuck yeah. My ass tightens as I slide inside her slick pussy.

"Mark," she says faintly. "I need you."

I slide slowly out and back in.

She turns her head. "Mark."

My head is spinning from her roused voice and I can't keep from driving faster.

"Yes!" she calls out as I attack her tits and thrust over her passionately. I have one knee on the floor and a hand on the window, but to hell if I'm going to stop fucking her because I'm uncomfortable. I've waited too long. It's been six weeks since I've had my dick in a woman—the longest I've gone without pussy since I was seventeen.

I hold her neck and demand to hear my name once more.

"Mark." The word shoots from her mouth like she's about to cum. "Mark." She reaches for her clit.

"Tell me how much you want me." I pant.

My nipples are grabbed and I'm pulled closer for a kiss. I'm done for. Opening up to her like this... the moment our lips touch... damn it; I'm a weakened mess from her pussy and tongue. This will be quick.

"Uh, fuck." My palm slaps the roof of her car as my legs convulse and cum fires out. "Fuck." I shove my cock further in. "You wicked woman."

What flows from my body is like the blood that streams from my victims. Both fluids are sticky, warm, and cause a loss of breath.

I fall over her, flush, with a hammering heart. I want more.

"Fucking hell, Jules."

"Mark." She pushes me off in a panic. "There's a guy outside the car!"

"Son of a bitch."

I reach for my gun, but she grasps my hand, saving my ass from making a tragic mistake. It's a cop. I can tell by the routine tap on the window and the flashlight shining in my eyes, and Julia was fully aware of who it was before I came to my senses. I bet she's been awakened a few times this way while sleeping in her car.

"Damn it, put your clothes on," I whisper while sliding quickly into my pants. "I knew this was gonna happen." Jules unlocks the car when the cop taps again. I place my hands on my legs as he opens the door and shines the light in both of our faces.

"Miss?" He looks at Jules. "You here against your will?" His voice is burly and direct.

"No, definitely not," she replies. "And I'm not a prostitute either."

The light does a dance through her car, darting along the front seats and around the floor.

"ID's," he says.

I keep a straight face, one hand on my leg while the other reaches for my wallet in my back pocket. He has his hand on his gun and I notice his car parked on the other side of the restroom. He must have arrived when I was cumming or I would've heard him drive up.

"Age?" he asks while looking at our drivers licenses.

"Twenty-two." She sighs.

"It's on my license," I reply.

"Don't get smart," he says. He shakes his head and shines the light into our faces again. "That your Tacoma parked just past the entrance?"

"Yes."

"The park's closed for the season, that's why the barricade's in place," he scolds.

I nod.

"Don't mean to scare you two, but a body was found along one of the western park trails earlier today. We're keeping a watchful eye out until we can figure out exactly what happened. I suggest you find another spot to..." He flashes the light on my suit then at Julia's beat up car. "I think you can at least treat this woman to a hotel room." He hands us back our ID's. "Right, Mr. Jameson?"

Asshole. I fucking hate cops.

"Yes," I respond.

"I don't want to come across either one of you in these parts again, at least not until the beach reopens in April." He turns off the light and steps back. "I'll follow you out." He waves his hand for us to get a move on. "Hurry up."

"Take me to my truck then go to my place," I whisper. "You're not going anywhere else, but home with me."

FIRST LIGHT

T he morning sun warms my feet. I'm in bed with one arm under Julia and a hand stroking her soft straight hair. I grin as her chest heaves from a thirty-minute workout with my tongue. It was something I wanted to do last night but we were both too exhausted to fool around. She fell asleep in my arms straightaway and slept soundly, probably for the first time in months.

"You off today?" I ask.

"Yeah, I was going to look for another job then unpack a few things." She rolls toward me. "If the offer still stands."

"I wouldn't have it any other way. You're staying in the room next to mine and I'm changing your schedule from six to eight hour shifts. That will give you full-time benefits. This wasn't a half-assed bargain to get laid, Jules. I want you here, safe and sound."

The astonished glow on her face affects my heart in unforeseen ways. "You're the nicest—"

"Don't say it." I stand and pull on my boxers with a grin. "You'll damage my ego."

"Does this mean you won't be fucking anyone else?"

"No need," I say under my breath.

I head downstairs and retrieve the breakfast cart, sip my juice, and bite into my daily dry toast. The local paper has arrived with the food and, just like the cop mentioned, the front-page headline announces that a body's been found. I was hoping a black bear would've devoured Roland before anyone came across the body. Too bad the bears missed out.

After reading that the cops have no leads, I toss the local paper but save the Los Angeles Times for later, bringing it and the rest of the food upstairs to Julia.

I hand her my glass and set the plate on the bed before running my fingers down the front of her chest, stopping over her pussy.

"It's nice waking up with a woman in my bed," I say, watching her eat a grape and sip her juice. "Have you been using the tanning beds by the weight room to keep your skin this bronze?"

She nods. "I hope that's alright. I thought you said staff could use the facilities."

"It is. I was just wondering."

"You mean wondering if I spent my money on frivolous things, like going to a tanning salon?"

"Of course not." I sit next to her. "Just thinking about you... you've been putting on a good show."

"How so?" She takes a bite of toast and another sip of juice.

"The way you've kept yourself together. Your

clothing, hair, and makeup are always in order and you smell like you recently showered whenever we're together."

"Well, I'm not a hobo."

"Yeah, but even your pussy's soft and clean."

"Duh, I wanted to impress you."

"Why?"

"Why not? And why would I show up at your door wearing my period panties?"

I laugh and walk over to my dresser. "I'm glad you're here, Jules."

"Good, now I get to ask you *why*. Why are you glad I'm here?"

"Because now I can eat your pussy whenever I want." I smirk.

"Ha! You can get it whenever you want even when I'm not living here. Try again."

"Nope."

"Mark." She wants an answer.

"Come on." I hold out my hand for her to follow me to the shower. "Let's get ready."

She follows me through the master bath, to the back where I turn on the light to my separate shower room. And as expected, she's wide-eyed and in awe of the mosaic scene of Lake Tahoe that covers the shower wall.

"Holy shit," she says and runs her hand along the tiles. "It's beautiful... and huge. You could fit four people in this shower."

I turn on the water and slip out of my boxers.

"Five."

She eyes my dick then shakes her head in disappointment of where it's been. "I don't want to hear about *that* experience."

"Not *every* story's sexual."

"With you it has been."

"Not this time. I promise. I know because when my sister and her family visited after the hotel first opened, her two kids wanted to know how many people could fit in the shower. The answer is five with room for more."

"Ahh, that's cute."

"Not really. Her kids are little a-holes," I say while she washes her hair. I step in, and for once, continue the conversation like I'm a normal human being. "One of her kids thought it'd be funny to turn on the water and soak everyone's clothing before he decided to take a piss."

"In here?" She looks down.

"It was a long time ago, trust me, my place is clean."

"I bet they're not that bad. What are their names?"

I lather my body and hers, taking my time with her tits before rinsing off and answering her question.

"Daxton Snow and Xavier Hail. The Everton boys, only they're nothing like my brother-in-law and it's a shame they have to carry his last name. I'm convinced they're a hundred percent Jameson."

"Are you making this up? Those can't be their names."

"You can't make this kind of shit up."

"And what's your sister's name? Like, Xandra Rain?"

"That's good. Clever." I smile while rinsing my hair. "Her name's Sophia, but her husband's name is Cove."

"Okay, now I know you're kidding. Cove? Do you even have a sister?"

"Trust me." I step out and towel off. "She's real."

"I'll believe you if you show me a photo."

I hand her a towel and dress, having other plans for the day besides looking at photographs of my fucked up family.

"You wouldn't be able to tell we're related from a photograph. She looks just like my father."

"Mark?" She slips into black silk panties and a red and black polka-dot bra. "Are you feeling okay? It's like I woke up next to a completely different man. You're actually talking to me and you haven't broken anything... yet."

"Isn't that what you wanted?"

"Yeah, but I never thought I'd make it to this point. And this discussion must be killing you right now."

I push her against the bathroom counter, forcing her to bend over. Her hair is wrapped around my hand in a tight grip and her head lifts to view our reflection in the mirror. "This better?" I kick her legs apart and rub my dick on her ass. "I'm still the same domineering bastard from yesterday, my head's constantly replaying that fuck from last night, and I can't wait for you to feel my cock again. The last time I had pussy as tight as yours, I was a teenager. You want to take a hard one now or later?"

"You're back." She laughs. "Later, please. I want to enjoy the nice side of you before it disappears... unless you just showed me it's already hidden away."

Turning her around and lifting her chin, I dish out my best look of adoration.

"Kiss me," she whispers.

"Ugh. Why are women so fucking obsessed with kissing?" I shrug her off and reach for my toothbrush.

"Damn it, I should've stopped while I was ahead."

"Porn stars don't kiss."

"Oh, is that what you call yourself, a porn star? Being with a lot of women doesn't make you a porn star, Mark Jameson. You're not *that* good."

"No, but working for Jameson Industries does. It was my life for years and you should know about it before you become too infatuated."

"What?" she whispers.

I lean against the counter with my arms crossed. "Look, I'm not used to a woman getting stuck in my head, and I'm trying not to be a prick. You're here and it's time to get some things out in the open, then you can decide whether or not you want to take the leap into my world, and if not, you still have a free room until you get back on your feet. Or, if you want me to shut the hell up, we can continue to fuck and forget about all the rest."

"Wait, you really were a porn star?"

"And what the hell do you mean, I'm not *that* good? I was one of my father's top men. Only second to my brother-in-law."

"What? This isn't even making any sense to me right now. Your father forced you to screw people in his company?"

"He didn't force me."

"And your sister's husband was in it too? I need to sit down." She paces, looking for a chair. "Jesus. I knew you were a man whore, but I didn't think you got paid for being one, like a prostitute. So you've been with hundreds of women?" She shakes her head.

"Over a thousand."

"And I've been with two men... only one by choice."

"Three, if you remember last night. And I think you're overreacting."

"Gah! Thank fuck you used a condom. Screw this, I can't compete with your past."

"It's not a contest, and I'm clean."

She pauses and digs through her bag for makeup. "You're absolutely right, it's not a contest." She puckers her lips and applies a coat of pink lipstick. "I wish I could get you out of my head."

"Is that what you want?"

"What I *want* is *not* to be one of *those* women. You've sampled an entire army of vaginas, but I guarantee the people who spread eagle for you don't give two shits about their bodies. I've always thought of myself as being better than that." She raises her hands and shows off her figure. "I want a guy who thinks I'm special, not someone who finds me weak or easy prey."

"You're not weak."

"And I'm not a sex toy." She puts her hands on her hips. "If I show you a good time you sure as hell better reciprocate."

"Of course." Fuck, she's in control again.

"That doesn't happen in porn. The guy gets off and the girl gets nothing. I won't allow you to treat me that way."

"You're taking this to an extreme."

"You were a fucking porn star! This sucks. I don't want someone who's going to fuck me then try to fuck my best friend the next day."

"That's not exactly what we do or what I did. It was years ago anyway."

"Oh yeah? So what *did* you do?"

My head shakes incessantly. There's no way I'm going to take this conversation that far. "It's not important."

"So why even bring it up?"

"I'm starting to ask myself the same question." I exhale. "Because I thought you wanted more from me and this is the simplest thing to start with."

"It's what? The *simplest* thing? For Christ's sake, next you're going to tell me you're a serial killer."

I laugh and look at the floor. "You know that's not true or you'd already be dead."

"Not funny."

"Whatever happened to liking me because I'm mysterious and a little dangerous? Don't you think it's cool in any way? The guy you're with is a former porn star. Your friends will find it fascinating." I smirk.

"No, it's gross." She sets her ass against the counter and rubs her temples, possibly thinking of a way to get out of this situation. It takes her forever to speak again. "Alright..."

I wait, but she doesn't say what that means.

"What? Alright, what?"

"*Alright*, I think I can handle this... maybe." Her hand touches my dick and our eyes lock. "I hate the fact that this thing has had so much fun without me, and I'd be lying if I said I'm not insecure about pleasuring you now, especially knowing *trained* women have had their way with you. I had hoped to impress you, but I guess that's impossible."

"Jules, you—"

"Shh." My cock's released, as I'm hushed. "But, I did impress you, didn't I? I'm the one standing next to you and not Chloe, or any of your past whores."

"You're like a breath of fresh air," I whisper. "Your reaction alone is enough to put a smile on my face, not to mention your maturity in wanting to try to move past this so quickly."

I can't believe these words are coming out of my mouth. If my father was still around and he heard this shit, he'd slam my head against a wall and call me pussy-whipped. Then he'd hand me a shot of liquor and tell me who to fuck next.

"Come here." I pull her closer and place my hand

on the side of her face. Her tongue glides across her lips, yearning for my mouth.

"So according to you, you're not a porn star anymore," she says. "They may not kiss, but real men sure as hell do. Show me. I want a long passionate one, not some short five second peck like you usually give me."

My lips press softly to hers and my dad instantly returns to my mind. The bastard will live inside my head forever.

• • •

He kicks in the door of one of the bedrooms in his mansion, pulling me off a new hire in his company. A woman no older than eighteen, scared shitless, and her first time on camera.

"You fucking son of a bitch. Get up," my father yells.

He pulls me out of the room and I'm pushed down the hall to his office where he slams and locks the door.

"What the fuck, Mark? Is it that hard to keep your lips off women when you fuck them? I'm starting to second-guess bringing you into this company. Maybe you need to go home to your pretty little wife and die an old man with your face puckered like a fish. Smooch, smooch. I hate that shit. You look like a dumbass. Stop wasting my money and get the scene right the first time."

"She's nervous."

"Too fucking bad, she's not here against her will. She

signed up for it, now fuck her, don't turn this into a love scene. This is about making money, nothing else. If this is too complicated for you or your mouth to handle, pack your bags and go home early. I don't need you around for an entire week if all I'm gonna do is babysit your ass."

My hands cover my limp dick, hiding it from the bastard. According to him, kissing and losing wood are two signs of weakness in a man.

"You're trying to buy a new house, right? That's why you came this time. Your wife's been nagging you? One week, Mark. A week and I'll help you out, but you gotta play the game. Fuck, are you soft?" He stares at my groin and shakes his head.

"How can you expect me to stay erect when I'm carted to your office and bitched at."

Shit, I know that look. He's furious... about to do something that makes me feel helpless, to show he's in control, the man owns me. I'm not his son... I'm his property.

He hands me a shot then fixes one for himself.

"Show me," he says.

"What, my dick?"

"That you can get it up."

"Get real. I'm not yanking my cock in front of you."

He places a call then points to a chair. "Sit," he says. "Someone's replacing you for the day."

I'm fucked.

"You like being here?" he asks.

"Most of the time. I like the money I'm bringing in. It's

triple what I made at my old job."

"And you understand this is a business?"

I nod.

"So if I ask you to show me you can get it up, stroke it and show me, don't mouth off. The cunt in that room is my money and so is your cock. It's a business."

"I'm not feeling well."

"You're fine."

"Did you put something in that shot?"

"You'll only be out for about an hour. When you wake, don't try to force your lips open, you'll tear the stitches. I'm shutting your mouth for you since you don't know how to do it yourself. It's the only way you're going to learn to keep your lips off women. I'll take the stitches out tomorrow."

"I promise I won't..." *My vision blurs and I slide out of the chair. "Dad."*

"Kissing makes you susceptible to a woman's control. You're the man in those rooms, Mark, it's time to act like one."

• • •

"Hot!" Julia's flush. "You can't tell me that kiss wasn't enjoyable."

"Give me a moment to use the bathroom," I say, locking her out without mentioning or even remembering the kiss.

Duct tape was covering my mouth when I woke up in my dad's office on the day I was drugged. He could've stitched it shut, but he didn't. He wanted to scare the shit out of me instead. The more I was afraid of him, the more control he had over me. That's what he did to everyone in his company and eventually I was so brainwashed I could barely function in the real world. I stopped fucking my wife, but stayed in the house because of my son, which did him more harm than good. And it's no wonder I'm an abusive fucker like my dad.

I touch the stubble on my face and raise my chin, feeling the area of my jugular vein while admiring the rest of my body in the mirror. I need to stay fit until the day I die. If my abs or dick ever goes slack, I'll cut this vein and end my life.

"Mark? Every time I'm here and you lock yourself in the bathroom, something ends up broken or you hurt yourself."

"Get dressed, I'll be out in a minute."

"I am dressed. What are you doing in there?"

"Just read the paper or something and give me a moment alone."

She sighs as I clasp my watch and fix my hair.

"Guess what, Dad?" I say softly. "I'm about to spend inheritance money on this woman. Yes, a *woman*. Some of that money's from my dick anyway, so I have every right to spend it however I see fit. I worked my ass off for it—literally. And since you're dead, there isn't anything you can do about it besides haunt my mind. I can handle that, but I bet you can't. I hope you turn in your grave when I buy her new clothes and jewelry." I lean closer to the mirror and grin. "And if I want to put my lips on hers, I'm gonna fucking do it. I don't give a shit if it makes me weak, or if I lose control and cum instantly because it feels so good, or if it's an act of *love* and unacceptable to you. Your heart's no longer beating and shit no longer flows from your mouth."

"I'm worried about you," she says. "What are you whispering?"

"I bet you didn't even have a heart inside that cold body of yours when you were alive, and sometimes I wonder if I'm the same way, or if there's a small chance mine may be able to beat again."

I open the door and walk past her, getting dressed then dragging her by the arm down the stairs.

"Let's go."

"Where?"

"I want to clear out your storage unit so you can get settled in your room. Then we're going shopping for the things you need and have done without, then we'll continue shopping for things you don't need, but that I want you to have, then we're going to talk... then we need to fuck some more."

"You've always gotten your way, haven't you?" she asks.

I put my arm through my shoulder holster and cover my gun with my suit jacket. Turning back, I see the photo of my son over the fireplace. "No, I haven't."

DISCHARGE

My son knows what a shitty father I am. He tells me on the phone once a month that I suck moose balls and he hopes I rot in Hell. When he was born, I told myself the age-old lie that I was going to be a better parent than my father was, but I'm just as horrible.

My son's a teenager now, and even if my wife agreed to fly him out for a visit, he wouldn't want to come. I deserve that and I'm proud of him for telling me off. Treating me like shit after all the years I ignored him and his mother is just fine. I send my monthly child support and sometimes even tell him he's a little prick for mouthing off, knowing our relationship is in a fast decline. He doesn't listen to me anyway. My words are meaningless.

Sometimes I'm bothered that I lost him, mainly because I hate to lose. I've offered to give him a couple hundred bucks to come for a visit, but "It's not enough," he says. I'd hate to have to bribe him with a grand. Dumbass kid.

Although my money can't seem to buy my son's love, it *can* buy other things.

"I have a king-size bed and a kitchenette! I feel like royalty." Jules grins in delight.

"So the room's big enough?"

"Are you kidding? It's like a castle compared to my car." She steps away from the window and admires the curtains I bought to make the room feel more like a home. "And I even have the Jameson Hotel signature flowers on the dresser." She sniffs the Mariposa lilies. "It's perfect!"

I lean back in the desk chair and study her movements. With quick steps, a budding smile, and her eagerness to unpack her new clothes, I'd say she's on cloud nine.

"Now that I've talked your ear off about my family and childhood, it's your turn to open up like you did this morning. I need to shut my mouth for the rest of the day," she says. "It's *your* turn."

I take off my coat and place my gun next to the television, then slip out of my shoes and unbutton my shirt. "I can tell by your expression how happy I've made you and it's obvious you're even happier now that you know I'm staying here for a while."

She blushes. "I am happy, but I'm wondering if you find me bland because I own so little? I have clothes, accessories, and books, but my apartments have always been furnished, so I don't have anything of substance. I could tell you were surprised by the size and contents of my storage unit... you know what? Forget it. I just answered my own question. I know I'm mediocre. That's okay. I have years ahead of me to change that."

"I love how your mind works." I laugh. "You process your own questions before I even have a chance to respond. And you seem satisfied with your answer, even though it may be different from what I was going to say." My fingers run over a box as she places a sweater into a drawer. "Our day was a heck of a lot easier than I imagined it was going to be. I thought we'd be making four or five trips with my truck and was worried I'd have to put you in a larger room, further away from my suite. If anything, what you own makes me feel at ease. And if it doesn't work between you and me, I can dispose of you and your things quite easily."

"Smartass," she says under her breath. "Are you gonna tell me more about yourself like I asked or do I have to listen to you being a dick until I finish unpacking?"

"Why don't *you* ask me what you want to know? That way I won't make the mistake of telling you something you don't want to hear."

"Alright, tell me more about your family."

"Very well." I put my shirt on the bed and pull off my belt. "My mother tried to commit suicide recently and she's in a psych ward. It's the fifth time. My sister has a house in St. Louis with her alcoholic husband; they own a wine bar. My father got a well-deserved bullet in his head and he's six-feet under. I took over his porn company for a while, but sold it after my divorce. My ex moved back to Philly with my son. It's our hometown... but, our relationship and the entire marriage was nothing. I was fucking her on and off for years, but the two of us were just friends. Then she got pregnant and decided against an abortion. I was young and ignorant, and she wanted to get married. I should've walked away. There was never a romantic moment between us, just loud sex that was cold and heartless."

She stops unpacking and closes her eyes. "Jesus, you weren't kidding that the porn was the simplest thing to discuss. I don't even know what to ask you after that."

"Keep it simple."

"Okay, where'd your sister meet her husband?"

"That's complicated."

"Why? Was she a porn star too?"

"Not by choice."

"What? That was supposed to be a joke. Your family's fucked up! Didn't you ever have a Sunday dinner together or go to the park, or on vacation, or anything with one another?"

"No."

She stands and places her hands on her hips. "Don't you crave normalcy?"

That one throws me off guard. "I've never really thought about it before."

"Think about it now." She takes off her clothes and points to the bed. "Sit."

"Yes, my sexy domineering one." I drop my pants

and sit on the edge of the bed.

"Mark, look at me. I'm pretty damn normal."

"You're the furthest thing from normal," I say, straight-faced with her hand in mine. "But if you insist that you're normal and you want to know if that's what I crave, then the answer is yes."

"You're agreeing to everything I say just to get laid."

I nod. "Is it working or do I need to take another approach? It hasn't been easy being a gentleman today, especially after last night." I shake my head. "And Jesus, when you were trying on clothes, all I could think about was how quickly I could rip the damn things off and fuck you again. My cock was a mammoth most of the day."

Her head tilts and she flashes a sarcastic smile. "Thanks. Glad to know my first time with a guy in the backseat of a car was as meaningful to him as it was for me."

"That's not what I meant," I whisper and run my hand down her back.

I take a moment to inhale deeply, smelling the cherry scent still on her wrists from the body lotion she sampled earlier.

"I need my flesh in yours so I can be one with you," I finally say.

"Better... but you still sound like a typical guy in the books that I read."

"Are you comparing me to a fictional character?"

"You could be the poster child for those men."

"What the fuck does that even mean? Is that where your desire to be whacked in the ass comes from?"

"Maybe." She laughs.

I pull her playfully to the bed and lie next to her, placing my hand on her taut stomach while my legs lock around hers.

The fuck in her car was selfish on my part, not to mention how restrained I felt in the space. Fast too, embarrassingly quicker than my usual twenty-minute run.

"I want to try something, if that's alright," I mumble, unsure if those words were meant for her, or me.

"As long as it's not painful." She faces me and rests her hands under her head with an expression of trust. "Make it fun for both of us."

Where do I even begin? I don't want to come across as a pansy ass to someone who's only experienced my commanding and abrasive side in bed. And I'm assuming she likes it that way or she wouldn't be here, so why fuck with what we've got?

Her lips tighten, unable to mask her enthusiasm while her face flushes in arousal. "It's nice being here in this soft bed next to you. Your blue eyes are full of life for once and your voice sounds frisky. It's exciting. You're exciting. Tell me what you want to try. You know I'm up for almost anything."

"Give me a second."

"Don't you dare disappear into the bathroom

again."

"I need the condoms we bought today."

"You mean the *boxes* of condoms we bought."

"I plan on using every last one of them too." I roll one on and rigidly inch over top of her. "If you don't like this, stop me. I can always go back to something you enjoy, like the belt."

"Enter slower this time, please. It hurt a little last night," she requests.

"I will," I whisper. "I'm doing everything differently tonight."

"Why?" she speaks quietly and wraps her legs around my hips.

"Because... do you think I'm cruel, Jules? Punishing? Selfish?" My arms rest next to her head as I stare into her eyes, waiting for an answer. Nothing. She's dead silent. "What about heartless?"

Still nothing.

"Can you feel this?" I rub my tip around her clit. "I never have a problem getting it up for you. Look at me... look... watch my face. Feel me sliding inside... gently... feel it... fuck, you're slippery wet for me," I say softly, while keeping my eyes focused on hers. "I'm almost in. Take me... accept me."

"Mmm." A faint sound leaves her mouth.

I drift slowly over her, once, twice, then clench my ass and push deeper inside. Her mouth drops open and her hands grab at my hair.

"Your lips are provocative. Teasing me," I whisper

in her ear. "Would they like some company?"

"Yes, please," she whispers back.

An explosion of moans fills the room as our lips touch. I take it gingerly at first, like I'm savoring rich chocolate, letting her melt in my mouth. She bites my tongue and my chest expands in a pant while her hips rise eagerly for my cock. Thank fuck this is doing something for her.

My waist lowers to hers, putting pressure on her clit with each drive.

"You feel incredible... what are you doing?"

I cradle her head in my hands, advancing forward, kissing her mouth, neck, and tits.

"I feel like I'm on fire," she says in a high voice.

I'm quiet now, gifting her short, gentle, and precise thrusts until our stomachs glide with sweat. Ten minutes later and both our hands are gripping the sheets while our mouths begin a greedy attack on one another.

"Mark." She pants. "I've never cum with a man inside me." Her head falls back, chin up, eyes closed. "I'm so turned on. I think it's going to happen."

That's for damn sure, it *will* happen. And I can't believe I'm allowing myself to caress a woman's sweet lips. Fuck, it's good, a renewed pleasure. One that heats my body, twists my head, and has my dick ready to spit. I'm not going to last much longer.

"You're being so... I'm not used to... oh fuck, I'm so close."

I nudge and kiss.

"Uh," she whispers.

Then lunge harder, getting lost in the erotic sounds in the room.

"Ohhh."

Quick jerks and warm tongues dancing, a whisper of how gorgeous she is, and a hand under her ass pushing her body into mine. That does it.

"Oh, oh." Her mouth is open. "I'm cumming, harder, yesss," she says faintly. "I'm cumming."

Her pussy tightens then runs wild with quick pulsations beating at my cock. I groan, bite her lip, hold my breath, and wait.

This is amazing.

I always pleasure myself first, shoot my load, then finger or eat a woman out to get her off. I haven't felt fluttering muscles in ages. And fuck, Jules' muscles are ferocious. Like a hand stoking my dick.

She trembles in my arms and all I want is to devote this moment to her, but I can't stop my release.

A lusty sound escapes my mouth then, "Damn it... it's coming... Christ, I can't stop it."

She's over her crest but still in a frenzy as my first strong shot escapes, then the second.

"Uh, fuck." My forehead rests on hers. I tighten my feet and close my eyes.

"Cum, cum for me," she says.

I collapse and our mouths join, kissing while a soft light glows over our heaving bodies.

"Holy hell," she says.

She owns me with an embrace, holding the gearshift in this relationship.

I roll onto my back with my dick drowning in a condom packed with cum. It's pulled quickly off and tossed on the floor. I pant, staring at the ceiling, disoriented, confused, and somewhat embarrassed by my tenderness. I noticed her. I felt her emotions. I allowed myself to get lost in a kiss and thought it was crucial to please her. What the fuck?

"You made love to me," she says softly.

I shiver.

"You made love to me, Mark. It was beautiful."

My fingers rest over my eyes and I suddenly feel unsettled. I need to get out of here without being too much of a prick.

"It was good." I pat her leg and get my ass dressed.

"Where are you going?"

"I forgot I have work to do."

"Crap. That was incredible for a second, but now I just feel used."

"Don't. I didn't use you. Seriously. I told you, it was nice, but I thought of some things that need to be done and they can't wait until tomorrow."

"The first thing you thought about after sex was work? That sucks. No, *you* suck."

"Sorry." I grab my gun, kiss her cheek, and walk out.

"Good night!" she yells, bitingly.

This woman has mangled my brain.

I enter my suite and slump onto the sofa. Shit. I did exactly what I wanted, so why am I so goddamn ashamed? I'm coming unhinged over making love?

A woman who owns your heart is the devil, and the only way to kill the devil is to fuck it in the ass, cut its throat, and bury it deep.

That's what my father used to say.

I'm surprised my mother's still alive after dealing with his bullshit. And my sister and I are poles apart whenever we discuss our childhood memories of him. He was nice to her, but hated me with a passion. Maybe she blocked it all out.

Fucker.

I kick the coffee table and an echoing crash fills the room. It's dismal in here and I need a shot to calm my nerves.

No, forget the liquor tonight. I need some weed. Luckily, I've got a few joints left in my bedroom and getting high might help me figure out what the fuck's going on in my head.

I smoke when I'm under stress and need to unwind, and usually it's a solitary experience. I don't enjoy people yacking in my ear when I'm stoned.

I take a black metal case from my dresser and turn on my favorite music to smoke to, *In the Pines*, a folk song from the 1800s. It's something that brings me peace.

After a long drag I close my eyes, sensing a massaging hand codling my brain. The pot soothes my muscles and alleviates my anxiety. I grin and take another hit before heading to my bedroom deck to marvel at the mountain pines.

Hell, this woman's turning me into a clod, forcing me into a world that I'm completely unschooled in. And to hell if my father didn't also turn me into a clod, forcing me into his world that I was unschooled in. Shit. I'm just too marred to escape either one.

In the pines, in the pines
Where the sun never shines
I shivered the whole night through

The melancholy voice lingers in the brisk night, seeping between the trees and down to the empty pool. The lights from the inhabited hotel rooms ignite the back property where the ash trees exhibit a few remaining leaves on their branches. It's simply sensational, especially the smell of the decaying leaves.

I love my property. Leaving the overpopulated city of Vegas and living in isolation was a dream I had for years, long before I ever got a divorce. I hated the smell of that dusty, polluted desert city. My father loved it. He was addicted to the twenty-four hour rush, his mansion full of people and his bed full of whores... bright lights, loud music, gambling, booze, and sex.

I tired of it after a decade. The money I was

bringing in was incredible, except I had little time to enjoy any of it. Not the way I wanted to. The parties were demanding and I felt suffocated by the company. I was overwhelmed by the stress to keep Jameson Industries number one and I hated being compared to my father by all the other porn company kings. The competition was fierce. Plus, my dad had the Rosen twins, Dayne and Doron, and their father, David Rosen, working by his side. They were a team of four. I had no one.

But that's my own damn fault. I wanted all the power. I couldn't stand having a partner. Still can't. I need total control of everything and everyone. I'd rather be a big fish in a little pond, then...

Where will you go
I'm going where the cold wind blows

"What the...?" I whisper as a tiny flashing light bounces along the railing next to my hand then travels up my arm. I know its source; it's coming from the opposite side of my hotel, the dark suite. This isn't the first time the figure is standing outside on the deck off the master bedroom, using the light to say hello. I point to go back inside but the fucker won't obey.

I tap my watch and bring up the walkie-talkie App we use to communicate. "Get inside, now." There's no reply, only a continual light on my body. I look down at it and shake my head. "Get the fuck inside so I know you're safe," I speak into my watch again. "I'm not up for games tonight or Morse code with the flashlights. Maybe another time."

The light vanishes, only to be replaced by another. This time, a small red light coming from the woods that gleams when it strikes my watch then quickly races up my stomach to my chest... it's a laser sight.

"Duck!" the voice from the other suite calls out. But I'm already down, just a split second before a shot from the pines thuds into my exterior wall.

"Fuck, fuck, fuck!" I crawl inside and pull the gun from my holster. "Fuck!"

"Get the fuck inside!" I yell into my watch.

Recess is over. How the hell did that bastard, Dayne, get a gun? He's not doing this shit to me. I'm coming for him. No one takes a shot at Mark Jameson and lives.

I run down my stairs and out my front door, slowing to a hurried pace in the hall and setting my gun back in its holster, not wanting to raise any suspicions from the guests.

"Mr. Jameson?" The voice of one of my security guards comes through my watch.

"It's okay," I answer.

"Did you hear that?"

"Let the guests know it's okay," I repeat. "It was a kid setting off a firecracker out back."

I'm so not amused, Dayne. If you had shot at the figure holding the flashlight from the dark suite instead of me... fuck, I can't even go there in my head.

I turn a corner and pound twice on the dark suite's door, waiting impatiently. Two knocks means an emergency and this door better open.

"What?" I hear a voice through the steel.

"What the fuck do you mean, what? Open the freakin' door," I say as calmly and discreetly as possible. At least I think I did. Everything sounds twenty times louder because I'm stoned. Plus my eyes are wavy and my heart's racing. I'm feeling paranoid. "Did you see what Dayne did? That's like shooting a man in the back. It was a cheap shot." I kick the door in an unreasonable state. I'm not chill and I know it won't be opened when I'm like this. No one wants to deal with a riled madman.

"I heard the shot. Do you think he's coming inside?"

"Keep this suite dark at all times and lock the back door. No one, you hear me, no one should be coming in or out on that deck. Listen to me and you'll be fine."

"I'm worried."

"Don't, the fucker will be dead soon."

There's a faint sigh. "I don't want to hear that you're a murderer."

"Fine, then a Jameson will be dead soon."

"Jesus, Mark."

"One or the other. I can't be a savior without being a killer." I look around the corner and down the quiet hall where two guests are walking at a distance. "Open the door."

"Is it necessary?"

"I'm itching to slap someone upside the head. There shouldn't be anyone on that back deck playing around with a flashlight while Dayne's in the area!"

"You know you'd get your ass kicked as soon as you raised your hand. The flashlight got your attention and saved your life. Just be gracious and don't think about slapping anyone."

I laugh and shake my head. "Give me the code so I can open your door in case there's another emergency."

"Fuck no. You said it was safer for you *not* to have it. No!"

"Just a test," I whisper. "Remember to keep the lights out and the doors and windows shut. Don't do anything stupid, either, like ordering take-out. You should have plenty of food." I look down the hall again and see it's empty. "It shouldn't take much longer," I mumble. "If I could figure out where he's staying it'd already be over and done with."

"Who's the woman?"

"What woman?"

"The one by the pool who you looked heartbroken over."

"No one."

"Bullshit."

"This door-side conversation has already lasted too long."

"You trust her?"

"What?"

"Mark. Do. You. Trust. Her? It's a simple question."

"I don't have any reason not to."

"I've never heard you say such an asinine thing. You know full well those are the ones who'll put a knife in your back. 'I don't have any reason not to?' Seriously? Why aren't you thinking straight?"

"Fuck off."

"Yep, fuck off and goodnight."

I exhale and linger back to the opposite end of the hotel. Everything seems to be in need of repair when I'm stoned. And I mean my life *and* this hotel. It's not something I notice unless I leave the peaceful solitude and dim lights of my suite.

I squint at the traditional damask patterned carpet that could use replacing, and the walls in need of a fresh coat of paint. I'm sure in the morning it'll all look brand spanking new, but right now I feel like I'm in a decrepit hell hole. I think I need more weed after a gunshot and a dazed discussion, but I also know I'm still high and shouldn't over do it when Dayne's around.

Fuck, I can't believe he took a shot from that distance. He's more of the type to shoot a man in the face at point blank range. What gives?

I stop at Julia's room and knock, still apprehensive of her control, but unable to stand the fact that she's in this room alone, not after what just happened.

"Don't expect to fuck me and just take off again," she says before the door is even open. "Next time you leave I'll follow you out and knee you in the nuts."

I smile, pulling her from her room, lifting her over my shoulder, and kidnapping her for the night.

"I want you in my place while I work, not to fuck, but so I can keep an eye on you. I warned you I'd get possessive once you arrived. Now no more fucking tonight. You can sleep while I track someone down on my laptop."

"Make love to, not fuck," she says playfully while kicking her feet on the way to my bedroom. "Admit it, you made love to me."

"Fine." I fling her onto the bed, lock my bedroom door that leads to the deck, and close my blinds. "You're the lucky winner of a mentally-ill, controlling cocksucker. Now stay in that bed and don't move your ass unless I tell you it's okay. That includes getting up to use the bathroom."

My bed is positioned away from the windows and door so I'm not too worried about a second shot, and considering the height of the suite, a bullet would never make this angle anyway, not unless Dayne climbed forty feet into one of those pines. But, I'm still being overly cautious. The bastard caught me in the perfect spot, and I wouldn't be surprised if he's been out there all day, waiting for that moment.

I'm going to figure out where the fuck he's hiding out.

"Have you ever done that before? Sucked cock?" She smiles, in a playful mood.

"That's not a conversation I want to get into when I'm about to work. Shut your eyes and try to get some sleep."

"Wow. So you have?"

"I didn't say that," I reply, sitting in a leather chair with my computer in my lap and my feet on the bed.

"You didn't say no. When? Recently?"

"Nope. Many years ago."

"Was it someone special?" She lies on her stomach with her hands under her chin and her legs waving in the air like a teenage girl.

"You're not tired, are you?"

"No." She rolls over and stares at the ceiling.

"You're fidgety."

"Can you use the computer and talk to me at the same time? And why does it smell like dope in here? Did you take off to get high and not invite me along? What's that all about? You slug."

"Will you calm the fuck down if I give you some? It's like you ate a bag of sugar after I left."

"I don't need any, I'm high on my orgasm." She rolls back over and kicks her feet once more. "Now I know why you have that dumbass grin on your face... so tell me about the cock. How old were you? Are you bi? Is that why you enjoy that cock mask you own?"

"Jules, shut it."

She's silent for a moment then asks the same questions over again.

In a huff, I take a joint out of the drawer and toss it

on the bed. "Inhale, deeply, or I'm gonna put a pillow over your face."

"Geez. What if I don't smoke?"

I give her a look of disbelief as I settle back into the chair.

"Fine."

"Remind me never to make love to you again."

"Ha! You said it!"

"The lighter's next to the bed, smoke it," I request while checking my email, bank accounts, and the system for the names of my guests. It's possible someone's here with Dayne and wouldn't I be the fool if his sidekick's staying in my hotel. I also need to search through some of my security cam footage to see what kind of car Dayne drives and the direction he took off in yesterday. I'll need to check the back property footage and live cams as well. I'm going hunting for this dickhead.

"You're gawking," I say, keeping my face in my computer. "I can feel your eyes burning a hole in my head."

"I can't remember the last time I've been this happy. Will you talk to me now?"

"I can talk as I run through some video."

Her feet rub against mine, causing my pulse to accelerate.

"Are you bi?" she asks in a mellower voice.

"Does it matter?"

"No, I'm just curious."

"No."

"So it's something you did for your dad's porn company then?"

I nod.

"Was it enjoyable?"

"Just with one."

I continue viewing footage and she sits quietly, still staring and waiting patiently for me to reveal more without her constant questioning. A few minutes pass before she eagerly nudges my feet.

"What?" I ask softly.

"Why only one? What made him different from all the rest?"

I exhale and decide to pay attention until her questions fade. Giving her what she desires, no matter how disturbing the answer. Eventually, she'll realize she doesn't want to hear anything about my past.

"My father was in love with him and I was jealous of that relationship. I was smitten because he was young and handsome, easy to control, and in need of saving."

"Did you?"

"What, save him?"

She nods.

"No. I fucked him when I was told then he disappeared for a while. I think the reason I was drawn to the guy was because I wished I could be him, but only based on my father's interest. I'm convinced my father wanted him as a son instead of me."

"That's sick, Mark."

"You asked."

"You still talk to him?"

"I don't have much choice since he married my sister."

"What?" She sits up unexpectedly with wide, red eyes.

"They didn't meet until a few years after I was with him. So it's not like I was screwing my brother-in-law. And I doubt my sister is even aware of all the details. The less she knows, the better."

"Holy fuck." She falls back on the bed. "You were with your sister's husband?"

"I already said it wasn't like that."

"Am I high? Like, totally high?"

"Yeah." I grin.

"Are you fucking with me? You are, right?"

I laugh. Maybe this *is* the perfect time to tell her all the shit she wants to hear. "Sometimes, I pretend like I'm in love with him and he freaks out, cowering like a dog. It's good fun."

"Good fun for him too? Is it a friendly relationship?"

"No, he gets pissed at me, and he hasn't a clue I adore him in a little brother kind of way. And he's got a few problems, like when he drinks, he's a jackass."

She covers her eyes with her forearm to block the bedroom light.

"Ohh, why did I ask?" She sighs. "Okay, new subject. Do you remember any of your dreams from when you were a kid?"

"What sort of dreams, you mean what I wanted to be when I grew up?" I question, dimming the lamp on the table next to us.

"No, actual dreams. Do you remember any of them? I always dreamt about falling. Falling off a cliff, out of hot air balloons, from trees. Falling, falling, falling. But dreams like that must be common."

"Where do these random questions come from?" I ask, getting no response.

I think for a moment, knowing one dream that has always haunted me, but unsure if she can handle something dark after the other crap. I probe for something else but nothing comes to mind.

"Anything?" she asks. "Anything at all?"

"A nightmare I had when I was seven or eight has always stuck with me, but I don't want you to get all freaked out if I tell you."

"Why, is it about me?" She peers out from her arm.

"No, I said I was a kid." I shake my head. "It was disturbing and since you're high..."

"Go ahead. I can handle disturbing."

"Remember, you asked." I place my hands on the arms of the chair and lean back. "In this dream, I entered the kitchen of my childhood home and my mother was taking a pie out of the oven. She asked me if I wanted a piece and when I looked to see what kind it was, I saw my sister's head baked inside. My mother began slicing it and I was fixed in terror, unable to run away, you know like those cartoons where the feet move but the character doesn't get anywhere? That was me. I woke up in a sweat and crept to the kitchen to see if it had really happened. The dream was so vivid; the smells, colors, voices, temperature of the oven, it was like I had actually witnessed it. I couldn't separate my dream from reality and became paranoid. I felt helpless and panicky for days."

"Jesus Christ, Mark. You *are* fucking with me, aren't you? You said that thing about reality and dreams because I'm stoned and now I can't figure out what *is* reality, here and now. You did that on purpose." She kicks my leg and stands. "You have any snacks?"

"Help yourself, but come right back. Bring whatever you find upstairs with you," I say on her way out. "And remind me not only to never make love to you again, but never to give you any of my weed either."

"Ha-ha, smart ass," she says from the stairs. "I swear half the shit that comes out of your mouth is a lie."

"It's all real, Jules. I'm not fucking with you!" I call downstairs. "What else do you want to know?"

"Mark, you don't have any food!" she yells.

"Check the pantry!"

She reappears a few minutes later and flops on the bed, holding a box of Saltines. "I can't believe this is all you have."

"I eat at the restaurant every day or have room service deliver food. You want me to call them?"

"No, this is fine. It's just odd that you have such an elegant kitchen and it's empty. And you really like storm cloud colors, don't you? Every wall in your place is dark grey, your furniture is all dark brown or black; even your kitchen cabinets are a blue-grey."

"Don't get crumbs on my *black* comforter."

She salutes me as a soldier would a senior officer and tastes the cracker. Next, I just know she'll need something to drink.

"Don't give me any more pot. I feel like an idiot and must sound like one too. Plus, my head's sizzling," she says. "How often do you smoke?"

"Not often." I continue rifling through the video. It's odd that she's not asking about Dayne. Maybe she got the drift last night when I refused to talk about him, but then again, that's never stopped her before.

I glance at her adoring face as she nibbles and swallows dryly, then nibbles again like a tiny bird. Her hands and feet are small and delicate. Her eyes gleam tenderly when she looks at me. I trust her.

I've checked all of her social media sites and didn't run across anything unusual. She's lived here her entire life and as far as I can tell, she has no connection to Vegas or Dayne.

"What?" she whispers.

"There's a glass in the bathroom if you need some water."

"You read my mind." She's slow to rise and starting to reach a more tranquil state for the night, kissing me on the top of the head as she walks by.

Now, if I could only... well, I'll be sucked, fucked,

and tattooed. Jackpot. There's a brief shot of Dayne from yesterday, getting into the passenger seat of an old orange Datsun pick-up truck, but the person behind the wheel is unrecognizable. I zoom in and still no luck. The truck is too far from the camera, the visor is down, and the face is blurred as they drive off in a rush.

At least my suspicions were right. Someone got that prick a gun and drove him here.

I fiddle with my watch and wonder if I should make a quick run through town to see if I can spot the truck, or if I should just wait 'til morning. He can't still be hiding out in the woods. Once he took the shot the bastard would've booked knowing I'm on full alert. And as long as everyone stays inside, it's safe for Jules and the other suite to be alone, but once outdoors everyone's an open target.

Real men don't drag shit out for days like pussies.

Yeah, Dad, I know.

"Jules, I need to check on the hotel and staff before I call it a night. Promise me you'll stay in this room."

"Will you be disappointed if I fall asleep?"

"I'd prefer it."

She undresses and burrows under the comforter, resting her head peacefully on the pillow. "I promise."

"I'll be gone for about an hour. Stay naked so we can fuck when I get back."

I pat my holster, making sure I have my gun, strap a

second one above my ankle, and pull a new switchblade from my dresser.

Julia's eyes are already closed when I turn off the light next to the bed and whisper in her ear, "Or, if you'd like, we can make *love*."

I sense her smile in the darkness as I walk out of the room.

Evil woman.

INTO THE DARKNESS

The orange Datsun is in plain sight; parked three short miles from my hotel at the ramshackle Pine Mountain Motor Lodge. It's a one-story shithole, painted dark green with black trim. The type of place that has weekly room rates for deadbeats like Dayne, or hourly rates for high school kids needing a place to lose their virginity.

I park less than a hundred feet away in a used car lot and walk behind the motel with my gun drawn, counting the small bathroom windows until I reach his room. I want to know who's with him and if there's a chance I know this other person. If I have to take both men down tonight, I will.

I'd expect the asshole to go after my sister and brother-in-law in St. Louis first. Dayne's a creature of habit and despises them both. But it looks like he's doing a one-eighty and starting with me. I guess if I'm out of the way then he's free to take his time torturing the rest of my family, but I never expected him to attempt a kill before finding out the truth about his father.

I take a deep breath, look around, and peer into the bathroom window.

Well, I'll be... tits. He's got a woman with him? Maybe she's a hooker, damn it, this could complicate things.

She's toweling her legs with her ass in the air and tits hanging down that look ready for a good suck. And knowing Dayne, that ass and those tits are well used.

Her skin is white as snow and blemish free, but I can't see her face when she stands and covers her head in the towel. She's short, curvy, and... fuck, there's a Jameson Industries tattoo on her shoulder, just like mine. She *is* flawed. The wench worked for my father.

Damn it.

I move away from the window, suddenly sick to my stomach, and oddly, I believe it's not because of the tat. I admit it; now that I'm so enamored by Jules, I feel guilty that I gazed at this woman's body.

"Stop being such a wussy boy," I whisper, rubbing my gun under my chin while figuring out what to do next. I have another look inside and notice the bathroom door's open, but I don't see Dayne or any weapons in the room. And if he were around, he'd be groping that woman's flesh. Since he's not here, I'll have to deal with the dick monkey later, alone, without getting the woman involved.

He probably took off to a bar. In which case he could be gone for hours. I'm not spending my entire night waiting around when I've got warm flesh in my bed. Anyway, it's fucking nasty behind this dump.

I walk cautiously to my truck, start the engine, and pull onto the highway.

"I hate it that you parked that Datsun in plain sight. You're waving the orange carrot in front of the rabbit's face. You gonna use the woman as a decoy? Fucker, you drew me in, now where's the trap?"

Crap in hell. The hotel... the private suites... my possessions. I bet he's there. I'm in a panic, feeling like an idiot, and unable to drive back quickly enough. He lured me away. But there's no way he could've gotten inside either place. No way. Fuck, I should've told Jules not to answer the door.

I'll contact her after this call to my second suite.

Come on, pick up. Pick up.

"Yeah?"

"Everything okay?" I ask. "The doors are closed and the lights are off?"

"Is he in the hotel?"

"Maybe. Just stay put."

"Jesus, Mark."

"I'm taking care of it."

"No fuck this, I'm coming out and I'll take care of him."

"Don't even think about moving your ass. Get real."

There's silence and a sigh.

"Stay put." I hang up then call Jules in a rush. No answer. Shit, I doubt she was carrying her cell when I took her to my place.

"Almost there, almost there." I tap the steering wheel.

The hotel's glowing in the woods as I drive up the dark road, veering to the right toward my private underground garage. I look around before opening the door, then shut it once inside.

I exhale, draw my gun, and step out of my truck.

"If he laid a finger on her..."

Two steps toward my door and I hear swift movements from the truck bed. There's the fucking trap. It's him.

I'm charged and a speedy fist hits my jaw.

My gun flies from my hand.

I'm down.

He's on my back and my head gets slammed into the concrete.

"You fuck!" he shouts.

Blood trickles down my forehead as I reach for the gun, but it's too far away.

"Fucking Jameson piece of shit!" He pulls my arm back and spits on the side of my face. "I'm gonna have a blast killing you."

My other hand reaches for my blade in my front pocket.

"No more using pussy ass guns, douchebag, that's too quick and easy."

I got the knife in my hand.

"I'm gonna take my time dismembering you, starting with your fingers, toes, then your arms..."

The blade opens and in a rush I swing my free arm back, forcing it in his side.

"Oww!"

I pull out and thrust in again.

"Fuck!" He releases my arm and in a quick turn, I'm able to jab it in his gut.

His jaw drops as he clutches my wrist. I turn the blade, causing an agonizing sound to erupt as he falls forward.

"Dubious, Dayne, you motherfucker." I push him to the ground.

Rolling on top, I put wounds in his thighs then stab each shoulder and force another deep cut into his stomach, trying not to hit a major artery. I want his blood to trickle out, not spurt. "Who's the woman at the motel?" I ask, taking a gun from his jacket pocket. I close my blade and cock the gun, pointing it at his head. "Damn, it's so easy to shoot a man, but the kill is too quick, isn't it?" I pause and look at the suffering in his face. "Tell me about the whore."

He stays quiet as blood tints his clothing.

"You don't look so hot. You should've just shot me. Then you wouldn't be in this predicament." I stand and he covers his gut with shaky hands then rolls on his side.

"What now?" He wheezes.

"You have to ask?"

"You're not your father, Mark."

I laugh and continue. "My garage is equipped with plenty of rope..."

"Your dad wasn't a meek pussy."

"And I'm decent at hog-tying..."

"*He* would've shot me dead a day ago."

"We can go on a road trip together..."

"You're nothing but a wannabe drowning in shoes too big to fill." He gasps from the pain. "A former Paul Jameson... bootlicking-groupie-stooge..." He inhales and mumbles, "...imperious prick porn star." His eyes shut then flutter back open. "You know he hated you... you're nothing."

My foot presses into his bleeding thigh and a groan hangs in the air. "No, Dayne. I'm exceptional."

"You got lucky, nothing more. I'm old and slow, just shoot me... kill the race horse with the broken leg and put it out of its misery," he requests with a stomach covered in blood.

I pace, trying to figure out how long he's got before he's dead. This asshole needs to experience something while he's still alive and I want him to tell me about the woman. I bet I have an hour or two before he fades away. That should be enough time.

He tries a final grab toward my neck, but falls short. I tie his feet and flip him over to tie his hands and elbows behind his back, then connect all three areas with a firm knot.

"Tell me why you killed my father," he says.

"Oh yeah, I forgot that's why you're here."

"You little dickhead. Why?"

I pat his greasy hair. "Now, now, Dayney boy, you

know full well your father was a rapist and not fit for this earth. All rapists should die. But, that doesn't mean *I* killed him. He made the right choice that day by committing suicide."

"You sick fuck. Your father was the rapist."

"Well, then. I guess it's a good thing they're both dead, right?" I pick my gun up off the floor and give him a hard kick to the abdomen, before unlocking the door to my stairwell. "Don't go anywhere." I laugh. "I'll be back with a friend."

My suite is two flights up and pleasantly serene when I enter. Jules is sound asleep.

Hoping she doesn't stir, I close the bathroom door and wash the blood off my face and the blade, then change quietly into a pair of jeans, a hoodie, and sneakers before giving her a light kiss on her soft cheek.

"My sleeping beauty," I whisper.

The blade is in the pocket of my hoodie and one gun is in my ankle holster. I keep Dayne's gun in the back waist of my pants and leave the other behind. I'm overcompensating with all these weapons for an incapacitated man who's nearly dead on my garage floor, but at the same time, I don't know anything about his woman.

I close the bedroom door and step silently downstairs to the corridor outside my suite. There's a late arrival in the hallway and I wait for the couple to enter their room before walking past. Blood drips down my forehead and gets wiped on my sleeve. My vision's blurry. Plus, my head's pounding. The fucker could've given me a concussion.

I put my head down and hood up then walk to the opposite end of the hotel. What I have to do next, asking for help, is going to sting more than a little.

"Let's get the show on the road," I whisper and knock three times on the door.

It's silent and I knock again.

"You're bleeding," a voice responds. "A lot."

"No shit," I say. "Open the door."

"Is it safe?"

"It's *safer*."

"What happened?"

"Open the fucking door." I lose my cool then regret the tone, not wanting to wake the guests. "Listen to me," I whisper with my fingers on the steel. "I need a second set of hands to put the fat shit in my truck."

"When?"

"Now. He's like a beached whale. Hurry up."

There's mumbling behind the door then silence.

"I'm not going to stand here and discuss this for twenty minutes. Get your ass out here."

"Give me a minute."

There's more mumbling then a lock clicks, the door opens, and my brother-in-law, Cove, steps out.

I shake my head at my sister before she quickly shuts the door in my face.

"Fuck, what's up her ass?" I ask. "And look at you, hot shot with the mountain man facial hair. Is that a new look or just a horrible disguise?" I place my hand on his back as we walk to my suite.

"Don't start, Mark. I'm not in the mood for your shit."

"And you're bathing in a new cologne." I inhale deeply. "*Vodka in the Woods,* perhaps? I hope you're sober enough to do this."

"I'm not drunk, but maybe I should be. What are we doing anyway?"

"What are we doing? We're living, Cove. Living the good life."

He pushes my hand away and strides forward.

It's too bad I needed to ask for his help, but I'm glad he's here with my sister and the kids. I know he'd never admit it, but my extra suite is the safest place for them. They were sitting ducks in St. Louis.

And it didn't take much persuading to get my sister on board with the idea. All I had to do was send her an image of Dayne's face and she was eager to be in *my* protective custody.

Sophia and I despised one another growing up, which isn't surprising. Our home life sucked. We even went a few years without speaking to one another when we were in our twenties. She finally came around to my dark humor and menacing personality a few years ago. We still bicker incessantly and have a love-hate relationship, but in her heart she knows I'm more of a guardian than her husband. I'll get the job done and I've always got her back. No one's going to hurt my little sister.

She also says I'm a control freak. And so what? I can admit to that.

"How the fuck did he manage to sneak his ass into your place?"

"Let's not discuss this in the corridor," I whisper, keeping Dayne's covert hideout in my truck bed a secret. "How you been?"

"Is that supposed to be a joke? You know I can't stand being locked inside a room."

"The suite's as big as a house."

"We've been in there for weeks and the boys are like savages. Sophia's been giving them new video games to play every two days, but she ran out a week ago. Now they're climbing the walls and it's been nearly impossible to keep them quiet."

"You ever hear of a thing called books? Why the hell didn't you bring a Kindle along?"

"They're ten. They refuse to read."

"That's your fault," I mumble. "Trust me, you made the right decision coming here. The bodyguard from your bar back in St. Louis couldn't protect you the way I can. Besides, this is a family issue."

"My guy back home *is* family which is why I wouldn't have put such a burden on him, not since he's got another kid on the way and a toddler in the house."

"Oh, I get it. I'm not family?" I laugh.

"Knock it off, Mark. We're here only because Sophia insisted you could fix the problem quickly. You know I'll do whatever the fuck she wants, especially if it means keeping Daxton and Xavier safe. But, I would've been fine taking care of my family on my own, without hiding out like a coward."

"Yeah, and I'd be perfectly fine letting you handle this on your own... in my dreams... or I guess that would be a nightmare," I say sarcastically while opening my suite.

"So what's going on? How'd you take him down?"

"Shh. I've got company upstairs."

"What company? Who?" he whispers.

I give him my best *you dumbass* look as I open the door to the stairwell and we head to my garage.

"Cove." I stop part way down and turn to him. "You know I love you, right?"

He puts up a hand so I stay back. "Is this another one of your fucked up pranks? Is Dayne here or not?"

I let out a disappointing sigh and look into his brown worrisome eyes, wanting to blow the dark wavy piece of hair from his forehead. He's pale, no doubt from being in the suite for so long, and skittish, but that's normal. All I ever think about when I see him is the abuse he endured as my father's number one star in the porn industry. That's what my dad called him. His *Star.* I want to comfort the guy, and at the same time I'd love to kick his ass and tell him to grow a pair.

"Mark," he whispers. "What's going on?"

"He's here, but we need to—"

"You didn't do anything drastic, right? Soph said

you mentioned killing him earlier. What the fuck is that all about? Can we pay him to disappear from our lives?" he speaks nervously. "He likes money. Everyone does. How much does he want? I'll give him anything, you know that, anything to keep Soph and the kids safe."

This time I exaggerate my sigh and continue the two flights down the stairwell. He's always been a submissive dainty boy and a bit gullible when it comes to things like this.

We're the same height and share the same muscular build, but our other characteristics are like night and day, in a bizarre sort of way. On the outside, I'm the blond palomino horse and he's the black stallion. Both exquisitely striking, stately, broad chested, and well hung. But on the inside, he's a Dandelion Puffball and I'm Deadly Nightshade, the toxic Belladonna.

"I need help lifting—"

"Jesus Christ!" Cove shouts as we enter the garage. "What the *fuck* happened?" He bends over and places his hands on his knees then stands and begins to pace. "Fuck, what the fuck!"

"Chill and keep your voice down."

"No. What did you do! Damn it! Did you stab him with something? Why is he covered in blood? What the hell happened?"

"When a dickwad like Dayne has me on the ground and says he's gonna cut me up, I'm gonna do something about it. What the fuck did you think was going to happen? It was him or me. And if he won you would've been next, then Sophia. Get real and fucking help me out. It's the least you can do."

"No, this is too gruesome."

"What the fuck? Where are you going?" I clutch his arm as he takes off for the stairs.

"I thought I was prepared to handle something like this, considering everything I've been through, but fuck no. Just, fuck no."

"What would you have done? Look at my head, Cove. I can feel the blood dripping. And you know he took a shot at me earlier." I pull him over to Dayne. "Get his legs and help me lift him onto the bed of my truck."

"I'm not placing a finger on him!"

"Fine, I'll pay your kids a hundred bucks a piece and they'll do it," I say sharply.

"This isn't a joke," he snaps back.

"I wasn't joking. Don't force me to dismember him. It's too messy, now grab his goddamn legs."

"What?" He starts to panic. "You're fucking insane! What are we gonna do with the body?"

"Good, you said *we*. And it's not a body. He's not dead yet." I place my foot on Dayne's shoulder and he comes alive with a groan.

"No," Cove says and steps back. "No, we're not... I'm not... damn it, Mark. How the hell can you ask me to do this?"

"You're an asswipe," Dayne whispers. "Both of you... asswipes."

"Fuck." Cove paces and runs his hand through his hair. This is his usual routine when he freaks out, and he's only going to get worse.

"Why don't you go back to your suite and send Sophia down."

"Screw you," he says. "You bastard. We didn't discuss this. I don't want to be in a room with a dying man."

"I just said I had no choice in how things played out. We're dealing with a demented mammoth who wanted a lot of people dead."

"Are you talking about Dayne or referring to yourself?"

"Real nice, dickhead. I thought you'd be more appreciative to the fact that I saved your ass... twice."

He places his hands in the air and turns away. "I don't even want to know what *that* means. Jesus! I knew you were a fucking monster!"

I close my eyes, exhale, and shake my bowed head in disappointment. This is exactly why I've always taken care of shit on my own. "Go back to your family," I whisper. "I'll figure out a way to make him disappear without your help."

"He's not dead, Mark."

"Neither is my sister, or you, or my nephews, and I'm surprised you're not focusing on that fact instead of the rodent on the floor. And I'm not dead either, in case you haven't noticed."

"I knew she was here," Dayne mumbles. "I knew the

whole family was here."

I take a roll of duct tape from my toolbox, open my blade and slice a piece for his mouth. "Any last words?" I ask, leaning over him.

"I hope you assholes sleep well... knowing I was going to force feed the meat on your bones to your offspring dipshit children." He struggles to breathe. "Sleep well... knowing someone else... will finish this for me."

I cover his mouth and he mumbles under the tape.

"Lift his legs," I demand while pulling him up by his armpits. Cove doesn't move an inch, still hanging on Dayne's last words. I start dragging the beast toward the truck, knowing I might be able to get him in the back by myself, but getting him from my truck, down a set of stairs, along a long dock, and into my boat is a whole other story.

I lay him face down then follow the trail of blood across the garage until my eyes land on Cove's distressed face.

"At one time I thought you had grown a backbone." Now I'm fucking irritated with him. "This is what it's come down to and you can't deny that you would've done the same thing if he had gotten to you first."

"I wouldn't have tortured him with multiple wounds and kept him suffering for all this time."

"Why? My feeling is you should treat people the way they treat others."

"You moron, it's treat people the way you want to

be—"

"Cove." I walk over and place my hands on his shoulders. "You and I have been beaten, called scum, and have had our asses ripped in two by men who purchased us for an hour of pleasure. My dad made a fortune selling our bodies. *I* did it because I fell in love with the money and I had the crackbrained idea that it would please my dad, and maybe, just maybe he'd start to like me, but I know *you* didn't have a choice." I turn back to Dayne. "That sleaze by the truck, my dad's heavy, he made sure you never left or got out of line. I overheard him and my father laughing one night about nearly drowning you... they said you shit your pants, and at that time, you were like nineteen or twenty. How many times did they torture and nearly kill you before that?"

"Shut up, Mark."

"Dayne used to stand outside the sex rooms in my dad's mansion with a mile wide grin on his face, listening to you getting your—"

"Enough!" he fumes.

"He drugged my sister, *your* wife, sat on top of her and gave her a Jameson Industries tat—"

"Alright!"

"Then he kept her locked away so he and my dad could do the same shit to her that they did to us."

"Shut the hell up!" He walks over to Dayne and grabs his legs. "Let's make this quick."

"I plan on it." I smile as we lift the moaning

buffoon onto the truck bed, cover him with a tarp, and pull out of the garage.

Cove doesn't speak the entire way to the lake and when I park in front of the path to the dock, he drops his head and sighs.

"Seriously? I thought you'd leave him in the woods to bleed out," he whispers. "You're gonna pull a Paul Jameson tonight, after you just went off on what a dick he was. Let's think of a better way then dumping him in the lake."

"Dayne's probably already dead and I'm not leaving any trace of him for the cops to come across. He's got too much of a connection to you and Sophia."

He rubs his face then laughs at the irony of the situation and steps out of the truck. He spent a good part of his life worrying that my dad was going to do this same shit to him.

"This area better be safe."

I nod as we secure the tarp around Dayne. "No one will be around this time of the night, not to mention this time of the year. It's a private area. I rent two of the six slips at this dock and the other four are rented by local hot shots. It's safe."

We're careful blood doesn't drip from the tarp when we carry him to my Cobalt. It's a good size boat with a step platform on the back—something that's helpful when rolling a body into the water. Once on board, I take a bucket of water to my truck and dump it in the bed to wash out any evidence of blood, just in case a cop happens to show up with a waving flashlight once again.

Cove's a mess when I return; his face is resting in his palms, his foot's tapping, and his entire body's twitchy. This will be good for him.

"Buck up, buddy," I say, starting the boat.

He shows his sickly face as we pull away from the dock.

"You had the boat uncovered and ready to go before we even arrived. This was planned, Mark. What the fuck?"

"And? So what?" I knew this is where Dayne was going to sink into the depths of Hell. I prepped the boat before my morning *appointment* with Roland.

Keeping a low speed, I head a mile out and turn off the motor. At this distance he'll sink about a thousand feet.

"Cove, open your eyes," I demand while removing the tarp from Dayne. "I've got two cement blocks in the back compartment with some rope. Tie one to his legs, make sure it's secure, and I'll get the other around his neck."

He moves hesitantly, but for once follows my instructions. I'm surprised he hasn't... yep, that's what I was waiting for. My brother-in-law's famous for vomiting under stress.

"Sophia make you and the kids SpaghettiOs for dinner?" I laugh and finish tying the knot. "Smells yummy."

"You need to be put away." He shakes his head and

wipes the puke from his lips, unquestionably upset.

"What? Like my mother? I'm saner than her and all the rest of you. I'm not living in some fantasy world."

"Tell me he's dead. I'll never sleep again if you roll him in while he's breathing."

"Get upfront, I'll finish this. And keep your eyes closed so you don't puke again."

"Gladly."

I sigh and place a hand on Dayne. I doubt he's still alive after I tied a knot around his neck. And why should I care? Especially since I watched him dispose of a few men from my father's boat on Lake Mead, only *they* were still alive, in tears, and pissing themselves. I think it's fitting for Dayne to die the same way that he made so many other men suffer. And I'm *not* sick, as Cove believes. People get what they deserve. Shit, the fucker almost shot me.

And Dayne's death isn't ghastly in any way, not like the ones I witnessed. If he's not dead already, he will be before he hits the water. I need to take extra precautions to get the gas and air out of him so he stays down. This isn't cruel. Drowning a person is cruel. What I'm doing is just a little unpleasant.

With the brute on his side, I open my blade and jab his lungs multiple times then impale his gut, making sure his stomach and intestines are pierced. Blood oozes from his body, seeps onto the back of the boat and flows into the water.

"Holy Jesus," Cove says in a faint whisper. "Stop.

Please just push him in and let's get the fuck out of here."

I give Cove my best *shut the fuck up* look and continue finishing this *my* way.

"Hang tight," I say while turning back to the body and putting my blade back in my pocket. "Let me tell you a bedtime story before you fall into infinite sleep," I whisper. "Once upon a time... there was a man named David Rosen. He had twin boys named Dayne and Doron, meatheads who were more muscles than brains. The three of them decided to start a porn company, only David knew he was in need of a front man, a face for the business, someone who would take the fall if the company ever went under. He knew his sons weren't bright enough so enter Paul Jameson. My dad. He became the king of porn, the head of Jameson Industries, and had complete control over David's sons."

"Mark, enough," Cove whispers.

"But one day, a lot of shit happened, and my father's bodyguard, you Dayne, you weren't watching over him. So why is that? What were you doing when my father got shot in the head?"

Cove stands and folds his arms.

"I heard you were too busy locking my sister in a room so your father could fuck her."

"Shit, I can't listen to this." He covers his ears and turns away.

"So we're just one big fucked up family, right? My dad raped the guy standing behind me, and your dad tried to rape my sister. And *you* came after us because of this shit, because a couple of dickhead rapists are dead? Was it worth it?"

"Start the boat. Stop talking, dump him, and start the boat," Cove says, attempting to pace in the small area behind the seats.

"When the cops investigated my father's death your arrest was justified. And your father got what he deserved when he sought revenge for your prison time on my sister and brother-in-law. *That's* what you wanted to hear. As far as I'm concerned, your father's death was necessary."

"Mark, *I* don't want to hear this."

I take Dayne's gun from my waist and toss it in the water, watching it vanish instantly. A third cement block gets tied around his chest as I continue my story.

"I had a gun pointed at you the other day in my hotel. With your strength you could've easily turned it on me, making it look like I shot myself in the head. The tale would be that I committed suicide... just like the story of your dad. Good old David Rosen. And now it's over. Damn, it seems so anticlimactic, doesn't it?" I set my hand on his chest, and start to loop the final knot. "I suppose I should at least sing you the troll song as a bon voyage... *I'm a troll...* "

"We're done here," Cove says and scrambles to the back, pushing Dayne hastily into the dark water.

"No!"

The loop of rope tightens around my hand and I'm

pulled in, sinking rapidly with him into the pitch-black lake.

The cold feels like razorblades piercing my flesh and my breath is driven instantly from my body.

I gasp.

The pain's sharp and crippling.

There's total darkness.

No! I'm not going to the grave with Dayne.

It can't end this way.

In a scramble, I pull my switchblade from my hoodie and slice away at the rope, sinking fast, starting to panic, concentrating on my breathing so I don't hyperventilate. Hurry, hurry, fuck!

My heart's pumping frantically and I could easily go into cardiac arrest. I need out!

At last, after cutting through the rope, I'm free.

I rush upward through the frigid water.

Everything's black.

I'm confused. Where's the boat?

Which way is up?

Fuck, I need a breath!

My chest... there's so much pressure... kick, kick, swim... upward.

Gasping for air when I break the surface, my body and mind are in a state of frenzy and shock.

Wheezing.

Coughing.

Confused.

I'm pulled onto the boat and covered in a blanket.

"Shit-ass mistake, Private Snafu." I pant with chattering teeth. "Shit-ass, mistake."

WATCHING YOU

"Don't give Sophia the details," I request. "She doesn't need any specifics."

"She already knows you're a psychopath like Paul."

"No. That's bullshit. I did the right thing. I *always* do the right thing and it's far from being psychotic."

"Yeah, you're a fucking saint, Mark. I'm not going to lie to my wife. If she wants to know, I'll tell her."

I ignore Cove's naive response as we step inside my suite. I'm in a shitload of pain, shivering, and my extremities are slightly numb, but I'm alive and able to walk on my own. I'm lucky it's only mild hypothermia.

"Thanks for washing off the boat platform and for lending me your shirt."

"Give me something to put on so I can get the hell away from you and back to my suite." He sounds and looks miserable, standing bare-chested in my living room.

"He was already dead. You didn't kill him, buddy."

"Shut up! I don't want to discuss this any more."

"Here." I unbutton the shirt and toss it at his chest. "Keep Sophia and the boys in the room until I talk to you tomorrow morning. We need to discuss something important before you leave."

"Whatever," he whispers, slamming the door on his way out.

"I did this for you, asshole!" I yell through the door.

"Mark?" Julia calls from the bedroom. "What's going on?" A set of footfalls echo through my suite then the bedroom door opens.

"Everything's fine."

"What time is it?" the dark silhouette asks.

"Don't know. Late. After one."

"You worked late. Did you get a lot done?"

She doesn't sound awake.

"Yes, a lot."

"Were you talking to someone?"

"My brother-in-law."

"Why is he... what? Is everything okay?"

"Just fine. My family's visiting. Maybe you'll meet them tomorrow." She wraps her arms around my body when I reach the landing.

"Oh my God, you feel like ice. What the hell happened?" She conceals my fingers in hers and blows warm air onto my skin.

My vision's still blurry and I'm sure the gash on my forehead isn't pretty. I'll need a story. Fast.

"I had to deal with an unruly drunk who was using the pool as a urinal. He ended up pushing me in and I hit my head. Luckily, my brother-in-law was with me and the two of us got the guy back to his room. It was a mess."

"But the pool's warm," she challenges.

"Yeah, but it's fucking cold outside and once I got out, my body temperature dropped."

She turns on the bedroom lamp. "Take off your wet pants and let me warm you... oh shit, your head." She sees the wound and reaches out.

"Is it bad? I haven't seen it yet."

"You have a small lump. There's a cut too, but it's not bleeding. When did this happen?"

"About an hour ago."

"You've been in wet clothes for that long? No wonder you're so cold. I'm surprised you didn't get knocked unconscious when you hit your head. Hurry up, take off your pants and get under the comforter."

I smile at her motherly commands. My ex never took care of me like this, and she never asked how I was, or if I needed anything. She couldn't even make me dinner. I'm sure Jules would do those things. She's a considerate woman and a good fuck. I hate lying to her, but the less she knows the safer she'll be.

"Will you blow on my cock like you just blew on my fingers? I doubt I'll be able to get it up for a while, but it might help."

"Anything," she whispers, helping me take off my pants and boxers. She sits nude on the edge of the bed, grabs my ass, and brings my shriveled dick closer to her mouth. Her smile as she looks into my eyes calms my jittery nerves.

I can't believe how close I came to death tonight. Thank fuck I had my blade and was able to think clearly enough to get out of the situation to come back to her.

It's in my blood to be a killer, but I might also have it in me to show Jules a little love. I'm going to try. I want this. My head is a goddamn whirlwind whenever I look into her golden honey eyes, and I can't get enough of her seductive words that do a number on my cock. She's irresistible.

"You're my first glimpse of the brilliant rays of sunrise," I say like a pussy, watching her hand drift slowly down my leg. She loosens my ankle holster and drops my gun to the floor then guides me under the comforter where I'm tucked into a tight cocoon.

"Do you have plans for me once I'm encased inside your silky web?" I ask.

She leans in and kisses my neck then gives me a chilling wink. I tremble, unsure if the shiver in my bones is from the cold water, or her.

"Close your eyes, Mark. I'm going to play some relaxing music and caress your body. You'll be sweltering and ready for me in no time."

I stare at her ass as she flips through the iPod connected to my sound system. I doubt any of my music is *relaxing*. I suppose she could put *In The Pines* back on, but I'd be surprised at her age if she's ever even heard of it.

"This okay?" she whispers and straddles my hips from on top of the comforter.

She's playing *Every Breath You Take* by The Police and I nod in approval. It's another one of my smoking songs.

"Close your eyes," she repeats. "Let me touch you."

I obey and savor her hands moving gently over my chest and arms, feeling relieved as the numbness in my fingers and toes starts to disappear.

"This is pacifying."

She hums and sings quietly along with the music. *"Every breath mmm mmm..."*

My blood vessels no longer feel constricted.

"Mmm, mmm watching you."

My heart beats normally.

"You belong..."

I open my eyes. "You belong to me, Jules."

Her response isn't subtle. "I've been watching you... I know."

"Know what?" I move like wildfire, tossing the covers, pushing her down, and restraining her wrists. She thinks this is a game and laughs, making me realize she's referring to my ownership over her, and not Dayne.

"It's nice being underneath you. Are you ready to feel the sticky silk of my web now?" she jokes. "Or do you need to be licked into shape first?"

"I wouldn't mind getting a little tongue action. My dick relishes being lost inside your mouth." I turn on my side and her face departs for my cock. She kisses the tip then does a nice swirl before flicking the ridge a few times until slowly, my flesh parts her lips and slides inside.

"That's it, beautiful. Keep working it 'til it reaches your throat."

My fingers flow lovingly along the side of her face and around to the back of her neck. Her warm mouth on my shaft steals sweet moans from my body with every lick.

It takes longer than usual to get erect because of the icy water, but once I'm hard...

"Shit, that's good." I hold her hair back, watching saliva drip from her mouth. "Let up now so we can fuck. This has been a stressful night and I need harsh play to let off some steam. Turn over." She lies on her stomach and I pull her hips upward, toward my cock. "Get ready for me." I smirk, reaching for a condom in my nightstand. "Don't try to be in control and don't speak. The only word you're permitted to say tonight is *Mark*. I don't want anything else leaving those plump lips of yours. My dick's going in and only my name's coming out... that and my cum."

I lick my fingers and moisten her pussy before rubbing my tip against her flesh.

"Mark," she whispers.

"That's it, say it."

Nudging inside causes her head to rise, exposing her small, vulnerable neck that I grip passionately. I pull her closer, needing to be immersed within this woman. The lake will never have my last breath; I'm saving it for her.

"You're beyond wonderful. It's startling how obsessed I am with you," I whisper.

Her back hits my chest and a hard rush of air fires from our mouths.

"Ride me," I demand. "Fucking ride me and make me cum."

Her ass rests on my upper thighs and my hands capture her breasts as she bounces rapidly on my dick.

"Uh." Her head falls onto my shoulder, exposing her face and open mouth in the soft light.

"You love my cock, don't you?" I pant while biting her shoulder. "You love it. Go ahead and beat it. Work the cum out of me."

I force her movements with one hand clutched to her tit and the other on her hip, thrusting her body onto mine.

"I can't wait for you to taste it."

She launches into her own wild ride, leaving me behind.

"What the fuck do you think you're doing?" I whisper and smack her hand away from her clit. "Don't you dare cum. Pleasure me, not yourself. Not yet."

Her motion ceases and she does an impressive one-eighty on my dick, a move that seems effortless and feels superb. I could get used to that.

She starts up again, coating my cock with her jellified pussy. It's slick and I bet she's aching for my fingers to get her off.

"I want you to eat my cum. Swallow my entire load, every last drop. Do it and you'll be rewarded."

"Yes, Mark!" Her voice is high and boisterous.

"Keep hammering me. Pound it. I deserve a good beating tonight... that's it. Fuck me, you little sex fiend."

"Uh," we say in sync.

Her springing tits get seized, sucked, bitten, pinched, and friskily slapped. She loves it. I can tell from the loud non-stop moans that fill the room.

"I'm on the verge... so close... keep fucking me."

She uses my shoulders to steady herself and moves faster, thrusting her hips to get me off.

"Yes..." I moan. "Uh... finish it... give me head and swallow."

I yank the condom off and push her head down, replacing one wet hole with the other.

"Hell, yeah." I grab her hair and lunge my hips forward. "Suck it."

Her head bobs and my warm semen starts to surge down her throat.

"Fuck!" My eyes clench and my fingernails dig tightly into her shoulders. "Uh," I mumble huskily as I fill her mouth. The thick fluid escapes and lands on my abdomen. "Jules, oh, that's good. Swallow for me." And she does. "I want to be all the way inside you. You're incredible. Fuck, that's badass... you're badass," I babble, releasing quick expirations while she laughs. "Oh, Jesus, that was terrific."

I open my eyes and see a devilish look on her face.

She's just as pleased with herself as I am with her, and my cold and clammy flesh has changed to a warm glow.

I'm back.

"Thanks for engaging in my rough games. I didn't hurt you, did I?"

She's silent, still acting... I think.

"Speak to me, Jules."

She leans forward with cum covered lips and adorns my face with soft kisses before a firm grip of my chin takes me off guard. My head is tilted upward to meet her eyes. Then, after a tranquil breath she addresses me candidly...

"I know about Dayne."

PART TWO

FIXING

"What did you say?"

Julia's delicate frame is restrained in a solid grip. She gasps with mammoth eyes, but doesn't fight to get away.

"What the fuck did you say?" I repeat.

"Be nice to me," she whispers. "I heard you and your brother-in-law in the garage and I think you're in need of fixing."

"What?" I push her away and get my ass out of bed, grab my gun and demand she get dressed.

"Fucking son of a bitch!" I shout.

"What? I don't understand. It didn't sound like you had much of a choice but to kill him."

"Put your goddamn clothes on."

"Mark—"

"I said put your fucking clothes on!" She dresses quietly under a watchful eye. Fuck, I really don't feel like killing another person tonight.

"You need help."

"What the hell does that mean? Help with what? You know... just shut the hell up, don't say anything right now. Let me think," I say. "Damn it, I wish you wouldn't have opened your mouth."

"Excuse me?" She stands and struts forward with a finger pointed toward my face.

"Sit down, Jules," I say sharply.

"No, you sit down, Mark."

"I said sit your ass down!"

She stops an inch from my face, places her hands on her hips, and stares into my eyes with a furious expression.

"Are you fucking kidding me?" I whisper.

"No," she says. "Stop acting like a dick, there's no reason to be afraid of me."

"What? Who the hell do you think you are? Afraid of *you*? Seriously, sit your ass down!"

She's motionless, showing no sign of backing down. "I'm not putting up with this shit," I say, lifting her into the air.

"Mark, put me down!"

"You're the one who should be scared." With my arms securely around hers, I carry her to my bathroom and slam the door. "Lock the door. Lock it!"

"What?" she asks in complete annoyance.

"Lock me out until I can clear my head! Do it!"

"Fuck's sake. I understand what happened. Dayne didn't give you a choice... and the things you said about your past, how do you even function after all that shit? Mark? Are you listening? I could've called the cops when you left, but I..."

Her voice fades as I reach the bottom of my

stairwell, in need of a drink. I take the cap off my bottle of whiskey and down two shots then carry the bottle back upstairs.

Maybe she's a figment of my imagination.

"Did you hear me? I'm coming out if you don't answer."

Nope. She's real.

"Jules." I stand naked outside the bathroom door with a gun in one hand, the bottle of whiskey in the other, and cum from our recent 'fuck and suck' crusted on the tip of my dick. "What you heard about my past is like a speck of sand in an endless desert. You don't have a clue."

"I want to know."

"No!"

Cold air floats across my flesh, causing the hair on the back of my neck to stand on end. I don't believe in ghosts, but every once in a while there's a moment when I sense someone's watching me, like my bastard father, although tonight this frigid air feels more like Dayne.

"Shelter yourself from me," I whisper.

"You're going about this all wrong." It sounds like she's pacing. "Who ever heard of this sort of kidnapping? I'm not supposed to lock *myself* up. Geez."

She's insane. I've fallen for a crazy woman who's playing Ping-Pong inside my head. "You're not kidnapped."

"Good, so I can open the door?"

This isn't working. She should be cowering and

pleading for her life.

"Mark, are you rubbing your chin with the barrel of your gun?"

How the hell does she know that?

"One of these days you're going to accidentally blow your head off!"

It won't be an accident.

"Are you there?"

"Tell me why you didn't call the cops?" I ask. "Is it because you didn't want to give up your free room?"

The door bursts open and she stomps toward me with her fist shaking in the air.

"You dickhead!" she shouts. "You're damn lucky I know how to restrain myself or you'd have a bloody nose right now. No, it's not because I've got a warm bed! God! I already told you I overheard you in the garage."

"And what the hell were you doing sneaking around and listening to a private conversation?"

Her finger is back in my face. "Don't interrupt me," she says. "You idiots were yelling, how could I not overhear? If you want to kill someone, do it in the privacy of your own home."

"This *is* my home! And what the fuck do you know about killing someone?"

Her mouth drops open, in shock that I would butt in again.

"As *I* was saying..." She pronounces each word slowly, taking charge of the conversation. "That guy, Roland, the one who hurt me... I've often replayed that night in my head. What if he had tried to kill me? What would've happened if he was worried about me going to the police and he wanted to shut me up? If he had attempted anything, I would've tried to take his life to save my own. That's what you did, right?"

I'm hesitant to answer.

"I think that's what happened. At least, I want to believe that's what went down." She sighs, sitting on the edge of the bed. "If I didn't know you, I would've called the police, however, my heart's involved and I'm being led by my feelings."

She *doesn't* know me, but those words just relieved the storm in my head. There's another person in this room with a hijacked heart. To hurt Jules because she overheard my big mouth would be absurd. It's my fault. Of course, I've killed for less, but never a woman. That's the main issue. I've never physically harmed or killed a woman. If it were life or death I would, except this isn't. Or maybe... shit, she better not be playing me. I take another sip of whiskey then hand her the bottle, but she turns it down.

"I'm too good for you," she says. "But I think you deserve a chance with me. You need a good woman to set you straight."

"Oh yeah?" I laugh, not knowing whether to lock her up or marry her. I guess they're one and the same anyway. "What do you mean by 'set me straight?'"

"If I'm open with you then you should be with me. No more lying. I know you didn't fall in the fucking pool."

"Screw that. You pretended to be asleep when I got in. Don't call me a liar, you hypocrite."

"Okay, see, this is good. We have a lot in common," she says approvingly. "We both lied earlier."

I shake my head and let out a deep exhale as I fall into the chair next to the bed. This woman has to be imaginary. Seriously. I mean, maybe I'm starting to hallucinate.

She crosses her legs and kicks her foot in the air as she speaks. "I'm sure this is hard on you. When I say you need to be set straight, I mean someone needs to help you through this mess. You're still in shock and unable to process the events of the night. I bet that's why you're so calm about it. Right?"

I offer a fake nod.

"And once you come around and reality sets in, you shouldn't have to deal with the stress on your own. It's not easy. Trust me... please, you need to trust me with everything. You know you can."

Wordy woman. She's speaking so quickly that I wonder if she's on speed.

"And you know I'm decent. I stayed, and the police weren't called. I didn't run away because you and I both know you'd be lost without me."

I pretend to rub my lips so she can't see the smile on my face.

"Oh, and by the way, you should be thanking me. I didn't say anything about Dayne until our fuck was over because I didn't want to be rude."

Yep, she's flat out cracked. Senseless and wild even when sober, like myself.

"Breathe," I request. "Relax for me."

She leans back with her arms stretched and takes a deep breath.

I'm doubtful I can trust a person who's perfectly fine with the fact that I just killed a man, but I'm not about to let her go. I'll have to sleep with one eye open for a while.

"Tell me you're okay," she whispers. "Does your head hurt? Is your brother-in-law alright?"

"Cove's fine. And yes, my head's pounding."

"Let me get you some ibuprofen."

"No." I stand, getting them from the bathroom myself.

She grins. "See, you're fearful of me."

"You're such a comedian," I say sarcastically. "I'm not worried about you drugging me, if that's what you think. I just don't feel like explaining where I keep them... and I don't need you to look after me."

"You're wrong. You not only need fixin', but lovin' too."

I place my hands on the bathroom counter and gaze at the mirror. Shit, my forehead looks like it was hit with a baseball bat. And I've got drowsy eyelids. What a fucked up day.

"I'm tired," she calls out. "Can we go to sleep now? Arguing with you is downright draining."

"Unbelievable," I whisper. That's it? She's done discussing Dayne and everything else? Just like that?

I leave the bathroom and open the door to my deck, allowing the crisp fall air to flow into the room.

"That's chilly."

"Good, you'll have to curl up next to me to keep warm." I lift the comforter and she crawls underneath, keeping her clothing on, but eyeing my dick as I slide in next to her.

"I need a while to recharge," I say. "But I've got other ways to get you off if you need a thrill."

"Actually, I'm pretty sore from earlier," she whispers. "I've never fucked liked that before. It was intense."

I apologize by weaving my legs with hers, running my toes along the arch of her foot, and massaging her back. She moans in appreciation and nuzzles her head against my chest.

She's really finished talking about this? Huh. This is baffling. And now she's humming The Police song again.

I'm her nest, shielding her from harm. But she's the one flying in, rebuilding my walls piece-by-piece so I stay intact. Fuck, I'm thinking about nests? What a pussy.

I sigh and stare at the open door, inhaling a deep breath before closing my eyes. My body's dog-tired, but my mind won't relax. I keep replaying the evening in my head. There were too many mistakes—Dayne in the truck, needing Cove's help, Julia eavesdropping, and getting snagged on the rope then nearly drowning. Fuck, this is the sloppiest I've ever been. I'll end up dead if I'm not careful... and who the hell was that woman in the sleazy motel? A random washed up porn star with my dad's old company tat on her shoulder. To hell with her if she comes looking for Dayne. I'm not worried about her though; I just want to know who the fuck she is.

And all of that shit is nothing compared to my biggest gaffe—the one drifting to sleep in my arms. I'm pussy-whipped and heart-hitched which has turned me into a half-wit.

My wicked woman breathes slowly and deeply. It appears that what just happened is an everyday occurrence to her. She's too calm. Her restfulness is disturbing. No, Julia Alison Barringer, I'm not afraid of you; I'm fucking terrified.

BREAKFAST

"Where the fuck is she?"

The bed's cold where Jules slept so I know she's been awake for a while. I check the shower, my deck, the kitchen, before noticing the open door. She's in my garage.

The scent of bleach snuffs out the fresh mountain air, causing my eyes to tear as I walk down the two flights of stairs. My plan was for us to have a loud morning fuck then eat breakfast together, but this is bullshit. I told her last night not to leave my bedroom. She's been snooping. The bleach is kept in my laundry room off the guest bedroom, and... wait. Hell, no. Bleach?

"For fuck's sake," I whisper, frozen on the stairs as she walks toward me. Her hair is in a ponytail and she's wearing nothing but panties and a pair of bloodstained yellow rubber gloves. She swings the bottle of bleach in one hand and carries a bucket in the other, whistling a happy tune with Dayne's blood on her knees.

"Morning." She nods and passes me on her way to

my suite.

Holy shit, she cleaned the blood.

"You left a mess," she says. "But's it's impeccable now. Your garage and truck are spotless."

I follow her into the laundry room, fully erect, and worshipping her every move as she dumps the bucket of bloody water and washes the gloves in my sink.

"I wasn't in the mood last night to tidy up. And didn't I tell you to stay in the bedroom?" I ask. "What made you think you could go downstairs?"

"Well." She rolls her eyes. "I was curious. And if you can stick your dick in me, I think it's okay for me to stick my head in your garage. It only seems fair. Besides, I wanted to do something nice for you."

"Why?"

She gives me a glaring look like I'm an idiot. "Do I even have to answer that question? Jesus, Mark. Because you're supposed to do nice things for the people you care about. Like, you gave me a roof over my head, so I—"

"So you cleaned up the blood of the man I killed? Yeah, that seems equivalent. I don't want you to be involved in this shit. It's bad enough you know about last night, and now you've got blood on your hands. Literally, Jules, blood on your fucking hands!"

"It's too late." She turns off the water and light, heading for my bedroom. "Nice morning wood, by the way."

I follow close behind, being led around like I'm her submissive. This obedient boy bullshit ends now. My balls have been tucked away since our argument last night.

"And what if I want to be involved?" she asks. "Think about it. Who in their right mind would want to spend their life doing the same boring crap each day? No offense, but I hope I'm not working your front desk when I'm sixty. I know some people get trapped. They end up doing the same shit day after day, then they die. Fuck that, what happened last night was electrifying. I felt like I was in a Quentin Tarantino film. Well, not all of it. That dream about your sister's head in a pie was crazy dark, but it was just that, a dream."

"And Dayne's blood in my garage isn't dark? This isn't a game you know. My guns and blades are real. This bump on my head hurts like a son of a bitch... and it's fucking real."

She looks at my head with her lips tightly pursed and arched on one side then slides out of her panties and turns on the shower. "I suppose you're right," she says under a heavy breath. "I need to get this bleach scent out of my hair. It's driving me nuts."

"Is that what's wrong with you? You're high on bleach fumes?"

"No, I think I'm in love."

"Oh." I blush. "So you don't care at all that I killed Dayne?"

"You're still alive... that's what I care about."

Steam rises and her body becomes a cloudy haze behind the glass door. I rub my eyes and let out a soft laugh, thinking about my freakishly outlandish life. "Jules?"

"Yes?"

She washes her neck and breasts and my hand reaches instantly for my dick. I'm surprised I didn't cum when she walked up from the garage donning Dayne's blood. That was hotter than Hell. I've never experienced anything more stimulating in my life.

"Yes?" she repeats.

My free hand rests on the glass as I continue jerking off; seduced by the figure being swallowed in a heated mist. Her head turns and she watches me, lathering her hair, rinsing, soaping her arms and legs, still watching, setting her hand over mine on the opposite side of the glass... she opens the door and pulls me in by my cock a moment before I'm about to cum.

"You haven't a clue what you do to me." I fight for a breath as she strokes my dick. "Fucking hell." My head drops back.

She moves closer, grabbing my ass and rubbing her pussy across my thigh. My legs are rigid, my abs firm, and her racing hand devoted to gifting me a temporary blackout.

"Uh. Fuck!"

Cum lands on her stomach.

Her hand slows.

My legs quiver.

Our lips touch.

I'm dazed and winded.

"Swoon," she whispers, turning off the water with a satisfied grin. "That was your fastest orgasm yet."

"It's your fault I have no self-control."

"Mine?" She laughs while toweling off.

"Come back." I hold out my hand. "That's two to zero, it's time to even things out."

"I'm good. I need to get some clean clothes from my room then eat. I worked up a pretty big appetite this morning."

"Exactly. You deserve a thank you."

She looks at me and waits.

"What?" I ask.

"I'm waiting for you to say thank you."

"Come on, you know what I mean." I shake my head. "Let me lick your pussy."

"You're weak," she calls back to me. "I don't need to cum every time you do. A verbal thank you would've been nice."

I turn the water back on and grab the soap. "Don't let the door hit you in the ass on your way out!"

"Hey Mark?" Her head pops back into the shower room.

"Huh?"

"Is it okay if I eat in the restaurant, or is that too weird? Do I need to hide that I'm living here from the other employees? Should I get something from McDonalds instead?"

"No, it's fine. Don't you dare eat one of those egg muffin things when I've got a healthy buffet waiting for us downstairs."

"Us? So I have to wait like two hours for you to get ready?"

I give her the finger then finish washing my body. "Thirty minutes. I'll meet you in your room."

"Great. It's a date!"

"No."

She walks out.

"It's not a date, Jules!" I yell after her. "We're not sixteen!"

And there's her head again, making another appearance. "Then stop acting like a sixteen-year-old." She laughs, disappearing this time for good.

Shit, she's playful.

I dry off and rush to get ready, putting on my favorite black cashmere sweater, a pair of faded jeans, and a baseball cap. Going casual is the only way to hide the lump on my forehead. I'd look odd wearing my Phillies hat with a suit. With a new switchblade in my pocket and my gun in my ankle holster, I'm ready to walk out my door.

A hair dryer whirrs as I pass Jules' room on my way to my other suite. It's time to discuss a few things with my sister and brother-in-law... if they're still around.

I can imagine they argued last night, and knowing Cove, he would've insisted they pack up and head home on the first open flight to St. Louis. Only my sister would've bitched him out and insisted they stay to say goodbye. I know when I knock on the door that this isn't going to be a pretty scene.

"What?" my sister says.

"You always say that. Sophia, open up."

The door unlocks and her chestnut brown eyes sparkle in the hallway light. She flashes a pretty smile, looking surprisingly well rested and perkier than she was when they first arrived.

"You just get laid or something?"

"Get in here." She pulls me inside. "I was so upset last night when you asked for Cove's help, but I'm thankful he came home in one piece. And no, I didn't just get laid. He passed out after a night of almost drinking himself to death."

"That figures."

"Thanks, by the way." She gives me a hug, something she hasn't done in years. "So you saved the day? Everything's taken care of?"

"Drunk boy didn't fill you in?"

"He said he couldn't."

"That's surprising."

"Yeah, he came home, grabbed a bottle, and sat on the back deck for an hour then stumbled inside and crashed."

"Wake him up. I want us to have breakfast together."

"Really?" She spins and her short sheer skirt and black blouse float away from her fit body. "God, I'm so excited to get the hell out of here. Boys!" she calls out. "Put on a pair of shorts and let's go for a swim!"

"No, wait. I said I wanted to have breakfast."

"Are you kidding? My kids need to enjoy the rays of the morning sun and get some fresh air."

"Yayyy!" Two high-pitched voices bounce off the walls. Daxton and Xavier race down the stairs, stepping into swim trunks and nearly falling on their ass as they hurry to the door.

"Fuck Soph, can't you—"

"Don't!" she scolds. "Watch your mouth, Mark. I just got them to stop using that word."

"Yeah, like they don't hear you and Cove swearing all day long."

"I love to say fuck!" Daxton laughs. "Xav, that's my fucking towel!"

"Fuck off!" Xavier yells as they play tug-o-war with a beach towel.

"Thanks, asshole," Sophia whispers while putting on a pair of sunglasses. "Let's go, boys, pool time." She takes her purse and opens the door.

"Yayyy!" They run out of the suite. "We love you, Uncle Mark," they say in unison, flying past me like a couple of mini tornados.

"Race you there, farthead," Daxton says.

Sophia looks at me then at the staircase leading to the master bedroom. "Get him out of bed and I'll meet you in the restaurant in a half-hour. Deal?"

"Do I have a choice?" I mumble, walking toward the stairs. "Keep an eye on your kids and come inside if you see a woman with big tits."

"What?"

I stop on the landing and peer down at her. "Just be safe. We'll talk over breakfast."

"I'm always looking out for them, that's why we're here." She closes the door and I'm left in a darkened suite.

My sister *is* a good parent. She prides herself on being the antithesis of our mother, who was both physically and verbally abusive, but more to Sophia than me. Victims of abuse often become abusers themselves and I always thought my sister would be a terrible mother. Shit, she proved me wrong. I've never seen her lose her cool with either of her sons. It's surprising since she has her hands full with the two beasts. They're not easy to deal with, especially at the age of ten. I can only imagine they'll be worse in a few years when they're teenagers. Fuck, she's screwed. She wanted more kids too, but has a hard enough time keeping these two in line. Daxton and Xavier where just born devious. It was the luck of the draw. Even when they try to act loving their voices go cold. They give me the creeps. And that's coming from a guy who enjoys killing people.

My son has problems as well, but he acts out because he feels abandoned. That's obvious... and different.

Maybe it's just the age. Swearing, belching, farting, and running wild are all big fun when you're ten. Or it could have something to do with being twins, or some sibling rivalry thing, or... it's a way to cope with their alcoholic father.

Cove is sleeping on top of the comforter, wearing only boxers and snoring like an ox. I observe him for a few minutes, noticing the bottle next to the bed, the smell of body odor in the room, and his dark tousled hair. He suffers from depression. No one's told me that, it's just evident after observing his behavior over the past decade.

I slip out of my shoes and lie alongside him, caressing his back until he stirs.

"Soph, I helped your brother," he says, completely hung over. "I'm going to hell for this."

My hand slides down his abdomen and rests over his dick. This knucklehead is so easy to tease.

"I'm not in the mood to fuck. Start packing your shit so we can leave."

I roll on top of him and press his head firmly into the pillow. "Wussy ingrate. Who cares if *you're* not in the mood? Don't you think I deserve to get laid after killing Dayne last night?"

"Get the fuck off me!" His fist makes contact with my chest then hits me square in the jaw, swinging frantically to be released. I set him free and laugh as he hurdles out of bed.

"Damn it, Mark, you bastard. How the fuck did you get in here? Where are Soph and the kids? What the hell time is it?"

He stomps off and slams the door of the bathroom, swearing up a storm as he takes a piss.

"They went for a swim," I call out. "Get dressed so we can have breakfast."

"Fuck no!" He flushes and opens the door. "Why?"

"Jesus Christ, because we're family, that's why. Don't you want to shoot the shit before you race away to your enchanted little life in St. Louis?"

"No."

I walk to the bathroom and lean against the doorframe, watching him stare into the mirror. He sighs before starting to trim and shave his facial hair. His hands shake, either from the alcohol or because he needs to chill after I just scared the shit out of him.

"You gonna look like your old self again?"

"I only grew a beard while in your captivity. Now that I'm free, I can—"

"Alright, buddy. I can tell you're being an ass to cover your embarrassment. But let me tell you something. Sophia knew you weren't man enough to take control of the situation and this time she turned to her big bro instead of her husband. Grow a pair and get over it."

"Your giant ego has smothered your ability to think clearly. My wife knows full well I can protect my family."

"Ah-huh." I grin.

"Mark, we're here because we knew if anything got fucked up that someone would go to prison, and Soph said that person should be you, not me."

"Is that so?"

"That's the truth," he says. "Sad, isn't it? That we'd throw you under the bus to save ourselves."

"See, that's disrespectful."

"Yep." He gets dressed and runs his fingers through his hair. "I'm assuming you've already told Sophia you want to eat breakfast together?"

"She said she couldn't wait."

"I bet." He shakes his head and douses his wrists with cologne.

"Did you ever tell the kids about Dayne?" I ask.

"Fuck no." I'm given a look like I'm crazy.

"Well, one of them warned me with a flashlight the other night that I was in danger, because a split second after the flashlight turned off, Dayne's red sight was on my chest. They must know something."

"I'm sure it was a coincidence. They think we're on a primitive skills vacation."

I chuckle. "That's what you told them? And primitive skills involves playing video games?"

"They play hunting games. We did the best we could. Look, they don't need to hear about this shit with Dayne or about your fucking father, ever. I'd hate for them to have nightmares. I told them the gunshots were an accident from a hunter. They're innocent boys. Only a few years younger..."

He stops mid-sentence and sighs then grabs his wallet from the dresser. I know exactly what he was about to say. His kids are only a few years younger than he was when my father raped him.

I place my hand on his back for comfort as we make our way out of the suite, but he does his usual brush off and steps away.

"They're still little boys," he whispers. "And as long as I'm alive, my children will remain untainted and unaware of Paul Jameson's disgusting life as well as your present gruesome way of living."

I'm silent as he locks the door. I should remind him that they sprouted from a Jameson. They're already infected with Jameson blood, but I won't set him off before breakfast.

"I'll meet you down there. Say you're with me and my staff will put you in one of the private eating areas overlooking the lake."

I turn and see Jules coming out of her room as Cove walks away.

I bet she's tired of waiting. She sashays toward me and is already dressed for work, looking radiant as always, wearing the new heels and short tight skirt I just bought her, carrying her Jameson blazer, and flaunting dark red lipstick. It's my favorite 'bend her over the desk, grip her hair, and fuck her doggy style' type of outfit. And when we meet in the corridor, my eyes drop to the cleavage emerging from her blouse before gifting her a kiss on the cheek.

"I love how your eyes devour me like I'm a piece of chocolate cake," she says.

"You're more like a mouthwatering steak dinner and a flavorsome glass of red wine. Meat that expands my cock and alcohol that warms my heart."

She laughs and follows me to the restaurant. "That was one of the nastiest, but most romantic things you've ever said to me."

"Thank you."

"No problem."

"I meant, thank you for everything this morning. I'm still amazed that you did all that shit for me."

"No problem," she says again before changing the subject. "Do you have French toast on the menu?"

"It's a breakfast buffet, so yes... Jules?"

"Hmm?" She locks her arm around mine as we walk side-by-side.

I want to tell her that I think we were made for one another, but it comes out all wrong. "I think you're a bit fucked in the head."

She sighs and passes along a scornful look. "Speaking of fucked in the head, I think I'll start calling you pie face."

"Well, speaking of pie face, I want you to meet my sister."

"Really?" She seems genuinely excited as I hold open the door to the restaurant.

"Yes, all of her, not just her head baked into a pie."

"The pie face comment was just a joke." She grins.

"I know."

The hostess leads us to one of the private dining areas where a pitcher of juice and a carafe of coffee are already on the table. Sophia is spreading jam on a piece of toast while her kids are using the butter knives to have a mini sword fight.

"Who's the ho, Uncle Mark?" Daxton asks.

"Dax," Sophia says. "That's impolite. How do you know that word?"

"It's in the video game you gave us. Bitches and hos, bitches and hos!" he says as my sister closes her eyes and shakes her head.

"Looks like you're the one who fucked up this time." I laugh at her.

"Mark, watch the language," she says hypocritically.

"Just let it go. You can't keep your kids from swearing. It's unrealistic," I say. "And if you just let them say whatever the hell they want, they'll eventually tire of using those words."

"Like you?" Jules cuts in.

Sophia puts out her hand with a smirk and says, "I like you. I'm Sophia, Mark's sister."

"Jules," she responds as they shake.

"These are my sons, Daxton and Xavier." She wipes their wavy dark hair from their foreheads and the two flash exaggerated smiles, showing dimples and white teeth. Fuck, they look so much like Cove. However, they do have my sister's eyes, the eyes of my father.

We sit and I ask the boys to get us each a plate of French toast and a hardboiled egg. They dash happily toward the buffet table, shirtless, with dripping wet shorts and only socks on their feet. Kids that age don't understand seasonal changes.

"Dad! You shaved the vagina off your face," Xavier shouts from a distance as Cove enters the room carrying the local newspaper. He nods toward his son and smiles apologetically to the guests before joining us in the back room at the table.

"My handsome husband's back," Sophia says dotingly. "Looking good, Babe."

He takes one of the Mariposa Lilies from the middle of the table and sets it in front of his wife. "Thanks, Dove," he responds with his favorite nickname for her before looking questionably over at Jules.

"I'm Jules."

"Cove," he says while glancing at his kids. "Soph, we're leaving this afternoon. My parents are getting back from their cruise in two days and our managers can't run our bar forever. Besides, the kids need to get their asses back in school."

"No they don't. I'm going to continue homeschooling them until December. They can go back after the holidays. And you know we won't be able to get a flight for a day or two."

I laugh, unaware my sister was *teaching* her kids at home.

"What, Mark?" she says defensively. "I graduated from Temple University, remember? I know a thing or two about fourth grade math and science and other *things*."

"I don't care about your degree. They still need to be in school for peer interaction, if nothing else."

"Anyway," Cove cuts in. "If there's anything left to discuss..." He pauses and looks at Jules.

"It's okay," I say. "We can talk in front of her. She knows."

"Knows what?" Cove raises his voice.

"Mark, what did you do?" Sophia sets her fork down with an evil eye. "What did you tell her?"

"I overheard everything last night," she explains. "I'm fine with it."

"Fine with what?" My sister questions with distrust.

"You know... the Dayne situation. It's okay. I understand."

"You don't understand jackshit," Cove snaps. "Mark, you asshole. What the fuck's going on with you? This is yet another thing we need to deal with."

I pull out my blade and slam it into the middle of the wooden table, demanding silence in the room. Startled and on guard, they straighten their backs and tighten their lips. "Stop bitching. I'm tired of it," I say. "Nothing needs *fixing*. Not me, or this situation. If I trust the woman sitting next to me then that should be good enough for the two of you. Fuck. You know me better than that. For Christ's sake, she cleaned up the blood in the garage."

Jules laughs as she pulls my blade from the table and places it in front of me. "What are you going to do, knife your family?" She smiles. "They just met me, Mark. Give them some time. There's no need to exaggerate your tough guy attitude just to impress me."

"Holy shit," Cove whispers, waiting for me to strike.

"Wow." Sophia covers her ears, knowing full well I'm not going to let another person dominate this table.

But I say nothing.

"Mark?" My sister prods me to respond.

"As I was saying..." I continue and ignore what just occurred. Jules will be punished in private for that one later.

"The two of you can trust her and we'll leave it at that."

"You mean we can trust her for as long as you do." Cove shakes his head. "And what happens when you get tired of her? Are you gonna take her for a ride in your boat? How many bodies do you have in that Lake anyway?"

"Did you put Dayne in the Lake?" Jules whispers.

"Some friendly advice." Cove stands and looks for the boys then turns back to Jules. "Get out now. Take off on a bus and start over. Don't look back, just get as far away from this fucker as you can." He pauses and searches the room with his eyes. "Where the hell are Dax and Xav?"

Sophia looks around then points toward the opposite end of the restaurant at the back window. "Ug, they're swimming in the pool again. Bring them inside, please. They need to eat."

Cove tosses the newspaper on the table then takes the towel from the back of the chair and walks away.

"What blood in the garage and what bodies?"

Sophia leans closer to me. "What the hell, Mark? I wish someone would fill me in. I'm the only one who doesn't know what happened."

"Oh, you should've seen it," Jules says in an animated tone. "There was a whole bunch of blood from Dayne on the garage floor and more leading to Mark's truck, not to mention the smears in his truck bed."

"Stop." I raise my hand. "That's enough."

"Fine, I'll just ask Cove for the details later." Sophia sighs, picking at her food before she turns to Jules. "How old are you?"

"Twenty-two."

Twenty-two? Sophia mouths to me.

"It's not like she can't see you doing that, Sophia."

"Sorry." She exhales. "I was a drunken fool at that age, but that was a long time ago."

"Yep, now you're just a fool." I smirk while pouring a cup of coffee.

"My brother has a thing for two's so twenty-two is a good age, I suppose. Do you have a job?"

"I work the front desk."

"You mean here?"

"Uh, yeah, I mean here." She sounds somewhat annoyed by my sister's dumbass questions. "I'll spare you having to ask. My full name is Julia Alison Barringer. I come from a middle class family and was born and raised here. I'm not much of an outdoors person, but I like to read and have a good time."

"Meaning what?" Sophia asks.

"Go to bars with my friends, hang out, drink, socialize, that type of stuff." She shrugs. "I've also never broken a bone or had a cavity. I enjoy Thai food, pretzels, and soda water. And I've been working at Mark's hotel for six weeks. Before that I worked in a grocery store and at a bread company. I have a degree in Art History which has proven to be useless, and I would like to start over and go to cosmetology school."

"You want to study space?" my sister says. "Talk about a useless degree."

Julia looks at me and rolls her eyes. "Soph, it's beauty school, you idiot." I laugh. "See, you shouldn't be homeschooling your kids."

"Oh." She blushes and waves a hand to continue.

"But I'm broke," Jules says. "Mark just gave me more hours and once I get back on my feet and save a little money maybe I'll be able to afford school again, but for now a roof over my head and food are my main priorities."

I place my hand on her leg, rubbing her upper thigh in devotion. "Why don't you get breakfast so I can discuss something with my sister."

"Thanks. I'll get you that egg you wanted." She kisses my cheek and as soon as she leaves the table, Sophia's hand is on mine and I'm yanked by her side.

"Holy assballs, Mark! You love her don't you? I've never seen you under anyone's control before."

"No, fuck that. This woman isn't ruling me in any way," I lie. "Trust me. Her little stunt with my knife didn't go unnoticed. I'm just waiting until we're alone to bitch her out, that's all."

"Okay, keep telling yourself that... hell, what's wrong with being in love? She's beautiful, smart, sassy, and she's got balls. This woman is your dream *girl*."

"I know she's young... you don't have to exaggerate the word *girl*, but for her age she seems more mature than you... and me for that matter." I look around then lean in. "New subject. I need to ask you something about Dayne. Or maybe I should ask Cove."

"Mom! You should see the floater Daxton left in the pool. It's his biggest one yet!"

The boys run to their chairs and begin eating as Cove towels their hair. Sophia looks to Cove and he nods that it's true.

"You shit in the pool?" I groan. "What the fuck? There's a bathroom twenty feet away from the water."

"Yeah but there were too many people in the water. Once I did it they all took off and Xav and I had the whole pool to ourselves."

"So your plan was to clear the pool?" I ask.

He nods.

"Unbelievable." I shake my head and bring up the front desk's number on my watch. "A ten-year-old is going to drive my guests away... hey, Chloe?" I speak into the watch.

"Yes, Mr. Jameson," she responds.

"Contact whichever pool attendant is here and ask him to take care of the *brown gift* in the water."

"Brown gift?" There's a pause then laughter. "Oh... will do."

I end the call and point my finger at my nephew. "Next time I'll make you clean it up yourself."

"There won't be a next time," Cove says, giving his son a stern look.

Jules returns and sets two plates of food on the table, much more than an egg and French toast. Her caring gesture generates a massive grin on my sister's face.

"She loves you too," she whispers.

"Yeah, she's sitting right next to me, Soph. I'm pretty sure she can hear you."

"Fine, I'll let it go. So what did you want to ask about Dayne?"

"Not now," Cove says, pouring juice for his kids and a coffee for himself.

"See, that right there is the problem," I say.

He scowls back at me. "Not with the kids around. I just told you that, you can talk to us in private."

"I'm referring to you pampering them. They can dry their own hair and pour their own damn juice. At ten, they shouldn't be shitting in the pool. That's what two-year-olds do. It's fucking ridiculous. They'll never be real men if you keep babying their asses."

"My dad does stuff for us because he loves us," Daxton says. "We're not babies, you asshole."

"We're badasses," Xavier chimes in.

Those words send shivers down my spine like they

where just spoken by my father. I stare into Xavier's dark eyes and swear my dad's hiding inside of that child.

"Leave them alone," my sister says. "Boys, eat your breakfast, please."

I pull out my wallet and place a hundred dollar bill on the table. "Well, I have a question for you *badasses*. Who was playing games with the flashlight on the deck, and why?"

"Mark, I said stop. We told them about the *hunter* in the woods. The gunshot was an accident." She winks.

"I wasn't playing games. I was warning you about the man," Dax says.

Cove crosses his arms and listens, totally perturbed by what he's hearing. "You didn't tell us that. You said you heard a shot and that was it."

"You didn't ask me what happened before the shot," he says. "I was just shining my flashlight in the water of the pool when a red light started fighting with mine. I saw the big guy in the woods. His light went all the way up to my stomach then disappeared."

"Jesus Christ," Cove mumbles.

"Then, Uncle Mark came outside and I flashed him because I saw the red light under his deck. Those red sights are in our video games. I knew the man was going to shoot."

"He saved your ass," Xavier says while leaning back in his chair. "You gonna pay him?"

"No," Cove says in a stern voice.

"You're a good bodyguard, Dax." I hand him the

hundred-dollar bill.

"Fuckin' A." Cove tosses the money back in my face. "Daxton and Xavier, take your plates, we're going upstairs."

"Dad, I want to stay down here."

"Now!"

The boys scramble off their chairs, grabbing their plates and walking out of the room.

"Don't you ever give my kids money and call them bodyguards. You fuck. I've had enough." He takes his coffee and paper then motions for Sophia to follow.

She ignores me, but says goodbye to Jules before following Cove out of the room.

"So that's your family?"

"Yeah, but don't be fooled by what you just witnessed. We really do love each other."

POMPOUS

The front page of the local newspaper has a brilliant story about Jules' ex-boyfriend, Roland, along with information on the bum that's been arrested for the crime. I caught a glimpse of it in Cove's hand before he took off from the breakfast table. I was finally able to read it on my own when Jules started her shift.

Two killings in one week and I got off scot-free on both. The homeless guy was covered in evidence and Dayne's disappearance will go unnoticed for eternity. His brother and sister don't give two shits about... but damn it, I keep forgetting about the woman at the motel.

She'll need to be dealt with at some point.

Dayne's murder can be ignored, but who knows if this woman has family and friends who care. This is when things can get tricky. It's a problem my father often ran into. If you kill someone, you have to make sure there's not a group of people lining up to find out what the fuck happened or why their son or daughter disappeared. And if a problem arises, make sure you can pin the crime on someone else. My dad taught me that the older the person, the fewer problems you're likely to have. Kill an eighteen-year-old and the entire town is on a manhunt, kill someone in their thirties or forties and it's the immediate family who are concerned, but kill a sixty-year-old with no wife or kids and you're pretty much in the clear.

I'd say by the size, shape, and hang of that women's tits, she's in her thirties, which means her parents are possibly still alive and she may have siblings. That sucks. I also noticed she had a flabby stomach, but no stretch marks, so no kids.

I'm wondering if she's still at the motel or if she took off when Dayne didn't return. I'll check to see if the Datsun's in the lot, maybe even knock on the door and introduce myself if she's still around.

But that will have to wait 'til I finish cleaning and covering my boat. There's still some blood on the stern and the quicker that's taken care of, the better. It will take part of the morning, and will give me plenty of time to think...

• • •

It's a dark summer night; no moon or stars are visible as I look up to the sky through the window of my father's car. I'm nervous. I must've fucked up again or he wouldn't have dragged me out of bed at three in the morning. I haven't a clue what the fuck's going on, and with him, it could be anything.

"You meet my new house whore?" he asks while pulling the car into a dirt lot.

"No," I whisper. "She nice?"

"If you mean a good fuck, then yeah, she's got a nice cunt. She's a moaner too, unlike the last one who never said shit when Dayne and I fucked her. I'll never waste my time with another one of those."

"So what is this place?"

We step out of the car and he takes me inside a building that's under construction.

"It's one of my new casinos."

"No shit?" I reply. "Another one?"

"No shit." He whistles, signaling for someone to come out of the darkness. A moment later, his bodyguard Dayne shows his face. "I didn't bring you here for a tour, Mark. You're here to do your part for the family business."

I stop dead in my tracks, worried about what the fuck he means. When I saw Dayne, I thought my father brought me here to rough me up, but he could've done that back at his mansion. Yeah, that really crossed my mind. I wouldn't put it past him to break my face. But then I notice a guy behind Dayne... no, two men behind him. Blindfolded, on their knees, with their hands tied behind their backs.

"What the fuck, Paul?" Dayne approaches with a grunt. "Why bring pussy boy here?"

"He's going to take care of this one. It'll be a good initiation into the adrenaline-charged side of the business." He pats my back. "You ready?"

My heart pounds in excitement... and fear. He wants

me to kill for him? My hands shake and my legs feel like Jell-O. Deep breaths, fuck, don't wuss out.

I'm in my mid-twenties and this is the first time I might have a chance to make my father proud, as long as I don't fuck up. Shit, I can't believe I'm about to do this. I'm choked up that he brought me here. He must trust me. This is a step in the right direction in our relationship.

"I don't want you to speak. Don't argue, talk back, or open your goddamn mouth for any reason," he says. "Do what I say and nothing more."

I nod.

Dayne takes out his gun, but my father shakes his head and picks up a shovel instead.

"I already dug the hole," Dayne says. "We can pile them both into it, no need to dig a second."

My father ignores his comment and motions for us to follow him over to the men.

Fuck. As we get closer, I recognize one of them. He's my father's top porn star, a guy I've fucked myself, just a young stud who my father refers to as his 'Star.' What the fuck did he do? He's just a kid, nineteen, maybe twenty, whimpering, and pleading for his life. This would be easier if I didn't know him, but maybe that's why my father brought me out. It's a test. Except the other guy isn't familiar, so maybe it's not. If I can kill him first as practice then the one I know won't be as difficult.

The older guy's face is already beaten to a pulp and he has a broken arm, definitely from Dayne. He's also quiet, accepting his fate, just waiting to be put out of his misery.

My father hands me the shovel and I stand behind the two men. "This is your special night. I promise when it's over your cock will be harder than the first time you got laid."

"Please don't," Star begs. "Paul, I'll do anything you ask, anything, please!"

"I'm not the one doing shit. You know I don't like getting my hands dirty. Watching is a hell of a lot better anyway. You're begging the wrong person. I'm not the one going to take your life away."

"Please don't do this." He starts to cry. "You can do anything you want to me and I won't complain. I'll be your slave. I'll suck you off anytime you want. I won't talk back. I won't..."

"Oh shut the fuck up!" Dayne kicks his back and he falls forward, sobbing in the dirt.

My father raises his hand for Dayne to stop then turns to me. "So you've got these two assholes in front of you. This one." He points to the guy with the broken arm. "He created his own porn site using my company name, it's a clone of my business. He's been raking in the dough... my money... he's a fucking pirate." My father spits on him. "And that one." He points to Star. "I'm just tired of his mouth, nothing more."

I nod again, staying silent as requested.

"So here's the plan. We've got this grave dug and I've got a cement crew arriving at six in the morning to pour a slab of concrete in this spot. It's your choice whether you want to put them in alive and fill in the hole with dirt or—"

"Don't!" Star shouts, trying to move away on his knees. Dayne takes out a roll of duct tape, but my father stops him from taping his mouth, getting off from the kid's pleading words.

"My handsome little Star, are you scared?"

"Yes," he cries. "I'll never complain again, Paul. I'm yours. You own me." He continues to inch away. "Take me back to your place. I don't care what you do just don't kill me. Take me home and fuck me if you want and I won't complain. I'll be good. Anything but this." He falls onto the rocky dirt and vomits in complete duress. "I love you, Paul," he sobs. "I love you."

Now I feel like shit. Killing the asshole that stole money from my dad is one thing, but killing someone because he mouths off is another.

"Star," my father whispers, hovering over him. "Your pal Dayne has a roll of duct tape in his hand. If we tape your mouth and you puke, all that steamy chunky fluid that comes up from your stomach will get stuck in your nose. Then you won't be able to breathe. You'll suffocate, just like if my friend puts you in the hole and covers your face with dirt. If I were you, I'd shut the fuck up."

"You own me, Paul," he whispers with a tremble.

It's interesting that he never says 'Let me go.' The poor kid's got Stockholm syndrome or something. If I were in this situation I wouldn't act like either one of these men. They're both pussies. I'd fight to the very end. Even on my knees with my hands behind my back I'd think of something, like biting into one of their dicks and not letting go. My head would be at the perfect height to do that sort of damage. I'd leave my teeth marks in their cocks forever.

My father sets his finger over Star's lips and whispers something in his ear then stands unemotionally and turns back to me. Damn, I wish I knew what he said.

"Your other choice is to kill 'em before you bury 'em. It all depends on how much you think they should suffer."

I motion for Dayne to hand me his gun, but my father cuts in again. "No, you're not thinking," he says. "Try another weapon, like the one in your hand."

My father frowns and I take it as a sign that I'm a moron. I just made my first mistake of the night. A gunshot would have the police swarming in a matter of minutes and I can see the disappointment in his eyes as he crosses his arms and waits. Fuck. Think, Mark, think. What will be the best way to do this? Maybe I should just bury him? No, too easy. I've got a gut feeling my dad wants something more from me, besides the shovel. I need to surprise him.

Crackling sounds leave the mouth of the man kneeling next to me. He's struggling to breathe and I think he has a collapsed lung.

I'm sweaty and my heart's pumping out of my chest. My father eggs me on with a smile and a wink.

I can do this.

I drop the shovel at my father's feet, shove the suffering man into the hole, and jump on top of him.

"Whoa," Dayne says.

The groaning stops when my hands tighten around his neck. I'm going to silence this guy and show my father I can *do it with my bare hands, not a fucking shovel. He's going to love me.*

"I love you Paul," Star says from above. "Please don't hurt me." His voice fades.

Shit, why won't he shut up? He's going to ruin my moment.

"Watch me," I whisper, gripping the man's neck. "Watch me." But when I turn to look at my father, he's gone. The fucking bastard walked away. "I'm doing this for you!" I call out.

Dayne looks into the grave and shakes his head. *My dad's not coming back and he left his shithead bodyguard to watch, like I need a fucking babysitter. I'm killing a man for him and he fucking took off. I'm pissed.*

"He's dead, let go of him," Dayne says.

The blindfold conceals the man's eyes, but his split-lipped mouth is open like a fish. *I missed it. The guy died in my hands and I failed to notice because I was so goddamn focused on pleasing my dad.*

"Fuck," I whisper. *I felt an adrenaline rush at the start, but it quickly changed to disappointment. Next time will be better. Strangling a guy isn't very satisfying, I know that now, but maybe a knife or a gun will leave me content.*

And where the hell did my father go? What an asshole.

"I wouldn't go over there," Dayne remarks after I climb out and head toward my father's car. "Get back here and fill in the hole. Trust me, Paul always gets off from this type of shit then he enjoys a good fuck. Don't interrupt him when he's with his boy toy."

"What?" I look at Dayne then to the car. The bastard would rather be with Star than me? To hell with this, not now, this is MY moment.

I walk to the opposite side of the car, only to see my sick father holding the back of the kid's head and forcing him to suck him off. That's right, he's the disturbed one here tonight, not me. I only strangled a guy; I'm not a fucking rapist.

"What the fuck?" I put my palms up, raising my hands in the air. "Just like that? You left?"

"I told you to keep your mouth shut." He pushes Star away and tucks his dick in his pants. The blindfold's still on when Star hits the rocky ground with a groan.

"Are you proud?" I whisper. "Say something to me. Tell me that you—"

My head is slammed onto the hood of his car before I have a chance to finish my sentence. Fuck, he can be so brutal. I want his power... I want to be just like him, but I hate his guts.

His cold breath drapes around my ear as he whispers his final words of the night.

"My dick got hard watching you grip that man's neck. That should be enough to make you happy."

• • •

Fuck my dad.

He adored Cove. His Star. He had no intention of killing him that night; he just wanted to fuck with his head... and that happened often.

I never told my brother-in-law I was there. He's unaware of how or if the guy was killed. He saw nothing. But he must've presumed the worst. That is, if he remembers. He's blocked out a lot of shit from that time period. It was a traumatic experience for him, one of many, and I'm sure many of those nights have melded together for the poor guy.

I envied the time he spent with my dad, even though he was raped and beaten by the man. I can't believe I never helped him, especially that night; I walked away instead. I think it's because the kid was already too far gone to be brought out of Jameson Industries. He had started in my father's business as a teen and would've been disposed of before he reached thirty.

There's a lot of shit I keep from him and my sister. Stuff they shouldn't know, like the fact I don't consider that to be my first kill. It wasn't satisfying.

The second one left me feeling the same. I shot a man in the head and was aggravated by the amount of blood that sprayed out. It was all over the walls and floor. I was quite displeased. Nevertheless, I carry a gun, ready to take a man down if he's about to do the same. Distant kills happen; they're just not very rewarding.

But when I used a switchblade for the first time... fuck, my dick was instantly hard and it was impossible to wipe the grin off my face for days. That's what my father meant when he said it would be better than the first time

I got laid.

I love the intimacy of using a blade. A close range kill, the victims breath in my face, the blood staying confined to the body as long as I don't hit any major arteries, and no splattering of brains. My blade sliding in and out of men like gliding my cock in and out of a pussy... it turns me into a starry-eyed and sexually aroused nutcase.

That's what I consider to be my first kill.

And there's been a reason behind each one. The men were all connected to my family in some way, not just random kills, although I do crave it enough that I could see myself slipping one day.

My father was kind enough to tell me all the things I did wrong that night, like leaving my DNA on the victim by not wearing gloves and killing the wrong guy first. Even though he didn't want Cove dead, he said you should always silence the one making the most noise to calm the scene then deal with the others after. He was also disappointed I reached for the gun, saying the blood would've been too difficult to clean up before the cement crew arrived, especially in the dark. Plus, I spoiled his fuck.

I did everything wrong.

And yet, everything I did was for him.

Damn it, I do everything for everyone else.

They're all fucking ingrates.

• • •

And that's the shit that goes through my mind while spiffing up my boat. At least *she's* appreciative of my care. She's back in order, clean as a whistle, and covered until the next outing.

Cove tossed her cover on hastily after we docked, but I wouldn't expect much more from him considering his desire to get home. He was also in a rush to get me out of the cold and into some warmer clothing.

Since he tried his best, I won't bring it up next time I see him, which will be soon since he couldn't book a flight out of the airport in Reno to St. Louis for two days. They're stuck with me. I love it. I get to spend more time with my baby sis and I can ask her and Cove if they remember any of Dayne's women. There are a number of house whores who fell head over heels for that dope.

Whoever she is, her orange Datsun is MIA when I pass the motel on my way home. And just as I'm pulling into my garage, a text comes through from Jules.

I saw the newspaper. Roland's dead.

Ladi-fucking-da. I text her back.

You need to be punished. She responds.

I smirk. Punished for my text or for Roland? It's difficult to figure out the meaning of some texts, but I bet this one's a joke. The article is clear that the police have someone in custody, so Jules is either happy about the situation and she wants to celebrate, or she believes I did it, in which case she also wants to celebrate. Either way, I doubt she cares much about Roland's death. She barely even knew the guy. It's not like murdering someone is a big deal to her; that was obvious by her morning actions. She's too fond of me to give a shit.

After changing into a clean black suit, I head downstairs to check on *things*. It's a busy afternoon and my hotel is booked solid for a three-day marathon that starts tomorrow morning.

I'm happy to see the place is spotless. The carpets have been cleaned, the wood shines, soft music plays in the lobby, the fireplaces burn, and every light is dim for a peaceful setting. Perfection.

Fresh Mariposa lilies have also arrived and Jules looks extravagant placing the white, newly picked, sweet smelling flowers into the vase on the front desk.

"The only punishment in our relationship will be me taking a belt to your ass," I whisper, pulling her into the back office where my hotel manager is speaking to another front desk worker. I nod for them to leave then shut and lock the door.

If I had more time to fool around, I'd take her upstairs to my private office or back to bed, but I'm waiting for a package and want to be around when it arrives. It's a special gift for someone.

"Did you kill Roland?" She puts her hand on my chest and looks at me with twinkling honey eyes. "If you did, then maybe it's time for you to admit that you did it out of love. Right? Is that why? Did you kill *another* man?"

My lip twitches as I unbuckle my belt, sliding it through my pant loops then snapping it between us. She doesn't flinch, there's not even a blink of an eye.

"I asked you a question," she says, snaking around my body like she's circling her prey. Her fingers move slowly across my chest, forearm, and around my back.

"I'm the one holding the belt," I remind her.

"But if I'm not mistaken, I'm the one holding all the cards in this office," she replies in a low, sexy voice. "Right, Mark?"

Fuck, I'm hard for her.

"Punish me later. It will be better if you wait. Besides, I'm not giving you everything you want whenever you ask, and now's not the time for this."

I grab her waist and pull her against my stiff cock. She smiles when she feels the erection and seizes my nuts through my pants.

"You're not listening," she says.

"Trust me, every word out of your mouth is causing my blood to pump through my veins like a fierce storm. It's apparent."

She looks down at my bulge. I can't believe I'm ready to go again. It's only been five hours since she jerked me off in the shower.

"Come straight to my suite when you get off today. Six o'clock?"

She nods and releases her grip. "I'll be ready for a little amusement."

"It won't be fun," I whisper, speaking slowly while

holding her chin. "Expect pain, prepare to scream, count on many moments when you beg me to let up, but know that I won't. Tonight, you'll learn to give me what I want."

WORSHIPPING THE PRINCESS

J ules is beautiful, elegant, and seductive, but she has a disobedient and wild side to her like a feral cat—my sinfully dark woman. She needs to learn how to behave, especially in front of my family.

She arrives exactly at one minute past six, strips out of her clothing, all except her heels, heads upstairs... slowly... not turning around... and sways her ass while walking into my bedroom.

"It's so dark in here," she whispers. "I can't see."

I light a candle, but leave the curtains closed and the lights off. She requests that I speak, but I'm in no mood for conversation. I have other plans.

Two leather cuffs have been fastened around the spindles of the foot of the bed and my belt is lying on my black comforter. She sees the cuffs and knows what to do, bending over and raising her arms to have her wrists securely restrained.

She's calm and compliant for once.

"Good girl."

My hand glides across her neck, down her back, and she's given one quick graze over her clit. Her ass and pussy lift, begging for a good smack. Fuck, this will be fun.

"Please be gentle," she whispers.

"Not tonight."

I take a small metal container from my dresser then sit and admire her soft golden skin flickering in the candlelight. I'm going to take my time and, no, I won't go easy.

"I'm unbuttoning and taking off my shirt so I don't get cum all over it," I say calmly, granting her a visual. I toss it next to her and lean back in my chair. "My dick's hard, Jules, but it's still confined in my pants. It's not coming out until you've been disciplined."

She's still and quiet; her head is bowed and her blonde hair conceals her face.

My finger traces my lips as I imagine crawling underneath her, fingering her pussy, and eating her out. She takes a deep breath, awaiting the belt while my hips rock like they're thrusting into her. Hell, I can't help but slide my hand under my pants and touch myself. I love seeing a nude woman strapped to my bed.

"I smell the pot, Mark."

And I smell her. I can smell every part of her. The fruity shampoo, flowery perfume, berry lip balm, and her sticky wet twat. She's one hundred percent woman.

"Please don't forget about me," she whispers.

"Smoke all you want, but remember I'm here, waiting, wanting this as much as you do."

I shake my head and sigh, taking a second hit before reaching for my belt. Forget about her? Never.

The belt snaps next to her ear, causing her to draw back in a playful attempt to flee.

"Secure yourself," I demand.

Her feet spread apart and her hands grip the dark mahogany spindles of my footboard. She moans when my leather belt glides down her spine, stopping over her clenched ass.

"Ready, steady," I whisper, standing next to her with my belt pulled back.

"Ow!" she wails with a quick rise of her head. "Mark, what the fuck..."

I strike her again and the sound of a powerful smack fills the room.

"Fuck! Not so hard!"

My hand trails her red flesh. Gorgeous. Simply stunning.

"You're not playing!" she whines.

"Nope." I crack the belt in the air then take another speedy swing, hitting her ass harder than before.

"Jesus!" she screams. Her confined hands yank at the cuffs.

"Julia, my darling Julia." I pace behind her, trailing the belt along the ground then forming it into a loop. "Tell me why the fuck you thought it was okay to touch my blade this morning." My belt touches her flesh and she leans forward in anticipation. "And tell me why you made me look like a fucking fool in front of my family." I strike again.

"Mark!"

The grin on my face must be as big as my erection. Fuck, I feel mighty.

"Guns are one thing, but fucking with my blades and my authority? Screw you."

She takes another hit.

"Uh!"

Like me, she won't back down... she's not telling me to stop, even with her flesh red and raw. I'm still pissed, but I decide to give her a moment, standing behind her, debating if she's had enough.

"Why the fuck won't you apologize?" I ask.

A deep exhale escapes her mouth. There's a blurry motion, and... shit! Her foot nails me in the nuts. A hard kick and I'm bent over in pain.

"Damn it, Jules."

That was unexpected.

"Fucker!" she shouts. "Why aren't you chill when you're stoned? I said go easy and I meant it. This should be pleasurable and it's not!"

"Fuck!" I gasp, with my hand over my dick. "What the hell?"

"Yeah, what the hell? I bet my ass looks like it's on fire." She kneels in front of the bed, no longer presenting her body for play. "You're supposed to pleasure me, not beat me."

"Jules, just fucking say you were wrong and that—"

"No! You're being a baby! So what if I touched your blade. Get bent!" she yells. "I told you before not to hurt me. This is supposed to be fun."

"This *is* fun!"

She turns to me with an open mouth and wide eyes. "Seriously?"

"Fucking back down and give me control!"

She does a double take, same expression, same open mouth and same wide eyes. Same words too. "Seriously?"

"Fuck." I toss my belt on the bed and rub my chin. "This isn't happening." I step to my door and let in the cool mountain air, needing to clear my head.

This is why I should smoke alone. What a dumbass mistake. It's so much better in private and when it's used to relax, not to screw. I thought it would keep me from going overboard with the belt, but just the opposite happened. Now I want to hurt, choke, fuck, and beat her ass, only I didn't expect her to attack back. Everything this woman does is different. My head is a clouded mess.

Her face is red and her hands fidget in the cuffs. She's fond of the belt, only I was cruel this time and may have ruined my chance of ever using it again. This wasn't BDSM in any way; it was pure punishment on my part. I had no plans of offering her any form of pleasure. Damn it. Wait... am I backing down? What the fuck? She's supposed to be begging me to stop. I want an apology. I want control.

"Nothing makes a man weaker than falling in love

with a woman," I whisper. Luckily she doesn't hear the shit that expels from my mouth.

I try staring her down with crossed arms and a stern look. That doesn't work. "Who the fuck are you and what have you done with my balls?" I finally say.

But shit, I wish I hadn't asked. The smile on her face and her laughter in this moment will stay with me forever. She owns me. Fuckin' A, she owns me.

"Julia Alison Barringer," she whispers. "Your balls hang on a necklace around my neck. You can have them back once you prove that you're a man."

Son of a bitch, I've been speared.

My dick's coming back to life. It went slack for a moment, but now it wants to rip into her. "For fuck's sake, put your head down, shut the fuck up, and get ready to fuck."

She smirks before her face disappears between her raised arms. "That's a lot of 'fucks' in one breath, Mark."

"Yes, and thanks for giving me an idea." I reach under my bed, digging through my sex toys, pushing my facemask aside and grabbing a strap-on. Jules sneaks a peek while I take off my pants and fasten it above my cock. It has a hole underneath that my dick slides through, allowing it to hang out.

Perfect. She's in for a double cock surprise.

"Whoa."

"Don't worry, it's a little one. I'm not going to initiate your first anal with a nine-incher."

"Oh my God." She puts her head down and exhales.

"I'm serious. Be gentle or you're dead meat."

I grab a bottle of lube and a condom from my nightstand then kneel behind her, excited that she's up for this after a harsh ass smacking.

"Did you hear me?"

"I think so... you said you wanted me to fuck you until I have red meat."

"Jesus, listen to me. My ass is already throbbing, go slow, okay?"

"You listen." I move her body closer to the bed then press my chest against her flesh. "You need to learn to back down and not be such a warrior all the time. Say stop, and I'll stop, but until I hear it, I'm going to fuck you the way I want."

"You dick." She tilts her head, persuading me to kiss her neck. "You need to worship your princess."

"Is that so?" I laugh. "Egotistical, are we?" I put on the condom then spread lube over the silicone cock. "Well, it's your lucky day. A princess in cuffs about to get fucked in the ass is indeed worth worshipping."

My dick nudges against her swollen lips. I grip the footboard, pause, and thrust. "Ah," I whisper in her ear. "That's one, Jules, one of two."

"Wait, I'm not sure if... ohhh! Holy hell! That hurts!"

Her head rises as my finger lubes her ass. She's tight and clenching.

"It hurts more if you do that. Just relax."

"Easy for you to say... not two, Mark. Uh!"

I slide a second finger in and she's stuffed—one dick in her pussy and two fingers in her ass. Nice. It's such a grand feeling to have your ass fucked, something I haven't experienced in years, but I'm sure she'd be game to return the favor if I asked.

"Here we go." I position the strap-on over her hole and push the tip inside. Her knuckles turn white as she clutches the spindles of the bed frame and whimpers.

"Breathe," I whisper, squeezing both my dick and the toy further inside. "Ahh yes. You made it. The first part is the most painful. How does it feel?"

I look down and admire the double penetration. The pressure is intense from my end, so I can only imagine the sensation must be even more extreme for her.

"It's incredible," she says. "I'll take this as a form of reprimand over the belt any day."

My cock sinks into her and the toy follows in a parallel motion, tracking each lunge, and rubbing against the top of my dick as it were in the same hole. With every push forward, she moans and says fuck. That's my plan. Moan and fuck.

For twenty minutes I tease her ass, listen to her heavy breathing, watch her hands tighten into fists as she tries to tolerate the pain, while graciously massaging her clit... waiting, hoping, and finally relieved when she cums.

"Fuck yeah. Beat my cock with your throbbing pussy. I'm in total control now. You're trapped in my arms, weak and powerless." I smile and watch my dick sliding into her shuddering body. "Scream while I'm inside you. Be loud. Tell me you love this. Speak."

"I'm cumming, Mark... I'm cumming," she whispers. "Fuck, you feel amazing."

"That's right." I kiss her neck. "Not only do I feel amazing, I *am* amazing."

"Don't stop."

My hands cling to her tits while we fuck. I feel them bounce with each slam and pinch her nipples when I want her to call out my name.

"Fuck it hurts, but it's incredible. Move faster. Cum for me!" she yells.

Screw taking this easy.

I seize her hair and pull her head back so her eyes are gazing at my mirrored ceiling. "Watch," I demand. My dick and the toy nail her hard and her engorged tits swing. "You're mine... watch... watch me... you have no control... no power... I own you... I... fuck, fuck, I'm gonna cum." I speed up, tightening my ass and clenching my abs. "Fuck, Jules, fuck."

I look up so she can see my face. "Watch," I say in a gnarled voice. Shit, it feels good... every shot, every last drop. "Damn." I fall forward, gripping the footboard. "Fuck."

Her head rests on her arms, waiting to be uncuffed. I slide out and hear a gasp, as her pussy and ass are free.

"That release of pressure is fabulous, isn't it?" I pant.

"All of it was fabulous, even the belt," she mumbles

toward the floor.

"Really? So you were fucking with me, trying to be all badass while I hit you?"

"I was and I won."

I unfasten the cuffs and she collapses to the floor with a massive smile plastered across her face.

"Indeed, you won, beautiful. Get dressed or we're gonna be late for dinner."

"No downtime?" she whispers.

"No."

"Mark?"

"Hmm?"

"Fucking kiss me, you bastard."

"Now? Why. We just finished. It's not like I can get it up again."

"God, you suck." She stands and rubs her wrists, watching me put on a black dress shirt and a dark grey sport coat. "What dinner?"

"My sister invited us over. But don't expect anything tasty, she can't cook."

"I thought Cove was annoyed at you this morning?"

"Are you kidding? That was nothing. The guy loves me. Don't let his snarling remarks and pissy attitude fool you."

She rolls her eyes, holds her ass, and starts to walk away, only to be surrounded in my arms a moment later. "Wait, I have a question."

"What?"

"You're always fucking with my head."

It's true. She makes me second-guess everything. I feel like a fool when she's around.

"That's not a question."

"I know. Look... I want to know how a man like Roland can hurt a woman like you? If I did anything like that you'd cut off my dick."

I graze her cheek and she looks past me then leans into my hand for comfort, kissing my thumb and the palm of my hand. She knows full well that I killed him. There's no doubt in my mind now. She knows.

"I was weak once in my life, but never again. If this was our first time together, and you held me down and was forcing me to do something I didn't enjoy, or I said no and you wouldn't stop, then we'd have a big problem."

"*I'd* have a big problem," I whisper.

She nods. "After Roland, I knew I'd never let that happen again. You waited a long time to fuck me and along the way, if I ever told you to stop, you did. I trust you. And I let you play with your toys because I enjoy them too... besides, I really like you. That makes a huge difference. I never developed any feelings for Roland." Her eyes return to mine and her soft fingers touch the bump on my head. "Don't get hurt, Mark, okay? Don't do anything stupid for me. Let the past be what it is and forget about all the brutes."

My fingers are under her chin, lifting her head so her lips can have the kiss they deserve. Our eyes close when we touch and a delightful, erotically sensual sigh flows through the air. My tongue coils around hers, turning, twisting, and sliding in and out. Next time I'll remember to kiss her during our fuck.

The strap-on sticks out from under my shirt, the used condom hangs off my shrunken dick, and my fingers skim across her flat stomach. Never in my life have I paid this much attention to a woman.

"I'm sorry," she whispers.

"What? Where the hell did that come from?" I'm taken aback by her words.

"I'm serious. I promise to behave in front of your family and I won't touch your switchblade."

"No shit?"

"No shit, Mark." She grins. "Now, I better get dressed if we're going out."

"Wait." I pull her back. "Sleep here tonight. Stay in my bed, next to me. Will you do that? Maybe we can fuck again, or at least I can get you off, or, I don't know, we could talk, maybe... no, I hate talking. Forget I said that. But stay."

"Shh." Her finger presses against my lips. "I love it that you need me... this is good," she says.

I kiss her again, exhaling a powerfully defeated breath.

This most definitely, is *not* good.

GIFT

"What's in the box?" Julia asks as we walk through the corridor toward my second suite where Cove and Sophia are waiting. We're late. It's ten past seven. But at least the time was well spent. Jules looks absolutely stunning. I watched her slip into a short black dress, a snug fit, so tight that she left her underwear behind, expressing her disdain for panty lines. But, I bet it's really because she has a sore ass.

Her hair is pulled back in a bun, she's in her usual black heels, and her makeup has the appearance of perfection—plum colored lipstick, black mascara, and a gold eye shadow. She's way overdressed for my family, but I'll take this look any day to a woman in jeans and a T-shirt. I'm never been a fan of the casual look, it reminds me too much of my mother.

"The box is a surprise for Cove," I say.

My sister's loud voice stops my hand in mid-air, right before I'm about to knock, then I hear my brother-in-law's usual disrespectful words as I wait and listen.

"I don't want that fuck to come over here. I can't

believe you're not listening to me!"

"Cove, he's the only family I have. We're here for two more days; can you try to be civil, at least for one night? He helped us out a great deal. We're safe and he didn't even charge us."

"Ha! Are you listening to yourself? Jesus Christ, Soph. What, like a contract killing? You think he—"

"Stop it! And watch your language. This is total crap. And no, I didn't mean charge us to take care of Dayne, I meant for the suite."

"Fuck, I hate him."

"Hate's such a strong word and I don't want you to use it with the boys around."

Jules whispers that maybe we should come back later, but I shake my head and knock.

"He loves me," I say under my breath.

The door opens and my sister smiles while Cove's in the background mixing a drink. He turns around and raises a glass to us, walking over to the dining room table, acting like he wants to get this over with as quickly as possible.

"You're late," Sophia says. "Hi Jules, you look pretty."

"Thanks, you too."

We walk inside and I see two room service carts in the kitchen area. Good. She didn't cook.

"Thanks for the invite, even though the dinner's from my own restaurant."

"I wanted to make sure you didn't complain about

the food." She laughs. "If you don't like it, then it's your problem, not mine. I take no responsibility if you don't enjoy the meal."

"I thought this space was used for storage. I didn't know it was another suite," Jules says. "It's the same layout as yours too, only brighter."

My sister has the blinds open, something she hasn't been able to do in weeks since I'd insisted they keep the rooms dark. But this evening, as the sun sets, the remaining rays of the day dance around us.

"Where are the boys?" I ask.

"Watching a movie upstairs. I thought we could use a little privacy tonight." She leans closer to me and whispers. "Cove's in a foul mood. I didn't want the boys here in case the two of you get in an argument."

I nod and look over at him in the dining room, running a finger around the rim of his glass. He frowns at me and I smile, walking into the room and placing the box on the table.

"It's a thank you. Open it."

"I don't want you buying me gifts, Mark."

"Cove, just open it," my sister says, rolling the dinner carts into the room. Julia helps her place the four chicken dinners on the table, along with bread and a peach pie for desert while Cove takes the top off the wooden box.

"No shit," he says with a grin.

"I thought you might be missing home. I ordered it from your place and had it shipped overnight."

"What is it?" Julia peeks into the box. "Wine?"

"My house wine from my bar in St. Louis, The Dark Scarlett."

"Just what he needs, more alcohol," Sophia mumbles.

"It's exactly what I need. The alcohol in this suite is pure sewage."

"That's bullshit." I take a seat across from Julia and Sophia sits across from Cove. "I only buy top-notch liquor for my hotel."

"Nothing compares to mine." He pours himself a glass, swirls it in the air, sniffs, then takes a big gulp. "Ahh."

"Three bottles enough?" I ask.

"It's plenty, thanks," my sister says. "He's fine until we return home."

Cove pours a glass for everyone and I can tell he's pleased. I mean; he's already on his second glass.

"Your head looks like shit," Cove says.

"Thanks, I know. I got lucky."

"You never told me what happened," Jules whispers, staring at my forehead.

"Yeah, I'd like to know as well," Sophia says.

"Tough guy, Dayne, jumped me from behind and bashed my head into the concrete floor. That's when I knifed him. At that moment I knew it was him or me, right?" They nod as I butter my bread.

"Cove told me what happened on the boat and I don't want to discuss this at the dinner table. New conversation," my sister says.

"So he told you he sunk Dayne? He rolled him off the boat to rest in the depths of Lake Tahoe? Your husband was one hell of a sidekick last night."

"What?"

"Sophia, don't get him started. Just eat your food," Cove says, sipping more wine.

"No, he didn't mention that," she fumes. "What the heck, Cove? I thought we agreed you were just going to help lift him, nothing more. What did you do?"

I laugh, which I shouldn't, but the shit these too bicker about...

"You fucking try standing next to Mark when he's gutting a guy like a fish and telling horrific stories of our family and see how long you last before you snap! I wanted it over with and your brother was taking his sweet ass time, then he got all weird and started singing that creepy troll song. I was *not* going to stand and listen to that shit, trapped in a boat, with a dead body at my feet, in the middle of the dark lake!"

"Okay." Sophia sighs. "I understand. I'm sorry."

"Thank you," he says sternly.

"Mark." Sophia takes my hand. "I've been telling you since we were kids that the troll song is bad luck. He dies in the end, remember?"

"I feel so lost," Jules says. "What troll song?"

"It's from Billy Goats Gruff. He's been singing it since I can remember." She shakes her head. "My mother used to chase us around the house while she sang it to us, then Mark started repeating it like it was big fun. But it creeped me out, as Cove said, it's a hair-raising song for children, and just plain strange for an adult to be singing. Flat out weird." She looks at me and releases my hand. "Did you hear me? The nasty, goat-eating troll dies. It's not fitting for you to think you're a troll, Mark... could be bad karma, or something."

"Keep singing it," Cove whispers with a smirk.

"You should call her," I say softly to my sister, referring to our mother. "She'd be thrilled to hear from you, even from the psych ward."

"When Hell freezes over." She chugs her wine and passes the empty glass to Cove for a refill. "It's been over a decade since we last spoke and the two of us have nothing to say to one another. She's a violent wench and I won't subject my kids to her abuse. Plus, I can't talk to her when she's all medicated and wants me to call her 'mommy.' It sends shivers down my spine."

"It's not a bad thing that she's getting help. Besides, any one of us could be in one of those places."

She laughs, trying to lighten the mood. "The doctors wouldn't know what to do with us."

"Fair enough," I agree.

"Anyway, mom loves *you*, not me."

"No, you just never stood up to her when we were kids. She appreciated my dominance in the house but preyed on you because you were weak."

"That's a shit ass excuse for her behavior. And I'm far from being weak now, but the woman still hates me."

"You don't know that because you don't talk to her."

"Yeah, I already told you, when Hell freezes over."

"Umm," Jules interrupts. "So this is what you guys discuss over dinner? In my house we talk about sports, and books or television shows, new movies that are out, and how things are at work."

"Damn, I'd love to be a fly on the wall at your house if you ever invite Mark over to meet your parents. He can tell them all about how he made his fortune by inheriting his father's porn company," Cove jokes.

"That will never happen. I'm not fifteen, going to meet the parents just to impress some chick so I can get laid... now Jules... go ahead." I raise my hand for her to take control. "Feel free to talk about whatever the fuck you want. I'm up for a normal conversation."

The three of us stare at her and I can tell she feels uncomfortable. She's trying to think about something to ask, but draws a blank when put on the spot.

"Never mind," she says. As promised, she's behaving in front of my family.

"Well, then, I'll change the subject." I turn to Cove. "You remember any of Dayne's women from back in the day?"

"Shit," he says, taking a bite of chicken and chewing slowly while he thinks. "There were hundreds that came and went from Paul's house. Why?"

"I don't know, what do you think? Have you wondered about how Dayne got here and was able to buy a gun so quickly after getting out of prison? Or pay for a motel room in town? The guy was living in my dad's house when he got arrested. He didn't have a dime to his name."

"There's always a way. He knew people in Vegas. And that's why *we* came here. We expected him to figure all that shit out. That's the kind of guy he was. Why? What are you saying?"

"He brought company."

Sophia sets down her fork. "Why the hell didn't you say something earlier, when my kids were alone in the pool? You asshole... do we have to stay here now, or what? Who is it? Do you know him?"

"It's not that big of a problem. You're safe. It's only a woman and she'll be easy to handle if I ever run into her. And no, I don't know her, I didn't recognize her tits, but she did have a Jameson tat on her shoulder."

"What tits?" Jules asks. "Wait a second. That tattoo you have... I thought..."

My sister looks at Cove with a furrowed brow. He shakes his head and whispers, "it's not her."

"Not who?" I ask.

"What did she look like?" Sophia asks.

"Mark, *what* tits?" Jules says in a bitter tone.

"I saw her through the bathroom window of Dayne's motel room. She was bent over, toweling her hair, but I never saw her face."

"Okay, so what did her tits look like?" my sister asks.

"You're not going to make an ID from the description of some woman's tits."

"Try me."

"Alright... too big to be cradled in my hands, they looked soft, round, short nipples, and her areolas were deep brown and large, like wider than two inches, a nice contrast to her ghost white skin."

"Big ass?" she questions.

"Yep."

"Mera Calloway."

"Ha, Mera? No. This woman was too big to be Mera Calloway, both her hips and her tits were huge. I remember Mera had a small frame and good size tits and a big ass years ago, but nothing extreme. Not like the woman I saw."

"Stop ignoring me," Jules says. "So that tat." She points to my shoulder. "You didn't get it because you're big-headed? Other people have the same one as you?"

I pull my collar down to reveal the Jameson Industries tattoo then Sophia does the same, moving the neckline of her brown dress to show the dove she had inked over my father's company logo. But of course, Cove sits in silence, not showing his flesh, and not wanting to discuss it in any great detail tonight.

"He had two tats from the company and covered the one on his chest with a black rose," I say, motioning toward Cove. "One was the company name and the other—"

"Stop," he requests.

"So all of you were branded?" she asks, ignoring my last comment.

"It was business," I respond. "It showed that my father owned us, I mean, it showed we worked for his company."

"You were right the first time," Cove says. "He owned us."

"That has to be illegal. It sounds like a form of slavery."

"Well, my dad's dead, so that's a logjam of a comment," I say.

"Illegal?" Cove chuckles. "You mean like killing? You're concerned about a forced tattoo being criminal, but not murder? She's a winner, Mark. Perfect for you."

"Fuck off and drink another glass before I beat your ass."

"Whatever," he says casually under his breath.

"Why didn't you change yours, like they did?" she asks me.

"You already answered your own question," Cove says, taking a big sip of wine before continuing. "He's big-headed."

"Enough," Sophia says. "It's Mera Calloway. I know it. She was the last person with Dayne before his arrest and I think she genuinely had a thing for him."

"No." I shake my head. "This woman was twice her size."

"You're such an idiot. When was the last time you saw her?" my sister asks.

She's right. It's been years. I remember a video of Dayne fucking her that was on one of my father's porn sites years ago, but I haven't seen her since.

"I know what you're thinking," Sophia says. "I meant in the flesh, Mark. When was the last time you saw her in person?"

"When the two of you were college roommates and you brought her to mom's house for dinner. Remember, Mom was aggravated that you didn't come alone."

"Yeah, that was like fifteen years ago. A woman who doesn't pack on the pounds from her early twenties to her mid-thirties is either working out 24/7 or an alien."

I look down at my sister's body... she must be an alien.

"Having to keep up with twin boys is like running ten miles a day. I'm in shape because of them."

"How the hell do you know what I'm thinking?"

"Sisters know."

"Alright, all knowing one, if it's Mera, I need more information about her. I only met her a few times and I never saw her when she worked for Dad. What do I need to know?"

"Beats the fuck out of me," she responds. "I haven't spoken to her since..."

Mera Calloway was my sister's roommate when she attended Temple University. They met as freshmen, shared a dorm room, became lovers, then got an apartment together. Both were total whores, bisexual, having an open relationship and sharing men. They remained best friends after graduation and moved to St. Louis where they partied hard—got drunk, laid, and didn't have a care in the world. It wasn't until my sister met Cove that her life started to change and she began maturing into a responsible adult, though that didn't happen by choice. My father played a big role in hooking the two of them up for his business. Cove and Sophia's relationship was a big moneymaker to him, but so was Mera Calloway. She had long dark hair and eyes the color of a Colorado sky. A small frame, big tits and ass, and from what I saw online, a great fuck. My dad had all three of them under his control and I heard through the grapevine that when Mera was brought to his mansion to become his new house whore, Dayne Rosen fell head over heels for her. That was some fucking messed up shit. I keep telling my sister, she needs to write a book about it.

"... then I saw her one night on the street. It was right when we all got back to St. Louis after our father was killed in Vegas. Haven't seen her since. What you need to know is she's tough, a real hard ass. I've witnessed her give a few bloody noses and a couple of black eyes to guys who fucked with her. She's a sneaky bitch too, a calculating, skillfully sly, money-grubbing, scheming wench. She had Dayne wrapped around her finger in a matter of days, and fooled my ass about her true self for years."

"Everyone has a weakness," I say.

"Not her," my sister replies.

"Can I ask something?"

"Go ahead," I say to Jules.

"Let me get this straight. You were with this woman, sexually, right?" she says to my sister and Sophia nods. "And she was your father's house whore, slept with him... and Dayne. She was with you, your dad, and Dayne?"

We nod.

"And your father was with Cove also? And you, Mark, were with Cove, and now Sophia's married to him?"

We nod.

"Just checking," she whispers and throws back an entire glass of wine, then gets a refill. "I understand why you drink," she says to Cove and he flashes a rare smile back.

"Trust me, I didn't sleep with three Jamesons by choice," he mutters.

"What should we do about Mera?" Sophia asks, ignoring how incredibly vile this must sound to Jules.

"Nothing. Like I mentioned, she's just a woman."

"Did you listen to anything I just said?"

"Yeah. She sounds weak, Sophia. Fat, slow, and weak."

"I agree," Cove says.

"Wow, you guys are fucking assholes," my sister scolds.

"I second that," Jules says. "A woman can easily harm, overpower, control, and eventually kill a man, in an emotional, sexual, or physical way... right Mark?" She flutters her thick eyelashes.

"Fuck yeah." Cove laughs, sounding a bit drunk. "She burned your ass, dipshit."

My foot wiggles between Jules' legs, under her dress, and presses into her pussy. "Watch it," I say.

She ignores me and slices a piece of chicken, stares into my eyes with her fork in the air, then gives the meat a big lick before placing it in her mouth.

"That was nasty hot," Cove whispers.

"I love her," Sophia says.

"I know," I respond.

Cove opens a second bottle, appearing more relaxed than when we first arrived. "I fucking love my wine," he says to himself. He continues to get comfortable by unbuttoning his shirt and resting his foot over his thigh.

"You guys should look this woman up. Do a search online and see what you find," Jules says.

"Good idea." My sister leaves the room then returns with an iPad in hand.

"I've done a lot of research on Dayne and her name never showed up," I say.

"Fucking hell."

"Watch the language, Dove," Cove says.

"What?" I ask my sister.

"Look." She passes the iPad my way and I repeat her words. "Yep, fucking hell. Mera's sticking around, that's for sure. I killed her husband."

"No shit? She married Dayne? Damn, you fucked

up," Cove says. "When did that happen?"

"This was posted two weeks ago in Vegas. It's on her Facebook site. She did gain weight."

"She got another boob job too. Those are much bigger than before. And Dayne looks... I don't remember him being that massive," Sophia says, turning away. "She must've kept in touch with him the entire time he was in prison."

I scroll through her site and see she used to work for a few different porn companies in Vegas, which isn't surprising. Once you get a taste of that lifestyle, it's easy to get hooked on the money that rolls in. Being a porn star is a decent job when you work for the right people. It can be shit for some, but it looks like she did fairly well. Now she lists an Italian restaurant in Vegas as her current place of employment. What a fucking joke, going from serving her pussy to serving pasta? Fuck, that sucks.

"She was thin up until a year ago, these earlier photos are how I remember her. The weight gain is pretty recent."

"She doesn't look all that big to me," Jules says. "And she's very pretty."

"But for a porn star, she's way past her prime... no longer marketable." I turn to Sophia. "She's nothing. I wouldn't worry about her."

"I'm not. She's a bitch, but not insane, like you."

"Thanks, sis."

"No, seriously, she's not going to shoot or stab

anyone, she'll just kick you in the balls and ask for a lot of money as payback for killing her husband. From what I remember, that's her style."

Cove leans closer to Jules and whispers, "Don't you love how nonchalant they are about all this shit? This entire table is full of dispassionate asshats."

"Uh, excuse me, Babe?" Sophia says melodramatically. "I am *far* from being dispassionate about anything." Then she turns to Jules with a smile. "You'll get used to all of this."

"No, you won't," Cove says.

"Stop being a fuckhead or you're not getting laid for a month."

"It's already been a week," he says.

"Jesus Christ, would you two shut the fuck up. Most of the time you numbnuts amuse me, only tonight you're getting on my nerves. I was just thinking about how mature you've become, Soph, but now you're acting like a fucking kid again. And Cove..." I shake my head.

"Mark, don't," my sister pleads as she watches Cove set his fork on the table and run his hand through his hair. "Mark, please, not tonight."

"I'd like to know what you were going to say," Cove prods.

The room is silent. Our eyes lock and he leans back in his chair, resting his interlaced fingers on his abdomen. Jules distracts me by placing her heel on my leg and when I turn, she gifts me with a gorgeous smile. Pretty thing. It's amazing how quickly my thoughts can change from wanting to beat the shit out of Cove for being so depressed, to the sight of this woman's face placating my mind. "I love you," I finally say, looking at Jules first, then turning quickly to Cove. "I love you, man. That's what I was going to say."

I join Jules and Sophia in a good laugh, but it takes a minute for Cove to crack a smile. He never finds me amusing. But, he does lighten up enough to call me a pussy a second later as he's reaching across the table to fill his wife's wine glass. One of these days he's going to beat the shit out of me... I can't wait. I'll stop ragging on him once he does.

"So what do all of you do for fun?" Jules asks.

"How does your ass feel?" I respond.

"Oh God." Sophia rolls her eyes. "I don't want to know what that means."

"I wasn't asking you, Mark," Julia says. "I already know what *you* enjoy." She smirks.

"What kind of fun?" I force her to be more specific.

"Well, anything... I'm not trying to be rude, if that's what you think, but the three of you appear to be... you're all... just..."

"We're what? Spit it out," I say.

"You seem shallow."

Cove's laugh fills the room as he stands and places his hand on my shoulder. "You wanna take her out on the boat now or later?" he jokes, putting his wine glass down and walking out of the room. "I'm checking on the boys," he calls back.

"You're funny, Jules." My sister grins. "Mark, she's amazing."

"I know she is. I hope she stays that way." I take a final bite of food, push the plate away, and stare into her eyes. "You're not going to change, are you? Like become a bitch overnight."

"I'm already a bitch."

"True. What about pushing me into marrying you or wanting kids?"

"Nope, can't say I'm ready for either one of those things with you."

"With me?"

"Yes, with you."

I nod. Fuck, she's good. "Okay, I'll keep you around for a while."

"Fine," she says.

"Fine," I say.

"Damn, no wedding anytime soon. I guess all that's left to do is eat some pie," Sophia says. "Cove! Tell the boys to come down for some pie!"

"No! No sugar this late at night!" he shouts.

"Yes! Pie!" Daxton calls out and rushes down to the main floor.

"I agree with your husband. They're going to be climbing the walls for hours."

"Listen to me," she says. "I hated my childhood and I'm going to make sure theirs is the complete opposite of what I experienced. My boys have the freedom to do whatever they want without having to fear stern punishment. They learn from their own mistakes without us disciplining them. They're loved, happy, and if I want to give them pie in the evening, I'm going to give them a slice of freakin' pie."

"Fucking, Mom. Freakin' sounds lame." Daxton takes a seat next to his mother and rests his head on her arm. "That movie was great."

"Dax, honey. Can you please stop using that word all the time? We've already discussed how it makes you sound like a street thug."

He nods, displaying a big dimply grin. "Love you mom... now can I have some fucking pie?"

I laugh at the little bastard. "Yeah, Sophia. Give the kid some fucking pie."

She serves each of us a slice and two pieces for the stragglers. "Where's your brother?"

"He's having penis problems. Dad's talking to him." He takes a big bite of dessert while his legs swing under the chair.

"What do you mean he's—"

"Mark." Sophia shakes her head. "Normal boy stuff. Let it go."

Normal boy stuff, as she calls it, isn't normal to a kid that age. I started jerking off when I was eight or nine and was obsessed with the sensation, but frustrated because my father walked in on my private moment and said I was doing it all wrong. Talk about a mind fuck at a young age. I hope Cove's not saying shit like that to him. My father left my mother a week after he caught me yanking it, which gave me another reason to believe he left because of me.

"Mark, stop thinking about it."

"Jesus, how do you always get inside my head?"

"You're just *shallow* and easy to read." She laughs.

"Yeah, I have a feeling that 'shallow' comment I made will haunt me forever," Jules says. "So tell me, Sophia. What was Mark like when he was a kid?"

"No." I point to my sister. "No stories."

She ignores me. "He was awful and he used to beat me up. We hated one another."

"No, I never hurt you," I lie.

"And he'd laugh at me whenever I got in trouble. We really didn't like one another until recently. Even now we argue. But, I do know he cares. It did take me a while to accept the way he shows his love... mmm, it's a bit awkward."

"Awkward?" I tease, knowing full well what she means.

"Yep. You express it in weird ways like trying to control people's lives. Head games are your specialty, but don't worry." She grins. "I realize it's purely out of love because you're nothing more than a twisted bastard." She covers her mouth, realizing her foul language in front of her son, but he's too busy eating his pie to notice. She turns back to Jules and continues with a different subject. "His favorite toy was a slingshot and I was his target."

"No, none of this is true."

"One time he managed to hit my back with a stone and it left a nasty welt."

"Sophia, stop," I request.

The four of us turn quickly as the sound of a high-pitched motor fills the room. A remote control toy helicopter flies above us and lands on the table. Xavier flies in next, sits next to Julia, and fills his mouth with a piece of pie.

"Hey girl, you wanna go for a ride in my copter?" he says, with peach syrup on his lips. That kid.

"Xav, be polite please," Cove requests, tousling his son's hair as he walks by. I assume when he sits and winks at his wife that all is well.

The boys eat quickly, like pigs at a trough. We enjoy a few minutes of silence while their mouths are full, until my sister sets down her fork and clears her throat.

I know something's on the way.

"Mark, Cove and I wanted to tell you how much we appreciate everything you've done for us and the boys, but..." She pauses and looks down at the napkin that's on her lap, lifting it to the table, unfolding then refolding it.

"But?"

Cove draws his attention away from the conversation by gliding a finger around the rim of glass and swirling the red liquid in the air, pretending not to listen, or care.

"We're leaving in the morning," she says.

"But you don't have a flight for days."

"I know." She exhales. "Cove wants us to stay in a hotel next to the airport in Reno until—"

"That's bullshit." I throw my napkin on the table.

"Yeah mom, bullshit," Dax says. "I want to stay here."

"Me too, I want to go swimming. We didn't have a family vote."

"Yeah, how come no family vote?" Dax frowns.

"It will be two against two," Cove says calmly to his son.

"That's a tie. We need to flip a coin like we usually do," Xavier whines.

"This isn't a coin toss situation. Your mother and I are older so we get the final vote. We leave in the morning."

"Ahh, this fucking sucks!" Daxton tosses his fork and pushes his chair away from the table, stomping off while his brother grabs his helicopter and follows close behind.

"They'll be fine," Cove says to Sophia.

"No, we won't!" One of them shouts at the top of his lungs.

I stand and motion for Julia to join me, just as peeved as their kids and wanting to leave. My brother-in-law is a rude fucker. A discourteous, insulting, flippant little shit who can't even give me a thank you for getting rid of Dayne Rosen.

"Nice meeting you," Jules says, with no response from Cove.

"Nice seeing you, Sophia," I say. "I'll talk to you soon, if we don't cross paths in the morning." I kiss her cheek then reach my hand to Cove. He shakes it, but neither one of us will look at the other. "Be safe," I say to them. "Keep your eyes open until you hear from me about Mera."

Sophia nods and walks us to the door, then pulls me close for a hug. "Thank you, Mark," she whispers. "I'm sorry. It's not easy, you know? I hate seeing him so miserable. He wasn't like this before we left... it's just... we've been inside this place for so long, and he's disturbed by what he saw on the boat... I am too, but he was actually there. I think he's traumatized."

"He's dealt with a lot worse shit than that, considering the things I know about Dad."

"Maybe so," she says softly. "He'll feel better once he gets back to St. Louis and can be around his business and friends. He's lost complete control of his life by being here. This was my idea, I forced him to come, so I think it's only fair that I should support him if he wants to stay in Reno and wait for a flight."

"Yeah, I get it, but I'm not as much of a prick as he makes me out to be. I truly care for all of you."

She nods. "I know, but you need to stop setting him off."

"I brought wine, didn't I?"

She pushes me into the corridor and closes the door. "Cove's concerned that certain parts of your life will rub off on the boys. They're at an impressionable age. Try to understand what he went through as a teenager and how worried he is that something could happen to them."

"You can't keep them in a bubble."

"We can try."

"Alright." I rub my chin with a sigh. "Maybe you can come out for Christmas. This area is beautiful and the hotel will have a forty-foot tree, plus I'll have everything decked out in lights."

"You should invite your son, not us, but we'll think about it." She turns to Jules and shakes her hand. "Keep my brother in line and out of prison. I'm rooting for you to stick around, but if he treats you like shit, feel free to break his face and leave the bastard."

"Nice." Jules laughs. "Thanks for your permission."

"Wonderful." I roll my eyes. "Come along, ol' red ass. We need to talk."

My sister and I say one last goodbye. She heads inside as Jules and I walk back to my suite in silence.

I'm nervous for some reason. My heart's racing, I have sweaty hands and blurred vision, and my breathing's erratic. Fuck, maybe I should've got this bump on my head checked out. No, that wouldn't account for all of these symptoms. I hope it's not food poisoning. Wouldn't that be ironic, if I got sick from the food in my own hotel? But, it's not that either.

Jules takes my hand as we approach my door and my heart skyrockets out of control. It's her. I'm feeling all dopey over a woman. I'd love to fuck her again, but I need at least another hour of downtime for my cock to work.

"Mark?"

"Hmm?" I mutter, punching my code into the door. She watches and I don't bother trying to hide the numbers; she can come and go whenever she wants.

"Cove hates you."

"No, Jules, he doesn't. He hates himself. People who go through what he went through are really fucked up. I'll spare you the details."

She nods. "So what did you want to talk to me about?"

I open the door and allow her to walk ahead of me, looking down the corridor before slamming the door shut and locking her inside.

DAYS END

Our flesh melds under my heavy comforter. I had her clothes off in less than five seconds and was on top of her a moment later. We kissed and I licked her pussy until she had an astonishing orgasm. That's what she called it. Astonishing. And now, my gun is pressed against the side of her head, the barrel caressing her temple, moving slowly toward her mouth.

"How much do you trust me?" I ask, pissed off that my dick isn't hard. I want to fuck her so badly I can almost taste semen in my mouth. It wants out, but it isn't flowing from my cock anytime soon, so it's seeping out of every pore and orifice of my body. At least it feels that way.

I could start with a strap on, but I'm hoping playtime with my gun will get me hard instead. A gun is just as phallic as a dildo.

"I trust you more than any man I've ever been with," she says.

"My princess." I use my most erotic voice, inching the barrel between her teeth. "Show me."

She takes the gun into her mouth, her eyes close, and she sucks it. Goddammit, she's fucking sucking my gun.

I pull out, enjoying her tongue gliding along the barrel while her eyes reopen, on a search to see if I'm pleased and if I want more.

"You feel that?" I ask, rubbing my groin into her pussy. "Do it again. I'm creeping up."

With the slide pulled, I place the gun back in her mouth. There's no cringe or wince present anywhere on her face. Swallowing hard, I watch her wet lips. She keeps her eyes on mine, flicks the tip then sets her hands to either side and takes it to the back of her throat.

"Uhh." I exhale. "Yeah, that did it."

The metal is drawn from her taut mouth and placed next to the bed.

"You liked that didn't you?" I whisper, putting on a condom then pulling the covers over our heads. "Do you need me?"

"I do. Yes."

Her orgasm was only a few minutes ago and when my finger slides into her sticky pussy, I can still feel the pulsations beating on my flesh. Being on top of her gives me the power I lost earlier. I deserve to do whatever the fuck I want right now, but she's turned me into a pansy ass. Instead of pressing her face into the pillow and ramming her doggy style, I trail my tongue around her lips while rubbing my dick gently across her clit. It's just as good... this is far from what my father would've ever allowed or how I remember fucking as a teen.

Her moans and warm breath caress my ear. Damn, I'm gonna cum before I even get inside her. I don't know what's wrong with me. I should be lasting a little longer since we've been fucking like rabbits.

My arms rest next to her head as she holds my dick steadily in front of her pussy. Lifting her hips, I'm guided slowly inside.

There's silence from both of us. We're in total darkness. I hold my breath and her mouth presses to mine. Bloody hell.

An eruption inside my head brings my cock to life. Shit, it's like that moment when Frankenstein gets shocked with a bolt of lightning. Fuck, I'm alive...

"Oh, Mark," she says in a quick gasp as my body slides over hers, making sure to rub her clit with each movement. "Uh."

But then, I slow to almost no motion at all. Yes... she wasn't expecting those quick jerks to suddenly be delayed. I bet she's never experienced a slow motion fuck. And I'm not talking about making love, I mean I'm fucking her in a gentle, gradual, dawdling way. It's all a tease, a tantalizing and tormenting way for me to have all the power. Her hips lurch in search of more dick, an animalistic craving for Marcus Wild, but all she gets are short, light nudges.

"Jesus, you're killing me."

I grin and put my hands under her ass, fusing our bodies as close as possible. Slowly, my shaft glides into her pussy, but I'm even slower on the way out. In... slowly... out... in... and... I'm driving her mad.

Her nails dig into my hips, trying to pilot me into motion. Then she surrenders to something I never felt coming—a second orgasm. Hell, yes.

We kiss and I absorb the whimpering noises exploding from her mouth. This moment, this fuck, it's all about being calm. No belts or other toys. No rough and forceful rides. Just us. Cool and composed.

I release her lips and the sounds stay at a whisper. "Uh," is barely audible, "Mark, I'm cumming," is a hushed huff.

"I know you are, sweet thing. Cum for me."

Her entire body is heated and tight while her breasts are engorged in my hands. She trembles and exhales, then pulls in a deep breath.

Our lips rejoin... we share deep kisses... but my body never ceases. She's sensitive as I continue in a tender motion, listening to her pant as we fuck.

She says nothing for some time. I hear only grunts, which come mainly from myself. The smell of sex is trapped under the comforter. Her chest and neck are sweaty and leave a salty taste on my lips while her pussy is fragrant like fresh flowers. It's the young ones that smell and feel the best. They're so warm and tight.

"Oh, fuck." I'm aroused to the point that my dick feels a hundred times its size. The veins on my shaft must be swelled beyond belief. I set my chest against hers and kiss her neck, her jaw, and her ears.

"You okay?" I whisper. "Tell me how you feel?"

She nods while my jaw presses into hers. Her head's back, and both our mouths are open, too emotional to kiss.

"Each time you move... it's like I'm having multiple orgasms. They won't stop..." Her voice trails off, but then returns in intermittent gasps. "This is passionate... you're so hard... I know you're gonna cum... I can tell by your faster pace. Put it on my chest."

"Fuck." I moan.

"Give me your hot cum."

I'm panting, getting nearer, shouting 'fuck,' holding her head in my hands and... tightening... clenching... now slowing...

I pull out and tug the condom off just a moment before my cum lands on her tit. With the covers thrown behind us, I watch an explosion of fluid batter her chest as a release gushes from my swollen tip. A sensual smile plasters her face when she rubs my gift over her torso and licks it from below her lip. Good, it hit her in the face.

"Hell... fuck... fuck..." I collapse over her, capturing another kiss while our chests pound into one another. "Damn, that was good... I'm so glad... my cock decided to work again. That was..."

"Wow."

"Wow, yeah. I know. I can't catch my breath... that was a head spinner... man, so good." I look at her with a giant grin. "You know... I hate that I feel this way. I hate you for doing this to me."

"Thanks, you too." She taps my cheek with the palm of her hand then pushes me off the bed.

I get up and grab a towel to wipe my stomach and dick before tossing the cum covered cloth on her chest.

"What did you want to talk to me about?" she asks.

"That was it." I spread out next to her with my hand behind my head and stare at my reflection in the mirrored ceiling. "I needed my dick in you... again. What a great night," I utter, finally catching my breath. "Chicken, wine, and pussy."

"Yes, cock, wine, and more cock for me." She pats my leg then walks toward the bathroom. "Can I turn on some music after I freshen up? I like to listen to it when I fall asleep."

"I don't."

"Fine." She places her hand on her hip. "I can just go back to my suite if you want."

"Uh, if you insist."

"Thank you."

"I meant you can go back to your suite," I joke.

"I guess you can keep me in a separate room forever." She disappears behind the door then calls out, "what time is it?"

"Only ten," I shout, noticing a text message from my son. I hope I didn't hit his contact number when Jules and I were fucking. I'd hate for my kid to... nope, his text says I'm a bastard for forgetting his birthday.

"Shit!" I sit up.

"What's wrong?" She opens the door and looks at

me curiously.

I step hastily into my boxers. "I'll be right back. I need to call my son."

"Isn't it like midnight in Philly?"

"He's awake. Trust me."

I walk down to my office, which is directly below my bedroom, and take a seat in the cold leather chair. For Christ's sake, I'm in for an earful. I place the call and begin a nervous swiveling movement while I wait to hear his voice.

"Hey, Jack. Happy—"

"Fuck off, Dad, you asshole. Why even bother calling at this point? You're nothing but lowlife scum. I hope you rot in Hell!"

I sigh and my son sighs back.

"What? A fucking sigh? That's what you give me?" he says. "Let me guess, you were too busy fucking some whore to remember me, right? That's what Mom said and I bet she was right."

"Jackie boy—"

"Don't fucking call me that! I'm not three! It's Jack! Just Jack! I hate you!"

"Calm the fuck down."

"No! How could you forget about me again? And where the fuck's my money!"

"Enough! I'm sorry. I have a card on the way with some cash."

"Yeah, the check's in the mail. Bullshit."

"Son, tell me what you need."

"I can't stand that title either. Just call me by my name, alright? Son sounds creepy, like you love me or something."

"Listen, *kid*. I *am* your father." Our conversations are always the same and I'll call him whatever the fuck I want. Like 'little prick' or 'little shit.' "Did you have a nice birthday? You doing okay?"

"My birthday was tight, thanks to Mom, not you."

I hear my ex-wife in the background and his cell goes mute. When he returns, he gives me more shit. Damn, I should've remembered his issues with profanity when I was being hard on my sister about her kids using the word fuck. She's right. This *is* an issue and I'm the worst role model when it comes to language—and other things.

"Listen... no Jack... would you... I... calm yourself... cut the shit!" I finally shout. "Damn it, you're like my clone."

"Screw you. If you knew anything about me you'd never say that!"

He's at that age where he's rebelling against his parents, well, me at least. I don't know what he's like with his mother. His language is what I'd expect to hear from prison inmates. My friends and I were the same way when I was a kid, only with each other, not in front of adults. But, that's just it. I haven't been a father to him and he treats me more like a person his age than someone he can look up to and respect.

"When we can have a peaceful conversation, I want

to discuss the holidays with you. It's time for you to visit."

"Ha! What? Are you insane? I'm not leaving my friends to stay in a shitty hotel room in the middle of fucking nowhere."

"This is a five star hotel. You'll be able to swim and ski."

"Fuck no."

"Jack."

"I'm so angry with you right now!"

"I know. I'm sorry."

"Not good enough, Dad."

"I'll pay for your friends to come along."

"Yeah, if I bring my girlfriend, I bet you won't allow her to stay in my room."

Jesus. "That's correct, I won't. How... you know, you're way too young for that kind of play."

"Hypocrite! That's bogus bullshit! You're just trying to buy my love with that idea anyway. I'm not stupid."

He's right. Throwing money his way is how I show him that I care, but it's not entirely out of love, it's also to put a goddamn pacifier in his mouth and to get him here.

"I'm not being hypocritical. I'm telling you that you're too young to share a room with a girl. You're not even legally old enough to drive." I lean forward and rest my chin in the palm of my hand. A photo of him from when he won his first karate trophy sits next to my laptop and another photo of the two of us on the Vegas strip is on a shelf above. "What's the girl's name?"

"Maria, and she's hotter than any bitch you've ever been with."

I toss my head back and exhale. My son's a rotten fucker, and at this moment, I'm not okay with taking the blame for screwing this kid up. Sophia's children seem like saints after dealing with this crap. And Cove's right, Dax and Xav are just little boys.

"Why don't you send me a couple grand this year to make up for being such a shitty father?"

I laugh. "You'll get the usual. Now put your mother on the line, would you?"

"That's what I thought you'd say. You know, I don't want to talk to you anymore tonight anyway. You're a dipshit."

"Call me that again and I'll send someone to your house to smack you upside the head."

"Yeah, that's right, cuz you can't come out here yourself."

"You know..." I exhale, again. I do that often when the two of us speak. "You're going to inherit this hotel one day, it'd be nice if you could come out so we can talk to one another face-to-face instead of shouting over the phone. Think about it. I'm not the one against us having a relationship."

"What? Hell no. You're not sticking me with that *thing*. You pocketed a ton of money when you left Vegas. Give me that, not the hotel. When are you kicking the bucket anyway?"

Christ. That was a telling reaction. No response to us working on being father and son, all he mentioned was my money.

A thought flashes through my head of my son cutting me in half with one of his swords. If things continue as they are, I could see that happening one day. That's terrible, I know, but everyone has wicked thoughts now and again, and my son surely knows how to stir them in my head.

I need to get those weapons away from him now that he's losing control. He started collecting swords when he was in his pre-teen pirate phase. It was cute at the time, like you'd picture a child from the '50s dressing up in a cowboy outfit and shooting his BB gun at neighborhood squirrels, only Jack used to slice and dice cacti in Vegas with his Authentic Pirate Cutlass. That chapter in his life was short-lived and a year later he decided he wanted to be a ninja, so I got him an assassin short sword which my ex bitched about because he kept 'surprising' her with it in the house. And now, now the little twerp talks about killing zombies, something I know nothing about. I bought him a 'zombie gutter' last Christmas, like he asked. It's much shorter than the other swords and something I'd enjoy using myself, only I'm not a teenager obsessed with the dead, or the living dead, or whatever he imagines them to be.

Jack's always been civilized with the weapons, displaying them in his bedroom more than putting them to any real use, but I'm beginning to worry as he gets older that his behavior could change. Hell, his behavior *is* changing. Something I didn't think all that much about until now. I guess someday I'll receive the *Most Asinine Parent of the Year Award.*

"I'm sorry, Jack. I'll make it up to you some day, but not with money."

"Is your cell next to your ass? Cuz those words aren't coming out of your mouth."

"Put your mother on the fucking phone and have a fun-fucking-tastic birthday, you little prick."

He hangs up and I immediately call their landline, but he hangs up a second time. I try my ex's cell and thankfully, she picks up after a few rings.

"I can't believe you forgot to wish him a happy birthday, Mark. That was one of the most inconsiderate things you've ever done."

"We need to discuss getting him some help."

"Why? Because he hurt your feelings? Boohoo. Look, he's a good kid who stays out of trouble and has high grades. I'm not concerned."

I laugh. "Did you hear what he said to me?" I know she did. "He needs to show a little respect."

"Says the man who didn't remember his own son's birthday. You're the only person he uses that language with and seriously, can you blame him? You're the one who needs some therapy, not my son."

"Our son."

"*My* son!"

"Mark? Do you have any..." Jules pokes her head in

my office, but stops when she sees I'm on the phone. "Oh, sorry."

"Wow, that one sounds young," my ex says. "A blonde with big tits, right?"

"Stay out of my private life."

"And you stay out of ours!" She ends the call in haste.

"Uh," I grumble. "What did you need?" I spin in my office chair to face her and see her hand is raised for me to follow her back upstairs.

"Everything okay?" she asks on our way to my bedroom, her ass still red from my belting before dinner and in need of attention.

"Fine."

"I came down for ice, but you don't have any in your freezer."

"This *is* a hotel. You know there's an ice machine in the hallway."

"I didn't feel like getting dressed."

"You need it for you ass?"

She nods and tries to turn far enough to see the area then looks at it in my full-length mirror. "It's been throbbing, you brute."

"I'm not sorry."

"I don't need an apology, I want you to fix it. Or kiss it."

"No." I step into my bathroom, looking for some lotion. "I think I've kissed your ass enough over the past couple of days. Is that why you wanted the ice?"

"Yes."

"A warm bath would be better than ice cubes. How about some Dream Cream instead? I use it for sunburn," I say, reading the label. "It's supposed to be good for irritated skin."

She lies on her stomach and rests her head on the pillow, waiting for me to spread it on.

"Seriously? You want me to pamper you?"

"Yep," she says, short of hesitation. "A man who pampers himself with something called Dream Cream should be able to pamper his woman too."

"Fuck."

"Please?" she whines.

I sit next to her and cake it on. "Don't turn over. I don't want it all over my sheets."

"But the crusty cum I'm laying on is okay?"

I ignore her as I massage the lotion gently over the red marks. It looks worse now than it did earlier. I really need to stop being such a hard ass to her soft ass.

She has such beautiful skin. One small mole is on her left cheek, but no other marks, scars or even a slight discoloration can be seen anywhere.

"It rubs the lotion on its skin," I whisper.

She's quiet for a moment then groans. "Oh God, Mark, please. No horror movie references tonight, okay? I've had enough of that shit for a while."

I move closer to her ear and say in my deepest, eeriest voice, "It rubs the lotion on its skin or else it gets the hose again."

She laughs, kicking her feet against the mattress. "Stop it! *Silence of the Lambs* was horrifying."

I continue caressing her soft flesh, moving up her back, all the way to her neck.

"Oh, and hey." She turns her head, looking back at me. "Why is all your music so old school? Haven't you updated your iPod in like the past ten years?"

"Funny." I smack her ass, causing her to shudder. "You didn't look at my playlists." I stand, needing to change what she has on. "There's no way I can fall asleep to this, it's too heavy. If we have to listen to music, at least let me put on Norah Jones."

"Norah? Men don't listen to her. Did your last girlfriend put her on there for you?" She laughs.

"I haven't had any girlfriends since my divorce," I remind her, turning off the light and spreading out on the bed.

"Yeah, I forgot... you know, Norah's another oldie."

"Shut up about the music, Jules, or I'll turn it off. You didn't need it to fall asleep yesterday and I'm sure you weren't playing it every night in your car."

She's silent, but only for a minute, as usual. "You forgot your son's birthday?"

"I'd rather talk about music."

I pull the comforter over our legs and stare into the darkness, the only light coming from my stereo. With my hand resting on Jules' warm back, I can feel her slow breathing. She's relaxed and seems happy, which makes me happy.

"You're shutting down on me again," she whispers. "I'm trying to start a conversation about something other than sex."

I feel filthy, but I'm too damn tired to shower after a day of cleaning my boat, talking to my staff and other work related business, two rounds of pussy, and the argument with my son.

"Are you ignoring me?"

My free hand massages the stubble along my chin as I think of what needs to be accomplished tomorrow morning before the massive influx of guests arrive for the marathon.

"I guess you are."

It's going to be a busy day and this place will be packed. I'm sure a few people will try to crowd into the rooms in order to save money.

"If I sigh super loud will you talk to me?"

That's pretty normal when big events like this one take place in town. The Jazz Festival each year is the worst in terms of the drunken unruly sorts. These athletic types aren't as bad. Hell, either way, a packed hotel brings in a shitload of money, especially in the evening when people crowd the hotel bar.

"I love how easy it is for you to snub me," she says.

"I was thinking."

"About?"

The room's cold tonight. I pull the comforter further up, trying not to smear the lotion off her ass. I have a lot of laundry to do soon.

"Do you do laundry?" I ask.

"What the fuck, Mark? No. That's what's on your mind? Fucking laundry?"

"You've got to think about it sometime."

"Argh, come on. What goes through that head of yours? You must be thinking about other things."

"Nope. I'm a shallow bastard, just like you mentioned at dinner."

"So that's it? I was right when I asked what you guys do for fun and no one answered. Everybody ignored me because there isn't anything?"

I feel like being a total dick. She knows that's not true. "I like money, pussy, and more money, then more pussy. Toss some liquor into that mix as well. Those are the best things in life."

A melodramatic sigh fills the room causing me to laugh. "Those items are high on my list, but I have a few other amusements in my life. You know? And I do think about other things, only most aren't all that pleasant. My father and my brother-in-law are always circling inside my head, but I'm not going to discuss my thoughts about them with you. It's private. Also, when I say I enjoy pussy, I'm referring to being with you, and not just to fuck. I plan on keeping you around for as long as possible, but when I get tired of you, I'll bury you under a layer of cement in my garage like my father used to do with his 'objects.'"

She kicks me and makes another dissatisfied grumbling sound. "Good, now I'm an object. I guess that's a step up from being a pussy."

I was hoping I didn't need to say how much I enjoy being with her like I did earlier; she already knows I want her in my life. Women don't need to hear loving crap vomiting from a man's mouth all the time. Yes, *loving* crap. Those two words can, and do, go together. And that's as intimate as I'm going to get right now, considering the mood I'm in after speaking to Jack. Besides, women fall for men who are dark and sinister over the pansy types who bring flowers, or worse, romantic greeting cards home. A woman will toss the latter by the wayside.

"I love you too," she whispers.

"That's not what I said a moment ago."

"Yes, I think you did." She turns and twists her fingers through my hair. I've adjusted to the darkness and can see her spirited eyes inches from mine. "I doubt you'll ever admit you killed Roland because of me. And it could just be a big coincidence. My mind might be in a world all it's own when it comes to what happened to him," she lies. I can sense that she's sure I did it, but she needs to talk it out, like she does with everything. "Daydreaming and being okay with the possibility that a man would do such a thing is something I'm still processing. And perhaps it is some weird fantasy... to be involved with a dangerous man, to be in precarious situations, to have actual blood on my hands... it's all about taking a chance and experiencing something no one else in this town ever will come to know in his or her lifetime... an escape from the mundane world."

I brush a strand of hair over her shoulder and take her hand in mine. "This isn't a fairy tale, Jules."

"No..." She pauses. "But if what I think happened, did, then your love for me was plastered across the front page of the local paper like a man who paid for a romantic message to stream behind a plane. That's what you did. You said it. You shouted it at the top of your lungs for the entire city to hear, yet it will forever remain a secret between us."

Norah Jones' haunting voice crawls through my room, across my body, and seeps into my ears as our lips touch softly in the dark of night. The music is replaced for a brief moment with Jules' final words before she falls into a deep sleep.

"You're wrong, Mark. This *is* a fairy tale."

BLEAK NIGHT

Unlike Jules, I can't fucking relax enough to fall asleep. It's midnight and I've been lying next to her for over an hour, listening to a faint whistling noise exiting her nose every time she exhales. It sounds like a distant train signal and was adorable for about five minutes. Now I'm irritated. But annoyed about many things, not just my woman's nose.

I'm thinking about my parents and Sophia. My mother really fucked with my sister's head, more so than my father ever did. I remember coming home from school and finding poor Soph locked in the basement or in a closet when she was a kid. She was alone and scared. It kills me to think back on it now, and I was just as cold-hearted to her as my mother was back then. I treated her the same way because I didn't know any better.

Kids do what they see.

My mom would smack Sophia. I'd laugh. She'd cry. My childhood was insane.

What's interesting is we were also punished for

swearing and we weren't allowed to have friends over. My mother was a recluse who tried to keep us isolated from the world. We couldn't discuss or even bring up the word 'sex' in the house. But my sister and I didn't let our mother stop us from having a little fun. We tiptoed out when we got older and fucked whomever the hell we wanted, when we wanted, without giving two shits about the person or ourselves. We weren't happy, well-rounded teens. We swore, drank, fucked, and hated life. Only Sophia was beaten as punishment. Kicked, yelled at, her hair was pulled, and she was forever pummeled with abusive comments. My mother chewed me out, but that was about it. Clearly, my sister and I weren't treated as equals.

It's on my mind because of my sister's comments during dinner, Jack's harsh words, and my nephews' antics. Our kids have the freedom to do whatever they want, are being raised in a very different environment, and have never been physically harmed. I've never laid a hand on my son and my threats to do so in order to gain some control in our relationship never seem to work.

So then, why are these kids just as fucked up as my sister and I? Shit, I can't stand it when I have no power over a situation. Sophia and Cove want to buffer their sons' lives, and I want to silence my son's foul mouth and his hatred for me, but the three kids are going to do whatever the fuck they want, just like we did. All I can do with Jack is be patient and step up my game. Show him I care instead of keeping him in the back of my mind. I can't believe I forgot about him today.

I'm definitely not going to have any more kids. One's already far too many.

"Uncle Mark?"

A high-pitched voice escapes my watch. Jules stirs as I sit up and hit a button to respond.

"What's up, Dax?"

"It's Xavier. Can you let me in? It's important. Please, hurry."

"What's wrong?" I jump out of bed and dress quickly.

"I need your help, let me in!"

He sounds frantic and almost in tears.

"I'm on my way. Hold tight."

"Is that your nephew?" Jules asks groggily.

"Yeah, stay here." I kiss her cheek and race down the stairs, opening the door to see matted hair and his sneakers covered in mud.

"What's wrong?"

"I can't find Dax." He starts to walk hurriedly toward his suite, waving me to follow. "We snuck outside to use our copters and his went into the woods. He went to find it, but never came out. I looked everywhere for him!"

"Okay. I'm sure he's fine. Did you tell your parents?" I follow him, in a jogging pace.

"You have to. I just came from there, but they're in their room. That's why I got you. We're not supposed to go in there when they're moaning."

Great.

"When did this happen?" I try to keep him talking so he stays calm, but I can hear a shake in his voice as if he's about to break down.

"Over an hour ago."

"Jesus, Xav."

"Well, I was looking for him!" he whines. "I thought he was playing a joke on me, but he would've come out by now. I can't find him!"

"Okay. Alright." We reach the door and he puts his hand up.

"Stay back, Uncle Mark. I need to punch in our code."

"Make it quick."

"Don't look!" He covers the keypad with one hand and presses the buttons. The door clicks and he runs inside then heads toward the stairs.

He follows me to the landing and points to the bedroom door. Their suite is dark and cold like mine, and just as full of the sounds of two people in the middle of a good fuck. Damn it, I don't want to do this.

Xavier covers his ears when he hears an 'uh.' I remove one of his hands and tell him to wait downstairs.

"Okay, but I bet Dax is cold. Get my dad for me so he can help," he whispers and rushes away.

I walk up to the door, about to knock, standing quietly, with my hand raised. This sucks.

I love you.

I hear.

I always lust for you. Every inch of you. Cove says. *You ready for me, Dove? I need to cum... I'm ready.*

Crap. Do I knock or wait? What the fuck am I supposed to do? Either way he's gonna throw a tantrum.

Shh. Shh.

Sophia hushes him and I turn away and pace. I don't want to hear my sister fucking someone. Damn it, hurry up.

I love you... Dove... yes. He whispers.

I love you too. Cum, Babe. Cum.

Ug. Disgusting... my little sister. It's so nasty to hear this. I love listening to people fuck, but not her. And I don't blame Xavier for not wanting to knock on this door. The poor kid.

Fuck. It's about time.

That was nice.

Finally. I tap at the door and hear a gasp.

Shit, Cove. I knew we were going to wake them.

"It's Mark. I need to talk..."

That fucker.

There's rustling in the room as the two of them get dressed.

It must be important... Mark, what's wrong?

"It's..."

The door swings open and Cove's hands are clenched, ready to strike. His face is red from either the fuck or his obvious anger that I'm here.

"Dad!" Xav runs up the stairs. "I can't find Daxton." He grabs his father's hand and pulls him out of the room.

"What do you mean... Soph, get out here, quick!" Cove shouts. "What the hell's going on?"

"We went out."

"What? What do you mean you went out... where?"

"Outside, to play. He's in the woods."

Sophia appears in a state of panic, rushing past me and up to her son.

"Try reaching him with the walkie-talkie App," she says to Cove then turns to her son. "Do you remember exactly where?"

He nods and we follow him, asking questions along the way, each of us trying to stay composed for the sake of everyone else, only I can tell my sister's beside herself, becoming visibly upset. Cove tries his son's cell watch but gets no response, then Xavier tries as well.

"I got Mom and Dad. This isn't funny! You better come out now or the mountain lions are going to eat you!"

"Oh my God." My sister gasps. "No, don't say that to him. Don't scare him."

"Fuck, Mom. Dax isn't afraid of anything."

"That's what I'm worried about," Cove says. "He's probably hiding because he doesn't want to leave."

"Dax, come out and talk to us. It's rainy and cold," Cove says into his cell. "I'm sorry if you're disappointed."

No answer.

"Call his watch. If he doesn't have the walkie-talkie

App turned on then maybe we'll at least be able to hear a ring."

"Right here." Xavier points toward the tall pines that line the edge of the hotel parking lot. "This is where we were playing."

"What were you two doing over this way?" I ask.

"Using the roofs of the cars as landing pads. But he flew his copter into the trees. I went inside to go pee while he was searching for it and when I came out he wasn't here."

Cove calls his son's watch, but there's no sound from the woods. He starts to walk in, looking at the ground for footprints.

"I already did that, Dad. I think a mountain lion ate him."

"Xavier, stop it, please. That's not funny," Sophia says with her hand over her mouth, turning her head frantically in all directions. "Daxton... Dax!" she shouts.

"Mark, you got a camera out this way?"

"Maybe not this far, but I can check."

"Go do it," Cove commands.

"Xavier, why did the two of you go out? Why?" my sister cries. "You're not supposed to be outside!"

"You let us out this morning," he says softly.

I touch my sister's bare arm as she stands wearing only a thin tank top, pajama bottoms, and no shoes. Drops of rain trickle down her face, mixing with her tears.

"We'll find him, don't worry."

She nods and I head back inside, running to my suite to check the camera footage. Xavier said this happened about an hour ago so I'll be able to bring it up quickly.

"Jules!" I yell upon entering my living room.

"What?"

"Get up. I need your help."

I hustle to my office and open the security footage on my desktop computer, searching for the west side camera.

"What's wrong?" she asks, walking into the room.

"Daxton's missing."

"Oh Jesus." She pauses. "You don't think that woman, Mera..."

"No. I don't. And don't mention her to my sister. He's just lost in the woods. I need you to do me a favor."

"Anything."

"Get dressed quickly, and take some clothes from my closet outside to my sister and Cove. Grab two sweatshirts and find some socks. Everyone is in the guest parking lot. Far west."

She rushes out and I check the area on screen from two hours ago, advancing ahead from there.

The kids are playing in the lot for some time, hitting and scraping my quests vehicles. Fuck, I hope there isn't any major damage to anyone's car. And Daxton... he walks on the hood of a Prius. Damn him. Next, the copter flies into the thick pines. Dax heads in that direction while Xavier runs toward the hotel.

I'm surprised he didn't just take a piss in the parking lot.

Five minutes later, Xav is back, flying his copter and calling for his brother. He looks continually toward the pines and after a few minutes, lands the toy and walks into the woods himself.

I fast forward, keeping an eye on the woods and the lot. Guests come and go. Two middle-aged women park and walk inside then a young couple arrive and do the same. A man gets in a Land Rover and drives off with a small dog. Asshole. I don't want pets in my place.

More rain. Darkness. Silence. And more rain.

Xavier finally reappears from the woods, muddy and wet, running toward the side door. I continue to watch, but there's nothing. No movement other than rain and leaves falling from a few ash trees.

Fifteen minutes later the four of us are on the scene.

Fuckin' A. Where is that kid?

I leave my suite and walk quickly through the hotel, once again, trying not to disturb my guests or cause a scene, and hoping to God my sister didn't call the cops. I know I'm a piece of shit for thinking so, but I don't want the fucking cops here. Not now, not when I've got so many guests here, not ever.

"You find him?" I call out, feeling nauseous when I see Sophia's face. She's standing at the edge of the pines with Jules by her side.

"I'm calling the police," she says when I approach.

"Give it a few. He'll show up."

"Mark," she pleads.

"Daxton!" I shout. "I'll give you five hundred dollars if you come out of these woods right now!"

I hear branches break and short legs running my way.

"I'll take the money, Uncle Mark," Xavier yells, running toward me.

Shit, for a second I thought that did it.

My sister pulls her son into her arms and holds him tightly. He squirms and breaks free, sprinting back into the woods toward his father's voice.

"Dax!" Cove calls for his son from deep within the forest.

"How big are these woods? Where do you think he is? Oh..." She sobs. "He must be cold... Dax!" Her hands cover her face and she breaks down. "Mark, please... call."

I look at the ground with my hands in my pockets and sigh.

"We need flashlights," I say.

Jules takes out her cell. "Call," she whispers. "Do it."

"We just need some light and we'll find him. Cove and I will find him."

Jules shakes her head and places the call while giving me her best *you bastard* look.

She's right.

"Cove!" I holler. "We need to talk!"

"Okay!" The voice echoing through the woods

becomes louder as his figure moves toward us. I listen for a response after each of his calls to his son, but the only reply is from the drops of rain hitting the pines.

It's chilly and pools of water are starting to form around our feet. The rain comes down harder and Xavier runs from the woods, shivering and complaining about the weather.

"Can we go back inside? I'm cold."

"Soon," I say. "Did your brother mention anything about running away?"

"No!" My sister smacks my arm. "He'd never do that, no matter how angry he was at us."

"No," he replies. "We'd never leave Mom and Dad."

"And you guys know not to go anywhere with strangers?"

"Of course, they do," she scolds.

"Yeah. Like Mom said."

"Then he's here."

"Of course he's here." She admonishes my thoughts. "He's here," she says with a forceful stomp of her feet. "Daxton Snow Everton! Get your butt out here right this minute!" she shouts.

Xavier's eyes widen in total shock at her tone. "Whoa, Mom. You never yell at us."

"I'm not angry. I'm frustrated."

"Hey, farthead," he speaks into his cell phone watch. "Mom's fucking furious."

"No, I'm not. Tell him I'm not angry."

"Mom and Dad are crazy in the head!"

"Enough. I know you're trying to help..."

"The police are on their way." Jules ends the call and takes my hand as Cove stumbles up to us.

"I can't find him anywhere," he says out of breath.

"We called the cops," Sophia whimpers and reaches out for him. They embrace and I'm lost as to what to do. Kids do nothing but confuse the hell out of me. I have one, but my wife was the one who raised him. They're whiny, upchucking, money-eating, weasels. But, my heart will split in two if something happens to him. It will also be the end of Cove. He won't be able to handle life anymore if his son doesn't come home, Sophia too.

"Can I ride in the police car?"

"No," I whisper, still watching my deeply pained family.

"Don't mention Mera when the cops get here," I say.

"What?" Cove releases his wife and they stare at me with tearful eyes, in disbelief that I would say such a thing. He steps forward, looking at his son then back at me.

"If they ask you," I say slowly, trying not to sound too much like a dick. "If we've seen any suspicious people or are aware of..."

And that was enough for a fist to swing, only to be caught by my hand.

"Goddammit!" I shout, pushing him against a tree.

"Stop it!" Sophia yells, while Xavier screams.

"Mark, don't!" Jules shouts.

"You listen to me." I press a finger into his chest and get in his face, trying to speak in a calm whisper so his son doesn't hear. "We can't explain why Mera's here. Think about it. She came with Dayne, right? And where is he? They'll want to know." I look back at Xavier who's talking into his watch, telling his brother there's a fight. "Don't fuck this up. If the cops search for her, you know..."

I spy the cop car pulling up the hotel drive from the corner of my eye. I release him and fix his sweatshirt, turning back to my sister so she can hear my final words before they arrive.

"He's in these woods, not with her. If the cops get a whiff of Mera, they'll search for Dayne, and they'll trace things back here..." I turn to Cove. "If anything comes up, we're talking death penalty. Do you hear me? Dax is coming back, but you need to be here for him when he does, not in some prison cell. You understand?" I turn and point to my sister. "And do you understand?" Then I eye Jules as well. "You all better fucking be aware of what we're dealing with here."

Cove brushes against me on his way to meet the cops. "Yeah, my son." He seethes. "This is why I hate you, Mark. Those would've been your father's exact words."

"You don't hate me."

"Shut up!" Sophia bursts into tears. "I can't believe this is happening and the two of you are arguing. Stop it!

My son is missing!"

I exhale and nod in agreement with my sister. "Jules, take Xavier and stand under the awning by the side door. Get him out of the rain and away from the cops."

"I need to be able to see him," Sophia says. "Stay outside, I don't want him out of my sight."

"I'm cold," he complains, following Jules to the overhang.

"Stay where I can see you!" she calls after them.

The cops park and we introduce ourselves before explaining the situation. They ask Cove and Sophia some routine questions.

Name? Date of birth? Height? Weight? Other identifiers? When did you notice he was missing? What was he wearing?

Sophia calls Xavier over and explains that they're identical twins. They study my nephew while taking notes and listening to Xav explain clothing details.

"He's wearing his jeans and a blue hoodie, like me."

"And they have the same sneakers." Sophia points to her son's feet. "Anything else, Xavier?"

"His Cardinals baseball cap, the red one."

The younger officer begins flashing a light into each vehicle in my lot. Checking to see if he's hiding out.

"Did you check the closets in the room you're staying in? Or other areas of the hotel? How about under the beds?"

"He's out here, not inside," I say. "I already viewed the security footage. My nephew walked into the woods but never came out."

The officer nods then notices my injured head and gives me a suspicious look.

"And what happened to you?"

I place my hand over the bump and come up with a quick lie. "I fell down the last couple of stairs leading to my garage and landed smack dab on my head."

He seems satisfied with that response, nods, and speaks into his push-to-talk headset. "We need a search dog brought out to the Jameson Hotel, North, off of Route 50."

"What?" Sophia gasps. "Is that good or bad?"

"It's good," Cove says. "The dogs will track his scent."

"But it's raining," she whispers, looking back into the woods.

"They still might be able to pick it up," I say, reassuringly.

"Are there any other relatives on the premises or in the area?"

"No," she says.

"Did he ever mention running away or was there a recent argument that would cause him to—"

"No," Cove says. "He didn't run away."

The officer who was searching the cars shines his flashlight into the woods.

"Check for footprints!" the cop next to us shouts.

"There're a lot of them!" he yells back.

The officer looks at us and Cove nods. "My son

Xavier and I were already in there, searching."

"Okay." He sighs while putting his pen away. "You should also report this to the National Center for Missing and Exploited Children and we'll contact the FBI. Standard procedures. I'll head in and see if I can follow any tracks. Let the dog team know what's going on when they arrive... and if I were you, I'd also check inside. Kids can be stealthy."

"Then what?" Sophia cries. "What if we can't find him?"

I walk up to my sister and offer the only comforting words I can gather.

"Then we keep looking."

HOLLOW

There's no other way to explain how I feel at this moment, except to say that I'm hollow. It's five in the morning and we're in the west end suite, the dinner carts from last night are still in the dining room, and three empty bottles of wine are on the kitchen counter. Xavier's in bed, Sophia's sobbing on the kitchen floor, Julia is by her side, Cove's pacing with a drink in hand, and I'm vacant.

Daxton Everton is nowhere to be found.

We had a brief moment of hope when I remembered the tracking devices in our watches. We picked up a signal that was coming from their suite and thought he was hiding out, only to be saddened when we found the watch on top of the bathroom counter. Cove said his sons usually take them off before they go to bed, and since they were tucked in at ten and sneaked out later; it's not unusual for him to not have it on.

And the dog was useless. It didn't pick up any scent of Dax. After two hours of trying to search in the pitch-black night, the cops said they'd be back at daybreak and that we shouldn't disturb the area.

Fuck.

"I want my son!" Sophia's head rests on the floor. "Where is he?" she cries.

"We need to do something, now," Cove snaps. "I can't be in this place any longer, just waiting. Give me your truck keys."

"No." I shake my head. "You're fucking tanked off your ass. Besides, where the hell are you gonna go?"

"We should be checking on Mera. What motel is she in?"

"No one's that stupid. She doesn't have him," I say, unsure if that's true, but not letting on that it's crossed my mind a number of times over the past five hours.

"We've got until six before the police return, just fucking drive me around town until then so we're doing something. I'm going to explode if we don't look for him. What if he's out on the road?"

"Someone would see him."

"Mark, give me your goddamn keys!"

"Alright," I mumble. "We'll go, but I'm gonna drive since you can hardly keep your balance. Jules, stay here with my sister."

"Okay. I'll make some coffee."

"What the hell's that going to do?" Cove mutters.

"Thanks," I say to her, pushing him out the door. "She's trying to help. Treat her like shit again and you'll be flat on your ass."

He's silent the rest of the way to my suite, down the

stairwell, and into the garage. He slides into my truck then stares at the area where Dayne once laid as I start the engine and pull out.

"I can't believe this shit is happening to us again," he whispers, running a hand through his hair. "You bring nothing but evil into our lives."

"What the fuck did *I* do?" I ask, looking directly at him.

He exhales and shakes his head. "You did everything... everything Paul told you to and now that he's gone you expect everyone to worship your every move. You're the next in command, right? Well, I'm not following your orders like my wife does."

"I know what I'm doing. Trust me."

"Oh yeah. You don't know shit."

I slam on the brakes and his body rocks back then juts forward.

"I understand now why my father always talked about wanting to put a bullet in that tiny brain of yours."

I step out of the truck and plod around to his side, opening the passenger door and pulling him out.

"All you ever fucking do is bitch and moan when you're drunk, like a woman on the rag. Now hit me."

"I'm not as drunk as you think... exhaustion's affecting my body more than the liquor."

"Hit me."

"What?"

"I said fucking hit me!" I shout and his fist smashes

into my jaw like a bolt of lightning. My head is forced to the side in a quick jerk and my immediate reaction is to set a hand over the aching spot. I didn't think he had it in him. I know he's got a lot of booze in his system, but he *is* sober enough to take a swing.

"Fuck, hit me again." I lower my hand with a grin and he does, nailing my nose next. Blood drips down and lands at my feet. Damn, it feels good. The pain is so much better than thinking about my nephew.

But then Cove attacks. I thought two swings would be enough to satisfy his anger and frustration, both for his kid and me, but the fucker starts wailing at my face. In a second, I hit the ground from another hard blow and he's circling my body like a shark.

"Alright!" I put up my hand. "Enough! I'm not going to strike you back, so let up!"

"Why not? You want to do this? Because I'm ready, asshole."

"I wanted you to get some of that pent up rage out of your system!" I yell, wiping the blood from my nose as I stand. He takes another swing and I duck, plowing head first into his stomach to take him to the ground. He swings heatedly and we grunt like wild animals. I try to defend without hitting him back. I'm in shock when he overpowers me, tossing me on my back where I'm vulnerable and being smothered by his weight.

"I thought you wanted to fight, Mark. No one can see us over here and Sophia's not around to stop us, so get on your feet and let's do this!"

"Don't treat me like garbage after all I've done for you and your kids!"

A second punch to my nose sends a splatter of blood onto my truck tire. Fuck, that one really hurt.

"Fuck!"

My hand grips his neck, turning his head toward the bloody rim. He catches a glimpse of his reflection in the truck and a low groan emerges.

"Pure evil. That's what you are and what I've now become, pure evil," he whispers. "Goddammit, where's my son?" He stands and kicks my leg. "Stand up and drive!"

"Get in the truck," I say, rolling to my knees and holding my shirt over my nose.

We're both out of breath dipshits. Nothing more. Just two grown men acting like boys.

I put the truck back in gear and hit the gas. "My sister deserves better," I say, giving him a monstrous look. "She should leave your ass."

He lets out a short laugh.

"You'll regret laughing once you sober up and see my nose all bloody and swollen, *if* you ever get sober. You stopped drinking for a year once, you can do it again. Your sons deserve better, not just Sophia. They're going to pick up your bad habits."

"Yeah, you're living proof of a son who's picked up bad habits."

"Fuck off, Cove." I exhale, pulling onto the main road from my hotel drive. "You're a bastard."

"Not always."

"I hope you feel better after pummeling my nose."

"A lot, actually."

"Good. Me too, for some odd reason."

He finally did it. I'm so proud of the guy. Damn, that was fun.

"So why are you such a dick to me all the time? I know you get this way after you toss back a few, but it's been non-stop lately."

He picks at the plastic armrest, ignoring my words. Cove can be a brat, but I know for a fact he's wonderful to my sister. I get annoyed and say stupid shit to him, like *Sophia should leave your ass*, except I don't mean it. I know he's a different person when I'm not around. I've watched them on my security cam. A few days ago the two of them were slow dancing in the living room after their sons fell asleep. He's good to her, but a total ass to me.

"I can be your best friend and protector, or your worst nightmare."

"You've been my worst nightmare since the day we met," he says.

"That's bullshit."

"Yeah? You think I wanted you and all those guys to fuck me?"

Ohhh. Here we go.

"Are you gonna start this shit again? Whenever you're drunk and under stress this is all you talk about, like it was yesterday. It was years ago, buddy. There's nothing you or I could've done back then... look, you've got to stop killing yourself with those memories. You'll end up with one foot in the grave if you don't," I say hypocritically.

"Fuck, I'm already neck deep in." He breathes heavily while staring out the window.

The road is empty this time of the morning and the roads are dark. At least the rain has stopped and it will be easier for the search team to find him today, and they *will* find him. I know it.

"Do you?" he asks softly.

"What?"

"Have those memories all the time?"

"Anyone would."

"But do *you*?"

I turn the radio on and he turns it off.

"I've talked to people," he says. "I've seen shrinks. That doesn't do shit for me."

"I know." I sigh, suddenly realizing why those memories are really in his head. "We're going to find your son, Cove. He wasn't taken by anyone like you were. This is a totally different situation. Just try to keep your shit together, do it for Sophia and Xavier."

"I can't take one more day here," he whispers. "I've been in that suite for too long. And I just about lost my mind watching you gut Dayne. How can you push a blade inside someone and not break down? I'd kill a guy if I had to, but fuck; I wouldn't be able to walk away like it was nothing, unlike you. Your cold eyes, steady hands, and that calm voice of yours when you were speaking to him... everything about you that night was heartless. Killing him didn't upset you at all?"

"It was Dayne Rosen, need I say more?"

"And now my son is missing. I'll never be able to sleep again without a drink. This can't be real. I'm either dreaming or losing my shit like the guy in *The Shining*. Your hotel is just as sickening as that place. Another day it will start to snow... then we'll all be trapped here for the winter."

"Look, I understand none of this is easy for you, but it's time for you to step away from the booze, you miserable drunk."

"It's better than being a violent drunk. At least I'd never beat the shit out of Sophia and the kids like Paul did to me whenever he got wasted. You know," he says, "your fucking father..."

Hell, he rambles on and on about Vegas, always reminding me of my biggest regret in life—that I turned my head whenever he was abused and I never stood up to my father. Fuck, that right there is enough reason for him to hate me, but no one helped me either. "Cove, get your head out of your ass, sit up, and look for your kid... and don't compare my place to that hotel in *The Shining*. I know you're a city boy, but I happen to enjoy being in these woods. This is a classy resort town bustling with tourists."

"Bustling? The road's empty."

"People *do* sleep."

"What if Mera has him?" he asks.

"I think your son would kick her ass, that's what if."

Ah-ha, laughter. Yes, he laughed. That's what he needed to hear; a little humor about Dax.

"Can you imagine?" I say, dabbing my bloody nose with my shirt. "Daxton's the type of kid who would bite her wrists, kick her shins, then pull her hair out, all while screaming that she's a bitch."

He smiles and nods with brighter eyes.

We drive through town, past the park, and along the main street. I take him by the motel Dayne and Mera were staying at, but the Datsun's not there. We drive a few miles west of the hotel, further into the mountains, and see nothing but an empty road cutting through a drenched landscape.

I know we won't come across him this way, but Cove was right, we needed to get out and do something, anything, if nothing else but to pass the time.

"If, by chance, *she* is involved in this, then there's nothing to worry about."

He turns, surprised that I would say such a thing.

"Cove, she'd use him as leverage to find out where Dayne is, nothing more. I can pay her off and we'll do a quick exchange."

"My son's not some bartering tool," he says with disdain.

"It'd be easy and he'd come home safe and sound."

"Nothing's easy! And he *is* coming home safe and sound."

I raise my hand for him to calm down. "You're right. Of course he is. I'm sure Mera Calloway's back in Vegas by now anyway, selling her pussy on the strip to any takers."

His whole body turns this time, not just his head, wanting to read me when he asks his next question. "Hey."

"Hey what?" Spit it out, Cove.

"Are you going to kill her?"

"Shit."

"I think you will," he says in a straightforward tone, continuing to stare.

I glance briefly at him then turn back to the road. "You honestly want to know?"

"No." He rolls down the window and feels the air, frowning at the temperature.

"God, I hope he's warm enough."

"He's okay."

"How cold was it last night?"

I don't want to tell him it was close to freezing.

"He'll be okay. It's going to be in the fifties today and the cops will follow his footprints. You wanna head back?" I ask, seeing a tear on his cheek.

"Yeah, I need to check on Sophia then I'm going into the woods."

"Just wait until the cops get here so we don't screw with the footprints. It's bad enough Xavier was in and out of those woods last night. Give them a chance to catch a trail before you go back in."

He nods and rubs his eyes.

An icy drizzle begins to coat the windshield as I'm turning the truck around. Fuck all this precipitation. I know we're in a drought, but screw it. Bring on the sun. I want my nephew out of this foul weather.

We drive back and my eyes follow the side of the road, examining the shallow ditch... just in case. If I spot anything, which I hope I don't, but if I do... I'd drop Cove off and come back to the area on my own. No father needs to see his son lying on the side of the road. I wouldn't even tell him until after the fact.

It's not wrong to want to protect him from such a sight.

But that's not going to happen.

"It's freezing," he says again. "Mark, it's fucking cold."

"Dax is dressed warmly and he's wearing a hat, plus he's got a hood he can use."

"Sophia's a mess."

"Well, fuck, you both are and you have every right to be."

"I wish you'd show some emotions. Show me that you care for once."

"Damn it, Cove! Someone has to hold it together. The only way to make it through these situations is for me to—"

"Shut up," he says.

I ignore his roller coaster of emotions. I'm trying to be the one who gets him through this and I don't know why the hell he can't see how much I love him and my family. What the fuck? And what does he want me to do? Change? Yeah, right. There's no point in even opening my mouth around the guy sometimes. No matter what I say, it's wrong... so I guess I should just say whatever the fuck I want since it doesn't seem to make any difference to our relationship anyway.

"I love you... and I'm serious when I say it. Soph and the kids too, although I'm undecided on whether or not I *like* you."

"Yeah, none of us are very likeable," he says.

"That's why it's important for our family to stick together."

He checks his watch then runs his hand through his hair.

"But Jules is," I say faintly. "She's likeable. She's laid-back and big-hearted, if you haven't noticed."

His head shakes as he speaks. "She's still young and you've brainwashed the poor girl."

"Far from it. Trust me, she's got a mind of her own and doesn't put up with any shit. I like that about her. She's a strong woman."

"Then you should set her free before you end up... before she becomes one of us."

"Too late. Besides, she's an incredible fuck. I'm not giving that up. Those are hard to find. She likes my toys and my cock... it's all good."

He shakes his head again.

"What?" I grin. "You can't tell me you'd be with

someone who didn't like to play. Seriously. A woman who's gonna lie in bed like a dead body is worthless to me."

"Again, that sounds like something your father would've said."

He stares ahead and thankfully doesn't mention anything sexual about my sister. And I suppose I'm getting off track by discussing Jules and sex instead of thinking about Daxton. I keep hoping one of our cells will ring with a call from my sister that he's home.

"I'd kill her," he says out of the blue. "If Mera or anyone else hurt my son, I'd kill that person."

I sigh, still holding my shirt to my nose. "I can't see that happening... so we're back on this subject now?"

"Would you?"

"You know I would. But Dax is in the forest and I bet Mera's not in town. So unfortunately I won't get to have any fun."

He closes the window and taps the armrest. His watch gets checked as he waits impatiently for the sun to appear. He taps... checks the time... sighs... then checks his watch again.

"She's here," he says under a soft breath. "She's not going anywhere until she figures out what happened to her husband. Think about it, would you?"

I shrug.

"Forget it. Maybe you would... so how old were you. I mean, the first time you killed someone. How old?" he asks.

"Hell, you don't want to hear about that."

"Then tell me *why* you did it."

He's as pushy as Jules, only this is her normal personality and Cove... he's just nervous and confused. He probably doesn't even know what he's asking.

"To impress my father."

"Uh." He exhales.

I turn into the hotel drive, only to get stuck behind a car that's moving slower than a sloth, an older couple, no doubt. I hit the horn and they speed ahead, allowing me to turn down the 'no admittance' drive to my private garage.

"What is that?" Cove whispers when my headlights shine toward the garage doors. "Tell me you ordered something."

Oh shit.

"Oh shit," he repeats my thought. "No." The word barely escapes his mouth. He tries to open the door, but I pull him back.

"No, stay here." I put the truck in park. "Stay here!"

He rushes out and I follow, grabbing his shirt and pushing him aside.

"Wait. Just stop! Stand back, Cove. Stand! Back!"

He looks at me then at the large box in front of my garage.

"Oh my God." His hands rest on his knees. He leans forward, staring at the ground, hyperventilating, looking at the box once more.

"Open it," he pleads.

I walk forward and listen, hoping to hear breathing, a cry, a sneeze, a cough, anything.

"Daxton," I whisper.

"Don't say his name! He's not in there!" Cove's panic-stricken and unable to move, frozen about ten feet behind me. "Open it!"

The box is large enough to fit a child, sopping wet, and covered in mud like it's just been unearthed.

I take another step forward.

"Please," Cove says under quick wheezing breaths. "Tell me that's not my son."

With a hand on one of the flaps, I close my eyes, asking whoever the fuck is listening to let this be anything but his kid. My stomach sinks. I know. I feel the dread in my heart.

I just know.

"Fuck."

PART THREE

OMEN

*D*ayne *warned me not to interrupt my father when he's busy fucking in his bedroom, but I've got a flight to catch and he owes me money. I didn't just work my dick off for a week to fly home empty-handed.*

Besides, Dayne always says the same old shit, and it's not like my dad hasn't fucked women in front of me before. Just yesterday...

A sharp crack of lightning rattles the house. Rolling thunder. Rain. All bad signs. A downpour pounds the roof. This is Vegas for fuck's sake. It doesn't storm like this here.

I'm nervous.

I'll just knock and ask him to step into his office where he can write a check then get back to his pussy. Just one minute of his time. One minute.

Smoke from his cigar floats out of the open bedroom door, irritating my nose. I glance inside to see dim lights and the cigar being placed on the nightstand. He doesn't notice me. I should knock and get this over with, instead of eavesdropping, but I lose my train of thought when he speaks.

"I love you like a son... more than a son... you're the one person in this house who knows how to satisfy my cock," *my father whispers. "You're a good little boy."*

Fuckin' A. He's talking to Star. It has to be him in that bed. My dad... the sick bastard. Of course he loves this kid more than me. The nineteen-year-old is a wimp and will do whatever the fuck my father wants.

"Mmmph."

I hear a muffled scream and another. He must be gagged.

I step back and stand on the top step, listening, debating, wanting to kill both of them. I should do it. Kill them. Just put my father and his boy toy out of their misery. They'd both be better off dead. But I feel sorry for the kid and what he has to go through in this place. It's not his fault he's weak.

"I'm taking this tie off from around your mouth. Now you can tell me how good my cock feels in your ass."

"Yes sir," *he whimpers.* "It's good."

"Call me Dad."

Thank fuck he doesn't.

"Say it."

There's a gagging noise.

"I've always wanted a boy who looks like me. Someone I could introduce as my son and people would see the resemblance. Someone to play with who looks like a younger version of myself."

I need to step in. The kid is choking. I can hear my dad strangling him.

"See. Open your eyes. See yourself in that mirror. See my face behind you. You're me. We look so much alike. Why do you think I love you so much? Why do you think I *chose you over all the other boys in my company?" My father groans with desire. "I'm so proud of you for making me so much money. Look at us... oh, I'm fucking myself. I'm fucking myself in the ass."*

This stops now. I walk down the stairs and pretend I just arrived.

"Paul!" *I call out.* "I need to talk to you."

"Jesus Christ!"

I hold my breath, waiting to get my ass kicked. Damn, that was hard on my ears.

He races down the stairs, tying his robe along the way, grabbing my arm then pulling me over to his desk. Furiously, he opens a drawer and slams his checkbook down, scratching out a check for eighty grand.

"That should be more than enough for whatever the fuck you wanted."

"Down payment on a house. And thanks." *It's a lot of money. More than I was expecting.*

"Yeah." *He slides the check forward, waiting for me to take it from his desk.*

"Were you gonna say goodbye?" *I ask.* "Or are you too busy with..." *I stare into his beady dark eyes then up the stairwell toward his bedroom door.*

He stands and leans in my face. "I'm not gay," *he whispers, gripping my collar.* "I enjoy pussy just like every real man in this world."

"Does he live here?" *I ask with a hard swallow.*

"For now, but not forever."

"Don't ask me to kill him next time I'm here."

"Why, are you in love with the boy or something?" He laughs. "Find your own fuck buddy. There're plenty in my company."

I pull away from his grasp wanting to rip the check in two. Maybe I shouldn't come back, but fuck, the money... I'd be insane not to. My father's loaded and his wallet's always open when I'm in need.

"My private life is none of your concern," he reminds me. "I don't say a word about your time being wasted in that marriage or your shitty life back in Philly, so don't inquire about where I stick my dick."

"Yeah, but what makes him so special?"

"He's not."

"You love him. He's 'something' to you."

"I don't love anyone."

I sigh and look at his bedroom again. "I'm your son," I whisper.

"I see, you're jealous. That's what this is about? You want to join us up there? You feel left out, you whiny baby. You want your father to fuck you?"

"Asshole."

He laughs and leans back in his chair, placing his hands behind his head like he's so damn proud of himself.

"That kid up there—"

"Call him Star."

"I know," I say. "He's one of the few guys in this company I like. Just don't dispose of him when you're finished playing."

He smirks, amused that I care about this kid. And it's

true; I don't want him to be tossed away just because my dad's bored. Sometimes you can't explain the connection you have with another person; you just know it's there.

"You've been here long enough to see how my company works. I'm not going to have him around when he's in his thirties. Eventually he'll have to retire, like you. Out with the old and in with the new keeps this company's cash flow steady."

"I won't kill him for you. Not this one."

"No?" He rocks in his chair with a euphoric face. "Someone will, and when the time comes you might change your mind. We'll make it a father-son outing, just the two of us. My friend from upstairs can ride in the trunk of my car. We'll pack a lunch and I'll show you how grand it feels to bury a man alive. I'll even let you do the honors of tying him up, placing him in a cardboard box, and burying him underneath two feet of desert sand."

Yeah, I can do the honors because my father won't lift a finger when someone's about to be killed.

"Then, we'll sit and listen to him scream until he suffocates, all while eating peanut butter and jelly sandwiches and drinking a beer. We'll form a splendid father and son bond when the time comes. You'd like that, wouldn't you?"

"Jesus, Paul." I know enough not to call him Dad in this moment. "I'll stick to killing the fuckers who mess with our family, not innocent men."

"Well, you have a few years to think about it. You may end up changing your pussy ass mind." He grins. "I've got *plenty of cardboard boxes in my garage when the time comes. He's even been duct taped inside a few already. It's one of my most enjoyable mindfucks to play on him."*

I inhale and shake head.

"Mug up, pal. Learn from me." With his hands on his desk, he pulls his chair forward. "If you want complete control over another person... you want to dominate someone's mind, place him in a fucking box, or a trunk, or a barrel. It's a cheap, rewarding thrill. The person won't come back from that type of manipulation. You'll be worshipped by the poor soul forever. Just make sure he's in the dark and about to suffocate before you pull him out. Be patient. When the time comes and the light shines in his eyes, smile down on him, he'll tell you that he loves you. The sensation you get when he says it is incredible." He reaches for a cigar on his desk and lights the end, puffing, puffing, puffing, exhaling, smiling, giving me a wink, and puffing again. The heavy smoke curls above us and hovers in the air. I think he's waiting for a response, but I have nothing left to say to the man. Not even see you later. The eighty grand is enough for a while... then I'll be back.

He points the cigar at my face, wholly delighted by his own words. "Get yourself a cardboard box, Marcus. Have a little fun for once."

DAXTON

I lift a flap on the box and see the legs of a young boy. Muddy jeans and the same sneakers his brother had on last night.

It's him.

There's no movement.

I pat his leg, whispering his name, but he doesn't respond.

Opening the other flap, I see his upper body wrapped securely in an army blanket... even his head. Half of his body is exposed and the other half looks mummified in green wool. His hands are tied behind his back, hanging out from underneath the bottom of the blanket. His chest isn't moving. Breathe, Daxton, breathe.

Never in my life have I had such a sickening feeling bind my body to the point where I can't catch a breath. Air won't enter my lungs.

I step back.

Oh fuck.

Turning to Cove, he senses that his worst fear is inside the box.

"No." He shakes his head. "No," he says with a flood of tears. "It's not him, Mark! It's not!"

He stumbles forward, only to be encased in my arms. I need to protect him from the sight.

"Shh, shh. Don't go over there. Don't. You'll never get the image out of your head. Don't look."

My hand rests on the back of his head but he fights to be released then collapses to the ground in a grief so savage, I swear I can hear his heart fracture inside his chest.

"Bring him to me. I want my son!" he cries. "Let me see him!" His voice echoes into the woods. "I want..." His hands cover his tear-laden face. "No! He's not dead!"

Careening forward, he gasps for air when he sees him inside the box. With one knee on the ground, he whispers, "Please Dax... please move. God, don't do this! Don't take my son!" he yells, while lifting him out.

I walk over and touch Dax's ankle. Cold. Limp. Still no movement.

"Let me remove the blanket," I whisper. "Give him to me, Cove. Don't look until I see what his face... I want to make sure you can handle this."

"Why?" He sobs. "How could this happen?!"

I open my garage door and place Daxton on the concrete, eerily reminded that Dayne was on this very floor not too long ago.

A suffering man weeps behind me as I unwrap his

son. This is the hardest thing I've ever done in my life. My nephew... he's ten for fuck's sake. I'm going to kill that bitch. I'll hunt her down and gut her. Take out her intestines and stuff 'em in her mouth so she can eat her own shit.

"Mark," Cove whispers. "Bring him back."

I'm unsure if that means he needs to hold him again, or if he wants me to breathe the life back into him. I don't think I can do either.

His lifeless eyes stare into mine. Get up, kid. Laugh, cry, crap in my pool if you want, just...

A blink.

He blinked.

"Cove!" I set him on the concrete and check his neck, feeling a strong pulse. "Thank fuck, you little shit, you're alive! Cove! Get over here!"

"What? Daxton!" Cove rushes over. "Dax, talk to me. Are you okay? Dax!"

He pulls him up by his shoulders and witnesses his son's eyes blinking while his face grimaces from the light.

"Thank fuck."

An exuberant smile and tearful laughter encompasses my brother-in-law as he hugs his son.

"Dax?" His hands frame his son's face, wiping the hair from the boy's eyes. "Talk to me."

"Let me cut him free," I whisper, his frozen fingers and arms flopping down upon release.

"I think the twine cut off his circulation, his hands are purple. And who knows how long she's had him outside. Damn, he's cold. Let's get him inside."

Cove carries him upstairs as I lock my truck and make a quick observation of the area. The sun's coming up which means a team of cops will be back on the scene. We've got a lot of work to do.

Lowering the garage door, I run up the stairs and let Cove and Dax into my living room.

"Put him on the sofa," I say, taking a fleece blanket from my hall closet. "Here, try to get his extremities warmed while I call Soph."

"Thanks." He covers his son and blows warm air onto his fingers. "What happened? Are you hurt?" Cove asks. "Please talk to me, I want to hear your voice."

My sister picks up her cell as I'm preparing to light a fire. "Mark?"

"We found him. We're in my suite. He's—" The call ends before I even have a chance to let her know he's okay.

"She's on her way," I say, placing kindling under the logs in the fireplace. "I'll get a bowl of warm water for his hands and feet after I get this lit."

"Why isn't he talking?"

"I'm sure he's in shock. Give him a few minutes."

"Something's wrong," Cove says. "Dax, look at me."

His son stares straight ahead, in his own little world, expressionless, with no movement accept for blinking eyelids and shallow breathing.

I hurry to the kitchen after getting the fire started, filling a large serving bowl with warm water and carrying it over to the fireplace. "Bring him here. Set him by the fire and get his sneakers off so we can warm his feet." I push a chair in front of the burning logs and Cove carries his son closer.

"Let me in!" My sister pounds on the door.

She rushes past me the moment it's opened with a sleepy-eyed Xavier by her side and Julia close behind.

"Oh my God!" she cries, giving him a hug. Xavier's eyes widen when he sees his brother and he quickly joins the embrace.

"You snot brain. You have to show me your hideout. I looked everywhere and couldn't find you! Fuck, you win this time! That was a good one, Dax, but you made Mom and Dad angry."

"We're not angry, not at all," my sister says. "I'm so happy you're safe... oh, you're cold, sweetheart." She kisses his cheek multiple times and rocks him in her arms.

"Yuck, mom," Xavier says. "Hey Dax, did you find your copter?"

Still nothing from my nephew, he's mute.

"What's wrong with him?" she whispers. "Where was he?"

Cove turns to me and I bite my lip. Fuck if I'm gonna say her son was tied, smothered, and left in a box.

"He was in front of Mark's garage when we returned," Cove says, leaving out the details. "I think he's cold and scared."

"Were you lost?" she asks in a gentle tone. "It's

okay. You're safe now and back with us."

Cove eases him into the chair and unties his sneakers as Sophia feels his body, looking for injuries.

"You're just cold, right baby? You okay?" she whispers. "He's okay." She turns to Cove. "Right? He's okay?"

Cove nods and places his son's feet into the bowl of water.

"Are the cops here?" I mumble into Jules' ear.

"What the fuck happened to you?" she asks.

"Answer my question."

"Two so far. They arrived about thirty minutes ago. Their captain was livid that they all left in the middle of the night. A few of them were supposed to stay on the scene until morning. Mark, what the fuck happened to your face?"

"Dog fight." I sigh, turning to Cove. "What are we going to do about the cops? I can't talk to them until I clean up and Dax needs to be able to function when they're around. If they see him like this, he'll be hospitalized."

"You don't need to talk to them, we will. And what's wrong with taking him to the hospital? He may have frostbite," Sophia says. "He was lost in the woods and should be examined." She continues to feel his arms and legs, looking for any reaction that he may be in pain, all while commenting on my face. "I take it there was a fight and Mark lost?"

I ignore her observation. The fight was good for our

relationship; a healthy pummeling between two men to let off some steam. It's a guy thing that women don't understand.

"I love you so much," Sophia says.

Daxton stands and pushes the blanket off his shoulders, making eye contact with his mother and father. Thank fuck, he's coming around.

"You lose your Cardinals cap?" Xavier asks.

He nods while unzipping his hoodie.

"Oh, leave it on until you warm up," my sister requests. "I hope you don't get sick from being out all night in the cold. You must be exhausted. We need to get you a filling breakfast then into a warm bed for the rest of the morning."

He drops the hoodie to the floor and takes off his shirt.

"Fuckin' A." Cove runs his hand through his hair. "Dax, what are you doing?"

"No, this is good," Sophia says, reassuring everyone that her son is fine while she disregards everyone's foul language. "He's showing us that he's okay. Look, no marks, scratches, broken bones. He's perfect. Everything's superb, my son is home."

I disagree in silence. Her words are calming only to herself. Something's certainly wrong with this kid. Cove and I have sensed it since we first set eyes on him. Then, feeling the warmth of Julia's hand and a firm squeeze... I know that she can tell too... we all know... all except my sister who's easily fooled. At this moment, she seems happy just to have him home and alive.

Daxton looks up, scanning the room, until his eyes rest on mine. He squints—his dark brown eyes nearly disappearing under his eyelids.

"I have a message for you," he says in a slow, icy voice. The words ricochet throughout my suite like a bomb just went off and a pile of rubble landed at my feet. He's speaking directly at me.

"What?" Sophia questions, ignorant to the fact that he's referring to Mera Calloway. If that bitch polluted his mind with anything about the porn industry...

Daxton turns around and Sophia gasps. No, it's worse. It's a message placed where my nephew can't read it, which means Mera likely didn't say a word to him about our past. But he can feel it. He knows it's there, that's for damn sure.

"Son of a bitch!" Cove explodes, kicking over a side table in a fit of rage. Xavier steps back by his father's reaction and covers his eyes, but Daxton... he stands motionless with his head bowed and his back exposed.

"I have a message," he says again.

She cut him. The fuckwench scrawled a note into his flesh.

Murderer

"Oh fuck, fuck!" Cove's hand flies through his wavy dark hair. He drops down next to his son and takes his hand. "I'm sorry," he says. "I'm so sorry."

My sister's speechless, standing with her hand over her mouth.

And Julia's expression turns venomous—a look I haven't seen until now. She heads to my bedroom saying, "barbarous bitch," along the way. I let her be, needing to deal with my family first.

"Okay, listen. We've got to—"

"No. We don't have to do anything, Mark." Cove examines the cuts then helps his son back into his shirt while Sophia remains a statue. He kneels directly in front of Dax and offers a comforting smile, trying to keep his cool for a child who's just been through hell. And I can't believe how calm Daxton is after being cut, bound, and placed in that box. I wonder what she said to him?

Cove presses his forehead to his son's and holds the back of his neck, keeping their bodies connected. "I'm proud of you for being so strong," he says. "We're going back to our suite then home, okay?"

Daxton nods, never letting out a whimper or mentioning that he's in any pain, while his brother is quiet and appears confused.

"You're filthy." Cove smiles, speaking softly to let his son feel relaxed and protected. "It's okay though. We'll run you a warm bath and find something to soothe your back. Then we can talk about what happened, okay?"

He nods.

"Just tell me if you're hurt anywhere else."

"No, just my back. What does it say?"

"Are you in pain?"

He nods.

"I'm sorry, son."

Cove looks at Sophia, shaking his head then smiles again at Dax. "Can you do something for me? A big favor?"

"Yes."

"The police have been searching for you. If they ask where you were, you need to tell them you were lost in the woods and nothing else."

"Dad, I *was* lost in the woods."

Cove nods. "And nothing else, okay? Don't say you were hurt, or anything about the box. Then we can leave."

"What box?" Sophia asks in a harsh tone. "What fucking box?"

"Mom, don't say fuck," Xavier scolds.

"Yeah." Daxton turns to her. "It makes you sound like a fucking street thug."

My sister's face is red in fury as she gives both Cove and me the *I'm on the warpath and I'm breaking both of your necks for lying,* all-out manic look... but she holds back in front of her sons.

"Barbarous bitch." Jules exhales, now headed down the stairs, through the living room, and out the door.

"She's only a wee bit perturbed," I say under my breath, but Cove and Sophia are too focused on Daxton to notice anything else happening in the room.

"I love you," Cove whispers to his son, tying sneakers then picking up his sweatshirt. He nods for Sophia to take the boys out of the room and into the corridor so the two of us can talk.

We wait for the door to shut before discussing the issue at hand.

"Listen." He leans against the sofa with crossed arms. I can see the look of relief in his eyes, but the rest of his body emanates anxiety over the suffering his son endured. He has utter contempt for the bitch that hurt him. "I know exactly what's going through your head. Mera turned my son into a walking billboard for the fucking crime we committed the other night. She's good. Smart. My son is now evidence that we killed Dayne and we'd never be able to explain his wounds to the cops without being thrown in prison for the rest of our lives. She knows that. I get it without you explaining it in front of my kids."

"Yeah, Mera knew when Dayne didn't make it back to their room that he was dead."

"Well, thank fuck Dax can't see that word on his back unless he looks in a mirror. Shit, Mark, he'll have that scar forever. And Xav will see it every time they get dressed. How the fuck am I going to explain this to them?"

"I don't know." I shrug. "The truth maybe."

"Hell no."

"The cuts don't look that deep, they're more like scratches, just enough for us to see the word. It will fade and disappear. Maybe you don't have to tell them much."

"This is... uhh, fuck." He rubs his eyes with a deep

sigh. "You have no idea how happy I am that he's alive."

"I do."

"I need to tell the cops he's home so they call off the search before they come across something, like that box downstairs."

"I'll take care of it."

"And I'll let the cops know we need to be on our way to have Daxton checked out so they don't hang around asking too many questions. They should clear out once they see that he's okay."

"I can't go over there." I motion to my nose.

"Yeah. Sorry."

"No you're not. Besides, I don't want you to be sorry."

"You're right, I'm not." He pauses. "Why don't you wash up and take care of any trail you can think of. I take it you cleaned and covered the boat already?"

This is when I adore Cove Everton, when he sobers up and his head clears enough to act like a man instead of a wimpy, ball-less toad. It's the fucking alcohol that makes him so spineless. I wish he could see the difference from two hours ago when he was being an ass, to now.

"The boat's fine. Go and take care of Dax."

We walk to the door and I can hear my sister's trembling voice as she speaks to her sons. She's trying to keep her shit together, but I know when she gets inside their suite she'll take a moment to cry her eyes out in private. Cove inhales deeply as he listens then exhales a request. "Kill her," he says.

"With pleasure. I was going to anyway."

He leaves my suite and takes his sons' hands, talking to both of them as they walk toward the opposite end of my hotel. I know they're being prepped. My sister *and* Cove are doing a grand job of masking their sadness and rage. Cove freaked for a moment, but then quickly regained his composure after seeing Xavier's horrified face. And now, if they can get through a chat with the cops, they'll have the privacy they need to get through an extremely difficult conversation with their kids.

And I'll be a fly on the wall the entire time.

I sprint downstairs and open my garage, pull the box and my truck inside, then check the surrounding area before lowering the door. That snake was waiting for the perfect moment to put Dax in front of my garage. I'm just relieved he wasn't there when I pulled out or I might've run him over. But maybe that was Mera's plan, to put him there so *I'd* end up killing him. Fuck, that bitch. I'm not going to spend my time daydreaming about what could've happened. It didn't pan out that way so why bother? I need to focus on the fresh hunt instead.

My bloodstained shirt gets tossed in the fireplace before I head upstairs to shower and change. The bed's unmade and my sheets are full of cum stains and greasy Dream Cream from Jules' ass. It's really too bad she doesn't do laundry.

While brushing my teeth and waiting for the shower to warm, I admire my beaten face. Damn, I'm gorgeous.

I'll have to thank Cove for making me so fucking beautiful. That's a remarkable swollen nose and one badass cut on my lip. It will be a thrill to fuck Jules with my new appearance, like I'm all gangster and shit. I can't wait to watch myself cum with a busted face.

I laugh at my foolish brain. I can't believe some of the crap that goes through my head. Always inappropriate thoughts at the wrong time—I'm thinking about my face and my dick instead of the word *murderer* on my nephew's back. I suppose I'm just exhausted and won't be able to function until I get some sleep.

The reddish brown water circles the drain and eventually runs clear as I finish a quick shower. I'm sure it's past six and my breakfast cart should be waiting. I need some down time. Dry toast, the morning paper, some wholesome spying on my family then much needed sleep.

I towel off, wrap one of my plush black Jameson Hotel robes around my flesh, and wink at myself in the mirror while gazing at my face one last time.

"I'm a troll, fol-de-rol..." I walk over to my bed with that wonderful song stuck in my head, picking up the condom that's crusted to the floor. After tossing it in the trash, I get my pot from my dresser drawer.

"I'm a troll, fol-de-rol... and I'll eat... you..."

Holy shit.

Where the fuck's my gun?

TAUNT

My princess needs to be punished; only this time her wounds may require a stitch job, unlike the laid-back belt to her ass routine that did little damage.

She promised not to touch my weapons. I warned her.

And where the fuck is she? Does she seriously believe she can kill Mera Calloway, or even find her in this town? Jesus, I can't think of any other reason why she'd take my gun.

I need you. Come home.

I text without mentioning the gun and wait for a response. She's got balls. I'll say that. Damn her.

Busy

What? That's her response? Busy?

No, fuck that. Get your ass home!

I take a bite of toast with a playful grin and swivel in my office chair while viewing my security cameras with the audio on. My eyes are on Cove and Daxton who have been talking to the police for the last twenty minutes. Two of the three police cars have already left and the final two guys are wrapping things up. Cove has a firm grip on his son's shoulder and he's his usual nervous self. Of course, we all are when we have to deal with cops. Even seeing them on the security camera makes me uneasy.

Busy

Shit, this woman cracks me up. I take a hit of my joint and text her back.

My sweet, darling Jules, I need your pussy. Come play with me.

Cove shakes hands with one of the cops and the last two men leave their suite, my hotel, and finally, my property. Goodbye, so long, and farewell. Don't fucking come back.

You had an overabundance of pussy yesterday. It's my turn.

What the fuck does that mean, Jules?

My entire life revolves around enjoying a plethora of pussy.

I smirk at my clever response while zooming in on the upstairs guest bedroom of my second suite. Sophia's running a bath for her son while Cove helps him undress, being careful not to touch his back. He's saddened when Dax tries to figure out the word in the dresser mirror.

• • •

"Re-re-drum. Re-redrum. Re-red-rum." Daxton peers over his shoulder.

"Talk about *The Shining*," Cove mutters under his breath.

"What, Babe?" Sophia asks, trying to hear over the running water.

"Nothing."

"Dad, what's reredrum mean? Why did she do that?"

Sophia sits on the edge of the tub and holds her head in the palms of her hands. I don't have a camera in that room, but I can see partway in and I can hear everything. This must be a nightmare for her. Especially since she was once in love with Mera. And I'm not surprised Mera changed, considering she was under the influence of Dayne.

• • •

You glutton!

Jules responds to my plethora of pussy remark. I can't disagree. Sometimes I do over-indulge, but...

Can you blame me for craving your exquisite pussy?

And thinking back to Mera, I suppose I may have changed Jules in the short amount of time we've known one another. People do crazy ass shit for love.

Julia Alison Barringer, I need you. My cock wants to play.

I take another bite of toast while watching the

screen.

• • •

"They're jumbled letters Dax, nothing more."

"But why? What did I do? Ouch!"

Cove places a warm washcloth on his son's back and pats away the blood.

"Soph, can you get some ibuprofen? It may ease the pain."

"I'm not a wimp."

"I know, you're the strongest ten-year-old in the world," Cove replies.

He takes his wife's place on the side of the tub and feels the water before telling his son to get in.

"Don't look," Dax says.

"I won't, buddy. Just tell me when you're ready so I can wash your back."

"No, don't touch it. It's fine... okay, I'm in."

Cove studies the cuts before pouring a cup of water over Dax's back, trying to clean the area without causing too much pain.

"I need to ask you some questions, son."

"Go for it."

"If you don't understand, just ask me to clarify, okay?"

"Okay," he says, soaping his arms.

"Was she waiting for you in the woods?"

"Sort of."

Daxton shudders as his father pours another cup of water over his cut flesh.

"Sorry," Cove says with compassion. "Can you explain in more detail? This is important."

"I went into the woods and saw her at a distance. She knew my name and kept calling me over. She said she was friends with mom. She knew mom's name too, mom's *real* name of Jameson. She waved me to follow her out of the woods, but when I did, I realized I wasn't in the parking lot. I was further down the drive of Uncle Mark's hotel, close to the road."

"So you walked for some time?"

"I guess so."

"You remember we told you no to go anywhere with strangers?"

"She wasn't. She knew my name and mom's. That's not a stranger."

Sophia returns, handing her son a pill and a cup of water. Cove sighs, giving his wife a look of disappointment then asks his son to continue.

"She grabbed me and put me in a truck. I tried to kick and scream like you taught me, but she taped my mouth and tied my hands behind my back." For the first time I hear a waver in his voice. "It sucked. I tried to kick her, but that only made her angry. She said..." He pauses and soaps his feet while his parents wait.

"What?"

He doesn't answer.

"Don't push him," Sophia says gently. "Maybe

that's enough."

"No. I want to talk to him while it's still fresh in his mind."

Daxton looks over his shoulder at his parents. "She said I have the same eyes as Paul. Who's Paul? And why did you and Uncle Mark kill her husband? She's mad and she took it out on me. For fuck's sake, Dad." He turns back around and continues bathing.

"Oh, hell," Cove says, looking to Sophia. He stands and walks out, heading for their bedroom with Sophia following close behind.

"Where are you going? We need to explain this to him," she says.

"Fuck, we're not telling him shit about Dayne. Go ahead and tell him Paul was your father, but that's it." He paces. "I think I'm going to be sick. Fuck!"

"And what's going on with a box? What's that all about?"

"She put him in a cardboard box." His voice shakes. "And left him outside of Mark's garage."

"Dad!" Daxton calls out. "I thought you wanted to talk?"

"I'm coming!" he responds then grips Sophia's shoulders. "Listen, how we handle this situation right now, at this very moment, is going to affect him for the rest of his life."

"I don't want to lie to our sons."

"Well, I don't want to either, but what the fuck choice do we have?"

"Dad!"

"Be right there, Daxton!"

• • •

Okay, I was wrong. Mera didn't keep her mouth shut. Fuck, what is it with women needing to be such gossip hounds about everything in their lives? *Did you see the size of Clarissa's ass? Do you think Dirk likes me? OMG, Brad has a big dick. I think I'm pregnant. Mark and Cove killed my husband. Blah, blah, blah.*

I wish Cove and Sophia would just blame me for this shit and move on. I mean, how difficult is it to say Uncle Mark's a prick and it's his fault? I wouldn't care. If I could call them and tell them that, I would.

Still Busy

Another text from Jules... what the hell is she up to?

I'm not going to sleep until we fuck. Is what you're doing more important than sitting on my dick?

Women. You can't live with 'em and you can't cut 'em in half and keep their lower torso to fuck because they start to smell after a few days. I should text her that, see how she responds.

Aren't you upset? She messages.

Does she mean about the gun, or Dax? I guess the latter.

Yes, but I'll fix the problem when the time is right, not now.

How could she do such a thing to a little boy?

No worries, it will toughen him up.

Okay, that last text from me was a bit cold and perhaps unnecessary.

What the fuck, Mark!!!

I ignore her last comment, but then think of a brilliant response.

Welcome to the family.

I look at the security cam and see Daxton's out of the tub, in a pair of jeans, and trying to view the word on his back. Sophia's checking on Xavier who's sound asleep on the living room sofa and Cove is standing outside his kids' bedroom, figuring out what the fuck he's gonna say.

• • •

"Dad?"

"I'm here."

"Who's Paul?"

"Your grandfather." He walks into the bedroom. "Your mother's father."

"I thought mom said she didn't have any parents."

"Well, she came from someone, just like you and Xavier."

"Oh... why did you and Uncle Mark kill that lady's husband?"

Cove rubs his face then leans against the dresser with crossed arms. "I didn't. We didn't," he lies.

His son tries to look at his back once more, but

finally gives up. Cove takes him into the bathroom and places ointment on the cuts, then covers the area with gauze. When finished, Dax pulls a Hurley sweatshirt over his head and places a black baseball cap on his head. "If you and Uncle Mark didn't do anything, then why did she hurt me?"

"She's sick, Dax. People who are sick in the head sometimes do mean things to others."

"But you always say Uncle Mark is sick in the head, so has he done things like this?"

He's silent, thrown off by his son's question and refuses to answer. Dax stares him down, but Cove won't open his mouth.

"You know what? I think you're full of shit, Dad."

"Hey, wait a minute." He takes his son by the arm. "Don't talk to me that way. There are some things you're just not old enough to understand or do. This is one of them. Telling your father he's full of shit is another."

"You wanted to talk so that means *you* need to answer *my* questions, too. Remember? You said we should never be afraid to tell you anything and that you'd do the same."

"You're right. Uh." Cove looks toward the ceiling. "My sons are now old enough to put me in my place. Can't you guys go back to riding tricycles and playing with bubbles?"

Daxton laughs and heads out of the room. "Bubbles are for babies."

"Where are you going? I still have a lot of

questions."

"I'm hungry." He races down the stairs and eyes his brother on the sofa, running over and sitting on his back. "Get up, farthead. Let's eat."

Xavier pushes him off with a moan.

"Xav's exhausted, let him sleep. And why aren't you tired? You've been up all night," Cove asks.

He ignores his father. "Mom! I want some cereal."

"Hey, did you sleep? Answer me."

He nods.

"Where?"

I don't remember.

"Dax, think."

"Cove." Sophia sets a box of cereal on the counter as her son gets a bowl and the milk. "Let him eat. He'll talk when he's ready. Please, just be happy he's okay."

"I am. What the fuck, Soph? Don't sugarcoat this shit like nothing happened."

"I know something happened!" she shouts, making Xavier rise from the sofa and rub his eyes.

"What the hell?" Dax says, taking his breakfast to the kitchen table. "Did I do something wrong? Why are you arguing?"

"We're not," Cove responds. "We're confused, that's all. We need answers, buddy. Think. Tell me what happened after you were tied and in the truck."

"Well," he says with a mouth full of Cheerios, swinging his legs under the chair. "She said she wanted Dayne... who's Dayne?"

"Her husband," Sophia answers.

"Yeah she said that too. She wanted her husband and she wanted Dayne."

"Her husband and Dayne are the same person, Dax."

"Yep, that's what she kept saying. Then, she drove somewhere, only I was lying on the seat and couldn't see out the window. It was dark, that's all I know. I didn't see any lights anywhere. She stopped and said I had to give Uncle Mark, Mom, and you a message. Then she raised my shirt and started scratching my back. She said you or Uncle Mark must've killed him."

Cove shakes his head continuously while listening. "What did she use to hurt you?"

He shrugs. "I can't see behind me, but it hurt. I kept kicking and screaming, only no one could hear me because of the tape over my mouth."

Sophia wipes a tear from her cheek as Cove closes his eyes and rubs his forehead.

"Did you hear anything? Traffic? Any noise?"

"I don't remember... no. I don't think so. I was too busy trying to get away. Then I fell asleep."

"What do you mean?"

"I kicked her. I got her good, right in her stomach. That made her really angry and she said she had a mean cat that was going to get me."

"A what?" Sophia asks.

"She poked me with a cat and said it was mean. A *cat that's mean*, she called it. But I didn't see or hear any cats. Then I fell asleep."

Cove stares at his son for a few minutes then walks over to Sophia and grips her arm, leaning in close to whisper in her ear. "I bet she fucking shot him up with Special K. That bitch. It was Ketamine, Cat Valium. She could've killed him."

"How do you feel right now, Dax?" he asks.

"Fine."

"Do you remember anything after that?"

He shrugs, taking another bite of cereal while reading the back of the box. "Oh yeah. I vomited. I was in a room for a while... I think she took a shower... there was a gun on a table... she was talking to herself... she said she was going to kill me... I think I saw her breasts."

"Wait, wait, slow down. Slow down. What?" Cove gasps. "What the fuck?"

"Jesus," Sophia says.

"You saw tits?" Xavier walks into the kitchen and takes a bowl out of the cupboard. "Like, real ones?"

"I think so. Maybe I was dreaming. I don't remember... oh, yeah, I did. She walked out of the bathroom right when I woke up. She had those big ones like we saw online."

"That big?" Xav asks.

"Wait a second, what the fuck are you two talking about? We've never given you internet access."

The boys point to their watches with a grin.

• • •

Oh shit, that's my fault. I didn't think I had to block any sites when I gave them those watches. Fuck, Sophia and Cove are gonna have my head. But, *they* should've thought of it themselves. And anyway, this is what I'm saying about trying to keep them in a bubble. It's impossible, so just come clean with the kids. I'm sure in a few years they'll come across the fact that we were all porn stars at one time.

And Mera Calloway, you stepped in some deep shit. I can't wait to kill your ass. Drugging my nephew? You and I are going to spend some quality time together, I promise you that.

You angry?

Ah, my Jules is back, and I'll assume she's referring to the gun. Sorry, I'm not going to mention it in a text. Some things shouldn't be put in writing. Twat and cock are fine, guns and drugs, not so much.

Yes, for many reasons. And I'm cranky from lack of sleep and lack of pussy.

lol!

Where'd you go with my tool?

Tool?

Fuck's sake, Jules. My TOOL.

The black one or the pink one?

Black. The pink one's in my hand.

Hmm. I guess I not only have your balls around my neck, but your TOOL as well. Poor Mark Jameson.

Wait. Is she playing me again or am I just high? I

read her text a second then a third time before responding.

I'm going to stick that TOOL where the sun doesn't shine if you don't watch your mouth.

The black one or the pink one? She texts back.

I grin. *Smartass. Come home and find out.*

I am home. The hotel is packed.

Thank fuck. I lean forward and bring up the other security cams in my hotel. Yeah, there's a swarm of people this morning getting ready for the marathon that starts in three hours. Damn, it's crowded. I'm glad the cop cars didn't scare anyone away.

Searching, searching... there's my beauty, walking in the front door through a crowd of people and heading toward the elevator. She looks dead-tired like the rest of us. I follow her to her room and get a surprise when she undresses to take a shower. Hell, I wish I could see through the curtain. I untie my robe and lean back with a hand on my cock. Her silhouette is well defined and fucking beautiful as always. It's amazing what a dark figure hidden behind a screen does to me. I stroke slowly, closing my eyes at times, breathing deeply, craving her, eager to feel her flesh... freakin' A, this is good.

This is my usual masturbation spot—in front of my computer screen while watching my guests. I open the top drawer to my desk and take out a bottle of lube.

"Shit, that's cold," I whisper, as the Astroglide runs down my shaft. I spread it around and jerk off again.

Much better. Slick and... uh... so good. The image of her pussy in my head is so sweet.

My free hand grips the armrest. I'm gonna cum on the screen. Wait 'til she steps out... then shoot my load on her chest.

"No, come on. I'm not ready."

She's finished, toweling off and getting dressed. Damn, too soon, Jules. I know her shift starts in an hour, but she can slow down a little bit. I want a show, just two more minutes.

Mmm, she's in her Jameson Hotel blazer and a short skirt... uh... fuck... uh, here we go. My hand jerks faster.

I lean closer to the screen, gazing, gawking, yanking it, then watching her walk back into the bathroom to put on a pad. Oh hell, I'm not gonna pass up cumming inside her if she's on her period.

I call her cell.

"Hi. You need something?"

"A few things, but first, get your ass over here."

"Are you mad about the gun? I don't want to come over if you're going to use the belt again. I need to heal first."

"Screw the gun, this is an emergency. Now!"

I end the call and wait at the door, my hand gliding over my dick as I keep an eye on the corridor through the peephole.

Two minutes later, "there's my woman," I whisper.

I open my door and pull her inside with my robe

open and my erection pointing toward her face.

"Cute."

"The next thirty seconds aren't going to be cute."

She's against the wall, her mouth in custody, and our tongues at war. My hand hurries to slide her underwear and pad to the side. Yes. Fuck, yes. My cock slips in and is instantly coated with her warm blood. I've got seconds before I cum.

"Mark, wait. I..."

"I don't care about it, just let me fuck you." I thrust harder. "Stain me with your blood." I grab her chin. "Look at my beaten face. Watch me, Jules. I'm gonna cum... I'm gonna cum." Her legs wrap around my hips as her back gets slammed into the wall. My eyes start to blur. My dick... exploding... "Uh! Uh! Fuck!"

Her nails pierce my back causing an intense heat to shoot through my body and surround my cock. I pant and huff while grabbing her hips with a tight squeeze.

Nothing will ever compare to a speedy fuck. Nothing.

"Wow, Mark."

"Damn, that was—"

"Gross," she says. "And you only lasted five seconds. You owe me. I want a long loving fuck next time, with lots of foreplay."

"Uhhh. I'll make it up to you someday. I can't promise it will be our next fuck, but eventually you'll get what you want." My head rests on her shoulder as we embrace. I continue panting while rocking her in my arms, thinking about nothing but her. We were made for one another. I've tried to tell her that before but it came out all wrong, and once again, I fuck it up.

"Your blood kicks ass."

"Um... thank you?"

I kiss her forehead and set her down, sliding my red dick out of her pussy. That's pure satisfaction—no condom, being able to share her thick flow, and the end result is that my flesh gets painted like the face of a warrior.

"Fucktard, you got blood on my skirt."

"I'll buy you a new one," I say, tying my robe. "Thanks for the quickie. Now where's my gun?"

"In my room." She sighs, licking her finger and trying to clean her clothing, not giving a shit that she took my weapon. "Fuck. You're a mess."

"I'll take that as a compliment."

"Your dick, your face, your head, the smell of pot that's hovering in the air... a total mess."

I pull her closer for a long, enduring kiss, running my hands down her chest and gripping her tits. She blushes when released and tightens her lips, holding back a smile.

"But?" I question. "I know there's more to your last comment."

"But... for some reason I love you more and more each day. I must be crazy, but I do," she whispers.

"I know," I say. "So, Jules? Tell me something, beautiful."

"What?"

"What would you have done if I had stabbed you with my knife instead of stabbing you with my dick?"

"I would've pulled it out of my body and shoved it in your ass," she replies without hesitation.

I nod. "I had that thought when I saw my gun was missing. I just wanted you to know that killing you crossed my mind."

She cocks her head and folds her arms, giving me an evil glare. "This bullshit about killing me is getting fucking ridiculous. Don't talk about it anymore unless you're going to do it. Now excuse me, I have to change my skirt, dry my hair, eat breakfast, and try to get through an eight-hour shift without any sleep."

A hardy laugh echoes through my suite. Shit, she's the best.

"Follow me." She motions. "I'll get your goddamn *tool* that you seem to be so infatuated with. I swear you love your weapons more than me. And when are you going to say that you love me anyway?"

"I thought I just did."

She rolls her eyes and exhales my name. "Oh, Mark. So whenever I tell you I love you, your response will be 'your blood kicks ass.' Fine, act like a teenager again, fuck if I care."

"So what *was* your plan when you left?" I ignore her neediness. "Or didn't you have one?"

"No plan. I was just furious when I saw Daxton's back. I wanted to hurt that woman."

"Dax is tough."

"That doesn't make it any better."

"I'll be handling Mera Calloway, no one else but me. You understand? Don't be dumb or get in the way and fuck things up. I'll know when the time is right."

"Like with Dayne?" she says under her breath, whispering while we're in the corridor.

"I never planned on taking care of him so quickly. I was hoping for more fun and games with the dickhead, but he left me no choice but to take him down. Mera will be different."

"What about your family? What if she goes after them to St. Louis?"

"I'll make sure she knows I'm the man she wants to do business with, not anyone else."

"How?"

"Like I said, let me take care of this," I whisper. "I'm not going to hunt her down over the next hour and put a knife in her chest then wipe my hands and walk away. That's pussy shit when dealing with a woman. Plus, it's personal... for her too. Besides, I need some drama in my life."

"So what's been happening isn't enough?"

"Jules, I'm not the only one who feels this way. It was obvious by the way she treated Dax that she wants to play. I'm up or it, rain or shine, her playing field or mine."

We enter her suite and she picks up her purse, pulling the gun out and dangling it on her finger. I grab it with an evil eye and check the safety, while Jules continues to bitch as she changes her skirt.

"Loving you is a bit overwhelming. My heart hurts when I think about you, in a good way, but my mind's still unsure about what the fuck's going on. I think we should break up."

"What? Where the fuck did that come from? And we're not even—"

"Dating. I know. Then I'll change my words so you understand... I think we shouldn't fuck anymore."

The barrel of my gun runs under my chin. She's kidding, right?

"Oh yeah?" I question.

"Stop it," she sighs and forces the gun away from my neck. "I need to be wined and dined every once in a while. I feel neglected."

"Really?" I make a mental note of today's date. I guess this is what I'm in for whenever she's ragging it.

With her hands on her hips, she raises her voice. "I may love you, but I'm also losing interest, so you better do something quick if you want to keep me."

"Well, fuck. If you're gonna be this much work..." I smirk. "I thought you liked this lifestyle. You said it was exciting. Now it's not?"

"Be serious for like two minutes, would you?"

If my dick wasn't happy I wouldn't be able to deal with her menstrual moan. "Alright. We've got a long day and I know we're both going to crash after work, but why don't we go for a jog in the morning? That's a good way to spend time together, and you could use the exercise."

"Huh." Her mouth drops open. "Huh," she expels again. "You know what? Give me back the gun. I feel like using it all of a sudden."

I smile and hide it playfully behind my back.

"Jules, do I honestly have to give up control of everything in this relationship? Should I have my tat re-inked to read *Property of Julia Barringer,* instead of *Property of Jameson Industries?*"

"Please?" she begs.

"Begging's good."

"Please?" she pleads with a sexy smile.

"Okay." I bow my head in defeat. "I forgot, I'm supposed to worship my princess, not just fuck her. Damn, you've captured my balls again."

I can tell I'm still high or I never would have agreed to... I don't even know what I've agreed to yet. Thank fuck she's not in high school or I'd find myself going to a dumbass prom.

"How about tomorrow night?" I exhale. "We'll do something special to celebrate your love for me."

"God, you're such a bastard." She drops her hands, presenting me with a more tranquil pose and a grin. "Fine, but no fucking again until after the date. Oh, and you *have* to use a condom. I know I can't get preggo on my period, but I sure as fuck don't want to pick up the hundreds of diseases you have."

I love this back and forth bantering shit. We're both

trying to have the last word.

"Too late, unless your blood has some special disease fighting antibiotics to ward off my dirty flesh and semen bugs, you're doomed."

"Uh!" She throws her hands in the air.

"Ha!" I retort.

Her hands are back on her hips and my arms are crossed. She scowls. I sneer. She steps forward. I step forward. She's in my face. I'm in hers.

"I hate it that I love you," she says.

"I love to be hated," I reply.

We stare.

I lick my lips.

We kiss.

She sighs.

I love her.

AN OFFERING

As expected, my family left in the middle of my busy workday, leaving no time for a long, drawn out goodbye, which I despise anyway. I hugged my sister, shook Cove's hand, tousled the hair of Dax and Xav, and gave them my usual sendoff, "don't get killed."

My nephews were still discussing tits when they got into the shuttle headed for Reno. I never heard the rest of the conversation in their suite, but I would say Mera either drugged Dax a second time before placing him in the box, or he was still coming off his first high when we found him. That would explain his confused and dazed state.

Hell, I'm glad he didn't suffocate.

The rest of the day was shit. I could barely keep my eyes open, even after four cups of coffee. My hotel lobby resembled a stampede and the restaurant was packed with people who weren't even registered guests. Tourists infested the place for the Marathon. I even had to call in a few extra workers to open the bar early. I was counting both dollar signs and sheep throughout the day.

I was disappointed there were only a few moments to admire Jules. When her shift was over she went straight to her room and crashed. I worked a longer day, but stayed mostly in the downstairs office with my hotel manager, keeping my swollen nose hidden from the guests. The bump on my forehead is practically gone, and soon my good-looking boy face will reappear. I'll have to enjoy my badass appearance while I can.

I managed to get a lead on Mera from one of the owners of hotel in the downtown district. She might be staying in his place under the name, Fantasia Cocker. Yeah, *Fantasia Cocker*. No shit. Sounds like a fucking porn name if you ask me. That's got to be her. Now I need to figure out what she wants. I'm guessing revenge over money, but who knows.

Somehow, after nearly falling asleep at my desk, I was able to make it to my bed. I remember touching Jules' door on my way to my suite, standing, listening, wanting to lie next to her... yet, I slept alone.

I woke up a number of times; my usual 1am, 3am, 5am, staring at the ceiling for a while then getting out of bed to drink and pace. I kept thinking about dumbass shit like my dad and that fucking box. I doubt Mera had any clue it was one of my father's favorite taming devices for Cove; she's not that cunning. It was just an easy way to keep Daxton hidden from the outside world until we found him. But even so, it was more than disturbing for my brother-in-law.

The amount of sleep I was able to get was plenty

and after a morning jog, my dry toast and coffee, jerking off in the shower, and sending a text to my sister, I was ready for a better day.

The second day of the Marathon was just as hectic, but tolerable, especially since I could view Jules' ass from the hotel's main office. She glowed... whenever I saw her eyes, they reflected the dancing sparks from the lobby fireplace. And her cheeks were flush in adoration for me. Those moments caused my dick to twitch.

With our workday finally over, my family on a plane to St. Louis after a day in Reno, Mera within reach and not much of a threat, and Dayne still at the bottom of the lake, I can spend the evening focusing on my woman.

And Fuck, I sure look good for her.

I'm sporting one of my finest black suits and a pair of Brunello Cucinelli Shoes, a brand that Cove drools over whenever he sees them on my feet. We share a love for collecting exquisite footwear and if he's lucky, I'll buy him a pair for Christmas, but only if I get a thank you for killing Dayne.

I gaze into the rearview mirror while pulling out of my garage, checking my hair and teeth. My wrists are dabbed with my finest cologne and an extra splash was added to my groin for our fuck tonight. We *will* fuck. I'm not looking my best without getting pussy. Hell, I even slipped into a brand new pair of boxers for her.

"Swanky, Mark. You look swanky," I say to myself.

I'm keeping the details of our date a secret. I sent

Jules a text that I'd pick her up in front of the hotel at seven, and to dress erotic, but elegant.

Sure enough, she doesn't disappoint. She appears in a black, off the shoulder, long sleeve, knee-length dress with black heels and holding a long double-breasted grey coat. Her hair is in a bun and she's wearing just the right amount of makeup. Total perfection. "Very nice, Jules," I whisper. "Sophisticated and fuckable."

I park and walk up to her with a grin, kissing her hand then leading the way to my truck.

"Good evening, Ms. Barringer." I wink, opening her door.

"Good evening, Mr. Jameson." She winks back then sees one of my signature lilies waiting for her on the passenger seat.

No, I'm not buying a woman flowers when my hotel is full of them. Besides, it's the thought that counts... and she seems delighted by the surprise.

"Ohhh," she says all starry-eyed, placing the lily on her lap after she gets inside. I guess she enjoys the ultimate cliché gift.

A few staff members have their eyes on the truck as I start the engine and pull away. I'm sure they're saying I'm a cradle robber, but I bet they won't pass up young meat when they're my age. No one would.

"Does it feel like we've been apart for days?" I ask, as we head out to Route 50.

"Yes, and we have."

She's staring at me.

"So you thought about me?" I ask.

"You bet I did."

"And you're happy that I'm taking you out?"

"Ecstatic, Mark. And I'm amused that some of the staff are jealous of our relationship."

"They're not being assholes to you, are they?" I catch a glimpse of her out of the corner of my eye.

"No, just teasing... and I like it. It's fun being the center of attention. I've never experienced that before."

She's still staring, perhaps noticing all my prep work for the *date*.

"You look beautiful." I take her hand.

"And you look like Paul Walker," she says.

"The actor who died?"

"He was incredible, super hot, and he didn't die. He's like Elvis, Michael Jackson, and Princess Diana. They live on some quiet island because they wanted to escape the media. He's with them."

"Why am I not surprised that you're starting the evening by telling me I look like a guy who died in a tragic car wreck."

"He was handsome, like you."

"But tough, right? Not just handsome, but Paul Walker was threatening as well?"

"Hmm, depends on what role he was in, maybe... no, he was pretty much just hot." She turns away, commenting that my face looks better before asking where we're going.

I squeeze her hand. "It's in town. A special place,

like you wanted. I promise it will be a night you'll always remember."

"I'm sure it will be fabulous... as long as it's not the restaurant in your hotel or a graveyard." She sniffs the flower as I laugh at her comment.

"It's not a graveyard."

"You know I grew up here, so I've been to every restaurant in town... can I guess?"

"Go for it."

"Maxwells? The fancy restaurant on the water."

"Nope."

"Okay, so it's Callie Kay's or The Red Lounge."

"No, sorry. You disappointed?"

"Chili's? Mountain Steakhouse? Pasta Pete's?" She looks at her outfit then shakes her head. "Am I overdressed?"

"No. You're perfect."

She'll never be able to figure out what I've got up my sleeve. I don't do anything half-heartedly and I sure as fuck don't enjoy the standard, run of the mill, dinner date. "Jules, this won't be some shitty evening in some shitty restaurant where we have to sit and listen to all the shitty tourists in town, talking shit."

She laughs. "Well, shit, Mark."

"The restaurants are booked solid anyway. I could buy my way in, but why? Dining with a hundred other people and being unable to hear one another isn't how we should spend the evening. Right?" I glance over and see a nod then turn back to the road. "Now are you disappointed?"

"No." She pulls the bottom of her dress further down and fidgets in the seat. "But, why did you ask me to dress this way?"

"For me." I bring her hand to my lips and place a soft kiss on her flower-scented skin. "For us," I whisper, turning into the Tahoe Mountain Pines Ski resort.

"Oh nice, I forgot this place has a restaurant. It's beautiful here, too bad there's no snow. I would've loved to see the people skiing down the slopes." She looks at me and asks, "Why isn't this place packed like all the rest?"

"It is." I grin, motioning to the parked cars. "We're not eating at the restaurant." I drive past the lodge, along a dirt road and through the pines, coming to a stop next to a van owned by the resort. I help Jules out of my truck, smiling proudly that she still hasn't a clue about our upcoming adventure.

"What kind of surprise is this?"

I stop myself from saying, *the kind that will make you want to fuck me at the drop of a hat*, and instead, respond like a pussy by saying, "the kind of surprise every good woman deserves." It hurt, God that hurt, but by her blushing cheeks I can tell I said the right thing this time.

"Wow." She grabs my arm when she finally notices the gondola air lift ride before us. "Wow," she says again. "Are you kidding me?"

Good. She's stunned. I was hoping for 'shock and

awe' tonight.

"Mark, wow. Are you serious?"

A man in a dark wool coat and black leather gloves opens the door as we approach. I nod in appreciation when I see everything I've requested is in place. A table has been set up with a black tablecloth. On top is a basket of bread, white dinner plates filled with pasta, and an open bottle of red wine. Our glasses are already filled and the pasta sauce smells magnificent. The gondola is lit with two candles and two orange roses glow next to the flame. They remind me of her—a glowing sunset. They're a nice touch and something I didn't ask for. I'd say the outrageous cost of setting this up was worth it.

"Mr. Jameson." The man pulls me closer to talk in private. "It will be a forty-five minute ride up the mountain and another forty-five down. I'll return at that time."

I nod and thank him as he shuts the door and locks us inside.

Julia's face is radiant.

"Here's your fairy tale," I whisper, pulling her chair out.

"This makes up for *everything*."

"I'm glad you're pleased."

"And you're being so nice. It's sexy. I think you even deserve bonus points. Damn, this must've cost a fortune."

"It would seem that I believe you're worth it."

"See, it's hot when you say things like that. This is

exactly what I wanted."

The car starts to move and she laughs in delight. "Mark, this is incredible. We get to have a nice meal together, just the two of us, riding up a mountain in a gondola lift, while viewing the mountains to the west, the lake to the north, and the lights of the city to the east. This is crazy!"

I smile and take a gulp of wine then another. Yes, I must be insane.

"You really do have a lot of money, don't you?"

That's a new question for her. She never asks about my money. "Yes. My father left me quite a bit, but I earned him that money, so it was mine in the first place. Then I made a fortune selling his porn company. Even after my wife took a chunk in the divorce battle, I'm still set for life."

"Whoa." She sets her elbow on the table with her chin in the palm of her hand and gawks. "So why do you have the hotel?"

"I like to be in control of things, I enjoy keeping busy and having a job, and I'm extremely fond of money. It's a good feeling knowing my bank account keeps growing each day. I don't believe I'd be able to sleep if I knew money wasn't coming in."

She nods, still gazing into my eyes.

"Plus, I've never been fond of big city life. My wife and I had a house in the burbs back in Philly, same in Vegas, but even that was too crowded and suffocating for me."

"You don't enjoy being around people, do you?"

"I'd be in the wrong business if I didn't enjoy being around people. I own a hotel after all. What I'm referring to is my private life. I have a few close friends, including my family, but other than being around them, I enjoy seclusion. Jameson Hotel seems to be the right business and is in the picture-perfect setting for my lifestyle."

We begin our meal, admiring the scenic view. It's dark, but the lights from the downtown area glitter and reflect into the shoreline of Lake Tahoe. I see a few cars curving along the mountain road then disappearing into the pines. Jules keeps repeating how romantic it is and that she never would've expected anything like this, especially from me.

"Are you friends with the owner of this resort?"

"Owners. There're two, and yes. They rent boat slips down where my boats are docked. I met them a year ago at the lake. They're brothers. A couple of potheads in their fifties. Good guys, laid back, and open-minded. The type who try to steer clear of the cops and who want to be left alone to live their lives in peace, like me."

"Do you buy your weed from them?" She takes a bite of pasta and dabs the corners of her mouth with her napkin, trying not to smudge her lipstick.

I nod. "I have some waiting for me when we leave. I was running low after such a stressful week. My supply usually lasts twice as long as this one did."

Her fingers twirl the silver and jade gemstone

necklace that's around her neck. It's in the shape of a heart and casts a green tint on the flesh under her chin. Earrings and a ring match the necklace, cluing me in to the fact that she prepped for this as much as I did. I can't wait to see what's under her dress.

"My mother made them." She takes a drink of wine then puts her fingers back on the necklace. "I saw you eyeing my jewelry. My mother made this set for my twenty-first birthday. She sells her pieces at some of the downtown galleries. It's a hobby for her, but I could see her doing it full-time. She's good."

I'm nervous now. I have a box... a special gift waiting for her in my pocket, only it may not be as meaningful to her as her mother's jewelry, and she won't be able to wear my present around her neck.

"The set's unique."

"She gets custom orders and tries to personalize the stone with the person she's making each piece for. This one." She takes the heart in her hand. "She said could be worn to attract love, but it would also provide me with balance and peace."

Yeah, I might hold out entirely on my gift. No, screw that. This is *our* night. I can do this.

"Sounds like the two of you have a decent relationship. I couldn't imagine my mother making something for Sophia or me."

"We've always been close. She's the type of mother who was very supportive, until she couldn't be anymore."

"Meaning?"

"Meaning you can't rely on your parents forever. It killed her that I was living in my car, but we both knew if she pulled me out of the situation I might come to rely on her whenever I was in need. There's an age when you have to break free and when your parents should cut the cord. It was time."

"But..." I start to reply, leaning back in my chair and adjusting my tie then feeling the box inside my pocket. No, not yet. "But... I pulled you out of the situation. Should I have left you in the car to sleep in thirty-degree weather, in pitch-black parking lots with a steak knife for protection at your feet? I disagree with your logic. Would you do that to your daughter?"

"Would you? Think of your son when he's twenty-two. Would you?"

My son knows karate, and at twenty-two with a sword collection, I can't imagine anyone's going to want to fuck with him. He'd be just fine living in his car. "Jack's a rebel."

"So am I," she says.

She's right and I'm sure her mother recognizes how strong she is. Most parents know what they're doing.

"Still, there's no way I could've left you alone in your car that night. It would've been wrong to walk away."

She smiles with flushed cheeks as I replenish our wine.

"But, if you weren't so fucking gorgeous, I would've

fucked you and left you there."

She kicks my leg, now with an even deeper shade of red on her cheeks. I'm on a roll tonight.

"You bastard."

Maybe not.

"You can ask my mother her reasoning when you meet her."

"Uh." I nearly choke. "No."

"She won't mind."

"I mean, I'm not meeting your parents. They'd have a shit fit that we're together. We must be close in age."

"No, they're forty-five."

"Yeah, I'm in my late thirties."

"But you don't act like it. You seem more like someone my age, or younger."

"That's not a compliment, Jules."

She laughs, obviously fucking with my head. "Is that a text?" she asks looking at my watch. I check the screen and see a message from my son.

Still no card. No money. You suck!

I exhale. Fuck, I did forget to mail it out again.

"Who is it?"

"My son. He's just saying hi." I put the text out of mind. I'll call him back as soon as I get a chance. Sometime tomorrow.

"So tell me, Julia Alison Barringer, what are your plans?"

"Like what? Tonight?" She finishes her pasta and cleans the sauce from her plate using a slice of bread like it's a sponge. I've never seen a woman eat as much as her.

"Not tonight, in the future, say five years from now?"

"Well, I'd be in heaven if I had my own salon, but five years is pushing that dream, especially considering I'm broke, so maybe ten... when I'm in my thirties. That would be nice." She sips her wine and smiles at the view then back at me. Her tongue licks the red liquid off her top lip and she swirls the glass before taking another drink. I can help her make that dream come true. "Mark, I know we're still in the beginning stages of this relationship, and I don't want to scare you off, but perhaps we'll still be together. I could see myself being happy with you for some time."

My fingers fiddle with her gift. I'm quiet, waiting and wanting to hear more. My heart pounds with anticipation, harder than it's ever beat in the past. Fiercer than when I kill and faster than when I fuck.

"But." She places her warm hand over mine. "Only if you allow me to have some control in this relationship. I won't stick around if you don't. You can restrain me when we play, other than that, we need to share the power or this will never work. I'll try not to dominate you, if you do the same for me."

Hell... her touch... those warm eyes... her soft voice and the strength of her words; I've been waiting for a woman like her my whole life.

I look down at the black box and place it slowly on the table. Her eyes widen as my fingers tap the top. A moment later, I slide it forward while holding my breath. Here we go.

"Mark?" she whispers, placing her elbows on the table and covering her mouth with two hands. She gazes at the velvet-covered gift, then at me.

I lean back and swallow hard. "Open it."

She doesn't. The candles flicker, the lift reaches the top of the mountain and stops, the darkness of the night surrounds us, but she doesn't move.

"Jules," I whisper. "I'm fine with us sharing the power. Believe me when I say I want you by my side. This is the most meaningful and heartfelt gift I've ever bought for a woman. Please, open it... be with me."

She touches the box with shaky hands and finally flips open the lid. "Beautiful," she says softly. "So beautiful."

Oh thank fuck.

Her eyes well with tears as she holds the Handmade Coltellerie Berti Italian Pocket Knife, a romantic offering, and a blade that was most commonly exchanged between a couple as a symbol of their engagement. Better than a fucking ring. I'm not going to tell her the significance; I'll wait for her to figure it out on her own. What she does know is it's a gift of devotion, and that's enough.

It has a black handle decorated with a white pattern and a four-inch blade engraved with entwined hearts. Her fingers run along the sharp edge, stopping when she sees her initials.

"I can't think of a more ideal trio of letters to be etched into my lover's blade," I say.

"JAB," she whispers. "It's stunning, Mark." She holds it next to the candle appreciative of the craftsmanship. I'm glad she approves, it's more expensive than any knife I've ever bought for my own collection.

"I love you," she says, still studying the heart design, entirely uninterested in a verbal response. The Berti says it all.

I move to her side, placing my hand on her shoulder and kissing her neck. "What are you thinking about?" I whisper in her ear.

She turns to me and runs her hand down the side of my face, stopping under my chin. I'll wait to kiss her lips until she answers my question.

"Is this something you want me to use?" she asks.

"What you do with it is your choice, not mine."

She looks back at the knife and nods then surges out of her chair, nearly tackling me to the ground. Our lips explode, and I rush to undress.

"I was hoping you'd do that." I strip out of my pants, ready to fuck. My jacket lands on the floor, then my gun, holster, tie, shirt, her dress... shit.

"Fuck, you're remarkable." She's wearing thigh highs and a black garter with lace underwear. "Fuck," I say again.

She grins at my reaction then reaches back to the table and takes the knife in her hand, driving me wild. I can't believe it... she runs the blade between her cleavage and with a quick jut forward, her bra is cut, releasing her tits.

With my cock in hand, I rub the pre-cum around my tip, showing her I'm ready. She places a finger in the air and motions in a scolding manner to not rush things. That's okay. I can wait.

The knife moves playfully down her stomach and disappears under her thong. When it comes back into sight, the lace garment is cut and on the floor.

"You're gorgeous," I whisper, looking over her youthful body. "Tell me what you need. This is your night."

"*Our* night," she whispers. "And what I need is you. I want us both to cum in the sky, hovering over these mountains. Can you do that for me?"

"Anything."

She stands before me, inches away, and I close my eyes.

"Touch me with it," I request.

The knife glides along my flesh, tracing my heart before moving up to my neck. I lift my chin, becoming even more stimulated by her tease. It runs along my jawline, down my abs, then back to my heart where she presses the tip against my flesh.

I offer myself to her, standing feet apart with my hands behind my back and my head bowed. She inhales... and the blade pierces my flesh; a small cut over my heart. I open my eyes and we both watch the drop of blood run down my chest. The deep red, warm release is my reward for the evening, and it's spectacular.

With my head still down, I raise my eyes to share my best menacing leer. "Take out your tampon and get ready to fuck," I command.

A moment later her back is pressed against the window and my cock is pleading to be inside her pussy. Our bodies ache to unite, but there's no movement. No. I want to look at her before we begin. I'm overwhelmed by her first cut, her first draw of blood... it was for me. I gave her the power of the blade and she shared it, now all I want is to marvel at her gleaming face, showing respect and devotion to her and our relationship.

"Thank you," she whispers. "For everything."

"You're adored." I grin, caressing the side of her face. My head tilts and our lips meet, a soft touch to set her off, then pressing harder and sliding my tongue along hers to encourage an outburst of groans. Success.

She clings to me, her legs squeezing my torso like an octopus seizing its prey. I bend my knees and grab her ass, lifting her onto my dick.

"Uh." I exhale into her ear. My two fingers raise her chin so she can see my eyes when I speak. "You're the first woman I've ever lusted for and the only one who's given me comfort. You put me at ease and pacify my heart."

"Mark," she whispers.

Our temples are locked, side-by-side as I stare through the window at the distant lights from the downtown district. Her fingertips stroke my neck and my hips thrust. Hard and fast I work my cock into her, kissing her shoulder and gripping her tits. My blood coats her chest. Her blood coats my dick. It's an impeccable fuck, only not rough enough for my liking.

My cock becomes cruel, digging into her with long and forceful drives.

"Talk to me," I demand. "Tell me what to do."

"Put your fingers over my clit," she says with her hands in my hair. "Can you feel how wet my pussy is?"

I moan with delight.

"Fuck me. Fuck me, Mark. Fuck me with your long stiff cock."

"Jesus." I bite her flesh while my free hand slides under her garter.

"Yes... give me that cock."

"Oh my God." I throw my head back. "That's it, Jules. Get nasty."

"Fuck me. Press harder."

My fingers work her clit. Fluttering across the engorged flesh, circling it, moving faster, until...

"Yeah, right there. Right..."

"Yes. Cum for me."

"Fuck!" she shouts. Our chests slide and my balls smack into her aroused flesh. Slamming. Pounding. Wanting more. Needing to hear her cum. She pulls me closer and speaks faintly. "Give it to me. Give it... give it." She fades and her legs tremble around my waist. "Don't stop." Her eyes glaze over. "Ah." A high-pitched sound escapes her mouth, then another and another.

"Let yourself go, beautiful." My hand moves from her garter and wraps playfully around her neck. "Disappear into that sensual world. Escape."

My chest is clawed the instant her vibrating pussy lays siege to my cock.

"Yes," I whisper. Her body is an earthquake swallowing me whole. I'm disappearing inside her. Following her. Being led by her seducing, beating muscles. "Yes," I say again. "Own it."

My tongue runs along her lips in a slow and suggestive manner. My dick was ready. I was ready. But I wanted her to relish this moment as her own. But now... now I can cum.

I hold her tightly, turning us around so she can look over the city while we fuck. I notice the tiny lights reflected in her eyes as she watches in bliss.

"I love the way your cock feels inside me."

I close my eyes and listen, knowing every word from her mouth is significant.

"Can you hear us?" she whispers. "Listen... listen to our bodies and our heavy breaths."

"Uh."

"Keep fucking me." She wraps her arms over my shoulders. "Your cock's so hard... grab me, Mark. Pull me closer. Cum inside me."

"I'm close."

"Fuck me with that big cock and fill me."

"Oh fuck." I pant. "Fuck, my dick becomes a giant when you talk like a dirty slut."

Her hand slides down my chest around to my ass... then... her finger sneaks inside.

"What do you think you're doing?"

"Fucking you." She grins.

I grasp the back of her sweaty neck and our heads connect. "Holy fuck!" I yell. My dick's gonna burst. I love her finger in my ass. Another quick jolt... one more thrust. One more. One more. "I'm cumming." Our eyes meet. "I'm cumming..." I clench her finger. "Fuck! Don't pull out. Don't!"

"That's my man."

My cock heaves cum into her pussy. Shot after shot. I call out, "I surrender," like a blithering idiot when her finger slides another inch inside. "You have all the power."

Standing on my tiptoes with tense legs, narrow vision, and a constricted heart, the only sounds left to escape are, "uh, ah, and oh."

"We both have the power," she whispers. "We're one."

I collapse onto the floor and she falls on top of me, both of us consumed by deep breathing and aching legs.

"Shit, that was good," I say, in a daze.

"Everything was."

"I can't believe I just came and I still want you."

She laughs. "That's telling."

"I guess so... I'm dizzy... hell... let's fuck like that again sometime, like tomorrow." I grin. "By the way, is your ass healed?"

"It's much better, thanks for asking." She takes a napkin from the table and wipes my dick.

"Oh, don't do that. Someone's going to wipe his mouth on it."

"Yeah, after it's washed." She shakes her head. "And since when do you care?"

"Trust me, I care about cleanliness. My hotel sheets are laundered after every guest, not every third guest like most hotels."

"Hotels do that?"

I nod and look at my watch. "Shit." I sit up. "We need to get dressed before we're putting on a show for some resort worker. We've got about five minutes left. Time flies when you're fucking in the air."

She places her cut underwear in her purse and reaches for her dress. "Do you think people saw us?"

"No. We were too high and the lift is dark."

"So are you about to explode from all of this?" She motions around the space. "You've been so kind, but this must be shrinking your balls to the size of a pea."

"I can't answer that because my balls have been missing for weeks." I smile, buttoning my shirt. "Come closer." I pull her by my side, fixing her wandering strands of hair. "You happy?"

"I'm happy, Mark."

"For how long?"

She laughs, even though it was a serious question. I let it go for now while I fix my hair and straighten my tie.

She's dressed and tucking her Berti into the box it was gifted in. I'm sort of jealous that I don't own such an attractive knife.

"There's no reason to touch my weapons now that you have your own."

She nods. "Can I ask you something and get a truthful answer?"

"No," I say, tying my shoes. "It depends on the question. What?"

"Are you the one who killed Roland?"

I stand and sigh, hovering over her, unsure why she needs to hear me say it. "You already know."

She looks down and thinks before asking, "Would you kill for me again?"

"When necessary, yes. For the right reason."

"What if Roland never hurt me? Would you have killed him anyway, if I had asked?"

"What?"

"Just answer the question."

The lift stops and the door opens. We're no longer alone.

"I just want to know how far you'd be willing to go. Did you 'get rid of' people based on their 'actions?' What they did? Or did you do it because of the way it made you feel? Which is it? Was it about you, or them?"

"Shh." We've got company. The guy could think we're talking about firing my employees, but still.

"It was probably both," she whispers, stepping into the bitter night. "And I don't blame you."

She walks joyfully ahead while swinging her gift, delighted by the way the date turned out. Her silhouette fades into the darkness as I slip into my jacket, noticing the cut on my chest has stained my shirt—a red bullseye over my heart.

She got her target, dead center.

UNSETTLED

J ules decided to sleep in her own room, separate from me, which pissed me off considering the three grand I spent on the fucking Berti. She said it'd be better if we ended the evening on a high-note and not to push it.

"It was perfect, Mark. Let's leave it at that," she said.

"Whatever." I sigh while lying in my dark bedroom. "I'm not even going to try to decipher what's going on in her head. I'll assume she's tired, nothing more."

That was three hours ago and once again I'm in my usual bothered state—staring at the ceiling, unable to sleep, thinking about my family, and listening to a shitload of people hanging out poolside in a drunken stupor. I'm glad they're happy, but they're keeping me awake, and if I'm awake, guests are too. I'm surprised I haven't heard from the front desk about any noise complaints.

While I enjoy the fresh air and nearly always prop open my bedroom door when I sleep, tonight may be one of those times I have to lock myself away from the outside world.

"Loud, obnoxious, fucks," I mutter.

I should get up and kill Mera to pass the time, or... I check my watch... past midnight... still early when you own a wine bar. Maybe my brother-in-law can keep me company for a while. I bring up Cove's office number at The Dark Scarlett then decide it's a bad idea, considering I just saw him yesterday. He needs a day of peace. Damn, one of these days I'm going to figure out a way to get him to fall in love with me. I've tried everything I can think of, but he refuses to appreciate my company.

I decide to send him a text instead, but keep it short, after all, I don't want to 'push it,' like Jules so eloquently said.

We make a great team. Can't wait to work with you again. Hope Dax is well. Come back soon, dickhead.

I sigh. Hell, I have to get out of bed and do something besides sending loving texts into cyberspace. If I don't, I'll go completely insane.

A text sounds as I'm tying my robe. That was fast. I didn't expect him to respond... ever.

Swim with me, Mark Jameson.

No shit.

I check the number, seeing it's from a Vegas area code. Damn her. That bitch Mera Calloway better not be in my pool.

I reply while heading to my deck. She must've picked up my number from Daxton the other night.

You wanna hang out in my suite? I'll show you a good time.

I'm too far away to see if she's really here. It could be a prank.

Neutral ground, in the pool, no weapons. She responds.

Fuck, I wish I could see her. Come on, get out of the pool and show your face.

Fog hovers over the warm water, causing the guests' heads to disappear. There're a lot less people than I thought, considering the amount of noise. Around ten total, some of them holding drinks from my bar, and luckily, they're dressed. Every once in a while I get a group of skinny dippers after a night of drinking. Glad these people know how to behave.

But I don't see any women, only men.

I'm up for this. I'll head down and have a little fun, if that's what she wants. I haven't been in my pool in ages and I should take more time to use the hotel facilities, especially since I own the fucking place.

Wearing my swim trunks under my Jameson Hotel robe, my black loafers, and my towel in hand, I make my way to Jules' suite, hoping she'll join me for a moonlight dip.

No answer.

Wait, a moan. She's stirring. I knock again. "Jules, it's me."

A muffled "huh" sounds.

"Open the door, princess."

A moment later my groggy-eyed woman opens her door in an unbuttoned pink pajama top with her tits hanging out and her tan flesh begging to be caressed.

"Nice."

"I was sleeping," she whispers.

"You wanna join me for a swim?"

"Now? No, Mark."

"Why not? It's a clear night. The moon and stars are out, and who knows, the pool may be full of surprises."

"Are you talking about your dick again?" she sighs.

"You should come down and find out."

"I already told you..."

I block her body as a guest walks by, bringing her closer to my chest. "I know, I know. Suit yourself," I whisper. "Sweet dreams. And if you change your mind, bring JAB along. Get used to carrying that weapon." I assert, tossing the towel over my shoulder and walking away. Her door closes as I head down the corridor, alone. Once she's out of her drowsy state she might decide to show her face, but for now, I'm on my own—just *Fantasia Cocker* and me. God, that's such a fucking ridiculously horrible fake name. Amateurish.

I take a detour and stop at my front desk, inspecting the guest list to see if she's checked in or just being a parasite on my property. There's no Mera, Fantasia, or any other name that looks familiar, so my guess is right—she's being a freeloader, taking advantage of my backyard oasis like it's some urine-filled public pool.

My second stop is the bar. I'm gonna take my time and get a beer, two beers. One for me and one for me, because real men swim with a beer in each hand.

Last, I walk out the side door, checking the parking lot for her truck. Sure enough, the orange rusted beast is parked next to a classic red Corvette.

"Like apples and oranges," I mumble, turning back inside and entering the hallway toward the pool. Whistling and thinking about trolls, I drink from one bottle then whistle and drink from the other. I didn't invite this bitch into my 'home.'

I'm a troll, fol-de-rol.

She's rushing this, just like Dayne, and dealing with a novice can irk the fuck out of me. She's trying to act tough, but doesn't have a clue what she's getting into; it's obvious with the text. Some people need a septic hose jammed down their throats to get the, 'my shit don't stink,' sucked out of their systems so they learn the world doesn't revolve around them.

"I'm going to eat you for supper, Mera," I whisper, exiting the door that leads outside, ignoring the *no alcoholic beverages in the pool area* sign.

I place my robe over a chair, slip out of my loafers, take both beers in hand, and stand on the stairs leading into the water. It's fucking colder than a witch's titty tonight and my cock is a shriveled nub, but the water feels like it's ninety degrees, making it easy to slip in quickly.

My pool is a decent size and the heads that appear next to me dissolve into the fog a moment later, moving from the shallow end to the deep end then back again... in and out. Everyone standing poolside, above the fog, is within view; it's the swimmers at the surface that are in a haze. I lean against the wall in the shallow area, spreading my arms wide, holding each beer, and waiting for my *friend*.

"Marco," I call out to announce my arrival.

"Polo," some drunken dude yells, hanging out poolside about six feet away. I raise my bottle and nod, getting a cheer from him and his friends as they start chanting Marco, Polo.

Fucking assholes.

I walk further in, my beers above the water, taking a swig every couple of feet, then stopping at the five foot mark.

"Mera," I say, directing my voice toward the deep end.

"Polo," the dumbass behind me shouts.

I look around, only catching glimpses of people here and there... a head bobbing, splashing, feet kicking, then... a woman swimming underwater. Black bikini, long dark hair flowing behind her body, six feet, four feet, two, a touch... hands sliding up my legs, over my abs and to my neck... a head surfacing a few inches from my face... her arms and legs wrapping around my body. I'm encased.

"Hello, Mark Jameson," she says in a sexy voice holding on to me like we're lovers. Her hair's slicked back and mascara is smeared under her bright blue eyes. "How's it hanging?" She grabs my dick and I almost vomit in her face.

"Looking good Mera Calloway." I smirk, taking a chug of beer, hoping to get drunk so I can handle her touch.

"I didn't realize you were so small."

I look down at her fondling fingers. "The chilly fall air will do that to a man."

"Ha." She taps my cheek, rubbing her slimy snatch across my leg. "I've heard that lie one too many times from men. Nice try, little Marky." Her hands slide over my hips and around my ass, patting me down like she's a cop. "No weapons... unless you're hiding something up your butthole, which wouldn't surprise me, being Paul's son and all."

"No weapons." I place the second bottle to my mouth and drink.

"One of those for me?"

"Fuck no. I was hoping to pick up a good-looking woman tonight, gift her a beer then take her back to my room and fuck... trust me, you're not her. I'll keep drinking both beers until my dream woman shows up."

She digs her nails into my back and I jerk forward, smashing into her chest. Our eyes are inches apart and her face smells like chlorine. I'm freed for a moment as she massages her tits, putting on a ridiculous show that does nothing but make me ill.

"Those are fake."

"You like 'em?" She unties the bikini strap from around her neck and lowers her top. Her tits are disgusting as far as I'm concerned, but they're a foot away and I can't help but look.

"What a woman," I whisper. "Now put them away, this isn't some fucking porn video. I've got kids staying in my hotel."

I watch her retie the top while I drink from one bottle then place the second to my mouth. She licks her lips as my tongue circles the rim before swallowing a mouthful.

"Hot," she says with a second tug at my cock. "Give me a drink."

"Tell me what you want and I might."

She moves in for the kill, running her tongue up my neck and to my ear. Fuck, I hate it. I swallow the vomit that gets caught in my throat, but next time it comes up, I'll kiss her and expel it into her mouth.

When her cold tongue reaches my ear, she whispers, "Where did you bury my husband?"

"How and why did you get mixed up with Dayne?" I give her a repulsed look while taking another drink. "That piece-of-shit was twenty-five years older than you. Your marriage wasn't real. Tell me what you were using him for?"

My nuts get clutched. "You're wrong. Dead wrong."

"Shit." I wince.

"Dead. Fucking. Wrong."

I take a deep breath to control the pain.

"Dayne loved me. He wrote to me almost every day over the past year and we had wild master and slut fucking conjugal visits. We made truffle butter together and would beast fuck until the morning sun came up. He treated me with respect too, unlike most men, including washed up porn stars like yourself, Marcus Wild."

I'm released from the bitch's wicked grip and seriously consider choking her, right here and now. Her head would be held underwater if we were the only two in this pool.

"It'd be insulting to every woman on this earth if I ever said that you were one. You're trash and nothing more. Too bad you ruined your life starting when you became one of my father's whores."

A hardy echoing blast of laughter exits her mouth and ricochets into the woods.

"You too, kiddo," she says, using one of my dad's favorite expressions.

I stare at her incoming crow's feet and the start of a double chin. She looks fifty, not thirty-something, and her flabby arms double in size when distorted in the water. After two more slugs of beer, I hold the second bottle above us, ready to pour it over the water. She sticks out her tongue, waiting for a drop to fall.

"Don't be so stingy," she says, as I bring it back to my mouth, stopping before the liquid touches my lips. She waits, watching me chug half of it down.

"You're not very upset about your husband," I say. Dayne may have loved her, but it's obvious she didn't feel the same way about him. Especially since she's more focused on the fucking alcohol than showing any emotion toward the guy. She reaches for the bottle and I finally hand it over, watching her take two big swallows.

"I can tell by the marks on your face that he didn't go down without a fight." I turn my head, repelling her attempt to touch my skin.

"Let me guess," I say, amazed to see Jules swimming a few feet away. She looks over, but I ignore her and luckily she does the same. She gets it. Good girl. I'm glad she woke up and decided to join me.

"What?" Mera asks. "Guess what?"

My hand touches her waist and I pull her closer. We both drink, looking into each other's eyes. She places the bottle on the concrete and links her hands behind my neck. "You're lonely," I whisper, inches from her face. "Approaching middle-age, no longer in the porn industry, probably broke..." I look at her arms, not seeing any track marks. "I'm sure you're addicted to something. Maybe the Special K you drugged Dax with. I know your type. You'll latch on to anyone because you have no one." I look at her arms again and grin. She lowers them and backs away. "What the fuck are you doing here? Do you think I'm letting this incident with Dax go? You haven't got a clue how fucking enraged I am about that." I shake my head. "Don't count on getting out of here. You should've just packed up and left town."

She laughs and treads closer, her legs around my waist and mouth next to my ear. In a faint voice she says, "I didn't love Dayne, but I knew he'd scare the shit out of Cove and Sophia enough to get a hefty chunk of money from those two. Money we could've had fun with for a few years, then I would've moved on to someone else. That's the way my world works. Men will always take care of me, like your father did. He paid for my college tuition, apartments, and gave me whatever the fuck I wanted when I was his house whore. There have been plenty like him and plenty more to come. Dax was punishment for ruining my plans."

"You're a fucking bitch, Mera, and getting too old for anyone to care. You know it and it scares the shit out of you. You're no longer noticed because your body and face are sagging. You try to stand out and return to your youth by getting new tits, but they don't do jack shit. If the things you said were true then you wouldn't be employed at some Italian restaurant in Vegas."

"I'm not anymore."

"Because of Dayne. He was your way out for a while. A dirty old man just out of prison is the best you could do." She slaps my face and I laugh, noticing my gorgeous blonde resurfacing a few feet away.

I keep an eye on Mera while Jules continues to make me proud, swimming around us, not making a scene or acting like a jealous kid. She's listening, but pretending to be a guest and leaving out the drama like she displayed the other morning with my gun. I don't hear the words 'barbarous bitch' or any sounds coming from her mouth. She's calm and mature, while the rest of the guests are rambunctious, but at least keeping to their own circles.

"You're a fool to believe Dayne was going to get money from any of us. He had nothing more on his mind other than taking our heads."

"He came here for you first, shithead. He knew you killed his father, he never thought it was Cove. Get serious. Cove Everton, kill someone? Ha!"

"I already knew that. My death would've been enough to get money from Cove and Sophia because they'd be scared shitless without me around. That's not news."

She smirks and runs a finger down the middle of my face, stopping under my chin and lifting my head. I swear she's going to kiss me. Fucking gold digger.

"I'm not next in line."

"You sure?" She rubs my unresponsive dick. "I do have some drugs in my Datsun. We could have a party tonight and you can show me that you fuck harder, faster, and dirtier than your daddy. Then we could take a shot of K and travel to a far off land together."

I push her away, repulsed by her contact and words. Fucking hagbag. And poor Jules is watching all of this, her face turning red, lips tight, shaking her head. Hold back, beautiful. Chill for just five more minutes then I'm going to cut this woman's throat. I just need to get her out of this pool.

Jules swims off as Mera responds to my shove with a burst of laughter, treading water then paddling toward her beer. The bitch cozies up next to me with her back against the wall, sipping from the bottle and laughing like a child.

"Touch me again and your hand will be the first thing I cut off," I say. "Your death's going to be much slower than Dayne's."

"I'm leaving... and you're not going to kill me. You have no reason to," she states with authority. "I only came here to say goodbye and to see if you wanted to have a little fun before I go, after all, you are Paul's son. If he were still around he'd cheerfully fuck me tonight. But, it doesn't seem like your cock's working so I may have to find someone else."

"My father wasn't cheerful about anything... and no reason to kill you?" I exhale. "Jesus, there's a ten-year-old's back I can't get out of my head that says differently."

"Fuck you." She treads in front of me. "I may not have loved Dayne, but he was still a friend. What I did to Dax wasn't even close to being tit for tat. You won. You killed him; I was only expressing my anger about the situation. It's over, move on."

I grab her neck and drive her against the wall, trying my best to contain my desire to break her neck. She's lucky to get a quick release before anyone sees. I just wanted her to know I'm not fucking around.

"He was supposed to return with some money, you fuck." She rubs her neck. "I was married to the guy and we were having a good time until you ruined it. Now I'm alone."

"I knew it," I say. "So why didn't you keep Daxton

and ask for a ransom if all you wanted was money?"

She looks at the side of my face and over my shoulder then down my chest, ignoring my question.

"Did Dayne cut you?"

"He did," I lie.

"But he doesn't use knives."

"He grabbed mine."

She swims in front of me with hopeful eyes, touching the knick over my heart with a gentle hand. "It looks fresh... is he still alive? This can't be more than a day old."

I don't respond.

"What did you do to him?"

"He's dead," is all I say.

Her hands fall in disappointment. Like all people who are missing someone from their lives, the hope that they could be out in the world lingers on until you see a body. The body is what makes death real. I didn't believe my father was dead until I saw him laid out in the morgue. Most of his face and head were blown apart, but his one eye was still intact. I'll never forget my father's eyes. No doubt, it was him.

"I can't kill a child," she whispers.

"Not many people can, but I would've given you money to get him back. That was fucked up on your part not to ask for it."

"You would've killed me and taken your money back anyway. Now that I didn't get anything from you, I'm safe."

I laugh with a hand on each of her shoulders, squeezing firmly. "You're stuck in a dream if that's what you believe. Christ's sake, I know a lot more about you than you think."

She shakes her head in disbelief.

"Alright bitch." My nose is against hers as I whisper with a clenched jaw. "You fucked with my sister, my father, and now my nephew. With this fog around us I could hold you underwater until your lungs fill with water and the cops would call it an accidental drowning."

"No asshat, you can't. My name is associated with Dayne and your father. You'd be fucked if my body were found in your pool. They'd ask about Dayne and wonder where he was and what I was doing here." She's an inch from my lips, about to bite. "*You'd* be fucked," she says. "F-U-C-K-E-D. And just like I can't kill a child, I bet you can't kill a woman. If I were afraid of you, I wouldn't be in this pool."

I release her, about to detonate. "Then I won't be leaving any trace of your body, just like Dayne's. The two of you will disappear from the face of this earth forever, never to be seen or heard from again."

With a headshake, she says faintly, "Bullshit. I keep thinking he's in your room or somewhere in this hotel." She turns, gazing at the glowing windows and the men standing around the pool. Looking up and around then back. "You're a murderer. I knew it the moment Dayne didn't return. I wanted to punish you, however, there's a chance you're lying, right?"

So she did show up to see if he was still alive.

"I don't lie," I lie.

Death can throw people into a state of confusion and disbelief. But just as quickly, someone like Mera snaps out of it and focuses on other shit.

"So this is all a facade?" She looks back at my remarkable architectural feat. Massive dark logs with hefty fieldstone emphasize the fireplaces, windows, and balconies, and warm lights from every room light the grounds. It's a sensational retreat at night. "Your hotel is supposedly elegant. I saw online that you have fresh Mariposa Lilies in every room and a grand restaurant. You've built your own haven in the mountains, isolating yourself from everyone and everything... hiding out from the rest of the world." Her eyes gaze at my suite then to the opposite end where my sister stayed. "You've tried to rebuild your life by creating your own world, but just because you built this place doesn't mean you've changed. You're still a shithead. If people knew the true you they'd call this place the Jameson Asylum." She turns with a grin. "How is your mother, by the way? She still alive?"

I grab her arm and pull her closer. "Don't say a fucking word about my family. And why the hell would I ever want to change? I'm quite fond of myself."

"Oh, that's right, I forgot you're vain, arrogant, egotistical... what a guy. I bet you're getting a lot of muff out here too... you must be the cream of the crop." She studies the men around the pool. "Yep, Marcus Wild, son of Paul and Elizabeth, brother of Sophia, and a piece of shit to all who cross your path, you're the big star in South Lake Tahoe." She laughs. "Did you think your life in Vegas wouldn't follow you out here? Who are you hiding from anyway?"

"I'm not hiding from anyone. Just think about the name of my hotel."

"Not hiding?" She doubts. "Only from yourself. And I'm not surprised you used your own name for your hotel, fucking narcissist." She swallows another gulp of beer then examines the contents of the bottle, swirling the liquid high in the air. "You drugged this, right?"

"Should've."

"Are you sure you didn't?"

"Sounds like you wanted me too. Are you looking for a date rape or something sick like that?"

"Wouldn't be the first time." She shrugs.

God, I despise her. My hands twitch in anger as I chug the rest of my beer. "Your comment disgusts me and, unlike you, I don't drug people to overpower them. I have other ways of doing it. Men who drug women are cowards."

My head shifts quickly to a guy expelling a catcall toward someone walking into the pool. Jules is back. She wades in and snubs the whistling fool.

"Nice ass," he says.

My fists clench, but I hold back.

"Hey, baby. What's your name?"

"Sarah," she says.

What the fuck is she doing?

"Saaarah!" the guy sings. "Saaarah, come back and show me your titters!"

"Knock it off!" I call out.

"Whoa, tough guy. Mind your own freakin' business while I'm doing my thing with the ladies."

"A real man would beat the shit out of that guy," Mera says.

"I'm not placing a hand on any of my guests and getting sued. When the time comes, I'll have him removed. I've got a business here and a reputation to uphold. I'm not smacking the guy around."

"Sarah, wait!" He steps into the pool, glass held high above the water while walking toward her. She gives him the finger only to get a grin in response.

"Sarah, baby. You telling me you wanna finger fuck? Let's go up to my room."

"Hey!" I shout. "One more time and your ass will be down your throat."

"Fuck off. I'm busy, shithead."

Mera snickers. "I thought you had a reputation to uphold. Dumbass. Hey, Sarah. Come over here and hang with us. We'll protect you from Howdy Doody."

"Clever," he says. "Like I haven't been called that before."

That's the perfect name for this guy; he looks just like the redheaded puppet.

Jules smiles and swims closer. "Hi," she says. "I

guess that guy's just like the rest of us out here tonight—drunk off our asses." She laughs. "Hope he doesn't cause a fight." She starts to swim away, but Mera tugs her back.

"Stay here for awhile. I'm Mera and this is Mark."

"Sarah." She nods as Mera offers her some beer. "Thanks, I'll have a few sips."

I'm fascinated with the show she's putting on and curious if she has a plan or if she's just along for the ride. I told her I'd take care of Mera, but a united kill could be the next step in our relationship. Like she said, we both have the power. We're one. It's why I asked her down here in the first place, not to kill, but to be a part of it. It would be like taking the plunge into a joint bank account.

"You here alone?" Mera asks.

"Yeah, traveling from California to Vegas. You?"

"I'm going to Vegas too... so what's your plan when you get there?"

Julia drinks and I can tell she's trying to think of a response. "I got a job at Peek's Lounge," she finally says.

"The strip joint?" Mera gasps. "That place pays well." She's intrigued, moving closer to Jules, placing a hand on her leg and smiling pretty at her new *friend*. And Jules is fucking working her better than I ever could. Shit, leave it to a woman to school another woman. But, how the fuck does she know about...

"Have you been to Peek's Lounge?" I ask.

Jules takes another long drink before responding.

"Yes, for an event called *One Night Stained.* Lots of cock on stage that night."

"Sounds like total stud action!" Mera becomes a wide-eyed kid. "Peek's makes a bundle off their women, but I never knew they had men there too."

"Yah." She nods and I can tell she's making this shit up, and doing a damn good job of it. She's lucky Mera doesn't catch on.

"Are they still hiring?" Mera asks.

She nods, placing the beer on the concrete behind us "You can follow me there in the morning if you'd like. I could use the company on the road, especially when I stop for gas and lunch."

"It's a date."

"Good, I love *dates.*" She smiles, gaining Mera's trust in less than five minutes, which confirms how lonesome Mera truly is.

"Saaarah!" The drunken shit returns. "Swim over here, baby. Let's talk about that finger of yours."

"Busy," Jules says. I pull her next to me and she wraps her legs around mine while Mera does the same on my opposite side.

"Hey shithead, is that your daughter?" The drunk sneers. "Let her go so she can be with someone her own age, unless you enjoy molesting your kid."

"You fuck." I rush forward.

The guy tosses his drink poolside and hurries out, running behind a lounger, yeah, like a wood chair's gonna protect him. That's what I thought, pussy. Who's the tough guy, now?

"Thanks," Jules says.

"I'll be right back." Mera swims off. "Need to pee."

Jules takes the beer and follows her. "I'm coming too."

"Wait," I whisper, hoping she has her Berti. Mera's a fucking moron, but it's possible she's playing right along with our game and knows Jules and I are together.

My eyes are glued on her as she walks through the water with the raised bottle, her head turned, giving me a reassuring smile. Come back to me.

"Be careful," I say.

"There's safety in numbers!" Mera calls out as she turns her nose up at the drunken asshole and walks into my hotel.

I know Jules understands my reference is to Mera and not the drunk.

"Sarah, your tits rock. Come hang... hang with my long schlong and me. Let me squeeze it between 'em."

That bastard. If he takes one more step...

"What do you say? Can I get a titty sandwich? I'll pay ya. Ten bucks."

"Get your hand off me." Jules frowns, glaring at his firm grip on her arm. She clenches a fist in preparation to strike.

"Don't hit him," I yell, calling security on my watch as I'm speeding through the water. "Pool area, now," I order. "If two of you are here tonight, I need you both out here."

"I've got a king suite and a king schlong that needs some lovin'. Let's party, baby." He starts to draw her inside, yanking her arm and gripping her neck. She pulls back, struggling to get away.

"Fucker! You're dead!" I shout.

A group of men by the door cheer, spurring him on. "Remember to follow the law!" One laughs. "Use a condom even if she says no."

I'm finally out and Joe, my security guard, is also on the scene, arriving a moment before I pound the shit out of the prick.

Jules is released and the drunk raises his hands, denying anything's wrong. She takes her sweatshirt and runs inside, heading toward the women's restroom.

"Hey, I'm just having a little fun, that's all."

Joe nods and looks at me. "What's the problem, Mr. Jameson?"

"Escort this idiot to his room so he can get his bags then lead him to the front desk to check out. I want him removed immediately. Write in the report that he was drunk, acting in an disorderly manner, touched a woman inappropriately, and is being obnoxious to guests."

"Shit, you own this place? Hey, bro, I didn't mean any harm. Seriously. I'll chill."

I ignore his request and slip into my robe, watching security escort him inside while the other guys around the pool scatter.

My nostrils flare. My walk is quick. My face peeved, knuckles white, blood pumping, breath rapid... the knife from my pocket in hand, maddened by this little shit. This isn't over.

I call security again. "Joe, tell me when he's checking out. I want to know as soon as he's off my premises."

"Will do, sir."

Damn it.

I pound my door on the way inside my suite. "Piece of shit asscock."

I fume, taking a shot of whiskey before I dress in a pair of jeans and my hoodie.

"Don't fuck with me... don't fuck with my woman."

I call Jules. No answer. Text her. No answer. I pace.

"Jesus, princess. What are you doing? Be safe."

My heart tells me she's okay. Maybe she'll go back to the pool with Mera. Or she'll take her to the bar and get her drunk. It's okay. It's all good. I have to keep telling myself that while I deal with this fucker, I need to believe we're a hell of a lot more dangerous to Mera than she is to us.

Fuck, fuck, fuck.

I grab my truck keys and race to my garage, starting the engine and pulling onto my private drive where I wait. I'm not letting this asshole go just so he can screw with some other women tomorrow or the next day.

A call comes in from security. "Mr. Jameson, he's at the desk now."

"Is it just him?"

"Yeah. He seems to be here alone, hold on."

I hear a conversation in the background, one-sided... sounds like the guy is talking on his cell. Joe gets back on the line and informs me he's talking to someone about driving to Reno for the night then heading to Vegas tomorrow afternoon.

"He's going off about having to drive when he's drunk," Joe says.

"Well, he's not staying here."

"I don't blame you. Is the woman okay?"

"He didn't hurt her, but he could've."

"Alright, he's headed out your front door now. Good riddance."

"Thanks, I appreciate it."

It's always better to handle things on your own so the cops don't have to be called to chaperon the unruly guests away.

I drive to the main road and turn around, parking on the side and at the end of my long hotel drive, waiting for his lights to shine in the darkness.

Oh, fuck yes... a text from Jules. She's okay.

I love our life together.

"Me too," I whisper.

Don't be Super Woman tonight. I text her back.

Wonder Woman. She replies.

Wonder Woman, Super Woman, whatever.

Here he comes. I toss my phone on the passenger seat, start the truck, and watch him swerve. He's driving like a ninety-year-old, blind man with no arms who's having a heart attack. He'd kill innocent people if I let him out on the road. Once again, I'm doing society a favor, in more ways than one.

Fifty feet. Inching along. Fuck, I can't wait to tear him from limb to limb. He's much smaller than me in height and weight. I'll crush him. Thirty feet. I think he's in a Suzuki Jimny. Made for women... what they would call 'cute'... a pussy vehicle.

"That car fits you, buddy."

Twenty feet away and I pull out, blocking the end of my drive. He brakes then flashes his headlights.

"Hey asshole." He rolls down his window and shouts, "Move out of the way."

I step out of the truck and walk calmly to the driver's side. He locks his door and rushes to roll up his window, leaving it open just a crack to talk.

"Hey," I say, leaning close to him with my hand on top of his car.

"Look, man. I'm sorry. I don't want any trouble. You mind backing up so I can get through? I'll leave peacefully. Just don't call the cops. I can't get arrested again." His voice is shaky.

I'm silent.

He's nervous.

His trembling fingers rub the steering wheel. That's right, my friend. Get your blood flowing one last time.

"What do you want from me?" he asks.

Staring into his frightened eyes, my fingertips over the top of the window and inside his car, I say, "You owe my wife an apology."

"Oh, shit." He laughs. .Your wife? Oh, man, I'm so sorry. I had no fucking idea she was your wife. Yeah, I can do that. Shit." He shakes his head with a grin. "Just my luck."

Yeah, just his luck. "Head down that private drive to our garage. I'll bring her out."

He nods and turns his feminine, powder blue vehicle around.

I tail him the distance to my garage, opening one of the two doors with my remote. It's like driving into a cavern—dark and isolated. There're no rooms or guest windows overlooking this area, nothing, just him, my blade, and me. I pull behind him while he parks in front of the opened door and gets out of his car.

"Dude. I'm sorry, man," he says, walking up to me as I step out of my truck. "I thought she was just gonna be some easy drunken lay. One, two, fuck her and toss her."

My fist strikes his jaw, taking him down in one swing.

"No." He rises slowly, rolling to his knees then swaying to his feet. He holds his jaw and places his hand in the air for me to stop. "Look, I deserved that, but shit, it's just pussy."

I smirk. "Now, I'm coming to gobble you up."

"What the fuck, man. Is there something wrong with you?"

"I'm a troll," I whisper, taking the blade in my hand.

"A what? A troll? What the fuck does that mean?"

"*And I'll eat you for supper,*" I sing, rushing the blade into his gut in one swift thrust.

"Uh!"

My hands claw his face as I push him into my garage with the knife still stuck in his flesh.

He screams, flailing his arms like a toddler in a tantrum as he calls for help.

"Shut the fuck up!" I cover his mouth, but he bites my finger, piercing my skin. "Goddammit, you shit!" I pull out the knife and front kick his knee, taking him down. His body smacks the concrete and he cries out for help. I straddle his waist, grab his hair and give him a second powerful blow to his face.

"Shut up!"

Blood runs from his nose.

"No, stop! Please!" he shouts. "Please don't, please don't!" He panics, starting to hyperventilate. "Don't hurt me! Please! I'm sorry... I'm... I'm..."

He cries and struggles to catch his breath.

"Don't kill me!"

I hold the knife steady and clutch his chin, pulling his mouth open.

"Nooo!" he mumbles, trying to kick free.

The garage door makes a loud jolting noise and closes, disrupting the moment. Jules is standing at the bottom of the stairwell, lowering her hand from the remote... wet from the pool, in flip-flops, a sweatshirt, and her bikini bottoms, hair slicked back... such a beautiful sight in such an ugly scene.

She doesn't move or tell me to stop. Her head doesn't shake 'no.' She doesn't try to grab the knife or ask me what the hell I'm doing. There're no feelings expressed. The only communication comes from her eyes and it's all curiosity and total fascination.

She's aware I'm about to kill... and she wants in.

"You ready for this?" I ask her.

"No." He gasps. "No!"

She steps closer, staring at the knife and his bloody gut, nodding with composure.

"Help me!" he shouts at Jules. "Sarah, please!"

I place a knee on each of his shoulders, pinning him down while restraining his lower jaw.

"I didn't know you guys were married." His words are garbled in my hand. "I would've picked someone else."

I turn to her with the struggling rat underneath me. "You can walk away. It won't change the way I feel about you."

"Fuck, please, please," he begs.

"First thing you need to do," I say, "is establish silence in the room. Even if you're going to keep someone around for days before you kill him, tape the mouth, gag 'em, or..."

My hand tightens, his mouth is open, and I cut out his tongue.

"Mmmph! Mmm, mmumma, mmumma!"

"You can plan on the guy mumbling for his mother

after his tongue is removed. I don't do this very often, but it's part of his punishment for speaking to you in such a way. His tongue needed to be removed."

"He's pissing himself," Jules whispers.

"That happens too. It's incredibly painful. Right, buddy?"

Tears stream down his face as he sobs and closes his eyes.

"Closing eyes signifies the guy knows death is coming. He's giving notice that he wants it to end."

He spits blood from his mouth and babbles nonsense.

"Sometimes they puke... you can always expect a lot of bodily fluids to escape. Blood, piss, shit, vomit. Solids and liquids will expel from every orifice of the body. But mostly it's blood. They can also become delirious from fear."

"What's he trying to say?" she asks.

"Kill me. Don't torture me. They always say that. When you've been doing this for as long as I have, it's easy to figure out the mumbling... the same way a parent can understand what their two-year-old is saying when no one else can." I toss his tongue, shift lower over his body and stab his chest. A loud cry fills my garage. "You see where I knifed him? It's below his heart. It won't kill him yet, but he'll suffer. That's what I want. I've known men like this... I'm doing this for his past victims. He's scum."

"Nooo." He starts to moan.

"Blood will spurt if you hit an artery, like the femoral artery in the groin. And it pulses when you cut the jugular in the neck. You'll experience a gush if you knife someone in the heart and twist the blade; otherwise it tends to leak slowly." I wipe the sweat from my forehead. "Some people get off from a spray or a surge of blood, some don't. My father always enjoyed watching it, he'd cheer and light a cigar in celebration if some showered my face. But I learned quickly the best places to drive a blade into a guy so it wouldn't happen. And down here." I point to his abdomen. "If you thrust in dead center you might hit the aorta or lower vena cava. That's a quick death. Only a minute or two, and a man's gone."

She listens carefully.

"I want to share this moment with you. Come closer," I say tenderly.

She kneels so our eyes are at the same level.

"Tell me what you smell."

"Chlorine," she whispers, inhaling deeply. "Blood... urine... sweat." She inhales again. "Rubber and oil, your cologne... but mainly, I smell his blood."

I look at his teary, bloodstained face, his freckles, his lips trembling and his face turning pale.

"What do you hear?" I ask.

She closes her eyes and touches my arm, listening to the sounds in the room.

"The buzz from your fluorescent lights." She pauses. "I hear his shallow breathing, his moans, and my heart beating." She listens. "The sounds from him... we're the last people to ever hear these noises, his words... no one else, just us."

I smile. It's gratifying that she can sit quietly and process what's happening in the room without being terrified of the situation, or of me. We're both calm, her finger moving in the shape of a heart on my arm... she's in control... she still loves me.

"What do you see?" I whisper.

She opens her eyes, raising her head toward me. I'm ready for her to be blunt, for her to tell me she sees a deranged man. I know she'll say I need fixing—'I love you, but you need help, Mark.' She'll be upfront. Do it. Say it.

"I see a man." She keeps a steady voice. "Who will protect me until the day that I die."

With a speedy jab my blade slides into the drunk's eye and disappears deep inside his head. I wait a minute then exhale.

"A stab through the eye kills almost instantly. It's quick and easy. Always remember that."

"He's dead?" she asks.

"Dead," I say.

"So now what?"

"Clean up." I stand and help her to her feet. "I need to pull his vehicle into my garage and dispose of the body then take care of the evidence."

"What are you going to do with his car?"

"Call a runner in Vegas."

"What?"

"I'll explain it another time. Are you okay?"

She glances at the floor and nods. "I think so."

"I meant with Mera."

"Let's take care of this one first."

"No. If she's sleeping in her truck I need to deal with her before daybreak. She's not gonna drive off and get away with her shit."

"Mark." She takes my hand. "Do you trust me?"

"Yeah."

She smiles. "You didn't even hesitate."

"I trust you. We're so far in at this point that we can't have a relationship without trust. And?"

"Deal with him first." She points to the body. "Mera's not going anywhere in the morning. We have time."

"I hope you didn't promise her my breakfast buffet."

She shakes her head, nudging the bloody tongue with her flip-flop. "How can I help?" she asks.

"You're changing the subject."

"The subject right now is the dead man laid out on your floor."

"Fine." I take a flashlight from my workbench and place it on his chest then raise the garage door. "I need to take him into the woods, the farther away from my hotel the better, at least a mile. But it's dark, so I want you to stay here."

"Mark," she complains.

"Shh, listen to me. I don't want you to fall and get hurt. I promise we can do this together another time, but not tonight. This was a spur-of-the-moment kill and I have a lot of stuff to—"

"Are you a serial killer?"

"What? No." My head shakes. "Of course not. No. I punish people who deserve to be punished."

"How did it start?"

"What are you doing? We're not having this conversation right now." I stand defensively with arms folded and my feet apart.

"How. Did. It. Start?" She puts her hand on her hip, her usual 'I mean business' stance, knocking my authoritative presence out of the water.

"I wanted to impress my father. Okay? Now let it go."

"You were seeking attention?"

"Maybe."

"So you've got Dayne in the Lake, this guy here, and Mera as a possible third victim. Oh, and Roland. What the fuck? That's like four people in a matter of weeks. And it feels good, right? You get a thrill out of it?"

"Yeah, I wouldn't do it if I didn't."

"Wait, I thought you just said it was to punish people who deserved it." She cocks her head and crosses her arms, mirroring my position. "So now it's more about you. See, this is what I was asking about during our date."

"What does it matter, and why are you making me

sound fucked in the head?"

She shrugs.

"And so what if I enjoy sinking my blade into people. I might be a little fucked up, but I'm a Jameson for Christ's sake."

"What does that even mean?"

"Jules." I look at my ceiling and exhale. "Stop. Please. It's the middle of the night and I've got things to take care of and people to call about this fucking vehicle. I know you get chatty, but now's not the time. Don't try to analyze me." I wave my hand at the body. "Or any of this."

"You said you were isolated as a child. Are you also a voyeur?"

"Fuck. Stop!"

"These are all traits of a serial killer."

"How do you know this shit?"

"I took abnormal psychology in college. This is basic—"

"I'm not a serial killer, I'm a vigilante. I take the law into my own hands because the cops don't, and won't, do anything about these creeps. I know every person who's ever been hurt by these fucks would praise me for what I do. My actions are justified."

"A vigilante? Like Robin Hood or some comic book character? And what, am I your faithful sidekick?"

"That would be great."

She stares at me, not amused by my response. "Is that why you bought me the knife? It's not for protection or for play or because you love me, it's just to kill?"

"Oh, fuck that. Why are you doing this to me? To us?"

"Answer me."

"I bought it because of the way I feel about you."

"I know," she says straight-faced.

Her body language has changed instantly. She's now relaxed, arms down, lip twitching as if she's holding back a smile, and her eyes are playful and full of excitement. Shit, she's joking.

"Are you fucking with me? You are. You're fucking with me, right?"

A burst of laughter echoes through the concrete garage as her face turns beet red.

"Goddammit, why do you have so much power?"

She laughs even harder.

"You just love torturing me, don't you?"

She smiles wildly as I'm embraced. Holding her in my arms, I look over her shoulder at the bloody scene and kiss the top of her head—her damp hair smelling of chlorine, her skin warm. She's precious.

My hand caresses her back as I reveal something about myself that I've never been able to say to anyone.

"I kill to protect the people that I love and to keep others from harm. I watch over people because no one ever watched over me. It's that simple," I whisper. "I've felt abandoned and alone my entire life."

She's breathing steadily and holding me tighter.

"My parents never loved me. Fuck, they never even liked me. They wanted a *different* son."

"That's sad." Her voice is muffled in my chest. "I'm sorry. I was only teasing you because I'm confused."

I lift her chin and look into her eyes. "About what? Us?"

She shakes her head. "No. It's him." She turns toward the guy on the floor. "And Dayne's blood and the desire I have to harm Mera. I enjoy all of this a little too much," she admits bravely. "Fuck, I don't know why I was delighted in seeing you kill him and why I'm not calling the cops, and it scares the crap out of me. Why is it so stimulating? Why does this fascinate me? That's why I asked you those questions. I was hoping you could give me an answer."

"You may never know." I try offering a comforting smile. "But you're not crazy, if that's what's going through your mind. My father was a psychopath, he was insane, not you or me."

"You sure?" She laughs. "I could be. I mean, think about it. I just poked a tongue with my foot and it didn't even faze me."

"Alright, maybe a wee bit," I tease, leaning closer as she closes her eyes for a kiss. Our lips touch lightly under the humming lights, her mouth unlocks, and a groan emerges when I slide inside. She touches my chest, running her fingers down to my groin and strokes over my jeans while our kisses grow powerful. I'm erect under her hand. Wanting her.

Don't disappear, my princess. Sleep in my bed so I can make love to you in the morning. Just two hours is all I need to take care of the body and vehicle then we can be together.

I keep my thoughts to myself as she heads to the stairwell in a slow, sexy, hip-swaying walk, stopping on the bottom step and pulling her Berti out of her sweatshirt pocket.

"I really wanted to spend the rest of the evening alone until I saw you beating the pulp out of this guy. Now I don't believe I ever want us to be apart. I never imagined a scene like that would turn me on, but seeing your hand clenching the knife, the blade covered in blood, the surprise in your eyes when you saw me, and how your expression changed quickly from hatred to affection... I'll be waiting for you when you get back. And in your words, Mark, I think we need to fuck."

DEVOTION

My expedition into the damp woods was tiresome. The guy was short and slim, so carrying him wasn't an issue, but keeping my footing in the mud was. The pines blocked the light of the moon, making it nearly impossible to see without the flashlight. I slipped twice and got my boot stuck, had to lay him down a few times, thought I was lost, then finally found a good place to put the body.

I'm lucky I didn't run into any mountain lions or black bears, but I'm certain *he* will.

Unfortunately, the vehicle is more of an issue than the dead guy. I called the three car runners I know in Vegas and when they heard it was a Suzuki Jimny and the possible second vehicle would be a rusted out Datsun, I pretty much got big "FU" from all three.

These are guys I knew through my father and they've helped me out for years when I lived in Vegas. If it's a nice car, they'll take it and sell it underground, making a decent buck. If it's a piece of shit, I can pay to have it left somewhere, like an empty lot or a dingy motel. The cars are wiped clean of prints, vacuumed, washed, the works. But no one wants to risk the seven-hour trip from South Lake Tahoe to Vegas for such worthless vehicles. Having a car disappear in a matter of minutes was easy in Vegas. It's one of the downsides of leaving that area.

I was able to finally make a deal with one of the men, but it's up to me to get the vehicles to him.

Shit, I'm in no mood for a road trip. I'll have to think of another solution, and quick.

Before heading to bed, I bring up my security cams and check to see how much of the incident at the pool was recorded. His snide remarks were caught, the firm grip on Jules' arm and neck, Joe and me on the scene, and the entire escort out. Nothing else. Good evidence if the cops come questioning why he was asked to leave, and yes, that he *did* leave. I have no cameras toward the end of my hotel drive or down to my private garage so nothing to erase or worry about there.

I check the current state of my grounds, too exhausted to take my usual walk through the hotel on foot. Mera's truck is still in the lot, the pool has cleared, and the corridors are empty.

"Fucking Mera Calloway. You've come a long way... sleeping in your truck, penniless, tweaking out on the drug Special K like you're some rave-happy teen. I wonder if you're in a trance right now? I could get inside your truck and you wouldn't even know I was there. I'd slice your throat open... but no, I'm not that dumb. Not in my visitor lot in open view of my guests. I'll let Jules continue whatever she started with you then step in sometime tomorrow." For now, I'm content letting the sleeping bitch lie.

Enough of this, I need to wake Jules for some pussy then get some sleep. Tomorrow's another day to think about Mera Calloway.

Of course my watch chimes with a text from my son as I'm on my way upstairs... it's not like I can ever have a free moment.

fukker mutherfucs

Yep, that's my boy, and I can tell by his misspelled words that he's wasted. "Alright," I whisper, taking a seat on the stairs and placing a call. "Time for another round of 'father knows best.'"

"Jack, it's your dad."

"I know whose the fluck yous is," he slurs, completely plastered.

"You okay? What are you drinking, buddy?"

He moans, once, twice, a third time, then heaves.

"Fuck, you sound like shit. What did you have and how much?"

"Wha?" he mutters. "Nothin'. I'm good."

"Are you at home? Is your mom around?"

"You hate me... you..." His voice trails. "I'm nothin'... you married mom cuz... waz pregnant."

"No." I sigh. "I need to know what you drank."

"Life... sucks."

"At your age it does, but it gets better. You're only

fifteen and—"

The call ends.

"Shit, I fucked that one up." I head down to my office then out to my kitchen, to my living room, pacing, pacing, through the dining area, back upstairs, parking my ass on the top step. Fuckin' hell, why can't kids skip the years from thirteen to twenty so parents don't have to deal with this teenage bullshit?

"Come on, pick up your cell. Wake up."

Three rings. Four. Five.

"Huh?" he answers.

"Do I need to call your mother or an ambulance?"

"No."

"So you're okay?"

"Where's my money?"

Yeah, he's fine. "Look, I'm sorry. I'm not trying to be an a-hole, I'm just busy."

"Ten grand... I'll visit... ten grand."

"We'll talk about it tomorrow, when you're sober." Ten fucking grand, and he'd only stay one day. Little prick.

"You... don't care," he says in two exaggerated breaths. "Liar."

I need a guide to conversing with a fifteen-year-old. There has to be instructions online or a video I could watch, maybe even one of those *For Dummies* books. *Dealing With Your Teenage Son For Dummies.* It's been two long decades since I was his age and none of this rings a bell.

"I married your mother because I thought it was the right thing to do and we thought the experience with you would be special."

"Thought? Wha... what the..."

"That's not what I was trying to say, you *are* special, Jack."

Crap. Cut off again. Silenced.

I lean back and stare at my log ceiling, wishing one of the beams would fall and smash my head. Then I'd sleep. Damn, I wish I knew how to fix our relationship. If only he'd come for a visit so we could talk in person. It's easier for him to fly out for a weekend than it is for me to go there. He knows it, but refuses to make the trip.

"Keep trying," Jules says, standing in the master bedroom doorway, wearing only a pair of sleep shorts with her hair still matted down from the pool. She must've heard the conversation. "Don't ask him what he drank, ask him why," she says.

"You look beautiful." I rise slowly, sore from the strenuous night.

"And you look exhausted... now call him back. It sounds like he needs you."

"I'll call him tomorrow after he sobers up."

"Promise?"

"In the afternoon after he's had some sleep, I promise."

"Everything else okay?" She leads me into the bedroom and lifts my bloody hoodie off, tossing it next to the bed then helping me out of my jeans. I allow her to care for me, whispering that everything is perfect as she takes my switchblade from my back pocket and places it on the nightstand.

"Socks next," she says.

I raise one foot, then the other, watching the socks fly through the air and land in a pile with the rest of my clothing. She kneels before me, slinking my boxers down then leisurely walking her fingers up to my expanding cock. She looks over the tip and into my eyes with her mouth open in a suggestively carnal way. I'm dog-tired, but wouldn't mind a slow and gentle fuck, as long as I don't have to hold her in the air, be on top, bring out my toys, fuck her like a wild beast, or... hell, as long as I don't have to move, this is gonna work.

Our eyes remain locked while her tongue glides up and down my dick before it's taken inside her mouth.

"Uh, Jules." Her name is said tenderly. "Yes."

She caresses my balls in one hand and strokes my wet dick with the other, her fingers following her mouth with every bob and twist. Her tongue swirls my tip when she rises and flattens against my shaft on her way down.

"Uh," I whisper, as I'm deepthroated. She gags occasionally, giving me fast and slow nods, long and short licks, sucking me off with her hot mouth.

"You like that?" She wipes her lips and smiles.

My hand rests on the back of her head as I guide her back in. Fuck, yeah, I like it.

"More." I nod. "Your mouth is so gorgeous when

you suck me off."

I babble in pleasure watching my cock slide down to the back of her throat. The firm stroke of her hand never ceases, even when she needs a break to catch her breath. She tongues my balls and is a master of pleasuring the underside of my shaft... she even blows my flesh. An actual blow that feels fucking incredible.

"This is flawless head," I say with satisfaction. "Perfect."

She keeps eye contact with an expression of adoration. All of her energy focused on my dick.

"Mmm." Garbled sounds come from her mouth.

"It's coming." I hold her hair back and direct the speed, needing a quicker suck. "Yeah." My legs tighten. "Yeah." My body shudders. "Fuck." My cock's massive. Engorged. Ready.

"Uh!"

She pulls back and opens her mouth, allowing my cum to fire inside. One shot, two, a third and she's flooded with the thick fluid running down her chin and onto her breasts.

My hand slows and I fall backward onto the bed in a winded state as she disappears into the bathroom to clean up.

Sounding like a caveman, "good," is all I can say. "Good... good."

She returns with tissues and wipes my dick then lies next to me.

"So it was good, I take it?"

"Good."

She laughs and massages my abdomen, waiting for my brain to come back to life, only I doubt that's going to happen. I could fall asleep at any moment.

"I can tell you're about to crash, no need to get me off."

"Thank you," I whisper.

"No, I'm thanking *you*. You deserved a reward for protecting me from another scumbag."

I grin. "So all I need to do to get incredible head is to kill a man? Done."

She smiles and kisses my chest. "So what's *my* reward if *I* kill someone?"

"Me."

"Not good enough," she teases. "Why don't you roll over so I can give you a back rub as a second reward before you fall asleep. You must be sore."

"Hell." I exhale. "I still wonder if you're a figment of my imagination." I roll onto my stomach and raise my arms above my head. "No one's ever treated me so well. Actually, no one's ever paid much attention to me at all."

"Shh. Don't think about the past. Close your eyes and relax so you can drift to sleep."

"There's massage oil in my nightstand."

"I know," she says, taking it from of the drawer and breaking open the seal. "I was snooping."

"Did you find anything unusual?"

The smell of cherries reaches my nose as the oil drips onto my back. She works it into my tight muscles, touching my flesh in a circling motion.

"The number of sex toys under your bed was a bit shocking... and exciting. But the unusual part was that you don't keep them in a drawer."

"When I need them, I'm usually in bed." I yawn. "Easy reach, quick access."

She kisses my neck while firmly working the tension from my shoulders. Her thumbs press into the sides of my spine... her palms knead my shoulder blades... it's pure heaven.

"I'm happy," she says faintly, although I'm the one who should be speaking those words. She hums a pleasant-sounding song, luring me to sleep while her fingers continue to pamper my back.

"I should've kissed you."

"Hmm?" She leans closer, trying to hear my muffled words.

I feel deprived of her mouth and crave a kiss. Those moments of our lips linking finally have meaning.

"I should've fisted you," I mutter into the pillow. Dozing in and out of consciousness.

"That's not what you said."

She needs to stay with me forever.

"Mark?" she whispers.

It's true. There's someone for everyone. Even us fucked up Jamesons can find love. Peace of mind, probably not, but love...

INAMORATA

E ight in the morning and she's gone.

"Fuck, you better not be cleaning the blood again."

I rise and slip into my robe, take a piss, then check to see if she's showered before heading downstairs. No sign of her.

"Jules."

Silence.

My fireplace is the only source of light in the dark room and I can tell it's been burning for some time because of the large embers glowing underneath the flaming wood. The breakfast cart is pulled into the living room, there's a piece of toast missing, and my coffee cup is used. I wonder if she's already left for work.

"Julia."

Nothing. Yeah, must be at work.

I take the remaining toast and check the garage, remembering the guy's Suzuki on my way down. What the fuck am I going to do with that thing? Maybe I need to bring in a digger to bury it. No. I should sink it in the lake, but then it could reappear in a year or two if the drought continues. That's not the best solution.

The change in water levels could be bad for business in a few years. And not just here... Lake Mead back in Vegas is disappearing quickly. Soon all the bodies my father deposited will show up and a massive graveyard will appear, with the concrete blocks symbolizing headstones.

"Whoa," I whisper, nearly choking on my toast when I reach the garage.

What the hell is Mera Calloway's truck doing here?

I search the garage, run upstairs and check every room on my ground floor, then race to the top floor, still holding the toast in my hand, wishing it were my knife. Where the fuck is my knife anyway?

"Nightstand."

Grab it... check the deck... then the bathroom again.

"Jules!"

And where is that bitch, Mera?

I stop, wait, breathe, listen... a muffled noise comes from the guest bedroom, then another. I hold the blade steady, walking cautiously past the guest bath then setting the palm of my hand against the bedroom door. It's opened a crack, not enough for me to see inside, but I can hear what's going on and I know the sound well, too well.

Someone's gagged.

But the sounds aren't high enough to be coming from Jules. It has to be Mera.

I open the door slowly, seeing Jules with her back turned, sitting at the foot of the bed. She's dressed in a sweatshirt and sleep shorts and Mera's next to her, lying down. She has her wrists and ankles cuffed and her mouth covered with one of my ties.

She got her. My woman brought me a gift.

The word 'goodbye' is sliced into her stomach and I can tell by the smears of blood that Jules wiped her blade on my sheets. It's enchanting and somewhat relaxing to watch this play out, being a spectator for once instead of in the ring.

I take a seat on the low dresser and chew my toast, continuing to enjoy the show.

"I can't believe you hurt a little boy," Jules says. There's no anger in her voice as I'd expect, but I do sense remorse. For one, she's hiding Mera out in this room, meaning she feels guilty or possibly regrets that she's here. She's also no longer holding her knife; it's on the windowsill, away from her victim.

"I know this will hurt like hell when you come off your high, and I'm sorry, but it's only going to get worse when Mark gets his hands on you."

The room smells like urine and damp clothing, the type of odor that reminds me of an animal shelter. Two towels are hanging off the bedpost and Mera's still in her bikini top, although her bottoms are on the rug next to the bed, replaced with a pair of sweatpants. Next to her leg is a small bottle, clear, half full, with a needle close by. She's not sobbing or thrashing to get away. She moans, but it's a definite doped up sound.

"You're cold and heartless for hurting Daxton," she continues. "He's an innocent child and the nephew of the man that I love... you deserve whatever he has in store for you, but... I get you first."

She stands and grabs the knife, moving back to Mera's body and raising it, about to stab...

"Marry me," I say, chewing my toast.

In a startled uncertainty, she turns rapidly, lowering the knife and holding it behind her back like a child caught with her hand in the cookie jar. She looks at Mera, the blood smears on the bed, then at me.

I smile and wink.

"I'm sorry."

"For what?" I ask.

"The mess. I didn't think about the fact that she might need to use the bathroom. And when I was trying to hurt her like she hurt Dax... I got lost in the moment and didn't realize until it was over that I was wiping the bloody blade on your sheets. I fucked up."

I laugh while taking another bite of toast. She hasn't responded to my proposal. "Marry me," I repeat, pointing my toast at her.

"What?"

"Yeah, we're perfect for one another. Just say yes then we'll deal with Mera."

Her jaw and arms drop the way they always do when she wants to tell me I'm being a total twit, like when I took her to my own restaurant for dinner, or when I told her the belt punishment was fun. Seriously, I think my proposal's romantic. I mean, five hours ago she delivered a round of phenomenal head and now she's holding a bloody blade over a bound women. I can't think of a better time to ask her to be my wife.

"You haven't even said you loved me yet, but you're proposing? Tell me how that works? You're the only person in this world who's asked someone to marry him without first professing his love."

Mera moans and I can't help but smile. I thought I professed my love with the Berti in her hand, but I can say the actual words if that's what she needs to hear.

"I love you." I look at my toast and take a final bite, wipe the crumbs from my fingertips then give it another go. "Now, marry me."

"No. This isn't how you propose to someone, Mark."

"Says who? Who the fuck has a franchise on proposals and says there's a right and a wrong way of doing it? That's bullshit, now marry me."

"No, I'm not ready."

"What do you mean, no?"

She exhales and walks closer, spreading my knees apart and shifting her body between my legs. My hands rest on the small of her back as we discuss this face-to-face.

"I'm sorry, I'm *not* ready."

"Hmm."

"Hmm? What does that mean? Are you angry?

Disappointed? What?"

"Do you think someone better's going to come along?" I'm uncertain that's the right thing to ask, seeing how it made her grin. "Alright, it doesn't matter, we'll just be engaged until we're dead."

Slowly, she leans closer, her head tilts, eyes close, I follow, wetting my lips before we kiss. My tongue gets a wet tease before she pulls back and whispers, "You're irreplaceable, but your relationship skills are downright tasteless." She places her arms around my neck and swings her hips. "I'm not waiting for someone *better* to come along, but I think we should live together before we get married. Besides, you were the one who said you weren't ready for us to share a place, that's why I have my own suite, remember? Are you taking all that back? Now you want to rush into a marriage?"

"It was before all this other shit happened, and no, I don't want to rush anything, but I'm also not going to lose a woman like you, that's for damn sure."

"Well, I'm not going anywhere, I promise. Not unless I want to end up under a layer of concrete in your garage, right?" she jokes.

She turns to Mera who's coming out of her junked-up state.

"What are you going to do with her?" she asks.

I check my watch and shake my head. "Right now? Not much. We can leave her here since the bed's already full of piss and blood. Then I'll deal with her at nightfall."

"We," Jules says. "You're not leaving me out this time."

"We'll discuss it later... so how'd you get her up here?"

"How'd you get that guy in your garage?"

"Easy, I told him he needed to give you an apology."

"Sweet."

I nod. "Most people are gullible and I'm assuming Mera was the same."

She gives me a wide-eyed look. "Oh my God, I can't believe how easy it was. I told her I had a family suite because it was all that was left when I checked in and if she wanted, she could stay in the extra bed 'til morning. She brought a few things from her truck and followed me straight up and inside. I didn't have to do a thing; it was crazy. I kept thinking to myself, wow, this must be how a lot of killers get their victims—act friendly to people and invite them over... then she offered me some of her Special K, but I declined, she shot up and was out. Done," she speaks enthusiastically. "Oh, I used the cuffs that were under your bed. I hope you don't mind."

"Nope. Don't mind a bit. So you've been keeping her drugged?"

"Yeah, I wanted you to get some sleep. I've been shooting her with the same amount I saw her take when she first arrived, it knocks her out, but it doesn't last all that long."

I nod. "It's a high dose if she's not moving or

communicating. I'm surprised she doesn't snort the stuff like most people. She has it in liquid form, which means it's likely from some vet's office instead of from the street. And I bet with the dose you gave her, she's entered a K-hole; it's like a near-death experience."

"So you've tried it?"

"It's a shitty drug I took at one of my father's parties back in Vegas that turned me into a drooling, graceless mess—something I'd never touch again. I'm sure Mera enjoys it because it puts her in a fantasy world where she imagines people are viewing her as a queen."

There's slight movement in the bed, a mumble, and a twitch of her foot.

"I'll tape her mouth for the rest of the day and check on her from time to time. Did anyone see you bring her truck around?"

She shakes her head. "It was four in the morning, after you went to bed. The hotel was quiet. What do we do with it? Should we drive it off a cliff?"

"No. This isn't a movie. Trust me, we want to take it back to where Mera came from, or where she was headed. Luckily, it's the same destination for her truck as the guy's car. I'll figure out the details today." I eye my watch again. "Sooner than later, I hope."

"I better get ready for work. You sure this is okay?"

"What? That you're not marrying me? Fuck no, it's not okay, but I'll drown my sorrows in a bottle of whiskey and forget about your ass by the end of the day."

"No." She laughs. "I meant—"

"I know what you were referring to." I take her hand, leading her to my front door. "You got your key card?"

She nods, taking it out of her sweatshirt.

"The rest of your clothing, shoes, towel, and other things?"

She looks down; what she has on is it.

"Do you have your third hand?"

She stares inquisitively, looking down at my dick then with a grin, she brings the Berti out and kisses it.

"Still have your sanity?" I ask lovingly, while brushing her cheek with the back of my hand.

Another nod.

"Everything you did was brilliant, from your maturity in the pool and the way you took control of the situation with Mera, to your cleverness afterward and your restraint in our relationship. I'm amazed you walked into my life."

"You're such a sweetheart this morning, but I'm not saying yes to your proposal."

I shrug. "It was worth another shot, now kiss me, you wickedly beautiful woman."

She smiles and grips my neck, bringing my mouth to hers in a marathon of tongue and hip action. We laugh with pressed lips, her wrists secured and raised above her head, my cock rubbing her pussy, and both of us inserting dirty talk into our moment of play.

"You have no idea how much you turn me on. Tell me you can't wait to feel my cock."

"You better fuck me hard with it tonight... fuck me until I call out your name and cum."

"Mmm." I pull her sweatshirt up and kiss her tits. "Spread your legs so I can fuck your pussy right now." I prod my dick toward her and clutch her chin.

"It's tempting, but I gotta go. My boss gets irritated when I'm late." She bats her eyelashes.

"Funny." I smirk.

She pulls her sweatshirt down, reaches under my robe and strokes my dick, then whispers, "Can't wait to see your cum face tonight," before walking out.

"Oh, she's good." I rest my head against the door, breathless, touching my cock.

"Sarah?"

"Damn it." I tighten my robe and peer toward the second floor. "Better get the duct tape."

"Hey, bitch!"

I can hear her all the way down to my garage, swearing up a storm as I'm looking for the tape, calling for help as I stare at the cars, and saying she's gonna kill someone if she's not set free. God, she's fucking loud. Good thing Jules' room is next to my suite and will be a buffer for some of the noise. It's amazing that one woman can sound like a herd of cattle.

When I walk upstairs and into the bedroom, she's grumbling 'bitch this' and 'bitch that' while trying to get out of bed.

"Good morning, Mera Calloway." I smile. "Welcome to my hotel. I hope you're enjoying your stay."

"Fuck!" She tilts her head back then tries a quick jut forward, trying to sit up; only she doesn't have the strength to do so.

"You look exactly like Dayne did before I killed him, a beached whale on dry land. Poor thing."

I take my blade out of my robe and she screams.

"Now, now, calm down. I'm only cutting the tape."

She looks at her stomach and screams for her 'friend.' "Sarah! What did you with her, Mark? Sarah! No..." She turns her head, trying to escape the tape.

"That's better," I say. "I never did find your loud, rowdy voice very attractive. Now shut the fuck up. I doubt my guests can hear you, but *I* sure as fuck can."

She winces and rolls to the opposite side of the bed, searching for an escape.

"Guess the cuffs aren't enough." I sigh and walk back to my garage for some rope.

I pour a cup of coffee after another long trip down and back up, carrying the cup and the rope with me into the bedroom. She's on the floor, wiggling like a worm on pavement after a heavy rain. I watch her for a while, sipping my morning coffee and slicing the rope into two pieces.

"It's a magnificent morning, don't you think?"

Her response is muffled under the tape.

"Too bad you can't enjoy it," I say, lifting her back into bed and tying her to the posts, aggravated that I got blood and urine on my robe.

I pick up my coffee and finish the morning alone, reading the paper in my bedroom, doing a set of sit-ups and push-ups, and showering off a days worth of blood, sweat, and sex.

Pussy boy.

My father's voice enters my head when I wipe the steamed mirror with a towel and gaze at my reflection.

If you were anything like me you'd be fucking that tied up bitch in your bed. Don't waste a free meal.

I place my hand on the mirror, covering my blue eyes like I'm silencing his mouth.

Bring your cock out and make her suck you off. Women dig that shit before you kill 'em.

"Get the fuck out of my head." I look away from the mirror, reaching for my cologne in need of a distraction. I dab a spot on each of my wrists and neck before putting on my watch, seeing a missed call from Jules.

Good, someone to talk to besides Paul Jameson. I call her back straightaway, hoping her voice clears my head.

"Hey, beautiful," I say. "You called? Everything okay downstairs?"

"It's busy, but no issues. Look, I thought of something I wanted to say to you, but I think I'll wait to tell you in person. Maybe tonight. You can forget I called."

I smile... she's going to say yes.

"It's not about the proposal."

I frown. Wrong again.

"Just tell me, I could use a diversion to my morning routine."

"Hold on." She talks to a guest then gets back on the line. "It's amazing how many people are leaving together after turning in a key card from one room. Some of them totally scammed you."

"I know, it happens all the time with events like this. The Marathon's over today and the hotel will be calm again until ski season begins... about two weeks." I stare at my reflection; a gold towel wrapped around my waist, my hair finger-combed into place, and my fingertips trailing over my abs and stomach.

I hooked your sister up with Star. Fuck, they made me a hell of a lot more money than you ever did. I don't know why I didn't think to bring her into my company sooner. I wasted years with you on camera when I should've just used you for the behind the scenes desk work. That's where you shine, right sunflower? Behind the scenes... a desk job? What... are you jealous? You've always been the jealous type, not the Jameson type.

My fists clench. "Fuck you."

"What?"

"Sorry." I turn away from my reflection. "Distract me," I request.

"Are you talking to your mirror again?"

"You know me so well." I exhale.

"I worry about you when you're alone in that bathroom, Mark. Get dressed and come downstairs would you? Please? I'd love to know you were in the office behind me instead of alone upstairs."

Desk job pussy.

"I'll be down soon," I whisper, ending the call and sliding down to the floor with my hands over my face.

I'd like to smash the mirror again, but it does nothing for me. I need to figure out a better way to put to rest some of this shit with my father. The one person I can talk to about him is Cove, except he's so fucked in the head because of my dad that our conversation would be an unhealthy, never-ending, bitch-fest about the man.

And I know these thoughts are my own, my father's not really in my head. The words are what I believe he'd say... it's not real, just like my relationship with him was a sham from the day I was born until he was killed.

I toy with my watch, bringing up my sister's cell number, then Cove's, sending him a text.

I love you.

I should've sent it to Jules, but he needs it more, even though it's something he'll ignore like the one from last night. When I think about my father, he's the next person who comes to mind. I can't help it, he just does.

"Fuck, you bastard. You never told me that you loved me," I say to my father, while resting my head against the bathroom cabinet. "I only needed to hear it one time, just once." I shake my head. "What would've made you proud of me? Anything? Or nothing... there's nothing I could've done... nothing. No matter how many people I fucked, killed, or how much money I made you, it wouldn't have mattered. I was nothing."

You needed to be an entirely different person for me to love you. Isn't that why you hate your own son?

"Fuck! I despise my mind sometimes."

Thank fuck my thoughts get sidetracked when I hear an incoming call from Jules.

"Hey sweet thing." I take a deep breath and massage my eyes with my thumb and forefinger, trying to clear my head of my father.

"Are you rubbing your gun under your chin?"

"No." I laugh. "Not this time."

"What are you doing?"

"Getting ready for work."

She doesn't respond, but I hear her heels clicking on my wood floor as she walks through the lobby. "Be right back, Chloe," she says before her footfalls soften, reaching the damask patterned carpet in the corridor.

"I wanted to tell you something," she says quietly. "You know I like you, right? I mean…"

"I'm in no mood to get dumped by someone over the phone like we're teenagers. You're right, if this is what you called about before, say it to my face."

"Mark, get real. I love you."

"Sorry, I'm a bit off right now. What is it?"

"You can't fix people, you can only join them."

I smile. "Oh yeah?"

"Just listen. You don't need fixing. Okay? I love you for who you are and I wouldn't want to change you. You haven't tried to change me and you didn't force me into your way of life. I've made my own choices of how far I wanted to be involved with you and all of this, I still am. I think you're incredible just the way you are, perhaps crazy, okay, definitely fucked up, but amazing too. You deserve happiness in your life and... hell, I can't believe I'm saying this... I think some of the things you do make you happy and I'd like to share those moments with you because I enjoy them too. I guess we're both fucked in the head, but neither one of us needs to change. Right? I know I'm right. Don't answer that. That's all. Nothing else. That's my opinion. No fixing. You're perfect in my eyes. Now get your ass down here so I can see you while I'm working."

I swallow hard, unable to respond with the baseball-size lump in my throat, but ready to follow her order. Standing, I end the call and look in the mirror wanting to see if the tear she placed in my eye is real.

"I'll be right down, love."

LADY OF THE NIGHT

"Hi."

My sister's cheerful voice comes through my cell as I take her call in the lobby of my hotel. I'm using my actual smartphone today, waiting on a private call from my guy in Vegas so he can give me a drop off address for the vehicles. No need to announce the situation in my garage to the world if I don't have to.

"Hey, Soph. You guys make it back okay?"

"Yeah, no offense, but it's so nice to be home."

"None taken."

"The boys are happy, I'm happy, Cove's happy, the wine bar's even happy to have us back." She laughs. "I've been in St. Louis now for over a decade and when I think of home, this is it, not Philly where we grew up."

I lean back in the gold stuffed chair next to the burning fireplace and watch the guests arriving for the evening check in. I nod to some of them, wearing one of my finest suits with my arm raised over top of the chair and my fingers dangling over the side while we chat.

"How's Daxton?"

"Oddly, he seems fine. Do you think that's okay? It's like he doesn't even care. I don't know what to do."

"Sometimes it's best not to do anything."

"Perhaps." She sighs. "That's why I'm calling. Can you do me a favor?"

"Another one... geez I don't know, Soph."

"No jokes, this is serious."

"You know I'll help you out any way I can. What's the favor?"

"Please stop taunting my husband."

"What? Fuck that." I look around to make sure no one heard my foul language and continue the conversation in a quieter tone. "Is that what he said?"

"He's at the Scarlett and doesn't know I'm calling you, this is between you and me, but, he does walk around the house mumbling about your texts so I know he's annoyed."

"Tell him to grow a pair and just admit we're family."

"Mark, stop."

I lower my arm and tap the armrest. "What's it gonna take?" I whisper. "I've tried everything over the years."

"That's just it, you try all the time, just leave him alone for a while. We've had this conversation time and time again, but this time I need you to listen."

Jules sends me a smile from across the room while she signs for the delivery of fresh lilies. She opens the long flower boxes and her shiny blonde hair falls forward, gracing the white petals. The head of housekeeping arrives to distribute them to the rooms as Jules saves a few for the front counter. Her face comes alive on the days when the flowers arrive, like they've been delivered specially for her.

"Mark?"

"I'm listening."

"What did I say?"

"That I needed to listen."

"Ergh."

"I heard you loud and clear, Sophia." I laugh. "Look, I'm your big brother, I'm supposed to tease you."

"Forever?"

"Forever."

"But you heard me?"

"Yes, I'll give it a rest."

"Thanks, now here's my second request."

"Oh, now there's another?"

"Listen, please."

"Shoot."

"That's the opposite of what I'm asking." She hesitates, aware her boys are in the background requesting dinner. "In a minute," she whispers to them before getting back on the line. "Cove mentioned some things to me last night and I want you to let it go."

"Be specific."

"Hold on." Her cell's muffled, but I can hear her ask Dax and Xav to play in their room until she's off the phone. A minute later, the boys' voices can no longer be heard and the line's silent. "Still there?"

"Yep."

"Don't kill Mera."

"Not over the phone," I warn her. "Poor choice of words."

"Okay, but we need to talk. Cove told me he requested it and I figured you'd do it anyway, but I want all of this to stop. I hate her. I fucking hate her with a passion for hurting my son, but someone needs to bring all of this bullshit to an end. Dayne was different; he wasn't going to walk away, but I think she will. Plus, she has a sister who will eventually start to wonder..."

"I know, and parents, and maybe friends. I'm not an idiot. Dad taught me... I know what I'm doing. And I firmly believe a person who hurts a child isn't fit for this world; ask your husband. He'll have an opinion about that. And I agree that she'll walk away, but who said she should?"

"Fuck, I want you to get better."

"That's funny, someone just told me I'm perfect just the way I am."

There's silence from both ends. I rest my foot over my thigh and whistle, setting my eyes on Jules as she walks over and places two flowers in the small vase on the coffee table in front of me. She points to her watch that it's almost time for her shift to end and I nod.

"I am getting better in some ways, but it's too late for the situation you're referring to," I say.

"Oh." Her voice cracks. "Just like that? That quickly?"

"Partly, I'll finish the rest tonight."

"Let her go," she whispers. "Please."

"I probably won't 'dispose' of her," I reply. "I'm not sure I have it in me to do *that* to a woman."

Jules places two fingers over her lips and blows me a kiss as she's on her way out of the lobby.

"Thank you," Sophia says.

"Someone else will take care of the situation for me."

"Don't you dare... I know what you're thinking, just don't. Everyone needs to go their separate ways and live life, not take it away."

"You *don't* know what I'm thinking, sis. Not this time."

"Mark—"

"Love you." I end the call and place the cell in my pocket, enjoying the warmth of the fireplace for a few minutes before following Jules upstairs. I hear the shower running as I pass by her room, deciding not to interrupt as I continue into my suite to see Mera. I plan on the three of us having a romantic evening together.

I take a shot of whiskey and head upstairs. My last check was two hours ago when I untied her hands and feet, allowing her to use the bathroom before roping her back to the bed. She's in the same position when I return, staring at the ceiling, mumbling through the tape that gets ripped off and tossed on the nightstand.

"Fucker. Untie me so I can cut off your balls."

"Manners, manners, Ms. Calloway, or is it Mrs. Rosen? Are you keeping Dayne's last name?"

"I never took it in the first place. Where's Sarah? Don't hurt her, you dick. She has nothing to do with the situation. And when are you going to untie me? I've suffered enough." She struggles to free her hands and feet.

"You're only going to hurt yourself."

"At least give me some K so I don't have to lie here bored to death."

"Last time you did drugs you got tied to a bed, sliced, and diced. Remember? Most people would've learned from that experience."

"Prick. You're not going to hurt me."

"Then why did you scream this morning? What were you afraid of? And look at your stomach."

"I was confused, that's all." She looks down. "And my stomach doesn't hurt. It's barely even a cut. You're terrible at this. Seriously, I bet Dayne is downstairs and tied to a chair because you're too much of a loser to take anyone down."

"Is that so? You're still in denial of everything?"

"I'm still here, aren't I? I know you're just fucking with me, so just untie me now instead of later."

"Bitch." I walk down to my kitchen, rummage through my cabinets, grab a container of salt, and stomp back upstairs. My suit jacket gets hung on the bedpost, my sleeves rolled, and my gun out of my shoulder holster

402

and placed on the dresser. "I'm quite good at what I do," I say, putting the tape back over her mouth and taking out my knife. I pull a chair over to her side and drag the blade along her flesh. Her eyes widen then scrunch shut when I reopen the shallow wounds. "You're right, the cuts didn't hurt much, but they sure as fuck will now." Taking the salt container from my jacket pocket, I pour some inside each slice then sit back and watch her squirm with muffled cries. I'll keep my sister's words in my head and *try* my best not to kill her, but it's not easy.

"Fuck Mera, you're a guest here, you don't have to be so fucking rude." I pick up my gun and jacket and walk out, needing to change and get high before Jules arrives.

With music playing in my bedroom, my back door open, and a joint in hand—I take a hit, admiring my property and the towering pines. Water splashes in the pool and a chilly breeze runs across my face. It's much colder tonight than it was yesterday and I'm hoping the muddy ground is frozen. It will make the walk through the woods a hell of a lot easier.

"Inhale deeply, Mark," I whisper, closing my eyes... not referring to the pot. I smell winter moving in, pine needles, and burning wood. "Breathe in again and relax before you make your decision."

Swimmers continue to kick in the heated pool and I swear I can feel water land on my nose from their fun. But then more cold drops melt on my eyelashes and cheeks.

It's snow.

I keep my eyes closed, feeling it, letting it wet my face as the sun sets for the day. I want it to touch me, coat me... shit, I'm fucking stoned.

I open my eyes and grin, watching the white flakes float down and melt as soon as they touch the ground. The area won't get a significant amount until November, but the first sight of it alters my mood. Winter at my hotel is grand with an overabundance of lights, soft holiday music, and plenty of tourists coming in from California and Nevada to ski. It makes me feel like I own a chalet in the Swiss Alps, with chestnuts roasting in the fireplace of my lobby and hot chocolate... okay, that's enough pot for now.

Fuck, but it is beautiful out here.

"Hey." Jules voice is gentle and mimics the snow, floating through the air and melting against my flesh. She looks different tonight, relaxed, happy, dressed in jeans and a furry long-sleeve black sweater. Her hair is dried and her makeup light and natural. She might've sensed we'll be going outdoors.

I raise my arm and she burrows against my side, enjoying the warmth and the scenery, but declining my offering of pot. I put the snuffed out joint in my pocket and kiss the top of her head, lingering over her clean hair before lifting my head toward the woods.

"It's pretty," she says.

"Yeah, I can't think of a better place to be right now."

Her hand slides under my shirt, slowly circling and caressing my back. "Did you figure out the cars?"

I nod. "Two people will be here tomorrow. I just need to give them instructions when they arrive, talk to my guy in Vegas for the delivery, and that problem is solved."

"And you called Jack?"

"I did, and as you suggested, I asked him *why* he was drinking last night, not how much."

"And?"

"His girlfriend dumped him. He has a teenage broken heart which is something I know very little about."

"But you talked to him, right?"

"The best I could."

She laughs. "Poor kid."

"Let's not discuss my son right now. It was another shitty conversation and I don't want that part of my life to change my mood. Just enjoy a minute alone with me."

She gazes at the tall pines, and smiles at the snow, taking it in her hand and watching it melt. "What are you listening to? It's eerie."

"It's called *In The Pines*, an old recording that's been my smoking song since I built this place. Eerie, yes, especially since I have it on repeat, but just listen, the lyrics are hypnotizing, especially with the low downhearted tone in the singer's voice... and the acoustic guitar and the bass together... it's a moody, lonely song that for some reason makes me feel calm and in control."

Her eyes remain closed as she leans into me and listens. I hum the instrumental part then sing softly into her ear...

Little girl, little girl, where will you go?
I'm going where the cold wind blows
In the pines, in the pines, where the sun never shines
I will shiver the whole night through.

Look up, look down that lonesome road
Hang down your head and cry
If you love me as I do you
Would you go with me or die.

"The voice *is* gorgeous."

"That it is... like a woman I know."

She blushes and shakes her head.

"What? Just look at this scene." I raise my hands. "Inhale it, feel it, hear it, remember this... I'm trying to be romantic, for fuck's sake."

She laughs and kisses my cheek. "I know; it's just amusing that not too long ago I had to beg for a kiss. You're funny sometimes... maybe it's because you're high again."

I shrug.

"But I like it," she whispers.

"Well, that's all you get for now," I say, pulling her inside. "The sun's down, let's take care of the bedroom situation."

"What are you doing with her?"

"Do you have comfortable shoes with you?"

"Yes, sneakers, downstairs."

"We're going on a short hike," I say, putting on a fleece sweater and my baseball cap. "You have a warm coat? Gloves? A hat?"

"I'll get some from my room." She heads for the stairs. "Don't leave without me."

"I won't, but hurry up, we have a lot of shit to do, especially down in the garage before the guys come for the cars. I still haven't picked up the tongue."

"This is exciting!" she exclaims, before exiting my suite.

"Yep, I'll make the popcorn." I grin, putting my two guns in their holsters, bringing a knife along, and the keys for the handcuffs. I turn out the lights in my bedroom and get Mera into an upright position, shoot her with K, then carry her to the garage. I nearly fall down the two flights from her weight and fidgeting, still waiting for the drug to kick in. Damn, this will be an exhausting jaunt. It's times like these when I wish I had a wheelbarrow.

I slip into my winter coat and wait for Jules, watching the pathetic bulky mass on the cold cement floor. She sees the blood, the body part, her truck, and groans. But with slowed movements as she slips into a paralyzed state, I'm able to take off the cuffs and dress her in one of my old flannel shirts that's in the garage... not that I give a shit that she'll be cold, but so I don't have to deal with her flesh and blood against my clothing.

Her eyes stay open, zoned out on the bloody scene.

"Don't worry, it's not Dayne's blood. His was wiped up last week. That's just some random fuckhead from last night."

"All set," Jules says, entering the garage.

"Carry the flashlight and the rope that's on my workbench; I won't be able to hold either tonight. And I also need you to take one of my guns."

"Why?"

"Bears."

She nods, following my requests as I open the garage door. "Close it once you're out, stick by my side, keep the gun out, and make sure you don't turn on the light until I tell you too, got it?"

"Got it."

We walk to the side of my garage and head into the darkness. The snow has stopped and the moon is out, but the dense pines block most of the light. Mera's silent, Jules is silent, and the woods are still. Branches snap under my boots and I sink into the thick layers of pine needles. I can see my breath and can feel the chill on my open neck. I'm beginning to feel my usual rush with Mera's body over my shoulder, her cold lifeless dangling legs in front of me; it's an interesting juxtaposition to the vibrant woman by my side.

I can imagine if Norman Rockwell was fucked in the head that this would be a fascinating painting for him to create. A man dressed in a winter outfit and cap carries a woman's body through the forested pines. With his faithful sidekick alongside, they travel under the moonlit sky on the first snowfall. The only thing missing is an axe and a dog.

"What are you thinking about?" she whispers.

"Norman Rockwell."

"What the fuck? Be serious."

"Turn on the light." I ignore her response. "This is where the land gets rocky and is difficult to walk."

She shines the light on the ground in front of me, moving it in a circular motion, saying "watch out," when she sees something I might trip over.

There's no trail, no flagged trees, all I have to lead the way is a gut feeling and an idea of where I was last night. But I'll know when I come to the right place. Like in Vegas and out on the lake, I'd drive then something inside me would tell me to stop. I never continue on after that, the first thought to stop is always the correct one.

"These woods go on forever."

"Yep, that's why I bought this property. You can see the lake and the populated area from parts of the hotel, but there's nothing but miles of woods off to this side." I lean against a tree, taking deep breaths.

"Do you know where your property stops and the National Forest begins?"

"Only when I look at a map, but it's all uninhabited so it doesn't much matter if we're on my property or not... keep the light up," I say, trekking onward.

"Sorry." She shines it a few feet ahead, maintaining a steady hand as she stays by my side. "Why didn't you kill her before we left?"

"Because I kill people the way they deserve to be killed. It's not always a jab in the eye and it's over. It depends on the person, what I know about his personality, and why I'm killing him in the first place. Over there." I point. "That's the spot for Mera."

There's a lone tree that I place her by in a small clearing with a creek about twenty feet away. The light of the moon breaks through the open area, shining upon her face.

"She looks like she's on stage."

"I know, this is the perfect setting for her," I say. "Hand me the rope."

I remove the cuffs from her ankles and wrists and loop the rope around her and the tree, tying a reliable knot—making sure her legs, arms, and waist are all secure. She's coming to, mumbling and turning her head.

"You have something you want to tell me?" I ask, pulling the tape from her mouth.

Her eyes are half-open as she tries to speak. "Cold... fucker."

Jules laughs. "Do you think she called you a cold fucker, or said she's cold then called you a fucker?"

"Probably the first." I smirk.

"Motherfucker," she utters.

"That time it was clear. Hey, Calloway." I tap the side of her face. "This is it, your final resting place. Sorry, there's no cable or room service, but you do have a beautiful view."

"What do you mean this is it? You're just leaving her here to starve?"

"She won't starve."

Mera looks at Jules and shakes her head, in disbelief that she fell for her trap.

"Hi," Jules says.

"Sarah, you... you bitch."

"It's Jules and I don't give a shit if you think I'm a bitch, bitch. You kidnapper, abuser, torturer, evil wench, cunt rag... hey, what are you doing?" she asks, distracted as I unzip my jeans.

"I'm not sucking... you off," Mera mumbles.

"Fuck." I laugh. "I don't want your filthy mouth on my dick, especially after it's been on Dayne's." A pool of urine forms at her feet, leaving a strong odor in the air. "I'm ringing the dinner bell." I turn back to Jules with a grin. "She won't be alive long enough to starve. A bear will eat her by morning."

"You asshole," she says, coming quickly to life. Jules moves in, putting the tape back over her mouth.

"You see that area over there?" I take the flashlight and shine it down by the creek, about a hundred feet from where we're standing. "What do you see?" I wave it left and right.

"Trees, the water, same as here."

"Yep, exactly."

"I don't get it."

"That's where I stopped last night."

"You mean with the guy? He's already gone?"

"The bears are preparing to hibernate this time of the year and are extremely active, eating twenty hours a day. This is like a food court for them. You've got the watering hole," I shine the light on the creek, "with the growth along the banks, this open area, and a guy like me giving them free handouts. They're drawn to this place."

Mera kicks, refusing to surrender to her fate while yielding muffled screams. I lean next to her and give her some friendly advice. "Shh, shh, listen. If you stay silent they'll walk right past you, unless they pick up a whiff of my piss, then you're fucked... hmm." I scratch my head, being a total ass and loving every minute of it. "I've heard they have the best sense of smell out of any animal on this earth, so yeah, F-U-C-K-E-D." I taunt her by patting the top of her head. "There're mountain lions out here too, so be very, very quiet tonight. They creep, so you won't know when one's going to strike... but in a flash it will latch onto your skull and puncture your brain or crush your trachea. Dead. But hey, I have an idea, let's play a game, you and me. See this?" I pull out one of my old knives and set it in the ground, just out of range of her feet. "We're leaving you here, but if you can figure out a way to get to the knife, you may be able to get out of this shitty situation you've found yourself in."

I take one last look at the moon before reaching for Jules' hand, wanting more than anything to get her back to my suite so we can fuck.

"You're not going to kill her?" she asks, taking the flashlight from my hand.

"I did kill her."

"What if she gets away?"

"She won't."

"What if—"

"Jules, do you have the gun?"

"Yes."

"Keep the light steady, okay?" I distract her, not wanting to discuss the fact that I did this partly for my sister, and partly because I'm a pussy and can't bring myself to kill a woman. A man? No fucking problem killing a guy, but I think a lot of bad shit would happen if I ever stuck my knife inside a woman's flesh. Like the devil would appear and shove his dick down my throat... or... or my father would finally tell me that he loved me.

I stop and think about that for a moment.

"What's up?" Jules turns and asks.

The woods turn even darker and colder than before. I sense his presence looming around us, suffocating me, mocking me because I just walked away from a kill. Looking back, I wonder if I need to finish this.

"Mark, what's wrong?"

My body trembles. I feel like I'm eight, being slapped around and told that I'm a pussy, wanting to fight back but too small to beat him. If only I could've killed the fucker in his sleep when I was a kid.

And I wonder again, would he tell me that he loved me if I go back and kill her? Would the voice in my head be silenced? That's what I search for with each kill, and maybe this is the one.

"You okay?" she whispers with a gentle touch to my arm.

"Only sometimes," I reply.

She nods like she understands, but she knows nothing about my father.

"Tell me what's on your mind."

"Changing the past, or if a choice in the present could change your perception of the past."

"I don't believe that's possible."

"I know this is a common question, but what would you change about your life? Your past?"

She looks down and shuffles her feet, digging into the pine needles with the toe of her sneaker until she reaches the soil. "Not much. I would've gone to school for something that would've given me a more stable income, and of course, I never would've gone out with Roland, but there wouldn't be many extreme changes besides those... I wouldn't have colored my hair dark auburn back in middle school, that was a bad idea, especially with my light eyebrows... if you're wondering about meeting you and my life now, I wouldn't change any of that. I can't think of much else." She puts the light under my chin, illuminating my face in the darkness. "What about you? What would you do differently?"

"I'd kill my father."

I say those words like they were shot out of a cannon, an explosive charge that hits her face and explodes. The light turns off and we're both silent until I feel an urge to repeat it.

"I'd kill him when I was a child, not as an adult. I'd stop him before he slipped out of our lives so he could never reappear years later. He should've been my first kill."

She's quiet, but remains by my side as Mera's muffled cries echo into the night. The light shines down to the tree, over the knife, to the creek then to the forest ahead of us.

"Stay here," I whisper.

"What?"

"I'll be right back."

"What are you doing?"

"Something that stays within my family. Don't move an inch. Don't turn on the light, just stand and wait. Give me three minutes."

I walk down to the tree, thinking about my father and Sophia with their voices stuck in my head.

"Kill her and I'll finally love you."

I'm a troll...

"Don't, Mark, this ends now."

I'm a troll...

"Did you hear me? The nasty, goat-eating troll dies. It's not fitting for you to think you're a troll... could be bad

karma."

"Kill her and make me proud."

Sometimes...

Sometimes you just never know what happens to people... they come and go from your life, reappearing years later or perhaps never to be heard from again. That could be me. I could go into hiding, have a down period, stop killing, then resurface... or maybe Mera Callaway walks away tonight, being set free into the woods, scurrying away like a rabbit... and maybe, just maybe my father's voice stays in these dark woods and doesn't follow me home because of what I just did.

"It's quiet," she says when I return.

"It is." I place my knife in my pocket.

"And cold," she says faintly, taking my hand and pulling me hastily back the way we came, never asking about my time away. But I think she knows what I did. It was the best thing to do. I have to tell myself that. I make good decisions. Always. "It's dark and we need to get the hell out of here before a wild animal shows up and devours us... thanks for putting all that fucking shit in my head."

My hand stays on her back as we walk through the tall pines, stepping over fallen branches, weaving around trees and large rocks, walking upward for a good mile until we see the lights of my hotel. There's a dusting of snow on the ground when we exit the woods, and it could've been snowing the entire time we were in the dense area, never reaching us because of the coverage from the trees.

"Are you still high?" she asks.

"Not for some time, no." I punch my code into my garage keypad and the door opens, displaying our next job.

"Can we warm up before we tackle this?" she asks.

"Yeah, why don't we fuck and have a drink then come back down." I close the garage door, leading the way upstairs.

"A shot first then a fuck."

"Liquor before cock?"

"Yep." She races playfully past me, taking off her coat and sweater before we even reach the living room.

"The liquor's in that cabinet, your choice. I'll get the glasses."

"Vodka?"

"Not my usual, but it's fine."

"Well, what do you want?"

I walk toward her with the two shot glasses in hand, admiring her red lace bra. "Take it off while we drink." I nod at her chest. "What I want is to see your gorgeous body."

Her young, golden tits appear then she takes off her jeans and touches her pussy. Fuckin' A. I lick my finger and slide two fingers between her folds, grab a bottle of whiskey and guide her to my bedroom; liquor in one hand, twat in the other.

"Take a mouthful," I demand, starting to undress. "Let's get wasted and fuck all night. Screw everything else in life. My dick's going in your pussy and you're going to cum. You're going to cum all fucking night from my cock, my cock, and my cock."

"Stop talking shit and get that cock of yours in me before I start without you."

"Do it." I say, pulling off my socks. "Touch yourself for me."

She leans back on the bed with her fingers over her clit, rubbing in a continuous motion. I kneel over her, taking her tits in my hands, sucking and kissing them aggressively.

"Stroke it," I command. "Give me long, firm drives." I watch her two-handed play, one for herself and one for me. "That's it. Smear my pre-cum." Her fingers offer so much pleasure, circling cum around the tip and down my swollen red head. "Fuck, I love it when I have control. I'm gonna cum all over your beautiful body, up your stomach, on your tits, and all over your face. I'm gonna fuck you and cum all over you."

"Oh, hell no." She releases my cock, squirms away, and friskily pushes me down on the bed. Her legs straddle my hips. My hands are held above my head. She smirks. I laugh. "Me first," she says.

"You first, princess," I say affectionately. "Go ahead, do your thing."

She uses my stiff dick to stimulate her clit. Rubbing the tip against her swollen flesh then placing it between her folds, sliding over my long shaft. She's slick, aroused, moving over me without my cock ever going inside.

"God, that feels good." I place my hands behind my head and watch the show. Her tits bounce, springing forward as she launches into rapid movements, powering into me. She runs her hands from my groin to my nipples, squeezing, circling, and flicking them... holding my shoulders for stability, thrusting over me, closing her eyes... her mouth opening in an erotically stunning signal that the sensation, the spot, the movement... all are magnificent. She's breathtaking.

"I'm close. Touch me."

My fingers caress her clit as she glides with greater control over my dick, her wet pussy coating my shaft, sliding effortlessly.

"Mark!"

"I feel you. Your muscles are tightening over my cock... your tits are engorged... cum for me."

My hand clutches her back, pulling her down. I seize her mouth with a rock-hard kiss, hold her in a tight embrace, and can feel the spasms shooting through her body. Her legs and arms tremble then give out as she collapses onto my chest. Gasping, panting, whispering my name.

"Mark, I'm cumming."

"Shit, I wasn't even inside you." I hold the back of her head, feeling her warm breath coat my ear. Her clit pulsates over my shaft like it's sucking my flesh, while her hands grip and tug at the sheets.

"More!" Her legs shoot upward with her toes pointed to the ceiling. "More." She huffs.

"Yeah, that's just the beginning. You haven't even felt my dick dive into you. Get in front of me, on your side."

She rolls, setting her back against my chest as I pull her leg over my thigh. Her period's light and there's still time to fuck without a condom, and since she doesn't stop me, I'm going in.

"Yes." I thrust. "Mmm, that's the pussy I love. Warm, slick, and made for my dick."

She laughs and forces her ass backward, urging me on.

"My cock's happy now. I think I'll keep it in you for days, maybe weeks. Your pussy puckered around my dick, squeezing it, keeping it secure like it's tucked away in a handbag... or I can call it a cockbag."

"Shut the hell up and fuck me. I want dirty, nasty sex... now!"

"Yesss." I hold her leg up and ram into her, watching my dick slide in and out, her tits moving in a swaying, swinging, dance while my lips are on her neck. "My entire body wants you, Jules. Not just my cock." I buck forward. "I enjoy the touch of your soft feet in the middle of the night." I lunge. "My ass loves your finger." Propel, sink, and attack. "My hands have a mind of their own, wanting to meld to your body whenever you're in sight." A wheezing, gasping, exhale. "My mind is full of fantasies of our lives together." I charge, faster, harder. "My heart..." Oh fuck, I'm so turned on. Fuck. "My heart is submerged with a drunken blood... the blood...

the blood pumping through my veins... every drop is intoxicated by you... poisoned by you."

I set my fingers over her clit, watching her stomach tighten, feeling a second approaching orgasm.

"I'm going to cum with you this time," I whisper. "Feel my dick, feel it, beautiful. Beat into me." Our bodies slam in unstoppable waves of lust.

"Cum with me," she says.

Her tits are detained and my chest moves closer and closer until there's no space between us. She's mine.

"Oh." She tenses. "Oh."

"Fuck," I call out, biting her neck as her pussy closes around my cock. "I'm cumming too. Here... take it..." A rigid jolt and I explode, seeping inside her. "Here, take all of me."

"Oh! God!" she shouts.

Her pussy and my cock beat viciously. I rest my fingers over her clit, feeling her pounding climax. We're both wildly out of control, out of breath, and a total mess... out of commission for a good five minutes.

My dick's flaccid when I can finally move, dropping out of her on its own. I fall back, eyeing my heaving chest and lingering cum trickling from my dick. Damn, that was good. She turns and swipes her hair from her eyes then leans in for a kiss, her mouth turning into a comforting after-dinner dessert.

"Good one... again, please," she mutters.

I look down at my dick and shake my head.

"You said all night," she teases.

"Yes, all night, don't doubt me. Give me a half-hour to an hour to recharge and I'll fuck you harder, longer, and in every position you can imagine. We'll start easy, doggy style, and move into anal. I'll order room service and we can eat and play with food, drink, and fuck again."

"Perfect."

I stare into her eyes and run my fingers through her hair, thinking the same word can be used to describe her. I found my match. A beautiful blonde, strong, nice body, egotistical, authoritative, energetic, loves my cock as much as I love my cock, shit, my woman's just like me. She even likes the knife I bought her and doesn't mind that I kill. My female version is here and she's fucking *perfect*.

"Jules, I really do love you."

"Yeah, I know," she says while fondling my dick. "You'd be a fool not to." With a sigh, she lies on her back and joins me in starring at the mirrored ceiling. We look at one another and smile, our hands interlaced with the other behind our heads like twins.

"Do you think our lives will calm down a bit now? Are things over?" she asks.

I turn my head, still smiling. "This is the beginning, not the end, and I'm referring to us and all parts of our lives. The time we've shared and what you've experienced is only a taste of what's still to come. Hell no, it's not over... I'm Mark Jameson, welcome to my hotel."

She laughs and kicks my feet. "Ha, you just said that like you were a used car salesman in a television commercial for your business."

"Well, I am selling used rooms."

Another hardy laugh fills the room before her face slowly changes to a composed and pacified expression. "Mark, I'd still like to help you, not fix, but help. You know I've heard you talking to yourself in the bathroom, that on top of what you said in the woods earlier about killing your father... he's deep inside you and fucking with your head. Next time, talk to me instead. Tell me what's wrong. It's better to feel my love than his hatred."

I'm unable to speak for a moment, giving her a nod, then a squeeze of her hand as a thank you before finally expressing the truth. "I may end up relying on you to be the strength I don't have in that situation."

She faces me, with an arm over my chest, conquering me physically and emotionally. "Will you tell me about him?"

"My father?" I look up, thinking about all my sessions in front of a mirror, going back to when I was just a little kid. "Not now."

"Someday I'd like to hear more about him and your past."

"Not today, princess."

I'm waiting to hear my father's voice as I gaze straight up at my reflection, but in this bed, with my protector at my side, he's silent.

"Someday, Jules, but not today."

NEVER A DULL MOMENT

I hate to lose.

I know, I'm supposed to get fucked up the ass, right? Someone needs to show up and kill me because I'm a dick. Well, screw that.

But someone sure as fuck came close and I was not only pained by the event, but insulted too.

It started when I ran into a problem...

My guys in Vegas who were supposed to show up to take Mera's truck and the other vehicle bailed on me. Even when I offered to pay triple the normal amount, they still said no. It was too risky, especially in Mera's Datsun, which they thought would break down on the road. They gave me suggestions for other guys, but I won't call someone I haven't worked with, not for a job like this. So I decided to drive the fucking things myself... with my son, like a father-son bonding activity. And yeah, I had to pay the little shit five grand to come out and do it, the same amount as a pick-up and drive-off in Vegas would've cost.

I thought it would be good for our relationship, just

the two of us, driving one behind the other on the open road, stopping for lunch and staying overnight in Vegas, taking a look at our old neighborhood, maybe doing a drive past my dad's former mansion. I haven't had an opportunity to spend time with my son in years. It was a grand solution to both problems.

Plus, I worked for my father and Jack can do some work for me now and again. Why the fuck not? He can earn the money he keeps asking for, just like I earned mine. No handouts. Do a job, get paid, and spend time with your dad.

But hell, when I told Jules my plan, her body language changed from love to wanting to beat the shit out of me. Partly because she found out about the trip when my son showed up at my door.

• • •

"That 'boy' downstairs in your living room is the 'man' you said you hired for the cars? For Christ's sake! You can't do this to him. He's not even legally old enough to drive, let alone be involved in something this dangerous."

"Like you? You're involved in it too."

"I'm an adult, Mark. I make my own decisions and can take responsibility for my actions. He doesn't understand what's going on. Goddammit, *he's* your son."

I open my mouth to speak and she snaps.

"Don't!" She presses her finger against my chest.

"He's family, like you always say, you protect your family and the people you love. This isn't protecting him, it's tossing him to the sharks!"

"Stay out of my relationship with my son, you know nothing about him, or us."

She crosses her arms with a look of disgust. "Why am I surprised by this, but not surprised at all? It's so like you."

"It's one time. One fucking time, that's it."

"Bullshit, I see the smirk on your face, you're enjoying this and it will happen again... and how much are you paying him?"

"The same amount I would've paid anyone else to drive to Vegas. Five grand."

She puts out her hand. "Give me the fucking money. I'll take the two trips and drive the damn cars."

"What?"

"Why the fuck didn't you just ask me instead of putting your son in danger?"

"I needed to see him."

"What?" She gasps. "Are you listening to yourself? What parent would—"

I put up my hand for her to stop, closing my eyes with a deep exhale. "You don't understand," I say slowly. "I'm going with him. He's not taking two trips, we're driving together."

"Seriously?"

"Yeah, I'm a fucking shit of a parent, and if I have to pay my son five grand for him to agree to go on a road trip with me, to be my partner in this, I will. I don't care anymore. That kid out there needs to love me like everyone else." She rolls her eyes like I'm crazy. "He said my offer for him to visit wasn't enough, so I made it worth his while. Now I win. This is how the world works. You pay your kids for their time."

"This is how *your* world works."

"That's exactly right."

"Fine," she says.

"Fine?"

"No, what I'd like to say is 'fuck you, dickhead,' but what would that accomplish? And I should smack you and stomp off to my room, but then I'd be a hypocrite since I said you don't need 'fixing.'" She crosses her arms. "You're not killing any more people for at least a month. You understand?"

I bite my lip, trying not to smile.

"Mark." She points authoritatively. "This after-party clean up gets too complicated."

I laugh, in need of repeating my new favorite expression to her. "Welcome to the family, princess."

"God, any other relationship after this one would bore me to death." She throws her hands in the air. "I'm fucking stuck with you." The door swings open and she leaves my bedroom, then my suite.

"That was my plan!" I call out to her. "There's never a dull moment with Mark Jameson!"

• • •

But then my son fucked me over. I treated the situation like a normal business deal, trying to teach him a thing or two about life, giving him half the cash when he arrived, and promising the rest when we got to Vegas. We were to leave early the next day. I woke up throughout the night to check on him, but at five in the morning, he was gone. And now I'm fully aware of how fucking easy it is for my kid to travel by plane without my knowledge. After taking a shuttle from my hotel to Reno, he purchased a ticket with cash from a booking agent at the airport. Yes, minors can do this. It was his plan all along... and he told his mom he came back early because I was being a dick. I hired him for a job and he stabbed me in the back. I was disrespected and if the little shit knows what's good for him he better show up at my door, groveling for forgiveness.

Fucking prick.

And I couldn't believe what he said to me in a text later in the day.

I'd rather take half the money and leave than have to deal with your shit for an entire day.

Hell, he killed me with those words. My son. My fucking son... he's going to be worse than me when he grows up. Although by being worse, he'd actually be better.

So Jules and I took a one-day trip, got the fucking cars to Vegas, paid my guy to make them disappear, then spent the night on the strip... where once again, even in front of the stunning Bellagio fountain, she refused to marry me.

That's alright, I can wait. And I decided when we do get married we're having a ribbon cutting ceremony after we exchange our vows, not a reception. We can place the ribbon across the entrance of my suite, cut it with our knives, walk inside, and fuck.

I keep planning all this shit in my head and some day it's going to come true.

I'm obsessed with my woman and I know she loves me; I'm sure of that. She carries her Berti wherever she goes and sleeps with it under her pillow. That's her *ring*, and whether she realizes it or not, we *are* engaged.

This is our beginning, just her and me, and no one's going to fuck with us.

No one.

Oh, and by the way, there's so much more to come...

JAMESON HOTEL
Parts 4–6 now available as a bundled set

About the Author

Aven Jayce was born in Buffalo, NY. She received her undergraduate degree from SUNY Fredonia and her graduate degree from the University of Colorado. Now in her mid-forties, she resigned her position as a college professor to enjoy life as an author, wife, optimistic introvert, and loving mama.

Aven Jayce's novels include:

The NOVA Trilogy
Fallen Snow (Book One)
Desert Star (Book Two)
Sunset Rush (Book Three)
The Dark Scarlett (A continuation of NOVA)
Jameson Hotel Series (Parts 1–6)
Long Shot Love Duet

www.facebook.com/AvenJayceAuthor

52717060R00243

Made in the USA
Columbia, SC
06 March 2019